FORGED IN THE JUNGLES OF BURMA

To: Rosemary

de Staylo

FORGED IN THE JUNGLES OF BURMA

D. C. Shaftoe

iUniverse, Inc.
New York Bloomington

Forged in the Jungles of Burma

Copyright © 2010 by D. C. Shaftoe

All rights reserved. No part of this book may be used or reproduced by any means, graphic, electronic, or mechanical, including photocopying, recording, taping or by any information storage retrieval system without the written permission of the publisher except in the case of brief quotations embodied in critical articles and reviews.

This is a work of fiction. All of the characters, names, incidents, organizations, and dialogue in this novel are either the products of the author's imagination or are used fictitiously.

iUniverse books may be ordered through booksellers or by contacting:

iUniverse
1663 Liberty Drive
Bloomington, IN 47403
www.iuniverse.com
1-800-Authors (1-800-288-4677)

Because of the dynamic nature of the Internet, any Web addresses or links contained in this book may have changed since publication and may no longer be valid. The views expressed in this work are solely those of the author and do not necessarily reflect the views of the publisher, and the publisher hereby disclaims any responsibility for them.

ISBN: 978-1-4502-4443-5 (sc)
ISBN: 978-1-4502-4444-2 (ebook)
ISBN: 978-1-4502-4445-9 (dj)

Printed in the United States of America

iUniverse rev. date: 7/30/2010

All Bible quotations taken from the New King James Version.

To my Beloved Husband for telling me to "write it down", for always supporting me and loving me.

To my children.

Come to Me, all you who labour and are heavy laden, and I will give you rest. Take My yoke upon you and learn from Me, for I am gentle and lowly in heart, and you will find rest for your souls. For My yoke is easy and My burden is light.
Matthew 11:28 -30 (NJKV)

ACKNOWLEDGEMENTS

My husband, Crispin, for supporting me, for listening to every idea, and for editing.

My children, Jared and Nate, for giving up time on the computer so I could write my novel.

To my parents for reading and editing the book; to my Mom for romantic advice and my Dad for keeping John alive through his time in prison.

To my friend, Carolyn, for reading the book even though it wasn't your thing and for helping me keep it authentic.

To Wes for reading the prologue.

To Glen, for the birds.

To Dave for his "broken ribs".

For everyone who encouraged me: Diane, Beth, Mariette and everyone else, too numerous to mention. Thank you.

PROLOGUE

Soaring above the majestic mountains, the Boeing-747 carried Caroline closer to Singapore. *Finally, I can step forward into this second life—this second life I didn't ask for but was given nonetheless.* Three years after her first love died, Caroline embarked on a new life. She pulled out her airline tickets to remind herself: Pearson Airport in Toronto to London, England; one week to tour the museums and galleries; then on to Singapore. *Administrating a school for missionaries' children, who would have thought?* She gazed out the airplane window at the dark and light clouds pillowed below her. A bump and a growl interrupted her thoughts. The next bump sent her hands flying to the opposing ends of her seatbelt, fastening them snugly across her middle.

"This is your Captain speaking. We are currently experiencing mechanical difficulties. In the interest of safety, we will be landing at the Yangon International Airport in Myanmar. Please fasten your seatbelts. Thank you."

A ripple of exclamations oscillated through the cabin: "What's happening?"; "Where are we?"; "Myanmar? Is that Thailand or Burma?" A barely heard, slightly exasperated growl of a whisper from her seat mate announced: "Myanmar is Burma, you ninnies." Another bump sent Caroline's hands to grip her armrests. The airplane was now sinking through the clouds, the cumulonimbus electricity jolting the passengers. Beside Caroline, the Australian businessman, Dane Fowler, seemed oblivious to the discomfort of his fellow travelers, continuing to make notes on his laptop while the others murmured in dismay.

Circling once, the airplane shuddered onto the tarmac, grinding to a halt beside the old terminal, styled more like a Buddhist temple than an airport terminal. The 747 dwarfed the several older regional carrier airplanes also parked nearby, while in the distance more familiar passenger airliners could be glimpsed parked in front of a more modern terminal. Through the window, Caroline watched an animated discussion between the officious looking airport staff and the very agitated airline staff, who, by their lively persuasion and perhaps a healthy bribe, finally won a limited liberty for the passengers. Disembarking, Caroline followed Dane's auburn head closely, seeing him as her only familiar contact in this alien land.

The ornate carvings and figures which formed the golden edges of the roofline were echoed in the heavy golden doors which were constructed to appear carved. The stewards led them in through these beautiful doors and over to a more austere area where sub-machine gun toting soldiers seemed randomly scattered around the rows of red plastic hard-backed chairs. While she could see some of the usual car rental desks in the distance, as well as several small souvenir or magazine stalls, this part of the airport, at least, had few amenities except what appeared to be some kind of restaurant off to the right of the area. This shoppe's entrance was graced by bright red columns bordering a forest green interior in which sat several people who looked like locals rather than tourists. Taking all this in, Caroline remained intimidated by the sight of so many soldiers in one place, and stood uncertainly near the edge of this uninviting foyer, humming nervously and reminding herself that she wasn't in Canada anymore.

Obviously very experienced world travelers, the unflappable Dane and his gold card invited Caroline and a few of the other wary and nervous passengers into the tea shoppe for a drink. The little tea shoppe contained five or six tables, each with four chairs, and an L shaped red formica-topped counter behind which the corpulent shoppe owner worked. Assorted foods were on display both on the counters and behind a glass partition. Caroline surveyed the assortment of fruits, the hot plates where various meats were simmering and the rice cooker steaming away. Dane handed over his credit card and indicated that the money would cover Caroline's drink as well as those of the other three passengers accompanying them. Caroline, not even coming close to understanding the language, ordered a milky tea by pointing at the picture on the menu. Dane ordered a deluxe tea boiled in condensed milk and the two of them adjourned to a small table at the front of the shoppe. The other three passengers sat at an empty table closer to the counter.

The burst of angry Burmese startled her and she turned to see two soldiers approaching a group of young women occupying a table in the darkest recess of the shoppe. One of the soldiers hauled a young woman from her seat, dragging her away from the table. Fear filled her expression as she thrust her arms against the man to free herself while, from under the table, a little girl rose, reaching for the woman's legs. Slapping the woman once, twice, three times, the soldier pushed her to the ground. As the other women rose from their chairs to help their companion, the tea shoppe owner yelled some sort of warning which drove them back to their seats. One of the soldiers quickly wrapped his arms around the little girl and picked her up as she screamed and reached for her mother. The young mother's face fell in despair as she leapt to her feet, reaching for her daughter, all the while screaming at the soldiers who began to laugh at their little game. One of the soldiers grasped the front of her dress tearing it then following up with a punch to her stomach, yet still she struggled against him. The soldier's companion continued to hold the child firmly and it looked as if they meant to take her from her mother.

Glancing around desperately, Caroline waited for someone to intervene. Each pair of eyes she glimpsed was averted, each face unsympathetic. Caroline stood, eager to get help, but was pulled back to her seat by Dane's hand on her arm. As the assault continued, Caroline felt compelled to act. She couldn't stand by while men stole a child. Standing quickly before Dane could grab her again, she strode over to the soldiers with no clear idea in her mind of what she was going to do. The shoppe owner grasped her shirt, gesticulating wildly and shouting at her in an incomprehensible language. Instinctively pulling away, her suddenly released hand sprang forward, slapping one of the soldiers in the face. Furious at his humiliation, he immediately produced a pair of plastic zipcuffs and securely bound her wrists while pushing her against the paneled wall. With her face planted against the paneling, she saw one of the young women slip out of the shoppe with the little girl while the soldiers were distracted. Removed from the shoppe at gunpoint, Caroline, protesting, found herself bundled into an army jeep and led away to jail where she was placed in a holding cell crowded with the human equivalent of leftovers. Tried in court the next morning, she was subsequently brought here, to Bourey prison, never having seen a lawyer and never given the opportunity to contact the Canadian, or any other, Embassy. As the cell door slammed shut, Caroline's confusion metamorphosed into terror.

CHAPTER 1

HIM

Caroline had lived two lives. She thought of her first life as "Henry". She grew up, went to University, met and fell in love with Henry Wells. She and Henry married and had children together. Her Henry life was good. Their love was forged from the storms of life. They learned to "fireproof" their marriage long before it was a catch phrase. They learned the foundations of a happy marriage: letting God lead; politeness; gratitude; communication; and choosing to love even in the unlovely moments. Her Henry life was very good.

Caroline's first life ended on the day the bush plane crashed. That crash left Caroline a childless widow, struggling to make sense of the loss; trusting that in all this there was a purpose.

Caroline's second life started with—*Him*.

The first she saw of *Him* was through the razor-wire fence surrounding the prison exercise yard as an escort of soldiers shoved and dragged him through the side entrance of Bourey Prison. The soldier bringing up the rear was clearly in charge.

He looked more Russian than Burmese, sporting an imperial beard on his triumphant face. When the prisoner stumbled, the Russian pushed through the soldiers and lifted him by his shirt collar, shaking him and grinning malevolently into his face before thrusting him forward through the door. The prisoners, scrutinizing the arrival, returned to their conversations, but Caroline pondered the presence of another foreigner behind the bars of Bourey.

Later, inside her prison cell, her morning was interrupted by the Warden of Bourey Prison, Captain Htet. As a prison guard pushed open the door of her cell, in walked Htet, his stocky frame filling the diminutive doorway, his eyes scanning the tiny space as Caroline took her place, standing in the middle of the room as decorum demanded. Bowing, she waited in silence, suspecting that the warden preferred his prisoners bowed to perpetuate an artificial feeling of height in his 5 foot 6 inch frame. Caroline nervously followed the steps of his burnished chestnut riding boots with her eyes as he paced across the room, alternately slapping his riding crop against his uniformed leg and the palm of his gloved hand.

"Well, my annoying *Christian* woman." He managed to imbue the word with all the malevolence his compact frame could contain. "You have been a most irritating addition to my prison. My guards complain that the women from your cell no longer feel the need to earn favours from them; that the women feel they have some sort of intrinsic value." Htet turned his head and spat. "The men—the lonely men—I placed you with next have also become difficult. They *help* one another. In the three months you have been in residence here, I have submitted a total of four reports to my superiors asking that you be removed—or released to me for punishment." Caroline began to quiver in fear. Htet seemed intoxicated by the power he felt over his prisoners' health and safety. "Unfortunately, my pleas have fallen on deaf ears. However, I believe I have formed a plan to repay you for your 'inconvenient' effect on my prisoners." He began to laugh sardonically. Continuing to laugh, he departed, the cell door clanging behind him, leaving Caroline collapsed against her bunk, shaking in trepidation. The laws of Myanmar varied in so many ways from the laws of Canada and the rules in the prison seemed to vary with the whim of the capricious Warden. *What does he have in mind for me?* Caroline moaned inwardly.

Gasping in apprehension, Caroline glanced around the cell, yet again taking in the size and shape of the room; the ten by ten foot cell contained two bunks—really just two five by two foot planks attached to opposite walls—a toilet and a small sink. The dingy white washed cinder block walls blended into the grimy concrete floor. Slumping onto her bunk, Caroline found herself agonizing over her second life and how it had strayed so far from what she'd planned. Here she was, an educated Canadian woman who had owned her own house and a snappy little red car, now incarcerated in Burma, renamed Myanmar by its military leadership, for political crimes against the state. *I didn't know there were still places in the world where a foreigner could be made to disappear without a trace. Will I ever know what happened to the other passengers at the tea shoppe? Did they report my arrest to the airline? What about Dane Fowler? He deliberately turned away as I passed him on the way out. He knew what would happen to me. Oh Father, there's some purpose in all this, isn't there? You haven't abandoned me to torment, have you?*

<><><><><>

The warden chuckled viciously all the way back to his office. His smile, however, was erased when he found an exalted, highly illegal visitor ensconced in his chair, feet firmly planted on his desk.

"Ah Warden Htet, how pleased I am to see you." A tall, powerfully built man sporting a grey-flecked imperial beard and a Russian accent spoke from Htet's chair.

"Vlad, it's so good to see you," Htet replied, sounding anything but pleased.

"Have you found a place to store my treasure yet?" Vlad inquired.

"I believe I have. When you have finished questioning him for today, we will introduce him to his new home," Htet replied.

"Shing is taking a great risk trusting a common Burmese official with this treasure. Are you certain you'll be able to contain knowledge of his presence here?" Vlad inquired, expressing his contempt for the lowly warden of a small prison.

Bristling at the insult, Htet retorted, "I am quite capable of fulfilling Colonel Shing's request. The Burmese and Chinese have a long history of cooperation."

Vlad snorted at this. "The Chinese command and the Burmese obey. Very good. That is exactly the type of 'cooperation' Shing is looking for. It is such a shame that the KGB was not able to establish a presence in your country. It would have done you so much good."

Htet bridled his rising fury. He hated this 'freelance' interrogator, this mercenary Shing had hired then imposed on him under threat of revealing Htet's little "side business" to the Burmese Military Intelligence. Htet was not the only prison warden who profited by allowing prisoners to buy their freedom by selling their daughters to 'work' in Thailand. However, Htet was not fool enough to believe that the local authorities would be too pleased at not receiving a portion of the profits. Not desiring to become a resident of his own prison, he had complied, agreeing to house the captured British spy and cooperate with Vlad in his interrogation—*Vlad the Impaler*, the violence of his nickname terrified Htet. Htet did not like this man. He did not like this plan. If Military Intelligence discovered this British spy here in Bourey Prison, being tortured for information for the Chinese rather than for the Burmese, his own head would be served up on a platter along with his hands and perhaps his genitals. Captain Htet, wanting to symbolically distance himself from this situation, left the room.

<><><><><>

When Caroline had first arrived in Bourey Prison, she was placed in a cell with five other women; three prostitutes, a drug addict and a teenager who had murdered her new-born baby. Terrified by their hardened coarseness, Caroline did her best to learn the rules quickly, hampered as she was by her lack of cultural reference and complete ignorance of the Burmese language. As a result, her teachers were the blows she received from the guards and other prisoners when she "didn't get it right".

Gradually, she came to see her cellmates through eyes of compassion rather than fear as she witnessed their toughness in a world that showed little respect for the female of the species. The prostitutes faced weekly "visits" from the guards from which they returned bruised and hollow. The young murderess was despised and outcast, spending her evenings weeping in despair. As Caroline began to see that the galvanized surface of the women's reactions covered a wounded centre, her compassionate heart prompted her to reach out with small acts of kindness. As the women began to see that the terrified incompetence of Caroline's reactions covered a compassionate heart, their icy rejection began to thaw. When they saw that Caroline never totally lost hope, they began to gain hope.

Three weeks in a cell with so-called political prisoners followed with the same results. Pastor Paul, the de facto leader of the group, protected Caroline from the other men's "loneliness". He spoke English and encouraged her to see the crucial importance of hope in a prison in a country ruled by terror and whim. Rather than despair as the warden had intended, Caroline renewed her hope thus reviving the hope of the men in the cell with her.

Now, here I am, alone and lonely in my own cell. I never thought my life had much impact on those around me, she thought, shaking her head in wonder at the path of her second life. *Father, please protect me, I'm only trying to follow your will.* **In this world you will have tribulation but be of good cheer, I have overcome the world.**

Caroline's thoughts were interrupted by the slam of the cell door. She took up her compulsory position in the centre of the room, waiting apprehensively. The open door revealed the Russian that Caroline had seen escorting the new prisoner. Two prison guards entered, gripping the arms of—*Him.* He was a handsome man, about six feet tall, with a powerful chest and fine, aquiline features. His head had been shaved but she guessed from the colour of his beard stubble that he was likely dark-haired. He wore black dress slacks, a white cotton dress shirt open at the neck and black dress socks. His outfit was a noticeable contrast to the uniforms worn by the other prisoners: grey cotton shirts; and light coloured longyi, really just a long strip of cloth tied at the waist to form a skirt or tucked up between the legs to form pants. As he stared at the wall behind Caroline's head, she noticed the muscles in his jaw clenching and unclenching. Aside from this movement, his face revealed no emotions. His arms were tied behind his back and he bore the emerging bruises of a recent beating.

Eloquently welcoming the prisoner to his new home, the Russian expressed his eager anticipation of the 'games to come'. As Vlad and the guards departed, the new prisoner inspected Caroline, casting his eyes coldly up and down her body, taking in her five foot three inch frame, short brown hair and soft body.

"Who are you?" he demanded, fixing her with an icy stare.

"My name is Caroline—Caroline Wells. What's your name?" she responded evenly, hugging her arms around herself to hold in her anxiety.

"George," he replied. "You're American!" He hurled the words at her.

"No. I'm Canadian. Why does everyone always assume I'm an American?" She inquired, annoyed by his attitude, and then stated matter-of-factly, "You're British."

His eyes narrowed, studying her, seeming to bore through her skin to her skeleton. "Why are you in this prison and why have they put me in here—with *you*?"

"I'm here because I interfered with some soldiers molesting a young woman and her daughter in a tea shoppe in Yangon. I do—" she began.

He interrupted. "That was an utterly daft thing to do! The shoppe owner was likely Military Intelligence. The woman was probably an activist."

"Yes, thank you," she retorted sarcastically. *He really is an arrogant jerk,* she thought. "I think I understand why Htet thought putting you in here would be a punishment for me," she continued wryly. His eyes widened a little in shock, then narrowed again.

"Untie me," he ordered. Caroline studied him for a time, her ire firmly in place at the back of her throat. **In quietness and confidence shall be your strength.** She took a deep breath to still the angry pounding of her heart and whispered, *Okay Father.* George watched her.

"If you turn around, I will try to untie the ropes," she replied as calmly as she could manage. As he turned, she saw his hands, reddened by the constriction of the ropes, his fingers occasionally twitching. Caroline worked at the tight ropes, eventually loosening them with her teeth, noting the rope burns surrounding his wrists.

George turned around, rubbing his hands to restore the circulation and examining the two identical bunks, each made up with military precision as Caroline had been instructed to do in her early days at the prison.

"Which is your bunk?" he asked with a flat, deadpan expression. Caroline pointed and watched him climb into the other bunk, roll away from her and go to sleep. Caroline shook her head, humming quietly to herself. She felt as if a storm had swept through the room—demanding, troublesome and ungrateful.

The following morning, Caroline was awakened by a guard entering the room and dragging George from bed. He met the guard's gaze with disdain. Handing him a pair of shabby grey shorts, the guard smacked George in the gut with his rifle butt and ordered him to "CHANGE". Glancing at Caroline, George seemed to blush a little. *Well, at least he's not completely self-absorbed*, she thought. Turning away, she gave him a little privacy to change his clothes. As he finished changing, Vlad entered the room.

"Dobry den, John Brock, kak vashi dela? How are you? I see you managed to remove your bonds. That will never do." Vlad turned to the accompanying guard. "Bind his wrists!"

"John?" Caroline's surprised whisper was ignored by Vlad but John gave her an enigmatic look as she flushed with anger, her eyes narrowing. *What a liar! He couldn't even tell me his real name. His name's not George. I wonder if it really is John.* Caroline's thoughts were interrupted when Vlad continued.

"We have many days together, I think, to truly get to know one another. Seycha, now the games begin!" As John was led from the prison cell, his posture conveyed confidence and calm.

Caroline's subsequent days fell into a pattern. John, *formerly known as George*, Caroline reminded herself, was removed every morning for questioning and returned every afternoon, looking daily more worn and oppressed, and usually sporting an extra set of bruises. She was expected to make up his bunk as he was usually dragged from bed still half asleep. In the evenings he was surly and difficult, snubbing all Caroline's attempts to make peace.

To make matters worse, when John was introduced to Caroline's cell, she had expected food rations to be doubled—but they weren't. John bullied Caroline over the meal portions until she coldly offered him half. An arrogant man, obviously accustomed to being in charge of others, he questioned her repeatedly about the reasons for her incarceration. She repeated the story again and again, hoping this would ease his irritability. It didn't.

So Caroline went to bed annoyed and hungry again. *When I first arrived here, I joked that prison food wasn't worth eating anyway. Now, it's not so funny. My body adjusted to less food. Will I be able to adjust to half of that? Father, help me.* Caroline prayed, lying in her bed, hugging her hungry belly. Gradually, she drifted off to sleep. In the middle of the night, Caroline was awakened by a voice—John's voice. She stepped over to see if he was speaking to her but saw that he was obviously talking in his sleep.

Firmly placing her hand on his shoulder, she remarked, "You're dreaming."

Immediately coming alert, John flew out of bed and grabbed her shoulders, demanding harshly, "What are you doing?"

"You were talking in your sleep," she replied unevenly.

"What did I say? What did you hear? Tell me right now!?" John yelled at her punctuating each sentence by shaking her violently. Fear flickered across her mind to be quickly replaced by iron.

"Get your hands off me!" Caroline hissed as she leaned into his angry face to accentuate her words. Clenching her fists, she pushed him away with all her strength, his knees buckling as they collided with the bunk behind him. "I have had enough of you! You have bullied me and lied to me—enough! You stay on your side and I'll stay on mine. And don't you **ever** touch me again!!!" Caroline returned to her bunk shaking with spent emotion. Climbing in, she rolled away from him as if to clearly end the encounter. John's stunned expression filled her mind. Eventually, she heard him climb back into his bunk and roll over to sleep. *Did he honestly think I would let him treat me that way? What a jerk!*

Caroline refused to look at John the next day. He was dragged away as usual in the morning and she waited impatiently for her turn in the exercise yard. Three times a week, Caroline was allowed to mix with the other "political prisoners" in the prison courtyard, a muddy, square space surrounded by coiled razor wire and prison guards, pacing and smoking foul smelling cigars. She was grateful for these times, guessing that Htet allowed them merely to have something to take away from her. How on earth did her small acts of kindness "damage" his prison?

Outside, Pastor Paul approached with a kind greeting, asking after her health.

"How are you today, my friend?" asked Paul.

"Hungry," Caroline replied. "They've cut my rations—well, not really, they just added a new person without increasing the food."

"I heard that there was a new prisoner in your cell."

"Yes," replied Caroline.

"Who is he?" he asked.

"He's a spy, I guess, a British spy." She gave as little information as she could to prevent her distaste from brimming over onto the kind and good man in front of her.

"You do not like him"—a statement rather than a question.

Caroline sighed in frustration. "No. He's rude and violent... and a liar. He told me his name was George but it's not. It's John—John Brock."

"He's a spy, yes? It's rather his job to be a liar, isn't it? Perhaps he feels that he has people to protect with his lies," Paul postulated.

Caroline sighed again. "I suppose. But truth has to be an end in itself, don't you think?"

"What would you say to save the people you care about, Caroline?" Paul gently rebuked her.

"You know I don't believe in conditional ethics," she replied firmly.

"But," Paul persisted, "if this man feels that his lies may save the lives of his people, then how harshly can we judge him?"

"Stop," she pleaded. "He was mean to me."

Paul laughed lightly. "'Blessed are you when they revile and persecute you for My sake', the Teacher said. 'Love thy neighbour', Caroline. 'Turn the other cheek'."

"You're right," she conceded quickly, putting up her hand to stop him, "You're right," she repeated, deflating before him. She remained in thought for a long time. *I don't like John but I guess that doesn't mean I can't be nice to him, sometimes.*

"I have heard that they are torturing him—the 'games' they call it." Paul rested his hand on Caroline's shoulder for a moment then left her alone with her thoughts.

Father, give me compassion for this man, she prayed. Caroline's anger at *George*'s rudeness and arrogance were transforming into compassion at *John*'s predicament. She knew what 'the games' were at this place. This building housed the vulnerable and the dangerous along with those who threatened the well-being of the powerful. John's day would not be a day of sprints, field goals and winning shots, but a day of torture: cruel and brutal. In spite of how she felt about him, she didn't think anyone deserved that fate.

Later, sitting on her bunk, Caroline awaited John's return with a renewed determination to show him compassion. Pushing John into the cell, the guards removed his bonds and departed. He moved awkwardly into the room, scowling at her and moving toward the toilet. Caroline turned away to give him some semblance of privacy.

Groaning, he moved to his bunk where he tried and failed to sit down, beginning instead to pace gingerly between the bunks, holding his shoulders stiffly. Still clad only in the grey shorts, Caroline noticed the red welts laddered along the backs of his legs as he passed by, plodding along the damp concrete floor in his bare feet. *No wonder he can't sit down. I'll bet those welts continue across his buttocks, poor man,* Caroline thought sympathetically.

"What did they do to you today?" she inquired gently.

Maintaining his pace, he glared at her, his jaw clenching and unclenching.

Swallowing her irritation, she tried again. "John, I can see they hurt you. Maybe I can help."

"Just leave me alone," he demanded through clenched teeth.

Her feelings of good will gained this afternoon were quickly evaporating but she had long ago learned that Christians were called to do the right thing in spite of feelings, not because of them. Reaching out tentatively, she touched his arm. He froze.

Uncertainly, she asked, "Are your shoulders sore? Maybe I can—"

Spinning to face her, he grabbed her shoulders in a vice-like grip, pulling her up off the bunk, hissing: "You want to know what they did to me?" He squeezed harder, pulling her face closer to his. "They tied a rope to my wrists and suspended me from the ceiling so that only my toes could touch the ground. Then they left me there—they left me there until it felt like my shoulders were being torn from my body." He gritted his teeth as he continued. "When they returned, they beat me with a switch. What can you do about that? Huh? Tell me." He was panting in his anger. "Just leave me alone!"

She hesitated, her eyes filling with tears of pity. Suddenly, he pulled her toward him, covering her mouth with his own, kissing her hard. Caroline struggled and when his grip loosened and his mouth softened, she shoved him in order to get away. He seemed to flinch back from her before he twisted away and edged onto his bunk.

Squeezing her arms around her knees, trying to still her quaking, Caroline sat on her bunk staring at John's back. *This is the one thing I've been so terrified of in here. Father, I thought you were going to protect me from that. I'm so frightened. Please protect me from this violent man!* Watching John's every move, she pushed a portion of the blanket against her mouth, sobbing out her fear and frustration. **Beloved, he who keeps you will not slumber. He who keeps Israel will neither slumber nor sleep.** With God's promise in her heart, Caroline began to relax and eventually succumbed to sleep.

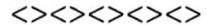

<><><><><>

Captain Htet sat chuckling, very pleased with himself as one of the guards told him of the spy's attack on the Christian missionary. *Wonderful! We'll see if this rogue can finally beat her ideas of compassion out of her. This should be most entertaining.*

Vlad entered the office without knocking, spoiling Htet's good mood. Without preamble, he began, "We will commence the sleep deprivation cycle tomorrow. Have you organized a guard rotation as I requested?"

Htet rose slowly from behind his desk. "Of course," he replied, "how do you intend to accomplish this?"

Gazing at Htet with disdain, Vlad explained slowly, as though to a child. "We interrogate him tomorrow and if he continues to resist, we keep him awake, all day and all night for seventy-two hours then we question him again."

Htet's body stiffened at the condescending tone in Vlad's voice. "I see," he ground out between his teeth. Htet called in his assistant and instructed him to be at Vlad's disposal for the next few hours. *Vlad the Impaler, indeed, more like Vlad the Idiot.* Htet amused himself with his thoughts.

<><><><><>

In the morning, John was again dragged from sleep into the waiting bonds of his captors. He had lain awake long into the night playing his actions and reactions over and over again in his mind until his need for sleep had overcome his self-reproach. When he had grabbed *her*, he had intended to push her away but the sight of her soft brown eyes filling with tears of pity *for him* had countered his will. He was unaccustomed to the feelings that brief kiss had evoked. He tried to find an excuse for his behaviour—but there was none. He had behaved appallingly. *What difference does it make?* He tried to justify his actions. *Maybe now she'll leave me alone. She's probably just a mole, put in here to get information from me.* John nursed his angry thoughts but no matter how loudly his mind screamed it couldn't drown out the question, *why does she make me feel this way?* At the memory of Caroline's stifled sobs, John's heart clenched in his chest, his guilty misery sitting like lead in his bowels. Glancing at Caroline as he exited the cell, he wondered again at her reaction to his kiss. Her strength and fortitude had surprised him.

Hauled into the drab, all too familiar interrogation room, his nose wrinkled at the rank smell of the place; the smell of perspiration, blood and hopelessness. Forcing himself to breathe deeply in order to calm his queasy stomach, John inhaled the thick air. He knew that, in time, he would become accustomed to the pungent odour which assaulted his senses like a punch in the face. The pock-marked grey walls which still echoed with the screams of its former captives, and the strange stains on the pitted concrete floor added to the stifling nature of the windowless space. The room was bedecked with despair.

Releasing John's wrists from their bonds, the guards roughly pushed him down onto a wooden chair where his wrists and ankles were shackled to the arms and legs of the chair. John lifted his chin in defiance even though inside, he quaked with fear. This was not the first time he had been captured by enemies; not the first time he had faced torture; however, he knew that his history with Vlad made this particular interrogator a very dangerous enemy. On arrival at the prison, he had recognized enough of the surrounding geography to realize he was somewhere in southern Myanmar, a country known for its political instability. When kidnapped and brought here, he'd been unable to leave any kind of message behind.

As he awaited the day's fresh torment, his hands were shaking but he thought this was probably more from the fact that he had hardly eaten in the past three days than the fear he was hiding. John looked up and blinked as a large man loomed in front of him and, immediately, he lost all interest in food.

<><><><><>

Upon John's return, Caroline attempted to ignore her cell mate as he seemed to ignore her, pretending that, within the tiny room, they could retreat from one another. That evening, Vlad entered Caroline's cell with two guards in tow. He ordered John and Caroline to sit on their bunks, watching

John gritting his teeth against the uncomfortable position with amusement, as Caroline sat on her bunk.

"Hurts a bit, does it?" Vlad inquired with a vile grin. John narrowed his eyes in response. "You will remain in this position until I return." Vlad departed but the guards remained, holding rubber truncheons in their hands. Quaking in fear, Caroline looked over at John questioningly then quickly looked away. His angry face reminded her too much of the other night.

Caroline could see that John knew what was coming. His eyes glazed over, staring at the space just above her head. Not realizing that she was making noise, Caroline began to hum until she was told firmly to "hsei"!

She tried to occupy her mind with memories and remembered stories but eventually, nature's call began to scream and she requested politely, "Excuse me, may I use the toilet?" Holding her breath, she waited anxiously for the guards' response. She saw John glance at her face as the guards exchanged a look and shrugged. Attempting to block out the fact that there were three men watching her, she relieved herself then returned to her bunk. John was still watching her but resumed his glazed staring once she settled. He was tapping out a rhythm on his leg with his fingertips as he gazed at the grimy wall.

As evening drew night around itself like a blanket, Caroline drifted toward sleep only to be awakened by a guard shaking her roughly. She opened her eyes in shock and fear to see John watching her again. She thought she glimpsed a look of fear or loathing dance briefly across his features before he quickly looked away.

Rotating the guards throughout the night, Vlad wandered into the room every few hours merely to gloat, smirking and stroking his beard. He seemed to know full well that the effects of sleeplessness wouldn't be evident until the next night but he clearly enjoyed the power he held over his victims. He obviously loved his job.

The guards allowed Caroline to relieve herself every few hours but she noticed that John hadn't moved. Every time she began to doze off, one of the guards would shake her awake. Her entire body spoke of her discomfort and fatigue; an aching back and screaming muscles in her legs gave way to exhaustion and she wanted to sleep—oh, how she wanted to sleep.

Finally, in the morning, Vlad announced that she could be allowed to sleep and, sliding sideways onto her bunk, she succumbed almost immediately. Awaking several hours later, she looked over to see John sitting in the same position, eyes distant, teeth clenched. *He must need to relieve himself by now,* she pondered. As she returned from using the toilet, she heard him groan in frustration.

"I need to go to the toilet," he said through clenched teeth. One of the guards grinned wickedly while nodding slowly. Uncurling himself, John rose stiffly from the bunk. He sighed as he finally relieved his bladder. As he moved back toward his bunk, the guard with the wicked grin stepped toward him, truncheon raised.

"What do you think you're doing, spy?" he hissed. "You were told not to move." Caroline looked up in surprise and confusion.

What's going on? They told him he could go. Studying John's face, she tried to discern the message printed there but all she could read was resignation. As she glanced back at the guard, he lunged at John, smacking him across the chest, knocking the wind out of him then following up with two strikes across John's back. Caroline cried out in surprise, rising from her bunk instinctively to protect the unarmed man. Drawing her body around John, she received the next blow on her shoulder. Crying out, she gripped John harder. Pulling out of her grasp, he grabbed her shoulders and pushed her away from him. A look resembling panic flitted across his features.

"What are you doing?" he demanded in rising dread.

"It's not right. He said you could get up," she replied, close to tears.

"Get back!" he insisted, shaking her in his alarm. "Don't ever do that again!" he exclaimed.

Dazed, she climbed into her bunk. The guard struck John twice more then ordered him back on the bunk. John sat, huddled over his bruised ribs, watching her uncomprehendingly. She was shaking in shock, her breath shuddering in her chest as she buried her face in her arms. *How can they treat him that way? Why does he hate it when I help him?*

As the moon crawled slowly across the face of Burma, John and Caroline kept silent vigil together. With the second and then the third night closing in, Caroline wandered toward sleep again, only to be awakened by a violent shaking.

"You know," she snapped, "all this shaking is not good for my cerebrum!" John chuckled, earning himself a hard slap.

In the evening, Vlad arrived again to gloat over his prisoners' suffering.

"Dubroye utro, Brock. You seem to have earned yourself a few extra bruises. Excellent!" he observed, spitefully. Nodding to the guard, he declared that the woman could sleep again. Caroline lay down, watching John carefully.

"Bind him!" The guards were commanded. Once the guards had bound John's hands behind his back, Vlad produced a noose. Swinging it loosely in his hands, he paced back and forth in front of John, delighted by the fear which briefly flickered across his features.

"So you know this game, do you?" Vlad sneered, stroking his pointed beard. "For the lady's benefit, I will explain." Turning to Caroline, he revealed his purpose. "First we thread this rope through the hook in the ceiling." Handing the rope to one of the guards, he paused as the guard demonstrated. "Then, we place the noose around our illustrious guest's neck." He paused again while the guard followed his instructions.

"Next, we tie the end of the rope around his ankles." The guard complied. "So you see that, if he falls asleep, he will slowly suffocate." Caroline watched in growing horror as the reality of John's predicament became dreadfully clear.

"Dobroy nochi, Shpion—good night, Mr. Spy." Vlad displayed an exaggerated bow and exited, gesturing to the guards to follow. Stopping short at the door, he paused and spun around. "And, my lady, if any of those ropes are removed, you will receive an invitation to my interrogation chamber!" he declared, maliciously, before turning briskly on his heel and exiting the room.

Caroline slowly pushed herself up to a seated position, her eyes tracing the course of the rope from John's feet, up and over the rusty eyehook in the ceiling to the knot around his neck. She stepped toward him, moving around to his back.

Watching Caroline carefully, he asked shakily, "What do you think you're doing?"

Caroline looked beyond him to the rope. "Maybe I can loosen the knot."

"Didn't you hear him?" he growled. "Look at me. Look at me!" he insisted authoritatively. Caroline paused in her advance, looking him directly in the eyes with a serious mien.

"The rope will be fixed in place. Just get away from me." John raised his voice, the emotion causing his body to sway. "Leave me alone!"

She began to pace around him again, studying the rope.

John gaped at her. "GET—AWAY—FROM—ME!" he yelled.

Fixing him with a determined stare, she challenged him, matching his tone of voice. "MAKE ME!" She stepped toward him. "Why do you hate it so much when I try to help you?!" she demanded, standing toe to toe with him.

His eyes widened with shock and disbelief. Quietly, he replied, "I don't hate it, but I can't let you risk this—not for me."

Silently deliberating, she began to examine the noose, testing it. *Maybe there's a reason for his anger. I know I'd be angry if people treated me this way.* Sadly, she returned to face him. "You're right. I can't loosen the knots. They've done something to fix them in place. What can I do to help?"

"Nothing!" he pleaded morosely. "There's nothing you can do. There's nothing anyone can do for me."

The sadness, almost despair, in his voice touched Caroline's heart. Shaking her head, she responded, "I can help keep you awake."

Climbing onto her bunk, she sat cross-legged at the end where she could look him in the face. "Well, you're not exactly forthcoming with information, so I suppose I'll have to do the talking." She readjusted her position to be a little less comfortable, hoping that would help keep her alert, and sent a prayer heavenward for wakefulness. "My name is Caroline Wells, as I've told you. I was waylaid in Burma on my way to Singapore to administrate a school for missionary children there. What you don't know is why I was travelling—why I left my home in Canada to travel across the world. Three years—"

Interrupting her, John implored, "Don't do this. You can't risk this—not for me." His words trailed off quietly.

Beginning again, Caroline stated, "As I said, John, three years ago—"

"Why are you doing this?" John beseeched her, as though losing the will to struggle against this bane of a woman who couldn't take 'no' for an answer. "You're daft—you make no sense! Why are you doing this?!"

"John." She noticed his eyes soften when she said his name. "My life has been ordinary. I've never done anything great or outstanding. That's why I decided to go to Singapore, because

I thought that would give me something I could point to and say, 'I did that'." She paused, snorting softly in self-ridicule. "I know now that it's not my lot in life to do anything great, but at least I can do the right thing." She raised her eyes to look at his face again. "That's what I'm doing here—now—I'm trying to do the right thing, in Jesus' name."

"But why?" he tried one last time.

"If my Henry had been in your position, I would hope that someone would be willing to do the same for him," she finished softly.

John stilled at her words. Caroline shrugged to gather her emotions then continued lightly, "Now John, shut up and listen." Grinning weakly in spite of himself, John was silent as she began her story again. "Three years ago, my life changed forever. My husband of fifteen years and my five children were killed in a plane crash…." As she told her story, Caroline was transported back in time to the day she waved goodbye to her children and husband as they boarded a northern charter bush plane to begin two weeks of camping in the Northwest Territories of Canada, the perfect wilderness camping trip—a true adventure. She was supposed to go with them but had come down with a nasty flu and was simply too ill to travel. Henry had offered to pay to fly her up in a week and she had planned to take him up on that. It would be expensive but, well, it was only money. How many times—so many times—she wished she had gotten on that plane. Then her pain would be over. She would be camping in heaven with her beloved husband and her children—at peace always.

Caroline trailed off as she became absorbed in her thoughts. *That had been the hardest part of coping after the crash. I just wanted to die, too. I would never have been so selfish as to wish them back from heaven. Henry and the children's eternities were set. I just wanted to be there with them.*

Quietly, John inquired. "Why do you still believe in God if he let that happen to you?"

"Look, John, compared to what Jesus suffered for us, I haven't been through anything," she explained. "Have you ever heard the song, 'Jesus Loves Me'?" John shook his head. Caroline began to sing, "Jesus loves me, this I know, for the Bible tells me so. Little ones to Him belong. They are weak but He is strong...." Finishing the song, Caroline was engulfed in a wave of exhaustion. She yawned loudly three times in a row. John watched her, tenderness flirting at the corners of his eyes.

"Why don't you get some sleep? I'll be okay now," John suggested gently.

Caroline shook her head, trying to escape the desire for sleep. "I'm fine. Um, let me see, what else can I tell you?" She yawned again, large enough to swallow her own head.

A soft smile escaped across John's mouth. "Caroline." Her heart fluttering in her chest, she looked up at the sound of her name on his lips. "Caroline. I'll be okay, now." He paused. "Thank you."

She studied him for a few minutes, assuring herself that he was sincere. Nodding once, she pulled her blanket around her shoulders and lay at the foot of her bed where she could still see his face. Sleep overtook her in seconds.

<><><><><>

John saw Caroline awaken as the guards entered the cell. Cutting John's bonds, they dragged him bodily from the room, his head bowed in exhaustion, his mind spinning with fatigue. John tried desperately to capture even a few minutes of sleep as the guards dragged him along the corridor to the interrogation room but his hands and feet stung with the blood returning to normal flow. The guards didn't bother to shackle him to the chair, knowing full well that he would be unable to stand for some time.

Vlad entered the room, stroking his beard and smirking viciously at the sight of his adversary slumped in his chair. John mentally steeled himself for this confrontation, trying to order his thoughts as Vlad advanced on him, but his thoughts kept drifting toward Caroline, sitting on her bunk talking to him, keeping him sane. Shaking his head, he admonished himself; *those are not my prescribed memories. I have to get to my 'happy place', to escape in my mind, as I was trained to do.* Thoughts of Caroline persisted until he surrendered and let the memory of her sweet voice envelope him.

John was conscious of a new person entering the interrogation room as Htet stopped by after his noon meal.

"He looks asleep," Htet observed wryly, slapping his riding crop against his leg.

Bristling, the disdain dripping from his voice, Vlad replied, "He is not asleep. He is unconscious." Turning to one of the guards, he ordered him to rouse the spook. The frigid water caused John to gasp and sputter as the icy stream hit him full in the face.

Moving closer, Vlad screamed, "Who is in your network?"

Mumbling, John replied, "Caroline", revealing his thoughts. Vlad spun around, clenching Htet's shirtfront in his fist, pulling him nose to nose, and hissed threateningly, "Are you certain the woman isn't helping him?" Htet turned his head slightly to avoid the interrogator's foul breath and disposition. The wary guards watched their warden closely to see if he was seeking their help with the Russian.

"Of course, I'm certain," he declared. Vlad released him in disgust. Pacing away from Vlad and near to John, Htet muttered, "Besides, breaking the spy is your job. The proper functioning of this prison is mine. If I'm going to continue to provide 'people' to my Thai associates, I need this woman to stop interfering with everyone else."

Vlad now paced over to John and commanded the guards, "Return him to his cell. No food for that cell today." As the guards looked back and forth between the ex-KGB agent and the prison warden, Htet nodded and while the guards approached John, Vlad punched him solidly in the face, knocking him out.

<><><><><>

Caroline found John dumped unconscious on the floor of the cell just inside the door when she returned from her time in the courtyard. Paul had been proud of her actions; reaching out to help her cellmate. His encouragement was as balm to a dry and weary spirit, refreshing her.

Kneeling beside John, she turned his head to wake him and saw the imprint of knuckles along his cheekbone. Wetting a rag at the tiny sink, she returned to bathe John's face. He roused suddenly, grabbing her wrist.

"What are you doing?" he demanded gruffly, glancing up as Caroline's face hardened at his reaction. Struggling to his feet, he continued to hold her wrist, using it for support as he rose. Confused, Caroline followed rather than retrieving her hand, waiting to see what he was doing. Edging carefully onto his bunk, he rolled onto his side, facing her.

"Thank you," he said, sounding truly grateful. "You should get some sleep." Releasing her hand, he rolled gingerly toward the wall and slipped into sleep. Shaking her head in wonder, Caroline crawled into her bunk, prayed and fell asleep.

<><><><><>

John could feel Vlad's frustration at his lack of progress in "breaking" him. Returned to the interrogation room, John was bound to a length of chain fastened to the wall behind him. Three inmates stood in a line in front of John. *This is something new. Vlad must be trying a different approach.* The Big Guy, as John thought of him, walked up and down the line with a bamboo pole as Vlad asked his question, his one and only question. When John didn't answer, the Big Guy began to beat the inmates as they cursed and begged. Gritting his teeth against the horror, John blocked the faces of the inmates from his mind, attempting to maintain his resolve not to speak. This grew more difficult as the day wore on and the beatings became more severe.

Vlad used the same tactic he had employed that day for two more days. John clung to his training because he didn't know what else to do. Allowing the few to suffer for the many was the code he and his colleagues lived by. Always look to the "greater good" was their mantra. He pushed the prisoners' faces out of his mind and escaped to his happy place.

He revived the image of his mother—his mother laughing at his pranks: the one with the spiders; the one with the white pillowcase; the one that resulted in a bucket of raw eggs being dumped on his father's head. His father had been furious with him and he remembered his mother practically dragging the man from the room before he finished removing his belt to lay it across John's back. When his parents reentered the room some time later, John was waiting. His father sat across from him with a frosty look in his eyes.

"Now John," his mother began. "Sometimes a joke can go too far, can't it son?"

John nodded, watching the stain on the rug between his feet.

She turned her gaze to her husband, seeming to wait for him to speak. When he didn't, she sighed.

"Okay then. I want you to apologize to your father and promise that this won't happen again"

"Sorry, Dad," John mumbled.

She waited again. "Go and do your chores." His mother ended the episode. He could still hear his parent's voices as he left the room.

"He really is a good boy, darling," his mother said.

"That boy is *no* good. You don't help by indulging his so-called 'sense of humour'," from his father.

John's mental escape slipped as the bamboo pole smacked against his chest. Vlad appeared before him. "Mr. Brock, I think you have not been listening to me". Vlad's fist connected with John's sternum but before he could hit the ground, the Big Guy hauled him up. As he gasped to regain his breath, his eyes locked with one of the prisoners kneeling before him. He was a small man, sleight in stature. This was no common thief or rebel. This man's eyes bespoke intelligence and peace, not fear and ignorance.

"I forgive you." The man spoke gently, straight to John.

"You will tell me your network, Brock. Tell me *now!*" Before John could answer, the bamboo pole struck the gentle man across the shoulders, knocking him down.

"You do not listen to me! Will you not answer to save this man's life? Do you have no honour, shpion?" Vlad motioned to the Big Guy to continue beating the gentle man. When they stopped, he was lying in a pool of his own blood.

"He's still conscious!" Vlad yelled at the Big Guy. "Resilient little blaggart. What is he saying?"

The big guy leaned down to listen but hesitated when he stood up.

"Well? What? Speak you idiot!" Vlad's temper was fast spinning out of control.

"Jesus loves me," the Big Guy answered simply.

Vlad's eyes narrowed in cold fury and he brought his boot down on the man's head.

"Not anymore" he hissed. "Now, Mr. Brock, we'll see how willing our missionary lady is to help you. This was *Pastor*

Paul," he spoke the name with blind hatred, "a friend—a *Christian* friend of our troublesome Canadian woman."

This kind man was a Christian. Is that how he met his fate with such calm? This gentle man was a friend of Caroline's. What did that mean? Caroline was troublesome to Vlad. Therefore, she wasn't his agent; she wasn't a mole! John wondered if Vlad realized the importance of the information he had just given him. But what would she say when she found out her friend was tortured because of him? John tightened his feelings around his heart like a belt and closed his mind lest he betray his inner turmoil.

<><><><><>

Caroline was puzzled by the change in John's behaviour. *I thought we'd made some progress toward a more amicable relationship but yesterday he wouldn't even look at me or talk to me. He didn't have any more bruises so he wasn't beaten. I can't figure him out!*

When John returned to the cell that afternoon, Caroline was determined to discover what was going on. Once John's bonds were removed and the guards departed, she stepped over to talk to him. When she reached out to touch his arm, he pushed her hand away and headed to the toilet, head down, jaw clenched.

As he returned, she stepped in front of him and asked, "John, what's wrong?" He stood, frozen, eyes down. She tried again, "I'm just trying to help."

"Get out of the way," he snarled in response.

Caroline's expression hardened in reaction to his tone of voice, and her annoyance slipped into her own tone of voice. "I can see that they haven't beaten you, so what gives you the right to behave this way?" His only response was to clench his fists. Because of her irritation with him, Caroline didn't notice the warning signs of his rising emotion. When she nudged him to provoke a reaction, she got one.

His eyes flew to her face and she could see fire blazing in his pupils just before he grabbed her shoulders and shoved her away, yelling, "LEAVE ME ALONE!!!"

Undecided on whether to feel angry, hurt or afraid, Caroline stood, speechless. She saw him squeeze his arms across his chest and take a few deep breaths. Once his breathing settled, he flopped onto his bunk and faced the wall.

"You're just a jerk, you know! You don't know anything about gratitude." Caroline spat the words at John's back.

"Gratitude?" He spun out of his bunk to face her across the room. "Gratitude for what? For being trapped in this hellhole? For being tortured? Grateful that you think I'm a jerk—whatever that is!"

"Shut up!" Caroline shouted back at him.

"Eloquent," John asserted wryly. Lying back down, he rolled away from her.

"I'd be happy to explain, if you like," she mumbled.

The following day, Caroline walked about the exercise yard looking for Paul, wondering why he hadn't come to find her. Normally, he sought her out, knowing that she needed his encouragement to face her days with John the spy. When she didn't find him, she approached the old priest, Rory.

"Where is Paul today, Reverend?" she inquired.

"You have not heard, then?" he replied. Caroline shook her head, as he explained. "He is in the infirmary, barely alive." The old man bowed his head as tears formed in his eyes.

"Wha-What happened?" Caroline asked, afraid to hear the answer.

"He was with your spy yesterday. Evidently, they used him and others in an attempt to force your spy to talk. When he wouldn't answer their questions, Paul was beaten nearly to death."

Caroline was shaking, "Has anyone been allowed to s-see him?"

"No, my girl, he is alone. We live in evil times." He walked away mumbling about the evils of this world.

Caroline stood frozen to the spot. She was still standing there when the guards called the prisoners in, barely noticing the slap she received for being tardy, though it did force her body into motion.

Caroline paced the cell, awaiting John's return, her mind a violent torment of scattered images. As John entered the room, she launched herself at him. The guards beat a hasty retreat, eager to report this new development to Captain Htet.

"Wha—" John's words were cut off by Caroline's fist. She grabbed his shoulders and shoved him against the wall, slapping him and slapping him again.

"You heartless coward! How could you?!" she screamed at him as he raised his arms to protect himself. Advancing on him, she slapped him again, continuing to beat on him as he sank to his knees. The blood pounded in her ears and she saw nothing but red as she followed him down with her fists. She could feel that he wasn't putting up any resistance but that fact didn't abate her anger.

A cold chuckle floated across the room bringing Caroline's movements to a halt. Vlad stood at the door watching with a huge smile on his face. When he saw her looking at him, he winked, shut the door and walked away.

Breathing hard, Caroline stood, fists clenched. John's coughing brought her around to see blood flowing from his nose. Turning on her heel, she stalked to her bunk.

"C-Caroline?" John wheezed. She froze, her back turned toward him, her fists still clenched at her side.

"Paul is a good man, John, a kind man," she stated evenly, and then softer, "he is my friend."

"Caroline—" he said again softly.

"Do you know why he's in here?" As she turned on him, he flinched back from her. "Do you?" She advanced on him but stopped short. "One of his parishioners got himself into debt with his employer who came to take the daughter as payment. A child as payment, John! Paul hid the child when they came to take her. That's it. He was arrested and brought here. And now his life is hanging by a thread! Because of *you!* He is my friend. He told me to be kind to you—to give you the benefit of the doubt!" Her voice increased in volume with every phrase.

"Caroline," John moaned. "I'm sorry."

"What did you say?" she replied ferociously.

John alleged earnestly, "I didn't want them to hurt him."

"You disgust me!" She spun around and rolled into her bed, covering her head with her blanket, trying to tune out his voice. She heard John haul himself into his bunk, and then he was silent. She cried long into the night.

For the next three days, the brutal, coercive pattern resumed. John was removed in the morning and returned in the afternoon, looking more pale and exhausted each day. Caroline completely ignored John. She stoked her anger and blanked her mind of anything that might soften her resolve to hate him. *Okay, God, I know I'm not supposed to hate him but I can't help it.* **Daughter, love one another as I have loved you.** Shaking her head, she made internal excuses to justify her hatred but she wasn't able to escape the memory of her own words to her own little son when he asked why he needed to forgive his brother. *"Holding a grudge hurts the holder even more than the other guy. Hate builds up inside you, making you unhappy. Forgiveness frees you from the hurt."* The flaming glow of her hatred began, very minutely, to cool.

<><><><>

On the third day, Vlad again changed strategies.

"Ah, Mr. Brock, I believe that we must keep the games fresh and exciting in honour of your illustrious success in 'resisting interrogation'. You remember do you not, when we met in Moscow at the Lubyanka, the games we played? I believe you are familiar with this game." Vlad moved aside gesturing to the tripod in the middle of the room with his outstretched arm. John's stomach churned in anticipation.

Vlad moved in close to John, breathing his foetid breath into his face. "You gave me considerable trouble at that time, if you recall." Vlad paced around John, hands slapping behind his back. "You know, of course, that I lost my privileges when you were rescued. I had not retrieved one useful piece of information from you when you were in my clutches." Grabbing John's face, Vlad used his thumb to force John's head back as he continued to speak into his face. "I have had to find an alternate use for my skills since that time or risk a one way trip to Chechnya." Here Vlad released John's head, thrusting him back a step. "But here—now—we have all the time in the world to play together. Your pathetic organization has no idea where you are or who has snatched their precious "shpion"—their precious spy. Begin!" This last word was directed to the guards who immediately reacted, forcing John roughly to the tripod and fastening his wrists to the bars.

"We shall begin with an easy one," began Vlad. "Again—tell me of your network."

John heard the crack of the whip a split second before he felt the searing pain across his back. He fell back on his training—take your consciousness away from the present situation. Clenching his teeth, he earned another crack of the whip as a reward for his silence as he took his mind away—away from this place, away from the sight, the smell—the pain. The memory of Caroline's gentle questions flashed across his mind but he pushed it aside. *I can't think of her now. She's so upset with me.* He found a happy memory and pursued escape, retreating into his mind to block out the discomfort, just as he had been taught. He didn't have many happy memories, and they all revolved around his mother, but he was able to keep his mind absent from the present, having been well trained in 'resistance to interrogation'.

He supposed that mothers were usually closer to their daughters but he knew his mother had always preferred him and his rambunctious behaviour to his more sedate sister. His mother was kind and gentle but strong enough to keep his wildness in check. The summer that he was eleven years old, the summer before she died, he and his mother travelled to Wales. They camped in a caravan park nestled amongst the hills. Hiking through the mountains, they spent their days searching for salamanders, insects, abandoned railway tunnels, anything that might be of interest to an eleven year old boy. In the afternoons, they lay on the grass on the hillsides, inventing knock-knock jokes—some of the worst ever composed, he was sure—and creating stories of knights and dragons. John loved his mother. His memories traveled the history of time with him.

He remembered the day his mother taught him to ride his bicycle. He must have been five years old. Tucking her skirt into her belt to create pants, she gripped the seat on his little two-wheeler and ran along behind him, shouting encouragement. "You can do it, John. Keep peddling, son." Heady with the sensation of rapid movement, he sped off, peddling furiously down the driveway and out onto the road in front of his house. Circling back to the house, he grinned in triumph at his mother who stood clapping her hands, cheering his efforts. Speeding into the driveway, he lost control of the bike as the asphalt changed to gravel beneath him. Heading straight for his mother, he swerved and landed in a heap in the flower bed, directly on top of his mother's prize roses.

As she extracted him from the thorny bushes, his father rounded the corner, taking in the bicycle in the flower bed and the crushed roses scattered around. He reached John in two strides and tore him from his mother's grasp. John's tears were stopped by the shock of his father's grip as he dragged John into the house while removing his belt. His mother pleaded with her husband, explaining that John had been trying to save her, but she was silenced with a look.

"You agreed that if I let you have children, I would be responsible for discipline," he stated. John could still remember the feeling that statement had had on him—the statement that your father had never wanted you. His mother stood by the door weeping silent tears as his father beat him. Once his father had exited the room and then the house, John's mother moved in to comfort him, holding him while he cried, whispering words of love and consolation. John had learned that day that he was valueless—only his actions mattered. He learned that good deeds were not rewarded.

They were so different, his mother and father. How had they ever come together? His mother was wild, a free spirit but his father was serious, a rule follower with no imagination and a frosty temper that silently froze you out when you transgressed any of his unspoken rules. Thoughts of his father made John's concentration slip. He was immediately conscious of a burning pain in his arm. The whip had snaked across his back and licked the sensitive skin under his arm. It was always harder to get back to his happy place when the pain was fresh. He braced himself for the next cut until, mercifully, he passed out from the pain—brief relief. His torturers did not allow him to regain consciousness on his own. He was certain they only gave him a few minutes wherein they could rest their weary arms, then they doused him in icy water to revive him—water to wake him but not to quench his thirst.

<><><><><>

The slam of the cell door marked John's return and though she was determined to ignore him, Caroline couldn't quite contain a gasp of surprise at what she saw: John hanging between the two guards, head down and breathing harshly through clenched teeth, his back laced with a dozen or so cuts, whip marks, she supposed.

They dropped him on the ground and walked out. Caroline battled with herself, her belly felt full of fear, fury and disgust, but her heart spoke pity as she watched John struggle to his feet, lurching to his bunk. He groaned loudly at the pain, a sob catching in his throat. Cautiously edging onto the bunk, he twisted onto his side, shivering in mild shock.

Torn between pity and anger she stood paralyzed, one hand on the wall at the foot of her bunk, humming softly to herself. **Tend my sheep.** *Father, no. He's a violent man. He's a liar. No.* **Tend my sheep.** Caroline shook her head, humming louder. She crawled into bed and rolled away from John, trying to roll away from his need. Tears continuing to fall, she pulled her blanket over her head and hummed even louder, attempting to drown out the turbulence of John's harsh breathing. The sound of his retching and loud groans invaded Caroline's mind like dragon's fire on a farmer's field as John made his way between the toilet and his bunk. *I don't want to help him. I don't want him in my life, Father. Take him away. Let someone else meet his needs,* Caroline beseeched the Good Shepherd. *Choose someone else, God. This is too hard for me.* **Let your light so shine before men, that they may see your good works, and glorify your Father which is in heaven.** As the words faded, images played across Caroline's mind, of Henry tied, stripped and beaten. **Daughter, I love you. Tend my sheep.**

Resigning herself to compassion, Caroline wet her small washrag and stepped over to John's side. Drawing a deep breath, she began to wipe the blood from his back.

Turning toward her in surprise at her first touch, he asked through his pain, "What are you doing?"

"I'm trying to help you," she informed him impatiently.

"I'm fine. I don't need your help," he stated instinctively, sounding irritated through his distress.

"Look, this isn't my idea. I think you're reprehensible but I'm going to do my job," she stated decisively, becoming annoyed at his stubbornness.

"Your job? Just leave me alone," he demanded but Caroline could hear the insincerity in his voice. When she didn't respond, he lay his head back down and waited to see what she would do. She hesitated. *Maybe there's more to him than I think.* She tightened her resolve and began to wash his back again. He flinched at her touch.

"Does that hurt?" she asked grimly.

"What do you think?" he muttered, not looking at her. She clenched her fist in anger around the cloth, the water sliding in a stream down his back, causing him to shudder at the sensation.

"Then shut up and stay still," she ordered. And he did.

When she had cleaned his wounds as best she could, she stepped back and watched him for a while. She began to see the faces of her husband and children in the man before her: Henry, Aleck, Gabe and the little ones. Then she saw the faces of the women and men who had shared her incarceration: Mya, Hla, Sanda, Paul, Rory. She shook her head and blinked away the tears that were leaking slowly from her eyes. The force of the emotion weakened her knees and she found herself sitting at the top of his bunk.

"You don't have to stay with me," John stated evenly.

"No, but I can't exactly go far either, can I?" Caroline said with an edge in her voice.

"No, I suppose not," he said quietly, then, after a pause, "thank you."

His gentle response surprised her and she touched his head letting her hand stroke across his bristly hair. He looked up at her in surprise and, perhaps, something that resembled fear. She moved away to her own bunk, guardedly reviewing the events of the last few days in her mind. *Father, what is it you're doing here?*

CHAPTER 2

SEVENTY TIMES SEVEN

The next morning, Caroline woke to find John watching her, his face a portrait of misery. The sight of his misery further weakened her angry resolve and she sat up, still facing him rather than turning away.

"Caroline?" She stiffened in response to his words but didn't answer. "I didn't want them to hurt him. I'm sorry."

"Why?" she asked, fiercely. "Why did they hurt him?"

"They want information from me, but if I tell them, many more people will die."

She watched him silently as her anger continued to dissipate. *Paul was right. He's protecting someone with his silence and lies.* **A good shepherd lays down his life for his sheep.**

"Caroline?" John asked softly. "What is a 'jerk'? You said you'd be happy to explain it to me."

A laugh burst forth unexpectedly. Feigning seriousness, Caroline responded, "Well, I guess a jerk is an idiot, a contemptible idiot." As she said the words, she saw the hurt that flashed briefly across John's eyes and she sobered.

"A 'tosser'? Yes, I know what that means," he replied sadly. "I'm sorry for being a 'jerk' when you've been so kind to me."

Caroline looked up sharply to if he was mocking her but saw only sadness in his eyes.

The following day, instead of being taken outside to the exercise yard as usual after the noon hour, Caroline was delivered to the infirmary, a sterile room with sparkling white-washed walls and drains in the concrete floor. The windowless walls were lined with white-sheeted cots filled with one, two or three prisoners each, groaning in pain or weeping in despair. The smell of antiseptic was so strong that Caroline felt she could taste it on the humid air; antiseptic covering the sweetly rotten scent of suppuration. Vlad was waiting for her, occupying a chair beside one of those beds.

"Good morning," he said in his most charming voice as he stood, stroking his beard. "There is someone here I wish for you to see." He led her up to the side of the pitiful man in the bed; the pitiful man lying wrapped in cuts, bruises and blood. Caroline gasped as she recognized Paul.

"You see now what our friend, the spy, is capable of. He would not give me even the smallest, most unimportant piece of information in order to save this man—this poor man." As Caroline began to cry, Vlad continued. "I'll leave you alone a few minutes to see Mr. Brock's handiwork." Vlad stepped back to take up a position in the doorway, leaning casually against the frame.

"Paul." Caroline wept his name, falling into the chair by his side. Weakly, he opened his eyes.

"Seventy times seven, my friend," he wheezed and closed his eyes.

"You want me to forgive him? For this?" Caroline gasped.

"The good Shepherd lays down His life for His sheep." Paul's whisper was fading as Caroline leaned closer to hear.

"You forgive him?" Caroline asked in wonder.

"Seventy times se—" Paul's voice trailed off.

Caroline wept at her friend's side until Vlad moved over to retrieve her.

"Ah, my poor lady, what do you think of our Mr. Brock now?" Vlad patted her shoulder in mock sympathy, handing her a tissue.

Wiping her eyes, she stated, "I think I see through him, clearly—very clearly."

Caroline sat on her bunk, anticipating John's return. Waiting as the guards cut the bonds on his wrists, she watched him move gingerly to the bunk opposite her.

"I saw Paul today," Caroline stated, a sob in her throat.

John's eyes filled with pain before he ducked his head. "I'm sorry, Caroline," he offered in a hoarse voice.

"He told me to forgive you." John's eyes snapped to her face. His astonishment made Caroline smile, just a little.

"He told me he forgave me just before they started to beat him. Why did he do that, Caroline? He was so calm. All the others begged and pleaded. They cursed and swore at me. He forgave me." John lapsed into silence.

"What else?" she prompted.

"He was singing 'Jesus Loves Me'. That enraged Vlad. Jesus loves me." John watched her thoughtfully. "What does it all mean?"

When Caroline hesitated, swallowing back her tears to clear her throat for speech, John retreated from the conversation. "You don't have to talk about it if you don't want to."

"John, why would you think that I wouldn't want to talk about it?"

"Well, you've never talked about the God stuff with me before," he answered quietly.

"We haven't exactly had an amicable relationship so far, have we? I guess I assumed you would despise anything

Christian. I'm sorry." She continued, "Paul's a Christian, John."

"But what does that really mean? I've known lots of people who go to church, cruel and hypocritical people, and I've known many good people who would never darken an ecclesiastical door. Obviously, 'Christian' means something different than I thought it did." John watched Caroline expectantly.

"You know all that stuff it says in the Bible about Jesus being the Son of God, Him coming to earth as a baby, growing up, teaching, dying on a cross for our sins and then rising again?" Caroline started.

"Yes" replied John.

"Well, being a Christian means you believe it. But not just 'believe it and move on', believe with your heart *and* your mind. Believe it with your life. God is real, John. He is a real being that everyone can talk to *and* listen to. He cares about us and has a plan for each one of us. I talk to Him every day and He shows me how to live, even when I don't really want to be shown. Jesus is the reason that Paul can forgive you." Caroline continued softly, meeting John's gaze. "Jesus is the reason that I can forgive you."

"Me? Why would you forgive me? I've repaid every kindness you've shown me with spite and anger," he replied, astounded

"Why, John?" Caroline asked.

"What do you mean?" John was confused.

"Why have you been so spiteful?"

John went quiet for a long time. Finally, he raised his eyes to her face and concluded, "You make me want to lower my shield—but caring is destruction to a spook."

<><><><><>

Captain Htet received Vlad into his office. The Russian paced up and down in front of the desk, fuming. Htet saw this as a wonderful opportunity to goad the arrogant man but was still afraid of the Impaler and so he kept quiet.

"It's not working!" Vlad stated. "The woman is no longer helping him, hates him in fact, but he's still resistant. I've cut his rations, deprived him of sleep, laid open his back, and executed three of your prisoners on his behalf and still, nothing."

Htet cleared his throat. Vlad speared him with his angry eyes as Htet asked tentatively, "Have you tried water torture?" Vlad narrowed his eyes.

Taking three quick steps toward the cowering warden, he clapped him on the shoulder and announced, "It's always good to remember the old ways! Send for Brock immediately."

<><><><><>

As the night guards entered the cell, they made their way to the right hand bunk. Rather than calling to the prisoner, they reached down and grabbed a handful of hair, removing the prisoner from the bed. Caroline startled awake and cried out in surprise and pain. Before her feet could touch the floor, the guard slapped her hard on the mouth. Tears stung her eyes as she tried to understand what was happening. Reaching down, he grabbed the front of her shirt, hauling her upright, and then, punching her in the stomach, he dropped her to the floor. He reached again for her hair but suddenly released her. The next sounds Caroline heard were a humph and a clatter as the guard landed on his backside against the far wall. The second guard had been watching all this in amusement until he saw his compatriot arrive beside him. He raised his gun and aimed it at her. *No, wait, not at me, at John!?* Caroline realized that John was standing over her in a fighting stance, his fists balled in anger, his jaw clenched.

Extending a finger at the guard with the gun, he yelled, "You tossers! Don't you *ever* touch her again! Get out of here, NOW!"

Realizing their mistake, the guards panicked and called for reinforcements from the corridor. Knowing they didn't dare kill the British spy, the guards charged in with fists and quickly subdued John, dragging him from the room before they slammed the door shut.

Caroline remained in the centre of the room, shaking and sobbing, "Oh Father, save us."

<><><><><>

John was taken into the interrogation room, empty except for a trough of water. Fastening his arms tightly behind his back, a guard led him over to the trough and forced him to his knees. Pain seared through his body as the position opened every wound anew. John felt nauseated but didn't fancy having his head dunked in his own vomit all night, so he swallowed several times, trying to calm his stomach. *Oh God, help me*, he thought. If Caroline was right and there was a god, John thought that maybe now would be a good time for him to act.

They say that when you're drowning, your life flashes before your eyes but why do I only see the worst parts? His mind traveled back to that day when he was twelve, his birthday. He and his buddy, Cal, had planned a great prank on their teacher. Revenge for, not only being paddled at school following some misdemeanor but also for calling John's father so that he received another whipping that night. He and Cal had spent a week collecting every snake they could find and storing them in tall five gallon plastic buckets in Cal's father's metal shed. Fifteen minutes before the teacher was due to arrive for his daily swim at the old quarry, the boys released every snake into the water then hid in a tree overhanging the water to wait. As expected, when the teacher approached the edge of the quarry, he confidently dove in, coming up for a breath to emerge face to face with not one but three snakes. The screams he uttered were truly hilarious to the two boys bent on revenge. The teacher, shrieking, escaped to the shore and ran from the spot leaving his clothes behind.

John and Cal laughed so hard that Cal lost his balance and fell into the water. Cal was not a very good swimmer and he floundered, panicking. John dove in to try and save his friend. And then, miraculously, John's mother emerged from the trees and quickly judged the situation. She surveyed the area, finding nothing to throw to the boys. Kicking off her shoes, she dove in.

Coming up for air beside her son, she instructed him sternly, "John! Swim to shore and run to get your father." John obeyed, fully confident in his mother's ability to save the day. John returned with his father who reached the shore in time to pull his wife and Cal from the water. When Cal was returned to his family, and John's mother was showered and wrapped up in her bed, John's father had come in to him. Grabbing the front of his shirt in his fists, he pulled his son close to his face.

"If anything happens to her, I'm holding you responsible," he growled menacingly into John's face. "You bring nothing but pain to those around you."

John had wanted to see his mother to apologize but his father wouldn't let him enter her room. The next time he'd seen his mother had been at her funeral. When he'd begun to cry, his father had seized him by the shoulders, shaking him and reminding him, "You bring nothing but pain!" Pulled back to the present, John was finally dragged away from the water trough, and dumped on the floor of the interrogation room where he laid, retching and coughing and swallowed up in misery.

<><><><><>

"Why is he soaking wet!" Caroline flung the comment indignantly at the guards as they returned John to her cell. She saw John's small smile. *Has no one ever stood up for him before?* "Why is he wet? Isn't it enough that you starve him and beat him! Do you have to drown him, too?" Caroline's obvious agitation seemed to bother the guards and they had trouble maintaining eye contact as she helped John into bed. She kept her glaring eyes on the guards until they sheepishly left the room.

"For goodness sakes!" she continued in a gentler voice. "You're freezing! What do they think they're doing? How are you supposed to tell them anything if you're dead of pneumonia? What possible purpose can there be in wanting any information from you when you obviously aren't going to tell them anything? Are they stupid, or what? Living on goofy beans?" Caroline looked over sharply as she heard John chuckle beside her.

"What do you think you're laughing at?!" she demanded.

"You are formidable when you're angry." John gazed at Caroline with an unfamiliar emotion behind his eyes. Sounding confused, he remarked, "I hope you're never that angry with me."

Eyes downcast, Caroline sighed. "What do you mean? I have been that angry with you."

When he went quiet, she looked over to glimpse the reason but saw only sorrow printed on his face. Wrapping him in his thin blanket, she retrieved her own blanket to put around his shoulders. When she offered him a drink of water, he jerked away, speeding to the toilet where he promptly vomited up what seemed like a gallon of water. Weakened by the effort, he stumbled as he returned to his bed. Caroline supported him, wrapping him up again as warmly as she could, and helping him lie down on his bed. She took up a position sitting on the top end of his bunk and let him rest his head on her lap.

"Tell me about your family, about growing up," John demanded, hoarsely.

Caroline gazed at his face thoughtfully and began to speak of her childhood.

"I was born in India. My parents were medical missionaries..." After a while she trailed off, caught up in her thoughts.

"What happened next?"

She jumped as she heard John's voice. "I thought you were asleep," she replied in surprise.

"My back hurts too much," he stated simply.

"Here, roll over and let me see," she ordered. Once he'd rolled over, she could see that every healing wound on his back had been opened and they were oozing various levels of blood and pus. Her belly clenching in pity, she asked, "What did they do to you, today?"

"Dunked me in water," he replied, simply.

"What do you mean?" she asked, in growing horror.

He shrugged, "They put you on your knees with your wrists bound behind your back and then they dunk your head in water until you almost drown, pull you up and then do it again."

Her voice shaking, Caroline confirmed the horrid thought growing in her mind, "You've been through this—this kind of thing—before?"

Turning his face toward her, he replied thoughtfully, "Yes, a few times," he paused, adding quietly, "but I've never had anyone to help me before." He turned his face back to the wall. Her hands quivering and her stomach feeling sick, Caroline retrieved a cloth and began to clean his wounds.

"Talk to me—please," John implored.

"Hmmm, I don't think I can concentrate on that and this too," she responded, her voice still shaking.

"Sing then—please."

He evidently isn't used to saying 'please', she mused, *as it always seems to come out as an afterthought.* Taking a deep breath, she sang to him while she washed his back, trying to help him escape the pain—physical and psychological—just for a little while. He didn't seem to mind if the songs were children's songs, hymns or rock and roll, he was soothed by them all. Once his wounds were taken care of, Caroline resumed her seat at the top end of the bunk, allowing John to once again rest his head on her lap. As John was too uncomfortable to sleep, Caroline kept up a steady stream of conversation to keep his mind off the pain. They discussed architecture, evolution, even global warming, anything that took their minds off prison and pain.

Responding to yet another of John's assertions, Caroline retorted, "No way is that a good idea!"

"Don't tell me you buy the propaganda? You're too bright for that!" John smiled, evidently enjoying the challenge of her mind.

"You're just winding me up, aren't you? You don't really believe in it any more than I do, do you? Do you, *Jonathon* Brock?" Caroline challenged.

"My name is Bernard John Brock." John spoke quietly, glancing briefly at Caroline's face as he finished, seeming to judge her reaction. "My mother admired Bernard Shaw because of his views on the obligation of people to help each other."

Caroline's heart beat faster, marveling at the gift he had given her: trust. He offered her a tiny bit of trust. She understood the importance of this piece of information, the first real piece of personal information he had shared with her. Waiting for him to look at her again, she smiled.

Breathing rapidly, he said, "Anyway, you're fun to argue with." Caroline nudged him gently and smiled again.

Once John fell asleep, Caroline returned to her bunk, looking forward to some sleep. However, once she lay down, she was overcome by a gnawing fear in the pit of her belly that forced her to her knees beside the bed. She felt a strong urge to pray for John—to pray for safety from some new fear.

The morning came all too quickly but even so, her tired ears picked up the noise in the corridor and she shuffled across the cell to help rouse John. He groaned as he moved about, letting Caroline help him, so that when the guards entered again, John was ready for them, looking defiant.

"You're late!" he admonished as he walked unaided out the door. The stunned looks of the guards made Caroline smile to herself. *Now that was impressive*, she thought.

In spite of John's mettle displayed in the morning, Caroline spent the entire day with fear in the pit of her stomach, pacing and praying all day, wondering what was going on. When she was led out to the exercise yard as usual she heard screams—screams followed by screams and, perhaps, crying?! What if that was John? Her heart quavered at the thought of her cell mate in that kind of pain. *Father, be with John. Help him find his way to you and rescue him from his pain.*

After her turn in the yard, Caroline was taken to an interrogation room rather than her cell where she was shoved roughly into the room and ordered to "clean up this mess". Caroline gasped as her hand flew to her face, attempting to shield her senses from the gory smell of the space. There was John in the middle of the room, stripped to his skin and fastened by the wrists and ankles to a large plinth. Caroline's heart was squeezed in her chest as she saw him bound there, covered in vomit and filth, with electrodes attached to all the sensitive parts of his body. In that moment, she excused all of John's anger and bile. *Poor John! Oh Father! No wonder he was so angry. How would I react if I had to suffer this, or worse yet, if I knew I could be the cause of others being forced to suffer this?* Here he was, powerless, completely unable to protect himself. No wonder he kept tight control of his feelings.

Vlad cursed her slowness and gestured that she should retrieve a bucket and cloth and clean the smelly mess. When she didn't immediately move, she was slapped. Then, quickly retrieving the soapy water, mop and bucket, she moved over to the plinth and began to gently wash John's face. He flinched at her touch and whimpered, his eyes unfocussed and staring straight through her. Singing very softly as she tended him, his eyes slowly focused on her face and he began to weep quietly. So overcome was she with compassion for this man that she leaned over quickly to brush a kiss on his cheek while whispering directly into his ear, "You can do it. I believe in you."

"Toropites' glupyj," Vlad interrupted from across the room. "Get back to work!"

Caroline continued using the rags to clean John's body and then mopped the floor. When she was nearly done, she was ordered out, the guards returning her roughly to her cell where she collapsed weeping just inside the door.

When John was returned that evening, his eyes were glazed and distant. He didn't seem to see Caroline or anything that was going on around him as she led him to his bunk and washed him. His silence and blank gaze frightened her. When she put the water to his lips, he drank reflexively but threw up when he smelled the food. Cleaning him again, she helped him lie down on the bunk, choking back tears at the sight of his belly and thighs covered in angry, red burns. Silent, he made no sound as she wrapped him in a blanket and held his shaking body, rocking him and singing songs of comfort and hope. When she ran out of songs to sing, she began to tell him Bible stories. She told stories until she was overcome with fatigue. She realized that she had fallen asleep when she awoke feeling cold. Glancing around the room, she realized that John was in the corner, vomiting. She sat quietly, allowing him some privacy.

When he turned back to the bed, she inquired, "Are you okay?"

"I feel like burnt toast—" he wheezed, "burnt toast that's been dropped on the ground and driven over by a 10 tonne dump truck."

"It's good to have you back." She smiled. "You were gone there for awhile."

John seemed to be thinking about what to say as he limped back over, sitting beside her. Wrapping her arm around his shoulder, she gently nudged him, giving him permission to set his head down on her lap.

"Did you mean what you said? About God and David?" he asked. "I'd always heard that David was an adulterer. Is he really called 'a man after God's own heart'?"

Caroline paused, intrigued by John's interest in the story. "Yes, David is called 'a man after God's own heart' and yes he did commit adultery. David was called that, not because he was a great warrior or a model husband and father, but because he earnestly wanted to follow God. When he failed, he was sincerely sorry—truly repentant. God isn't looking for perfect people to bring into His kingdom. He wants us— broken, bruised, imperfect us. God takes us as we are where we are, and transforms us into something beautiful." John was silent for a long time and Caroline left him alone with his thoughts.

"When I was being shocked today—well, in between times—the words 'oh God, oh God' kept going through my head. I realized I was just sending those words off into space. I decided that, if *you* could believe that God was really at work here in this prison then maybe I should give him a chance, so I asked him to send me help." He retreated into silence again, looking off into the distance. Caroline waited patiently for him to gather his thoughts. "That was when you came into the room. At first, I thought they were going to hurt you, and that made me lose hope. But then you came to me and washed me and—and comforted me—" he paused while he tried to gain control of his breathing. "—and—and believed in me, and I—well, I didn't know what to think." John paused, turning his face to look up at Caroline. "Maybe God is real."

Caroline chose to be silent, allowing John time to think. After a while, John spoke again, "I'll be okay now. Why don't you get some sleep—and, Caroline—thank you for helping me." He sat up, reached over and tenderly brushed his fingers along her cheek. "Good night." Her heart raced at his touch and his quiet words

The next morning started in the usual way but once John heard footsteps in the corridor, he began to panic.

"I can't do this again, Caroline. If they electrocute me again, I'll tell them everything they want to know!"

Moving closer to him, she took him by the shoulders and shook him gently until his gaze fell on her face. "Pray John. Tell God what you want then trust Him." He continued to look panicked until she drew in closer and kissed him lightly on the cheek. His look of surprise made her smile.

"You can do this, John. Just hold on for one more day. I believe in you."

John straightened a little and went forward to meet his tormentors.

John was returned after only a few hours, his face a little bloodied and bruised but he seemed almost happy with his new wounds. After the guards exited, he walked over to Caroline and gave her a quick hug.

"John, what on earth is going on?" Caroline asked in wonder.

"I prayed. I prayed like you told me. I told God that I couldn't hold out any longer under that torture." He positively beamed at Caroline through his bruised and cut lips.

"Well?" asked Caroline searchingly.

"The machine broke. They had me all trussed up, connected and ready but the machine wouldn't work." John was laughing—actually laughing—as he told Caroline. "They argued and ordered and the big guy with the mean left hook got smacked about by Vlad," here John chuckled. "They finally untied me, knocked me about a bit and brought me back here." John moved over to Caroline and grabbed her in his arms to twirl her around until he groaned and folded over on himself as his battered body protested this kind of treatment. "My people will come, Caroline. My people will come and get us out of here! Today!"

"Today, John. Are you certain? Why today?"

"Well, maybe today, maybe tomorrow—maybe we'll have to escape but we ARE getting out of here!" John spoke with such assurance that Caroline began to believe he might be right!

CHAPTER 3

ESCAPE TO NOWHERE

John's prediction about release today was a little off the mark. Come morning, John and Caroline remained in their cell in the prison. They could hear thunder rumbling outside, hailing the heavy storms of the monsoon, the rainy season. However, something odd did happen—or rather—did not happen. The guards did not come to get John. They did not bring food. There was shouting and running in the corridor but John and Caroline seemed to be ignored.

"Tell me about your family, John," Caroline said to pass the time, buoyed by John's good mood. Immediately, a closed look played across his face. Assuming he had reverted to his shuttered attitude, Caroline saddened at his reaction. *Why did I do that? Why was I so foolish as to believe that this between us was friendship?* Moving across the room to John, she laid her hand gently on his shoulder and said, "Never mind. I won't ask again." Before John could respond, the room was rocked by a blast followed by another. John leapt up, grabbed Caroline and pulled her under her bunk with him. The next blast was followed by screaming and gunshots.

"Stay here!" John shouted over the din. "I'll be back"

"John!" Caroline's voice followed him across the room.

Cautiously testing the door to their cell, he found it knocked off its hinges. With a little strength, he was able to make a space to move through the doorway as Caroline waited, barely breathing. Relief spread through her when he re-entered the cell a few minutes later. Motioning for her to come, he announced, "Rebels! It looks like the Chin Liberation Army has come to rescue its people. They've blown a large hole in the wall and are releasing prisoners. Come! This is our chance!"

Creeping quietly down the corridors, they watched for guards, dodging anyone with a gun. As they approached the outer wall it looked that, if they timed it right, they should be able to sneak past the guards and the rebels and flee into the jungle. John moved a few paces forward and turned to motion Caroline to follow. The punch that connected with John's throat came out of nowhere. Stunned by the blow, John staggered back against a wall, clutching his throat and gasping for breath.

"Oh no you don't, my star prisoner. YOU WILL NOT LEAVE!"

VLAD! Following up with three hard punches to John's chest, Caroline heard ribs break. Swallowing the bile in her throat, she frantically searched the area for a weapon, her gaze falling on a broken chair leg. Grabbing it and rising up behind Vlad, she watched in horror as his fist connected with John's temple causing his head to bounce off the wall. Caroline brought the chair leg down with all her might on Vlad's skull. The crunch of bone made her nauseous but she swung again to be sure and when she looked, Vlad's head lay in a pool of blood. Retching at the sight, she tore her eyes from the interrogator to his victim, John, whose limp body lay sprawled on the ground.

Now what, she thought. This was their one chance of escape and it was up to her to save them. Moving over to John, she tried unsuccessfully to rouse him. Realizing that he probably had a concussion and needed to be moved carefully, she looked skyward for inspiration. As her gaze returned to John, she saw it, a stretcher lying against the wall which must have housed the prison infirmary. *Thank you!* Grabbing it, and setting it alongside John, she rolled him onto it.

Now, she thought, *where do I take him?* Grabbing the handles of the stretcher, she began to drag him, travois-style, toward the opening in the wall. As she moved them closer, she noticed trucks outside onto which the rebels seemed to be herding the prisoners. She didn't know whether or not the rebels would be better than the prison guards but there really seemed to be no other choice. Besides, if the guards ever discovered that she was the one who had attacked Vlad, then her life wouldn't be worth a pittance. As she pulled the stretcher up to one of the trucks, a rebel soldier looked from her to the stretcher and pushed her away.

"No," he said.

"Please," she replied.

He slapped her across the face, "No!"

"Please!" she responded.

The rebel soldier began to curse and scream at her, gesticulating all the while with his hands and machine gun.

"Please!" She yelled, "PLEASE PLEASE PLEASE!!! NOW!" Called away from his post, the rebel soldier finally waved her onto the truck, obviously not willing to be distracted with this crazy foreign lady and her injured man.

Caroline wanted to quickly take advantage of this leniency but she honestly didn't know how she was going to carry John by herself. In her worry, Caroline missed the look that passed between a woman on the truck and the man sitting beside her. The woman was Hla, one of the prisoners who had shared Caroline's cell during her early days at Bourey Prison. Hopping down, the man lifted John's shoulders, waiting for Caroline to lift his legs and together they shifted John onto the back of the vehicle. As Caroline climbed aboard, she recognized Hla and tears of gratitude filled her eyes as she clasped her hands around Hla's, thanking her again and again.

At the first crossroads, each truck in the convict convoy sought a different route away from the prison in order to confuse pursuit. The truck transporting Caroline and John proceeded northeast along a lesser road. Caroline huddled against the rain in the back of the truck with the other refugees of Bourey as the rain fell in torrents, covering everyone in gloom. Outside, hazy trees fled past in a murky blur as they drove on and on, taking increasingly remote and narrow roads.

Skidding, the truck lurched to a halt in front of a jeep which was parked sideways in the road. Several men with rifles emerged, greeting the men driving the truck. A hasty conversation took place followed by a soggy examination of the individuals clustered in the truck bed. The sight of John, unconscious on the floor, led to an animated discussion which filled Caroline with dread. Alerted by the men's angry tones, Caroline used all her linguistic powers to follow the conversation.

"... European ... prisoner...."

"...unconscious...no harm..."

"Form 10...disappear... not inconspicuous..."

"No! ... leave..."

"Abandon? ... against military intelligence..."

"... Too risky..."

"... No!...leave...NOW!"

The conversation ended when a soldier with a sub-machine gun jumped aboard and, lifting John bodily, dumped him in the road. Caroline sat, astonished. Regaining his position on the truck, the soldier grabbed Caroline by the arm and, pointing down into the road, insisted she get "down". Caroline complied, tears in her eyes. Climbing aboard their respective vehicles, the soldiers resumed their journey.

Dressed in thin prison clothes and shivering with cold and horror, Caroline watched the truck disappearing into the mist. Seeking shelter from the driving rain under the canopy of the trees bordering the road, she pulled John along with her. Sitting under the wide, dripping leaves of the trees, the world was much darker and far more frightening. Grief and panic overtook Caroline and she began to cry, deep wrenching sobs that rose from her throat as she wept in despair and loneliness. Soon, her distress was interrupted by a noise down the road. At first frozen in trepidation, self-preservation soon kicked in as the growling engine noise drew closer and she hurriedly dragged John further into the bush until they were well-concealed. Common sense told her that if she was already this far, she might as well remove the risk of pursuit even further. Dragging John, she pushed her way through the verdant undergrowth until she found what Henry would have called a deer path. She followed the trail until her last reserve of strength was extinguished. Collapsing, she lay beside John under a bush near the muddy, narrow track, curling into a ball and succumbing to grief.

Eventually, the end of the rain checked Caroline's misery. **Daughter, tend my sheep.** "John!" she cried. Darkness had descended without her notice, creating a smothering, terrifying world. Patting around in the darkness of the sodden undergrowth, with panic rising in her chest, her hand finally landed on something soft and yielding—John. He was shivering. Caroline realized that as she had indulged her own wretchedness, John was left completely vulnerable to the elements. Rubbing her hands along his arms, legs and chest, she encouraged some warmth into his body. Knowing it would be futile to try to get anywhere in the darkness, she gently rolled John onto his side and curled her body around his, sliding one arm under his head and wrapping one arm across his chest, her hand flat over his heart. Before long, exhaustion claimed her.

"Ame. Lady."
"Lady!"
Startled awake by the prodding of a little toe in her back, Caroline rolled over to find a young Burmese boy standing beside her, arms behind his back and poking her repeatedly with his toe. He was a slender lad, about eight or nine years old. His jet-black hair swept across his forehead so that he was constantly brushing it from his eyes. Looking past him up at the sky, she realized that the sun was peeking through the trees. The addition of another voice to the strange scene made Caroline look over to see a slightly older girl a few feet away who motioned for the boy to come. Caroline simply didn't know what to do. Could she get help from these children? Should she run away and hide? How was she to do that? John still hadn't stirred. She couldn't carry him. What on earth was she to do?

Before she had a chance to decide, the children ran off. In the shady daylight, Caroline took a moment to examine John. Shivering and pale, he sported several large bruises, one on his left temple, a huge bruise on his ribcage and a large bruise coming out on his throat. Caroline stood quickly as she heard footsteps approaching through the jungle. Casting her eyes about for a weapon, she flinched when, along the trail, the children burst into view again. The boy who had woken her was pulling a man by the arm, a man clad in a longyi, shirt and traditional Burmese flip flops—his father, perhaps? Nodding briefly to Caroline, he called behind him. Three additional men, also wearing the traditional longyi, emerged from the bush. Stalking over to Caroline, they ignored her and lifted John, carrying him away through the trees. In an agony of indecision, Caroline shifted from foot to foot.

"Lady. Come." The little boy urged, taking Caroline's hand and pulling her.

Caroline followed. "Father, show me what to do," she murmured as she stumbled along in exhaustion beside the boy. Afterwards, she could never tell how many roads, rivers and streams they crossed.

Eventually the long and winding path opened into a clearing. Caroline stopped to take in the strangeness of the scene before her. In the midst of the trees stood a row of elevated wooden structures; low-walled, with wooden shingles on the roof, the rectangular abodes perched above the jungle floor. Each supporting beam continued below the floor to act as a stilt, raising the house above the floods of the monsoon and the creatures of the jungle. Wooden projections supported the wide eaves of the roof. The eaves hung low, providing partial covering for the window openings in the wooden walls. Each house was reached by either a ladder or wooden steps projecting up through the middle of the floor. A dirt path encircled the buildings, holding back the encroaching jungle.

Searching left and right, Caroline caught a glimpse of the men lifting John into the furthest house to the right. Releasing the boy's hand, she jogged to the structure which had swallowed John. By the time she arrived, the men were exiting the structure. Waiting as the men descended the ladder, Caroline ascended to find a gloomy single room above. John was lying on a simple wooden bed with a woven rope mattress. There were two other similar beds in the one room house. In the corner, Caroline saw a wash basin and stand, a cooking area, a table and four wooden chairs. A small Buddha rested in the corner, surrounded by lights and flowers, a plate of food lying in front of it.

Humming and hugging her arms around herself, she moved closer to John. She turned as the little boy entered the house through the trapdoor in the middle of the room followed by a young woman and a grandmother. The two women were young and old opposites. The younger woman was tall and slender with short black hair that rested neatly behind her ears. Her fingers were narrow and long, although obviously used to hard labour. The older woman was heavy-set and short with long, white hair swept into a bun. Her eyes sparkled with a continuous joy. The grandmother quickly took charge of the situation, ordering the boy to retrieve the pitcher of water from next to the wash basin and some clean rags. Surveying the damage to John's chest, head and neck grimly, she gasped in surprise as she rolled him onto his side, revealing the whip cuts on his back and the fading bruises on his legs. The young woman moved behind her, hand covering her mouth exclaiming,

"... No...torture...Form 10..."

The grandmother shushed her and motioned the boy over. Beginning to clean the wounds, she ignored her daughter-in-laws protests. Moving closer, Caroline wet a rag and copied the older woman's actions until John had been washed from top to toe. Rising slowly on her arthritic knees, the grandmother fetched a roll of blankets, placing a few beneath John and a few more over him. She started to roll him onto his back but Caroline interfered, resting him in a recovery position on his uninjured side, his right knee bent forward for balance. This position kept pressure off his injured ribs, his back and would keep his airway open.

Shaking her head, the younger woman left but soon returned with a middle aged Burmese man carrying a small black bag. He stood with confidence, taking in the scene laid out before him. His dark brown eyes displayed intelligence and the lines on his face looked equally able to express sorrow or joy. He walked over to Caroline, bowing and shaking her hand.

"My name is Ye," the man said.

"You speak English!" Caroline exclaimed, still gripping his hand.

"Some. I am a nurse." He waited.

Caroline's hopes lifted. "Please, come. My name is Caroline." She led him to the bed. "This is John. He's badly hurt."

Lowering the blanket, Ye tutted as he saw the wounds.

"Tortured?" he inquired.

Caroline's eyes filled with tears. *If I tell him who John is, will he turn us in? I don't want to go back to prison. Father, help me. Give me strength.* Nervously humming and hugging her arms around herself, she considered her options. Taking a deep breath, she responded, "He was illegally detained and tortured." Holding her breath, she watched Ye closely, uncertain of his response.

"Unfortunately, in my country, we know much about torture. Foreigners sometimes are caught up in our troubles." Caroline held his gaze as he continued, "The people here, of this zanapou—this village are of the Chin. They know injustice. They know torture."

As Ye examined John, Caroline kept talking, an out-flowing of her fear, "I noticed the little Buddha in the corner."

"Yes. This village is Buddhist but the grandmother of this house is Christian. Many Chin are Christians." Caroline's relief showed on her face. Ye queried, "You also, you are Christian?"

"Yes." Caroline waited to see his reaction to her reply.

He nodded, "As am I. I travel to these zanapou—uh—remote villages in order to bring—uh—medical care in the name of Tha ta ba ga na—the Great Physician." Bowing to his work, Ye retrieved some salve from his bag. Showing Caroline how to apply it to the wounds on John's back, he asked her to continue while he used his stethoscope to listen to John's chest.

Removing the stethoscope from his ears and folding it into his bag, he gave Caroline a summary of John's injuries.

"He has concussion, htin—I think, three pau—broken ribs and a bruising on his throat, perhaps affecting his speaking. I am not able to tell. Some of the cuts on his back are infected, accounting for his mild hpja—fever. However, due to the broken ribs, he may develop quite a high hpja—fever in the next few days. If he develops pneumonia, he could become quite ill. I can leave you some amoxicillin—"

Caroline interrupted, "What do mean?" She felt panic grip her belly. "Aren't you staying? Won't you stay and help him?" She rose from the bedside, gripping her arms more tightly around herself.

Ye moved closer to her and set his hand on her shoulder. Stepping back, he replied, "I must leave in time to reach home by nine o'clock tonight. Because of Form 10, all guests must be registered with the palei—uh, police by that time each day. If I am registered as being here, the police will want to know who is requiring my attention." Here he took Caroline firmly by the shoulders. "If they find pji pa—foreign nationals here, particularly foreigners allegedly freed from prison by the Chin Liberation Army," Caroline gaped in awe at this man who could read events so perceptively then, looking down, she saw her prison uniform clearly indicating her origins, "they will arrest you, John, the family in this home and, perhaps, the entire village. The bwa—old mother here can insist that her son extend you his htwe na—hospitality but she will have little influence over the military. As Chin, these people have no rights." Caroline stared back at him, terrified.

"I will not be able to return here for several weeks as we are now moving into mou thoun lei—the heaviest time of rainfall in the year. For the same reasons that I cannot return, the army, too, will stay away. God has led you here, Caroline. This village is set apart. It is surrounded by mountains and rivers; it will be tein mjou—inaccessible soon. The people of this village only emerge a few times a year to sell what little they can spare, so they make little impact on the communities around them. That is how they stumbled upon you and John. It was their last trip out before the mou thoun lei." Ye collected his instruments and packed his bag.

"Use the salve twice a day. Keep him hydrated, lots of boiled water and tea. If he develops a fever, you will need to inject the amoxicillin. If his breath becomes heavy—lots of coughing—because of the broken ribs, you will need to help him when he coughs. Do as I do." He showed her how to hold John's side to help splint his ribs. "Do you have questions?" She sadly shook her head, fighting back her tears.

Squeezing her elbow to comfort her, Ye departed. Collapsing on the floor beside John's bed, Caroline wept. *Father, why is this happening? Why did you abandon me here—with him?* **I will never leave you nor forsake you.** Caroline continued to pray as she sat, seeking comfort from the God of the Universe. If you can't get support from those around you, rely on the King Himself. Here in this strange jungle village beside this strange man, as forsaken as she felt, she knew she wasn't alone.

John's moans brought her out of her reverie. Wrapping a blanket more tightly around his shoulders, she sat stroking his forehead for a time. Brushing her hand across the softening bristle of his hair, she began to wonder, *who, exactly, is this man?* She had seen him demonstrate spite, hardness and bile. She had also seen him demonstrate courage and fortitude—and, briefly, remorse. *Father, what are you doing here? His life is far too complex for me. I don't want to get involved.* **Tend my sheep.** *That, I can do. Just protect my heart, please!*

The rest of the family returned after a time. As the younger woman prepared the evening meal, the grandmother brought her son over and introduced him to Caroline. Rising as they approached, Caroline bowed her head, hoping this was suitable. She pointed to herself, "Caroline" and to John, "John" she said.

The grandmother named herself, "Grace" and pointed to her son, "Zeya", her grandson, "Khin", the boy who had rescued Caroline, and to her daughter-in-law, "Cho". The grandmother, bwa Grace, spoke to Khin and he returned with some green tea in small, painted clay cups. Zeya, a square shaped man with powerful arms, moved a chair over beside the bed. Grace sat upon it and spooned some tea into John's mouth. Khin took Caroline's hand and led her over to the table where he produced a game board and several white and black disks. The disks were spread across the board, leaving one space empty. Khin patiently showed Caroline how each piece moved, reset the board and began. Each move he made was accompanied by a swish of his hair, clearing his vision for a moment. To Caroline, the game seemed a combination of chess and checkers. Reluctantly playing with Khin until supper was prepared, Caroline remained at the table for the meal. Each time her plate seemed empty, more food was added until she felt satisfied—more satisfied than she had felt in four months. The food was similar to the food served in the prison but much fresher and more flavourful.

After the meal, Khin dashed off to play with his friends outside, collecting his chinlon ball along the way; a ball constructed of the resilient fibres of the sugar cane plant. Zeya gathered some firewood from a pile stored beneath the house and Caroline helped Cho tidy the house. Grace brought over a new longyi for Caroline to wear to replace her prison issue grey. The longyi was a beautiful sky blue with white star-shaped flowers printed across it. Grace also provided her with new, slightly used undergarments, flip flops to replace the shredded pair she was wearing now and an indigo blue shirt. Caroline thanked her humbly, enjoying the finer feel of the fabric as compared to the coarse roughness of the prison uniform.

Remembering Ye's instructions, Caroline applied the salve to John's back. Tracing her fingers along his strong shoulders, she remembered the day he'd returned to the cell after being strung up by the arms and caned. He'd been so angry that day. *Why was he so angry? Why did he kiss me?* Her mind full of the confusing memories, Caroline wandered to the window opening and watched the children playing, tossing the wickerwork ball, trying to keep it in the air using their heads, shoulders, knees and toes. But watching the children caused her heart to pain. She'd done everything in her power to avoid spending too much time with children since the plane crash. It all just hurt too much.

Once night descended, the family rolled out a mat for Caroline to sleep on. Zeya and Cho shared a double bed and Khin and Grace shared another. After her bunk in the prison, the floor seemed wide and spacious and the mat felt soft beneath her. Grace checked John again, covering him with mosquito netting before crawling into her own bed.

Caroline slept fitfully, playing music in her mind to try and calm her anxiety. The noises of the night were disconcerting after the evening silence of the prison. Insects and owls filled the air around her with eerie, unfamiliar sounds. She was very concerned about John but didn't *want* to feel concerned about him. In the end, it was the rustling that propelled her into wakefulness and, in that confused state between sleeping and waking, she tried to still her breathing so she could listen past the furious beating of her heart and try to make sense of what she was hearing. The sound was coming from across the room, from John's direction. *John!* If something had gotten into the house, John would be easy prey. He was helpless!

Because of the darkness in the room, Caroline crawled across the floor, avoiding furniture and the trapdoor in the middle of the room. When she reached John, she saw that his blankets had fallen on the floor beside him. Restless and warm to the touch, he batted at her hands as she reached for him. In his delirium, Caroline was afraid he would aggravate his injuries so, sitting on the floor at the head of the bed, she began to sing quietly and stroke his hair. The sound of her voice seemed to calm him and, when he had settled enough, she retrieved his blankets and covered him. As she moved away, he began to whimper and groan, becoming agitated again, so she moved her bedroll to the floor beside his bed and continued her vigil at his side, singing once more. When she reached for his shoulder, he grabbed her hand, holding it firmly. For the rest of the night, every time she drifted off to sleep on the floor beside him, he would wake her in his agitation until finally, she crawled into bed with him, holding him close. He settled at once, drifting into a deep sleep. Caroline drifted off beside him.

Caroline woke to the sounds of murmured prayers addressed to the tiny Buddha in the corner. Cho and Zeya knelt before the statue offering a portion of food and drink. Grace sat apart from her son and daughter-in-law, praying to tha ta bag a na, Jehovah God, creator of heaven and earth. As Caroline's gaze fell on Grace, she moved over to her, smiling down at her with eyes twinkling in amusement. Realizing where she was, Caroline began to stammer a response.

"He was restless, feverish, agitated in the night. I—uh—I just—well, I was so tired it was just easier to crawl into the bed. He settled right away." Caroline blushed and stuttered through her explanation even though she knew that Grace couldn't understand a word she was saying. Caroline was embarrassed to be found in bed with this man who was not her husband, but Grace was clearly amused by Caroline's embarrassment. Handing her a wash basin, Grace patted her cheek and smiled. Standing uncertainly Caroline looked around the room, seeking an exit from this humiliating situation until John's pitiful moan captured her attention. The sight of this strong, proud man humbled in sickness, saddened her and her compassionate heart sent an arrow of pity to her belly.

After washing him, she spoon fed him the tea that Cho brought over. Hard rain began to fall, sending a breeze wafting through the house, the slight chill causing John to shiver. *His fever is rising. When should I give him the antibiotics?* As she felt his forehead, testing his temperature, she allowed her fingers to stroke his hair. His hair was long enough now to be soft to the touch and she caught herself enjoying the feel of it, noticing how he calmed whenever she touched him or spoke to him.

As the day progressed, John's breathing became strident and he developed a cough. Caroline finally injected him with the amoxicillin, knowing that it would take a few days for it to have full effect. She supported his ribs when he coughed just as Ye had shown her. Over the next thirty-six hours, his fever rose higher and higher. Caroline stayed constantly by his side because he became quite agitated when she wasn't near.

The force of the coughing and the high fever were taking a toll on John's already weakened body and he lay like an infant on his bed. Caroline kept vigil at his side, bathing his forehead and using her hands to splint his chest for his almost constant coughing. She even took to sleeping with her hand firmly over the broken ribs.

On the fourth day after arriving in the village, John's fever broke. Caroline wiped him down and moved away to make him some tea. When she returned, he gazed up at her, his eyes widening in recognition. He seemed to smile briefly before his eyes fluttered closed again. Later that day, John awoke again as Caroline was washing him. When he reached over weakly and grabbed her arm, she turned to face him, smiling to see him awake again.

"I'd forgotten what colour your eyes are," Caroline said with a smile. "How are you feeling?" He opened his mouth to speak but, when only a gasp escaped, his eyes widened in panic and he grasped his throat. Caroline reached over to smooth her hand over his hair and forced a smile onto her face to cover her own fear. "You were hit in the throat. I think your vocal chords are bruised. It should resolve in a few days as you begin to heal." John seemed to relax a little and reached up to weakly brush her cheek. Helping him sit up in bed, Caroline braced his ribs with one hand and offered him some tea, as much as he could stand. He grimaced at the bitterness but took what was offered. "Are you hungry?" Caroline asked. John shook his head. "You should get some more sleep," Caroline suggested. John rolled onto his side and Caroline pulled the blankets up around his shoulders. "Welcome back," she whispered and quieter, "I missed you".

The next morning, Caroline awoke to find John staring at her with a mischievous smile in his eyes. Blushing, she quickly stood up, realizing that she had fallen asleep on the edge of the bed again, her hand firmly clamped over John's side.

Avoiding direct eye contact, Caroline set about making John some broth and tea. Sitting on the edge of his bed to feed him, she looked away as he watched her, too embarrassed to meet his gaze. Clamping her hand over the fractures, she helped him sit up a little in bed. Bringing the spoon of broth to his mouth, he pressed his lips together.

"John. You need to get some calories into you. You've been very sick," she cajoled, studying the spoon in front of her. Trying again, she met his pursed lips once more. Sighing in annoyance, she looked up to find him watching her with a tender gaze. When she made eye contact, he mouthed "hi" and smiled at her, opening his mouth to receive his breakfast. Offering a small smile in return, Caroline fed him the broth. After a few sips of tea, she could see that he was wearying and needed more rest. Helping him recline fully, she pulled his blankets up around his shoulders. As she stood to leave, he grasped her shirt hem, pulling gently to encourage her to return.

"What's wrong?" she asked, concerned. Furrowing his brow, he reached for her hand and pulled her closer. "I just need to use the toilet, okay, and then I'll come back. Okay?" She tried to appease him, assuming he would fall asleep while she was away but he was awake and waiting when she returned. Smiling, she sat on the edge of the bed again taking his hand. Withdrawing his hand, he gently touched her lips. Confused at first by his gesture, realization dawned on her, "You want me to sing?" she asked. He nodded, pleased that she understood. She sang to him until his even breathing told her he was asleep and then, rather than leaving him, she sat gazing at his features, distinct and sharpened after his illness. *Father, what is happening here? This new feeling about John is confusing. Do I care for him or am I just clinging to the only familiar thing in my environment? Is this just a Florence Nightingale situation? But then Florence never fell for her patients, they only fell for her.* "Oh Father," she sighed. "Grant me peace". And He did. She felt a bath of peace wash over her and a voice in her heart said simply, **Trust me**.

Caroline awoke to someone shaking her shoulder. Wearily, she rolled over to find John awake. Suddenly alert, she sat up.

"Are you okay?" she asked, concerned. He shook his head, nodding toward the far corner of the room. Glancing over, Caroline was confused. "What's wrong?" she asked. Frowning at her in obvious annoyance, John pointed in frustration toward the corner again. "You need to use the toilet?" she inquired. He responded with a terse nod. "Okay, then, get up. I'll help you over." Lifting the corner of his blanket he shook his head in irritation. Caroline had forgotten that he was still naked. There had seemed no point in constantly changing his clothes when he was feverish. Retrieving a spare longyi, she helped John out of bed and wrapped the cloth around him like a bath towel, knotting it at the waist. Helping him to the corner, she stabilized him, while turning her head away so he could have a semblance of dignity while he relieved himself. Returning him to bed, she fixed him some porridge and tea for breakfast. He reached for the bowl but was unable to deal with his ribs, and the bowl and the spoon. Clearly displeased, he allowed Caroline to feed him.

The obvious difficulty of clothes for John became apparent after his early morning toilet trip. Finding a longyi was no problem and Grace gave him one of Zeya's to wear. The longyi was dark brown with no adornment of any kind, perfect for someone who desired to go unnoticed. Grace used the prison issue boxer shorts as a model and made John a pair of undershorts from a brilliantly striped material which made Caroline laugh, commenting, "At least they're not covered in red hearts." A shirt proved to be more of a challenge. John was much taller than Zeya and with Zeya's square build and thick arms, the proportions of the two men didn't match in any way. Finally, Grace pulled the buttons off an old, worn shirt of Zeya's and sewed a custom-fit shirt for John. She chose a jade green fabric and cut the shirt as short sleeved.

Now able to move about the house from a clothing point of view, John was still too weak to care for himself. This forced dependence seemed to bring out the worst in his temperament. John demanded her attention and, when she wasn't at his side, his eyes followed her every move as she tended to his needs. He was having nightmares once or twice a night, waking Caroline with his movements and groans. Usually, if Caroline stroked his hair or sang to him, he would calm and fall back to sleep. Often, he didn't wake fully. While he napped in the afternoons, Caroline felt obligated to assist Cho with household chores to help show her appreciation for their hospitality.

Within a few days, John's cough was much reduced. As he began to feel stronger and stronger, though, his confinement began to chafe. His ribs had healed well enough that he could sit up in bed or in a chair for brief periods of time but he always wanted to do more than his body was ready for. As a result, he was permanently uncomfortable and frequently in pain. Still not speaking in more than the occasional whisper, he quickly became frustrated when he was not understood. All this contrived to bring out the very worst in his temperament. He was grumpy! He was a grumpy and petulant patient and Caroline frequently thought about carrying him off into the jungle and leaving him there. However, she tried to remind herself of how difficult it must be for a man of action to be so dependent—particularly dependent on someone he barely knew and that, only in a prison.

One morning, about ten days after they'd arrived in the village, Caroline was again awakened by a hand on her shoulder, shaking her. However, this morning, she was in the middle of a most pleasurable dream, full of chocolate cake and Henry. Rolling away from John's bed, she tried to recapture her pleasant thoughts when a pillow roll hit her square in the head, launching her unwillingly into the morning. Infuriated, she leapt up and turned on John who was scowling at her fiercely. Rising to her full height above him, she pointed a rigid finger at his chest, his face morphing into a look of shock and awareness that the line in the sand was the one he had crossed. She was shaking with emotion and he sat, frozen in place under her stare. She did not pause as she lit into him.

"What is **wrong** with *you*?! I have spent the last ten days cleaning you, feeding you, toileting you, making you tea, broth, porridge, cleaning up after you and comforting you when you wake me up in the night—every single night!!!" Caroline ticked off each point on her fingers. "I'm tired. You get to sleep all day but I have to try and pay the debt we owe these people for sheltering us while *you* get well!" Here she waved her arms around the room. "I'm tired!" She advanced on him and he flinched back away from her. "GROW UP!" she yelled. Spinning about, she stormed out of the house, down the ladder and into the driving rain.

Caroline stormed into the jungle. Within ten steps she was soaked to the skin. Striding along beside the turbulent river, she walked and walked, using her angst to fuel her steps. Too angry to cry, too angry to pray, but knowing that God would understand her thoughts, she just repeated "help me" in her head. This was not a humble request for assistance but an assertive request for God to stop her from going back and smacking John.

As her anger cooled, she realized that if she wandered too far, she was likely to get lost in the torrential downpour. Retracing her steps she arrived back at Grace's house. Assaulted by feelings of embarrassment and anger, Caroline couldn't quite bring herself to climb the ladder and face the family—and John—again. Shivering in the cold and wet, she finally decided that a little embarrassment would be a suitable exchange for warmth and dry clothes. Ascending the steps, she realized that Grace and the others were not in the house. Ignoring John, she headed over to the corner and began to strip off her clothes, drying herself and pulling on a fresh longyi and shirt from the pile Grace kept.

Caroline heard John shuffling toward her but still she jumped and turned to face him when he grasped her elbow. Sighing in annoyance, she protested, "Leave me alone, John. I'll get you some breakfast, later". His hand dropped limply to his side but then he grasped her arm again and waved his other hand. She ripped her arm from his grasp in irritation. He doubled over in pain, gasping. Sighing, she wrapped her arms around his shoulders and led him back to his bed. Tears of exasperation threatened to engulf her again. Once they reached the bed, John pulled back slightly, motioning at the bed.

"John, just get in bed. I need to get warm, and sleep, just a little," she demanded. Instead of crawling into bed, he reached for her chin and tilted her face to look at him. His misery plainly visible on his face, Caroline watched him closely. Leaning forward, he rested his forehead against hers and closed his eyes. Suddenly, inspiration lit his features. Caroline acquiesced as John slowly dragged her across the room to Khin's checkers game. Caroline watched as he used the tiles to spell out, S-O-R-R-Y. Reading the letters, her eyes softened and stepping closer, she rested her head on his chest as he wrapped his arms around her in a warm embrace. Sighing, she gently hugged him back. Brushing his fingers gently along her cheek, he reached down and took her hand, leading her back to the bed. He drew back the covers and gestured for her to climb in. Caroline looked back at his face to be sure she understood. Smiling, he nodded at the bed again. Squeezing his fingers in thanks, she climbed in and curled up in the warm blankets.

Tired but still too full of John's apology to relax into sleep, Caroline lay watching him through hooded eyelids. She watched him standing, as he watched her sleep. She could see that standing was too difficult a position for him to sustain for long. He soon searched for a chair, perching there for a little while before that clearly became uncomfortable and he wandered back toward the bed. Caroline could see the pain etched into his features.

"John," she called softly. Looking surprised, he gazed down at her. Gesturing him closer, she lifted the covers, inviting him to share her warmth. Caroline saw the excitement that streaked across his eyes and saw the gulp as he calmed himself. Smiling briefly at his obvious glee, she waited patiently for him to curl up chastely behind her. Wrapping his arm around her middle, he planted an innocent kiss on her cheek. Sighing contentedly, they fell asleep—cozy and chaste with a new understanding between them.

Caroline woke, confused by the weight she felt across her ribs and the warmth along her back. Looking down, she saw John's arm still holding her to him and, breathing in sleep, she could feel his chest press against her back. As she moved to leave the bed, he tightened his grip, kissing her lightly on the neck. Rolling over to face him, she reached out and touched his cheek.

"You okay?" she asked. He nodded. Shifting his hand up along her arm, he slid his fingers into her hair, pulling her to him, breathing into her neck. Hugging, they clung together, needing to feel the other's need for familiarity and affection. As he pulled back, he seemed to study her and she smiled a small smile in response.

Kissing his forehead, she said, "I guess we better get you washed and fed". Moving away, she got up and started the day's routine, leaving behind a contented-looking John. Caroline's body felt cold as she walked away, but her heart felt warm. *Maybe there is good in him.*

The family returned in the evening to a calmly domestic scene. Caroline stirred soup while John sat at the table arranging tiles on the checker board. Khin dashed over and challenged John to a game. Walking over to Caroline, Grace patted her shoulder affectionately, eyes twinkling. Things would be different from now on.

CHAPTER 4

A NEW UNDERSTANDING

By the time they had spent two and a half weeks in the village, John's voice was returning and he had largely recovered from his illness. He told Caroline that his broken ribs ached all the time but when he was jarred, it felt like a jolt of lightning coursing through his chest. Aside from a change in his health, Caroline also noticed a change in his behaviour. He vacated the bed each afternoon and insisted she have a nap to catch up on the sleep she lost tending him in the night. In fact, before long, he gave up the bed to her and took over the bedroll she had been using. He seemed much more patient and never asked for anything to be done immediately. He smiled at her, encouraging smiles, and thanked her for every kindness. She noticed, too, that, at times, he even seemed to read her well enough to tell when she needed comfort or needed space. She, in turn, met his every need patiently. She gave him the care he needed and the independence he craved. She learned to ask when she needed his help and gently refuse when she felt overwhelmed.

As the days passed, the rains began to lessen and the villagers returned to their regular past-times and, as a result, Caroline and John were left more and more on their own. Becoming stronger each day, John's enforced 'captivity' was coming to an end and he was determined to get back to strength quickly. Although his ribs still caused him pain, careful movements minimized the sharp stabs made obvious by his abrupt intake of breath. He encouraged Caroline to join him on walks around the village; sixteen raised huts scattered about with forest creeping close to the margins. The cleared area of the village proper was populated by small children, chickens, a few pigs, two water buffaloes and a gaur; a cross between a water buffalo and a bullock—yielding a delicious T-bone steak. As they passed between the houses in the mornings, they passed by the daily life of the people: mothers bathing infants in basins; children feeding and herding the livestock; grandfathers sitting at the base of the houses, chatting and chewing betel-nuts, the red juices staining their teeth. Education was replaced by labour. Soon John and Caroline advanced to walks along the river, watching the young men fishing along the river in their hollowed wooden boats, steering with their feet on the rudder and their hands entangled in fishing nets.

Taking their morning walk by the river one day, they decided to pass by the rice fields, the paddies, on their way back to the house. They stood and watched the men and women, longyi hiked up above their knees, and wide-brimmed straw hats protecting their heads, standing up to their calves in chilly water, bending at the waist repeatedly to grasp and pull, harvesting the rice plants. Feeling guilty at watching others work, Caroline pulled John along, determined to offer more help to Cho from now on.

As they rounded an overgrown bend in the path along the river, the startling whirr of the pheasant wings alarmed Caroline, causing her to leap back as the vermilion hooded, azure missiles scattered to the air around her. Her heart beat rapidly in response to their surprising presence in the bush. Settling back onto the path, she lowered her gaze to find John watching her with a smile in his eyes. In a few more steps, her pulse returned to normal and she worked up the courage to ask the question that had been on her mind for some time.

"John?" she began shyly.

"Yes?" he replied slowly.

Reaching to rest against a smooth-barked tree, Caroline inquired, "John, why are you here in Burma? I mean, I know you're an MI-5 agent but—" Caroline's words were halted by John's solid grip on her wrist, spinning her away and sending her smacking against a second tree. Dazed, she cried out, falling to the ground. Tears of hurt forming in her eyes, she turned to see John swinging a stick at the tree she had intended to lean against. Two whacks of the stick and Caroline saw the small snake fall. John picked it up and flung it into the bush.

"Russell's viper—very poisonous," he explained in his hoarse voice. Caroline gasped, drawing an unsteady breath—two surprises in the last two minutes—too much! Eyes wide with shock, tears brimmed and spilled over. John rushed to her side and, holding her face in his hands, he asked, "You all right?"

Nodding, she couldn't meet his gaze. "I thought—You hit me!—A snake?—What happened?" she said, trying to organize her scattered emotions—fear, anger, surprise.

John pushed her hair back from her face lightly touching the red mark where her head had glanced off the tree he had flung her against.

"I'm sorry. I'm so sorry, sweetheart. I saw the viper hanging down just above you in the tree. If you had leaned in, it would have struck. I just reacted. I didn't mean to hurt you. I'm sorry." He kissed her temple, soothing the emerging bruise. Caroline cried as he murmured, "I'm so sorry, sweetheart." Reaching up, she pulled him close, clinging to him.

Hiccoughing as her breathing settled, she tried to gain control and, as her tears slowed, she released him, feeling embarrassed by her overreaction. "S-sorry. Shock—surprised me—thank you." Drawing a shuddering breath, she reached for him again. "Thank you." John lifted her face gently, giving her a tender smile. As he moved back toward her, she startled, bringing her lips in line with his. *Pull out. Pull out*, her mind commanded but her body refused to obey. As she moved back, he released her, studying her with a concerned look on his face.

"You know," she began, smiling shyly, "if you didn't want to tell me, you could have just refused. You didn't have to attack me with a tree." Her smile grew. Laughing in relief, John hugged her and, bracing his arms across his still tender ribs, he stood and helped her to her feet. They returned to the house, hand in hand.

About one month after they had arrived in the village, John awoke to find his ribs had finally healed. Greeting Caroline with a huge grin, he spun her around, reveling in the sensation of movement without pain.

"You're feeling better, then?" she asked, grinning at his infectious joy.

"I'm going for a jog," he announced. "I'll be back for breakfast."

"Okay," she agreed.

Over the next several days, John spent more and more time in 'training' as he called it. The physical activity seemed to buoy his spirits with an infectious enthusiasm but even so, as the month changed, Caroline couldn't resist a descent into sadness. The rains were lessening and John sought more and more time outside, cajoling Caroline into accompanying him. However, the more enthusiastic and persuasive he became, the more depressed Caroline felt because it only heightened her loneliness. *He's a good companion but he obviously doesn't care or he would have noticed how sad I feel.* Gloomy thoughts filled her mind.

After his morning jog, on which Caroline had again declined to accompany him, John entered the house and announced, "That felt great! I'm ready to tuck in."

Caroline turned on him, yelling, "If you want immediate service, try a drive-thru!" Throwing the spoon at his feet, she stormed out of the house and down to the river. Sitting on the riverbank, morosely tossing pebbles into the water, Caroline wept silently, reviewing everything that was wrong with her life. *My husband and my children are dead. I was thrown in prison in Burma, of all places, for helping someone. I was placed in a cell with an obnoxious, overbearing spy and then abandoned in the jungle alone with him. Why did you ever send me here, God? Why did you do this to me? I don't want to do this anymore. Can't you send me back to Canada? I promise I'll be happy with a boring job and a boring husband.* So lost in her thoughts and prayers was she, that Caroline didn't hear John's approach until he sat beside her on the rock by the riverbank. Tapping out a rhythm on his leg with his fingertips, he waited. When she didn't respond, he nudged her gently with his shoulder. She sighed loudly as silent tears slid down her cheeks.

"What's wrong?" he asked. Shrugging, she sighed again. "Khin says you've been sad lately, that you've been crying under the house. He says you sent him away when he saw you." John waited but she only sighed once more. "When I asked him why you were sad, Grace told me it was my duty to find out." He stopped speaking, watching her. She turned her head towards him a little, surprised by what he was saying.

"How do you know how to speak Burmese so well?" she asked, avoiding the question he'd asked. "I mean, I've been here longer than you and I only have a very basic grasp of the language."

Pausing before he spoke, she could feel him staring at her. "I worked in this region at one point and needed to learn the language."

"What other languages can you speak?" she inquired, still studying the pebbles at her feet.

Again, he was slow to respond. "My Hindi and Mandarin are very basic but I found Burmese rather fascinating. It's so different from the other languages spoken in this area of the world, so I mastered it more quickly and more fully."

Caroline slipped her right foot out of her flip-flop and began tracing geometric patterns in the dirt.

"Caroline?" John prompted her, "What's wrong?"

"Why did Grace tell you it was your job to find out?"

"I asked her why, and she said that you had given much to care for me and now it was my turn to care for you." He paused.

"And—" Caroline prompted, her interest piqued by Grace's words.

"When you threw your wobbly—yelled at me and stormed out of the house, I thought you were just being a woman—too sensitive." Caroline stiffened at his words but he continued, "I was h—I didn't understand your anger. I don't really understand much about caring or friendship or—or you. I can analyze terrorist threats but not you. You make no sense to me." Caroline began to protest but he cut her off. "You've done so much for me and I don't understand why. I've simply never met anyone like you before." Caroline sat beside John trying to decide whether to be pleased or upset by what he'd said. Taking her hand, he tried again, "I know you're sad. Please tell me why."

Sighing, she capitulated. "My wedding anniversary is coming up. The last few years, I've visited our favourite spots and rented our favourite movies to watch and cry over. Then I cry the tears I hold in during the rest of the year. I miss them so much, John."

A stunned look masked John's face. As Caroline began to weep in earnest, he wrapped his arms around her and held her close, gently kissing her hair. When she was able to gain control of her emotions again, Caroline thanked him. Then she stood up to head back to the house. As John stood to join her, he wiped a stray tear from her cheek with his thumb. She turned her head, kissing the palm of his hand where it rested against her face. Caroline started back but John remained frozen. Realizing he wasn't following, Caroline looked back and called to him. He started to move toward her and when he caught up, he took her hand and they returned to the house together. She decided not to pry into why that small kiss had seemed to affect him so profoundly.

After Caroline went to bed that evening, John sought out Zeya and they left the house together. John returned, whistling. The next few mornings, John waited until Caroline was occupied before going jogging. She accompanied him on his afternoon swim but when she looked for him in the evening for a walk, he was gone again. This new abandonment was very hurtful to Caroline. She had appreciated his sympathy the other day; following her to the river. But now he seemed drawn away from her, again. Rather than the companionship she thought was developing, she often caught him watching her from a distance whereupon he turned away.

Once again returning to the house after Caroline was abed, she heard him whistling happily as he emerged through the trapdoor. Caroline pretended she was asleep. *Why did I think there was anything between us? Has he found another woman? Another woman? Hah! I'm not his woman. I'm not anything but his nurse.* Caroline began to weep. Stifling her cries with a blanket, she rolled away from John so that he wouldn't hear her. Her tears were interrupted by a hand on her shoulder, firmly turning her.

"Caroline?" he whispered, sitting on the edge of the bed.

Forged in the Jungles of Burma

"Nothing, I'm fine," she said between gasps

"You're not fine. Caroline. Sweetheart?" Worry played across his features.

"Don't call me that," Caroline said quietly. Confused, he looked at her. Tersely, she repeated, "Don't—call—me—that. I don't mean anything to you, do I? I'm just your nurse—but now that you're better, I'm just an incon—" John clamped his hand over her mouth. She shook her head fiercely but he wouldn't release her.

"Stop!" he commanded, quietly. "Don't say something you'll regret." He watched her narrowly. "Do you trust me?"

His question confounded her. "What do you mean?" she murmured past his fingers.

"Do you trust me?" John's features softened as he repeated his question.

Prying his hand from her mouth angrily, she responded, "Why should I? What have you ever done to make me trust you?"

He pulled back, shock blatantly written on his features. Obviously floundering, he quickly collected himself and blurted out, "My mother died when I was 12." Furrowing her brows, Caroline settled. He continued, "My father hated me. He never wanted me and when she died, well—after that I never had a happy moment in my life—" he paused, "until I met you. You stayed with me in the prison, keeping me awake, giving me hope. You nursed me back to health," here Caroline frowned and he spoke more rapidly in response, "but more than any of that, you've been my friend—a real friend. I've not had many of those in my life and definitely no one like you." Brushing his fingers across her cheek, he tenderly demanded, "Tell me. Tell me why you're upset—please."

Caroline waited thoughtfully, considering what he had just given her: another small gift of trust; trust in her. She entertained a brief flicker of a smile and acquiesced. "You've been avoiding me."

John grinned a small grin. "Will you trust me?"

Sighing, she agreed. "How long?"

"Just until tomorrow, I promise." He held her gaze, eyes wide with hope.

"Okay. Now go to bed and leave me alone," she commanded with a wry smile.

He grinned back at her. "Not until you're asleep," he said, crawling into bed next to her on top of the blankets. Considering her next move for a moment, she shrugged and curled beneath the covers, pulling his arm around her middle and settling for sleep.

The next morning, John and Caroline ate breakfast together. Before leaving for his morning jog, John pulled her aside.

"I need to make one stop after my jog. Will you meet me at the riverbank in an hour?" John watched her reaction.

"Okay," she consented, sadly.

Waiting impatiently at the riverbank, Caroline brightened as John arrived and presented her with a rolled scroll of softened tree bark. Caroline unrolled the little scroll and saw, in charcoal letters,

C,
U R kind
U R brave
U R beautiful
Thank you,
J

Caroline looked at John through tear filled eyes. "Do you mean it?" she asked. John nodded and smiled in response. Her heart swelled in response to his smile. "Thank you," she whispered. John handed her his second gift which was wrapped in a strip of cloth and tied with thread.

"The gentleman in the furthest hut is a craftsman, a carver," John explained. "I drew a picture for him and he was able to carve it out of teak wood for me—well, for you. This is my gift to you. I had to work in the rice fields for four days to pay for the carving. That's where I've been going lately."

Caroline opened the present and gasped as she saw the small wooden figure inside. It was a carving of five children standing side by side, arms wrapped around each others' shoulders. She ran her fingers over the pieces. She could feel the hair on each head. Each child was wearing a different t-shirt, shorts and little toes on bare feet. Caroline kissed the figures and then she reached up and kissed John. "Thank you. Thank you very much." Excitement filled his eyes.

Before she lost herself to tears, John prompted her, "Tell me".

"Well," began Caroline, "This one is Aleck. He's the oldest. He has dark brown hair and brown eyes. He's the thinker. He always wants to know everything and is always equipped with questions no one can answer. This one is Gabe. His hair is lighter than Aleck's but his eyes are darker. He's the doer. If it moves, he'll chase it. If it makes noise, he'll bang it. This one is Teddy. His hair is much lighter than his brothers and he's the musician. He has the ability to find every harmonica, flute, drum, trumpet, anywhere. He makes up his own songs in the bath. This one is Titus. He's the boss. He is definitely bound to be the director of whatever board room they have in heaven. Caleb is the youngest. He spends his days running after the older boys and I spend a lot of time helping him find himself amidst the chaos of 4 brothers."

Caroline groaned and began to sob loudly. John pulled back as she started to cry, overwhelmed by the force of her tears. "Maybe it was a mistake to remind her in such a concrete way?" he muttered to himself, wearing a grim look and tapping at a furious pace. Caroline, fortunately, wasn't worried about the "best way" to handle this moment, she just wrapped her arms around John and buried her face in his shirt. He calmed then. Holding her tightly, he brushed the occasional kiss across her hair. "I can do this," he mumbled into her hair. Eventually, Caroline calmed but rather than move away, she continued to sit in John's arms, resting her face against his chest, listening to his heartbeat.

"Thank you, John. That was absolutely the sweetest thing anyone has ever done for me. I will keep this always." Drawing back so she could look him in the eyes, she hugged the carving close to her chest and held his gaze. Vulnerable and open in her grief, she stayed still as John leaned in to kiss her. Rather than pulling away as she supposed she should, Caroline wrapped her arms around his shoulders and pulled him closer, seeking reassurance in his embrace. Her heart skipped a beat at the heady sensation as he deepened the kiss, running his fingers through her hair as she moaned lightly, encouraging him to continue. Sliding his hands along her sides, he released his hold on her mouth in order to reposition himself closer to her and kissed her again—a kiss that held more than friendship and caring—a kiss that held passion and the hint of a deeper love. Caroline brought one hand around to touch his cheek and slid it down over his chest. John moaned as she found the spaces between his buttons.

"Hello." Khin chimed brightly. John and Caroline jumped apart.

Wiping her mouth with her hand, Caroline replied nervously, "Hello Khin."

"Ame, tou sa—time to eat," the boy reported.

John took him by the arm and led him away explaining about 'right moments' to speak and 'right moments' to go away. Caroline trailed after them, chuckling in a thrilling combination of humour and wonder. *I haven't been kissed like that in a very long time!*

As the next days passed, and the rains became less and less frequent, John and Caroline spent much more of their time together, although they seemed to be maintaining a bit more physical distance than before. They both worked in the rice fields every day to try and pay back some of the debt they owed Grace's family. John explained that the government was forcing the people to grow an extra harvest of crops each year and sell it at a reduced price. Most farmers were losing money because of this demand and it interfered with time that would otherwise be spent hunting and fishing. Many villages were on the brink of starvation due to this practice.

One afternoon, after their turn in the rice paddies, Caroline sat on the riverbank beside John after their daily swim. Deciding to bask in the warmth outside, John had set his shirt on the ground and flopped down on his stomach. Now, his head turned away from Caroline, he lay resting on his arms as he dozed in the sun. Caroline could see the scars crisscrossing his back and began to lazily trace them. John continued to snooze quietly under her tender touch.

How long have we been here? Caroline wondered. *John's wounds have healed. His ribs are strong—there's no evidence they were ever broken.* She gently traced over his ribs. John shifted in his sleep turning his head toward Caroline. *He was so very sick for so long and now he seems whole. It must be six or eight weeks since we arrived here. We've passed through the height of the monsoon and the rains are less fierce and less frequent now. It feels like we're on another planet, cut off from the rest of the world.* Caroline continued tracing the scars, following one around his side and across to his arm. John wiggled, bringing his arm down to protect the tender space.

"Sorry. Did I hurt you?" she asked. He opened his eyes and looked up at her. "Well, does that hurt?" She tickled him this time and as he shifted away from her, a smile flitted across his lips. "Ah, ticklish are we?" A mischievous grin played across Caroline's face and she began to tickle him in earnest. In a flash he was up and had flipped her onto her back, smiling above her, her arms pinned with his hands and his knees on either side of her legs, pinning them. He hovered above her.

"Now who's in charge?" he asked, grinning. Caroline flushed at the feelings his proximity were evoking. She wriggled but couldn't get loose. She smiled up at him, daring him to try anything as he slowly lowered himself until his face was a breath from hers, then he dove down and began nibbling her neck. She laughed and wiggled but couldn't break free.

"Stop, John, stop!" she said laughing uncontrollably. He stopped immediately but didn't release her.

"I'm the boss here, John. You just do as you're told and let me up." She pouted in pretend annoyance. He slowly shook his head, never breaking eye contact with her as he lowered his head again. Caroline began to wiggle again in anticipation.

"No!" she cried, laughing already. He dove to the opposite side of her neck and began to nibble. She was shrieking with laughter.

"Stop!" she admonished, breathlessly. He stopped immediately, grinning from ear to ear. Still laughing she began, "Now, John, we have to save your stren—" He cut her off, grabbing her earlobe between his teeth and gently nibbling. She squealed. "Stop stop stop!" and he did. The sensation of his lips on her skin was intoxicating. John reached across to grab both her wrists in his left hand while he moved his right hand to her belly and began to crawl across it, leaving her wiggling to get away from his sweetly agonizing touch. As he leaned down to her neck, his hand began to creep up her belly to her ribs. His tickling fingers stilled as he stroked the palm of his hand up higher still. His mouth had ceased to nibble and begun to kiss her neck as the blood poured like lava through her veins. As his kisses became more intense, his hold on her wrists lightened and she moved her hands down to his shoulders and around to his back where she smoothed over the marks she had been tracing earlier. John kissed along her jaw and gazed longingly into her eyes, as though waiting for permission. She pulled him closer.

"You are so beautiful," he murmured. He brought his lips down on top of hers, closing his eyes and breathing in her breath. When he pulled back, her eyes fluttered open and she looked him in the eye. Sitting back on his knees, he seemed to be waiting to see her reaction. She pushed up on her elbows, flushed and warm, studying his body, examining the scar above his right eyebrow, his deep brown eyes that made her want to reach out and stroke them, his almost straight nose and his mouth, the perfect shape. She traced her eyes down his chest watching the muscles play beneath his tanned skin. Her breath was hot and rapid as she looked down along his belly, wrinkled in that position, hiding his belly button. When her eyes reached his hips, she gasped and quickly glanced up at his face. He shifted back away from her as a blush suffused his cheeks. He kept his eyes on her, as though searching her face for her reaction. Caroline pushed up onto her knees and reached for his face.

"That's the biggest compliment I've had in a long time. Thank you." She kissed him on the cheek and walked back to the village, leaving John on the riverbank with his thoughts.

CHAPTER 5

HOW SOME MEN TREAT WOMEN

That night, Caroline woke up afraid. Unidentified noises drifted through the trapdoor to her ears. She whispered, "John". Rising from his prone position by the door, he put a finger to his lips, motioning for her to come. She crept silently nearer and lay down beside him on the floor. "Trouble?" she whispered. John nodded and pressed a finger to her lips.

Once the voices had moved away and Zeya had reentered the darkened, moonlit house, John took Caroline's hand and led her to the bed. Sitting beside her, he whispered directly into her ear, "That was some local men coming to warn the village that Military Intelligence is planning a raid in two days." Caroline heard his words in terror. "If they find us here, they won't just kill us; they'll torture and kill us and the entire village. We have to leave first thing in the morning." Then he said, more to himself. "I *knew* we had stayed too long."

"If we stay, we'll put Grace and her family in more danger?" Caroline asked, shakily.

Distantly, he responded, "If we stay we'll likely be captured."

Confused by his response, Caroline turned into his arms seeking comfort. Holding her tightly until she calmed, he then ordered her to bed while he went to converse with Zeya.

At first light, John roused Caroline. Cho had prepared some food wrapped in leaves and packed in a small, canvas satchel for their journey and Grace had rolled some blankets and tied them with rope, the sparkle extinguished from her eyes. Zeya approached tentatively, something concealed behind his back. Bobbing his head, keeping his eyes on the floor, he presented John with a sturdy, wooden-handled hunting knife. John froze for a moment as though in battle with himself. Then he quickly accepted it, offering a sincere "chezu ba"—thank you. With a quick good-bye and expressions of deepest gratitude, John and Caroline departed, leaving the family to erase all traces of their company.

Travelling northwest away from the village, they moved into the trees along the riverbank. It felt as though they had walked out of the land of people and into the world of birds, surrounded as they were by the vibrations of chirps, tweets and whistles. At a point where the river narrowed, they swam across then plunged westward into the jungle. The trees were thick and lush with flattened oval leafs that grew from ground to tip, making walking difficult. The sunlight reflected off the waxy leaves giving the forest floor a dim but dazzling glow. Bunching along the ground, the mottled, spearheaded leaves of the bushes grabbed at their legs and hands as they walked but, here and there in the clear spaces grew the most beautiful white, star-shaped flowers. John quickly found a sturdy branch for himself and one for Caroline to use to help push aside the verdant growth so they could pass through.

Stopping after a few hours to rest, John slumped down in frustration.

"What I wouldn't give for a machete!" he exclaimed.

Sitting beside him, Caroline reached over and squeezed his hand. "Where are we going?" she asked.

"West," he replied, taking a sip of water.

Caroline frowned, "Yes, and—" she gestured, letting him know that she expected more information.

"Yes, and—nothing. I don't know where we are. They don't know where they are. What kind of man doesn't know where he lives?" John was ranting. "I asked him where the Irrawaday River ran. He pointed. Can you believe it, he pointed?! And not a precise, follow this path and you'll find it, but a sweeping hand gesture!"

Caroline could tell that she wasn't really a necessary part of this treatise. Frustrated, she interrupted, "They don't exactly have much freedom to travel here, you know. That Form 10 thing is hugely prohibitive." Fixing him with a hard stare, she asked again, "Well, where are we going?"

Narrowing his eyes, John responded, "West."

"John!" She reprimanded him. "Where west? Going where? Why? Where's home?" She raised her voice at each question.

Sarcastically, he replied, standing and sweeping his arm like a compass point. "Canada—that way."

"I don't mean necessarily Canada. I just mean 'away from Burma'. Why are you being so difficult?" Annoyed, she flopped back to the ground.

"Difficult? Me difficult? I'm not the one—" He stopped. "Never mind, let's go."

Caroline leapt to her feet. "No, wait. I want to hear this. What? I'm not the one who can't speak the language, doesn't know the culture and cries all the time?" Her voice rose in anger, "I'm not the one who's a displaced spy, bringing danger and frustration to everyone he meets, using whatever he comes across as a resource—telling a woman that he cares for her so she'll do his bidding. Is that what you mean? Is it?!" Caroline's face was suffused with red, her fists clenched in frustration.

"Is that what you think?" John, incredulous and angry, spun and stalked away from her. After ten steps he stopped. In the densely, tangled growth, they could lose each other in no time. Caroline watched him clenching and unclenching his fists, his back turned to her. She slid to the ground, curling her arms around her knees. A volcanic eruption wouldn't have created more heat than their anger blazing along the forest floor.

Caroline cooled her anger first, calling out to him, "John." She sighed, reluctantly apologizing. "I'm sorry." Unmoved as he was, she got up and walked over to him. *I hate swallowing my pride but I really have been unfair to him. He has been very kind to me.* Reaching out she touched his arm lightly.

He turned on her, grinding out, "You don't sound sorry." Flinching, she expected to see his eyes blazing with anger but his face was a mask of misery.

"Oh John," she said in sympathy. "I *am* sorry." Reaching out tentatively, she slid her hand along his forearm.

"I don't know what you want from me!" he exclaimed gruffly, still holding his body stiffly upright. Caroline mused that most people thought that a man like John, a 'real ladies' man', wanted a string of beautiful women to use and leave. She knew that, in truth, what a real man actually desired was one woman who could make him feel truly special, and good enough to keep. Caroline wondered if John was capable of love. She knew he could kiss. He was very good at kissing, but what did it take to get beneath the surface of his emotions?

Uncertain what to say, she tried, "I—well—I just want you to be honest with me. Honest and open. Tell me what you're thinking."

"I don't know what to say." He began, reaching for her hand. "I've known plenty of women in my life." Caroline hardened her stare and grabbed her hand away. "But I've never felt this way before." He waited, as though willing her to reply—to tell him what he should do.

Caroline sighed. "I need to know if your kisses mean something, John, or is this just 'a guy with the only girl available'." She turned to face him then looked away again. "Are you just using me?" she added more quietly, watching his face carefully.

"I'm not using you," he replied, insulted. Sighing, he muttered with a hint of despair in his voice. "If this were about sex, I'd know what to do."

"What would you do?" she asked, seriously. He leaned in to kiss her but she put her hand on his chest, stopping him. "Tell me," she said.

"I'd seduce you," he finished simply.

"John, sex isn't love. I won't make love to you. Sex is an enhancement not a covenant. You're worth more than that—and so am I."

"I'm not just looking for sex." He paused, struggling to continue. "I don't know if I'm capable of love," he murmured, very softly then continued, slightly louder, "You're the first person I've met who makes me feel special just because of who I am. I haven't felt like that in a very, very long time. You're not impressed by the things that impress most women and you give me a lot of aggro about things that most women don't care about." He paused and she could see the struggle in his face. "I'm a good spy. I'm very good at what I do but my job pretty much put paid to my—my emotional education. I know I'm rubbish at all this but I also know that the thought of being away from you makes my chest hurt." His shoulders slumped. His confession seemed to have taken all the fight out of him.

Now Caroline reached for his hand, reiterating, "Is this—this between us—is it a relationship?"

"I don't know," John replied sadly. "I'm attracted to you. I enjoy being with you but I seem to annoy you without really

Forged in the Jungles of Burma

knowing why. You are a bit barmy," he smiled, "but I find I quite enjoy barmy, when it's you." He watched her face, as though looking for reassurance.

"I assume you're telling me I'm just a little bit crazy?" She smiled, enjoying the idea of that. When he grinned in response, she continued, "I really like you, too, and I do find you frustrating but—"

She stopped, uncertain how to explain what she wanted to say. They remained in an uneasy silence for a time, avoiding each other's eyes.

Suddenly, John sucked in a breath and said in a flurry, "But you don't want anything to do with me. I should get you out of here and let you return to your nice, safe life. I'm really not 'your cup of tea'."

She laughed a bitter laugh. "My nice, safe life landed me in a prison in Burma. No thanks, I don't need that again. John, I'm trying to explain something but I just don't know how to say it." She paused, gathering her thoughts. "I'm terrified." She glanced at him then studied the ground between her toes.

He looked up in surprise, "Of me?" He watched her, his face revealing the shock he felt at her statement.

She smiled and looked up at him shyly. "No, not of *you*, of love." John sighed, leaning back against a nearby tree as she continued. "Henry and I were very happy but marriage is hard work. Henry came from a pretty rotten home and we had lots to work through before we got to the really happy times. Love, more than anything, is a choice. It's a choice to love even in the unlovely moments—then eventually, the choice to love becomes automatic. Once the romance fades, it's the choice that brings it back. Most couples give up at this point but we didn't and, as a result we had a happy marriage and a happy family." Caroline reached out to take John's hand. "I worked hard to get to 'happy' and then in one fell swoop it was ripped from me and I was left in an agony of loneliness. I just don't know if I can do that again."

"You mean you're not sure if I'm worth it," he stated bitterly.

Caroline stroked his face with the palm of her hand. "I *know* you're worth it, Bernard John. I just don't know if I'm brave enough to be who you need."

John's eyes rose slowly to hers. "I need *you*." He turned his head to kiss the palm of her hand as it lay along his cheek. "I don't have a clue how to do *this*," he gestured between them, "but, if you're willing to be patient with me, I'd like to try. I don't want to lose this—um—opportunity—to lose you." John leaned forward slipping his hands around her waist and pulling her close.

She whispered into his ear before kissing it, "There's no one else I would do this for". Resting her forehead against his, she demanded, "So, we move forward together?" She waited until she felt him nodding.

"Yes," he replied as his lips met hers. After their tender kisses, John pulled back, watching the vibrant flush of her cheeks.

"John?" Her voice was tentative.

He looked directly at her, "Yes?"

"You know as a Christian I believe God's word and when he says that we shouldn't have sex outside of marriage, I believe Him and also that marriage is the end result of a romantic relationship and that's what we'd be moving toward and—and—and I know you're very attractive but you probably already know that and it's nothing special for me to think you're sexy but—" John's hand over her mouth cut her off and, moving his mouth close to her ear, he whispered, "Tell me."

Her blush reached from her toes to the roots of her hair now. She couldn't look away because he was holding her face so she closed her eyes. Sighing around his fingers, she muttered, "Do you find me attractive?" She waited, eyes closed for his response but he wasn't answering. Opening her eyes, she prepared herself to view rejection in his face, but he was smiling—a huge wide happy smile that twinkled in the corners of his eyes.

"Well?" she questioned in her smallest voice.

"You think I'm sexy?" he asked, still smiling.

"Yes, but we're not feeding your ego, you're supposed to be reassuring me," she replied with humour in her voice.

His face became serious and she wondered at what he would say. "You are beautiful. Your hair is the richest brown falling along your face. I always want to brush it away so I can see your soft cheek beneath it. Your eyes are pools I could drown in with the greatest joy. Every curve on your body begs to be touched and sometimes I don't know how I can keep my hands off you."

Caroline flushed again, this time in pleasure. "I know I'm not exactly the poster girl for beauty. I imagine a man like you, a real live action hero, has probably had the opportunity of many beautiful women."

John placed his hands on her cheeks, running his thumbs along hers eyes, down along the ridge of her nose and across her lips. "You are Beauty." He held her face until she looked him in the eyes. "You are Beauty," he said again and kissed her tenderly, as her eyes fluttered closed.

Sighing, Caroline slowly opened her eyes and in a dreamy tone asked, "So, then, where are we going?"

John laughed aloud, pulling her into a hug. "Fine," he said. "We're travelling west across the Bago Yoma wildlife preserve. If we have a great deal of luck, we may find the Ranger station where we should be able to acquire a map of Burma—if we're not detained or reported by the Rangers first. I have a contact along the Myitmaka River. If we can make it there, we should be able to get some money and provisions. The problem is, as I don't know exactly where we are, I have no idea where we're going to emerge. Most settlement occurs along the major rivers so we can't afford to travel up and down the roads there for fear of being noticed. However, if we don't get some money soon, we're probably going to starve." He paused, raising her hand to his lips. "Are you still glad to know what's going on?"

Smiling, she nodded, "I know I've cried a lot lately but I really can cope. I'm not a complete neophyte when it comes to camping and survival. I've been in the Canadian bush." He nodded then hugged her again. They set off.

They trudged along throughout the day, each kilometre taking ages to cross as they had to push through the thick undergrowth. Water was plentiful, and food abounded if you could catch it. Toward evening, John suggested they set some snares and showed her how to use vines and green supple branches to create a spring loaded trap. Afterwards, they built a shelter together to avoid the daily drenching that was still occurring every afternoon. John suggested the shelter needed to be raised above the jungle floor in order to keep them safe from predatory insects, and drier than the sodden ground. John found a couple of trees in close proximity between which he lashed branches, binding them with the vines he cut with the hunting knife. Carefully explaining as he constructed the hide, he showed Caroline how to find strong logs that would hold their weight and how to select vines that were green and sturdy not brown and brittle. Overhanging the platform he'd constructed, John fastened large leafy branches to form a canopy to keep the rain off.

Venturing out again in the evening, they found two squirrels and a hare in their snares. John dispatched them quickly and set about preparing them for supper. Using the knife, John prepared the animals for cooking, opting to bury them in the midst of the coals, using their hides as "survivor tinfoil". The smell of burning fur was most unpleasant but Caroline changed her expression when she tasted the cooked meat.

"How do you know how to do all this stuff—this survival stuff? Were you a Boy Scout?" Caroline inquired as she ate.

"Army," he replied between mouthfuls. "I was a Boy Scout and then I served in the army, Special Forces, as well."

"Just like that superhero guy—captain whatever?" she teased. Reaching over, he snatched her squirrel leg and sucked the meat into his mouth.

"Hey!" she exclaimed, launching herself at him to retrieve her portion. They tussled around in the grass for a while, sitting up when their stomachs began to hurt from laughter.

"Thief," she accused.

Grinning through greasy lips, he replied, "Perhaps." She stuck her tongue out at him, playfully.

As night descended, John noticed that Caroline had become fidgety and quiet. As he rolled out the blanket, she stood back, tapping her leg with her fist and humming a tuneless melody. Turning to invite her in, he watched as a blush crept along her face.

"What's wrong?" he asked. She shook her head and continued standing, tapping and humming. John snorted. "That's not an answer. I'm knackered, let's go to bed." Waiting for her to move, he tried again when she didn't. "Ca~ro~line," he sang her name. She stopped tapping and was silent.

"I—uh—I—uh— you—bed—" she stammered.

Inspiration dawned. "I'm not an animal, you know," he proclaimed.

Confused, Caroline moved closer to him. "What?" she inquired.

"I can control myself," he added, beginning to blush himself.

His reaction comforted Caroline, reassuring her that he was as disconcerted as she was. Standing beside him, she tried again. "I understand that we're likely going to need to share a sleeping space for a while and, I know we care about each other—are attracted to each other but—I just—I want—I need—"

John chuckled. "This is utterly ridiculous. We're two grown adults, fighting for survival in hostile territory and our biggest concern is how we're going to sleep." He chuckled again. "Caroline, what do you think of this idea: I'll be in charge of spying and survival and you can be in charge of everything else? So, you make the rules and I'll follow them. I give you my word." He gripped her hand tightly.

"Including sleeping and—and—not sleeping?" John grinned and nodded at her. "Okay, then we just follow God's rules—that's always the best way. No sex outside of marriage. Marriage is for life with no 'get out' clause. I used to tell Henry that, when I married him, it was for life, but it wasn't enough just to stay together, we had to be happy—even if it killed us." Caroline smiled.

John laughed. "Even if you kill me?"

Swatting him playfully on the arm, she exclaimed, "Now you're getting the idea!"

"I can live with that," he declared. They crawled into the shelter together, curled up and slept, each fully trusting the other to keep their word.

During the next few days, John and Caroline walked, ate, walked and slept. They saw wildlife all around them: langurs, tapirs, wild boars and barking deer. Long-eared hares launched their bodies into the bush while red-furred squirrels fled to the trees as the travelers journeyed on. The occasional rustle and hiss sent lightning bolts of fear through Caroline's body and usually sped her steps to match John's stride, clinging to his hand for reassurance. Caroline laughed to think of people who paid to attract wildlife. She would gladly pay to keep the leopards, snakes and tigers away.

Unexpectedly, they reached a paved road parallel to a narrow band of water. Confused, John muttered, "A paved road in the bush? Which road? Don't know…Beside a river… Too small to be the Myitmaka…the Dawe?…Thought that was further south." Caroline held back, watching him think.

Turning to her, he announced, "I didn't expect to cross a road at this point. Let's follow the road for a while and see if I can figure out where we are." Nodding, she took his offered hand and they walked along the road, the going so much easier than trekking through the bush. When the road ended near a lake, John asked Caroline to wait while he scouted the area. Spreading a blanket in an open, grassy section near the road to rest, she basked in the warmth of the sun. John set off, skirting the western shore of the lake. More tired than she thought, she quickly fell asleep, drifting into a dream about riding the roller coaster at that sea park she and Henry had visited when they were dating. Up she rode, pausing at the top before rushing down the other side, looping and twisting then slowing and easing into the uphill path. At the top, once again, she plunged down, down…until, there at the bottom of the hill was a figure all in black, caliginous and arcane, reaching for her, until his clawed hand grasped her face—Caroline woke with a start, looking directly into the eyes of a Burmese soldier grinning lasciviously at her and grasping her face in his dirty hand, obstructing her breathing with his palm. Striking out to push him away, she found her arms imprisoned at her sides by another soldier. The horrifying gleam of lust and violence in his eyes filled her with dread.

As she struggled to escape, the soldiers yanked her to her feet, dragging her toward the water. Amused at first by her determination, they soon became irritated when she managed to clip one of them on the side of the head with her flailing arms. Punching her several times, they flung her into the lake and then followed her in, dunking her head under the water. At first, the icy chill revived her and she struck out, screaming, "Get your filthy hands off me!" but the continued dunking drained her energy. Dragging her out of the water, the soldiers dumped her on the ground as they prepared for more 'entertainment'. *Oh God, help me,* her heart cried out as she sat retching and sputtering on the grass. *Please send John! Where is he?*

Rising to stand, Caroline fell back to the ground when one of the soldiers slapped her hard, yelling, "Foreign whore!" He followed up his slap by kicking her. Dodging, she managed to catch his boot on her leg rather than her stomach. Infuriated, he removed his belt and, pinning her arms above her head, he used it to bind her wrists together.

"John! Help me!" she screamed and was rewarded with a filthy cloth shoved into her open mouth. The soldier at her head knelt on the belt pinning her arms to the ground above her head. He reached along her arms, forcing her shoulders to the ground. Caroline retched again as his foul odour assaulted her. The soldier at her feet kicked her ankles apart and, grinning maliciously began to unbuckle his belt.

"NO!"

Caroline couldn't see her rescuer but she recognized John's thrilling baritone. She heard the soldier at her feet protest and heard his body hit the ground. The surprise on her captor's face alerted her that he was next. As he fell, the pressure on Caroline's arms was released and she curled onto her side, ripping the filthy cloth out of her mouth and sliding her hands out of the belt. Closing her eyes, she hugged her arms across her chest, shaking uncontrollably.

When John touched her, she flinched, scrambling to be away. She couldn't tell if her eyes were opened or closed; the world seemed to be swallowed up in a fog, a fog of violence and fear. She couldn't tell how long she had been lying there but gradually the familiar tune wended through the fog bringing with it the words of hope and comfort she had learned as a child. "Jesus loves me, this I know..." Slowly, the fog darkened and resolved to reveal John lying on the ground beside her. It was his voice singing the words of hope. As her eyes fluttered, he reached out to tuck a lock of hair behind her ear. Shivering at his touch, she squeezed her eyes shut and opened them again, just to be sure it was really him.

"God," she heard him say. "I'm no fool. I've seen enough here in Burma to know that you are real. I always thought that believing in You was a sign of weakness; that a real man made his own salvation. But this lady trusts you. She loves you. She loves you enough to care for me in your name. Please help me to help her."

Reaching out, Caroline touched the moisture on John's face, drawing her fingertips back to study the dampness between her finger and thumb. Looking back to his face, she saw the agony on his features, agony he felt for her. When he opened his arms, she crawled across the space between them and curled into a ball within his protective embrace.

She was never sure how long they lay there but it was long enough that the angle of the sun changed. When she moved to sit up, John released her from the hug and came to crouch in front of her. Studying her intently, he very slowly reached across the space between them and tilted her face to look directly into her eyes. Her gaze travelled beyond him until he tentatively called her name, drawing her focus to his face.

"Caroline? Can you stand up?" he asked gently. She shook her head, beginning to shake again. "All right, it's all right." Gently placing his hands on her upper arms, he slowly drew her closer to him, embracing her firmly until her arms reached around him and hugged him back.

"Caroline? Can you stand?" he asked again. This time, she nodded. He reached for her hand, helping her up. Maintaining her hold on him, she followed him to a jeep. Searching the ground, he found the blankets, wrapping them snugly around her.

"Caroline? I need to deal with these soldiers. Stay here by the road. I'll be right back." She clutched at his arm in panic, terror printed across her eyes. "I will be right back,

I promise. Will you trust me?" he inquired softly. Her eyes filled with unshed tears. "Do you want to come with me?" She nodded, still clutching his arm. "All right." He settled her in the passenger seat of the jeep and then drove them to the lake to get the soldiers' bodies.

"Caroline?" he explained. "I have to dispose of these bodies. If I can contrive some sort of convincing accident, we'll be much safer. Do you think you can help me?" Panicked, she vigorously shook her head, grasping at his shirt. He firmly placed his hands over her fists and stilled their movement. "It's all right." Kissing each of her hands, he placed them gently on her lap. Reaching around her, he brought the blanket up over her head like a hood, gently stroking his fingers along her cheek. "Stay here but don't watch." When he saw the panic return to her gaze, he promised, "I'll sing, all right? I'll sing so you can hear me, then you'll know I'm here. All right?" She nodded slowly, the panic leaving her eyes. As he stepped away, she pulled the blanket further over her head so that it blocked her vision completely. She heard the sounds of John dragging something heavy, felt the jeep sway as something was placed in the back but above it all she heard John singing to her. Returning to the driver's seat, John reached out to push the blanket off Caroline's face. Turning to face him, she pressed his hand to her cheek, holding him there for a time. When she released him, he turned to the steering wheel.

"Hopefully, they were an isolated patrol," he said. "If I can make a believable accident, with any luck, no one will question events. There is a rickety bridge over there, spanning the river. I saw some whiskey in the back of the jeep. Maybe I can make it look like they were drunk and drove off the bridge."

Driving over to the bridge, John helped Caroline out of the jeep. Propping the soldiers in the front seats, he poured the whiskey into their mouths and down their shirts. Caroline moved away at the smell. Starting the jeep, he jammed the 'drivers' boot onto the gas pedal and released the clutch. The vehicle bounced along the dirt road, directly at the rotting railing, flipping and flinging the bodies into the river.

Rinsing his hands in the river water, John returned to Caroline. He placed the map, the canteen and the knife he had removed from the jeep into their satchel, and, taking her by the hand, he led her back to the lake where he erased all traces of their presence that he was able. When he was finished, he wrapped his arms around her, hugging her.

Pulling back and looking directly into her face, he said, "Caroline? We need to get somewhere safer. Are you ready to leave?" She nodded, her eyes welling with tears. She took his offered hand and followed him. They walked back toward the Bago River, crossing the rickety bridge and continuing into the bush on the other side. Caroline shivered as they passed the spot where the bodies of the dead soldiers drifted torpidly downstream.

John kept them walking long into the night. Caroline walked silently by his side, stopping when he stopped and moving when he moved. When the forest floor was veiled with night, John began searching for somewhere to hide. Casting about, he located an overgrowth of vines laced together that formed a perfect cave. He asked Caroline to wait as he poked around to make sure there were no snakes or other creepy crawlies inside. As he turned to get her, she was right behind him, having silently followed him in. Taking Caroline by the hand, he encouraged her to sit by him on the ground and, pulling her to his chest, wrapped his arms tightly around her. She soon escaped into a dreamless sleep, breathing in the scent of John with every breath. She felt him shift position from time to time and, somewhere in her brain, it registered that he was still awake.

Morning came and the sunlight filtered through the leaves, the flickering shadows disturbing Caroline, causing her to shift around as she slowly woke. She startled as John spoke to her. "Good morning. How are you feeling?" Caroline shrugged in response and continued to look at the ground. "I'm just going to go out and check around to make sure we're alone. Stay here. I'll be right back," John said. Panic ricocheted around Caroline's belly. She grabbed his hand and clutched it to her with all her strength. John came back to kneel in front of her, allowing her to continue holding his hand.

"Caroline," he said gently, then "Caroline" a little more firmly as he lifted her chin. "Caroline, my darling, I promise I will protect you." At the endearment, Caroline reached out a shaky hand to trace his lips. Leaning in, he kissed her fingers very gently. The tender gesture cracked the dam restraining her emotions and she began to weep; great, shaking, gut wrenching sobs as John sat back down, wrapping his arms around her and rocking her. Hiccoughing, she tried to calm her breathing.

"Caroline, we're safe. I will protect you—just as you've protected and cared for me." John leaned in and kissed her again, more firmly this time. "I need to scout the area but I want to be sure that you're safe, so please stay here until I return. I promise that I will return as quickly as possible, all right?" John spoke calmly and evenly as though speaking to a child. He waited until Caroline met his eyes and nodded before he left. Caroline curled into a ball again, rocking and praying, *please bring him back—please bring him back—please bring him back*. Time stretched out. Then, even though he called out to her first, she flinched as his head appeared in the opening but moved toward him when he reached out his hand.

"I found a stream," he reported, leading her to it. "We're quite safe. Can you hear the birds? They wouldn't be singing if there was danger about." As they emerged from the bush and into the open along the stream, John turned to her.

"Come," he said, "we'll bathe in the stream". Reaching down, he started to lift her top but she pulled away, clamping her shirt back down. "We need to check your injuries," he stated mildly as she continued to look at him dubiously.

Trying another tack, he said, "I don't remember being allowed to refuse when *I* was the patient!" Caroline grinned weakly at him and removed her top. Sighing, she removed her longyi as well, standing before him in her undergarments, her arms crossed in front of her. Taking her hand before she resisted, he led her into the water.

"I'm really only bruised, I think," she said shyly.

John's face lit up when she spoke. "It's good to hear your voice again," he commented lightly. Moving back into shallower water, John examined her wounds more closely. An angry flush suffused his cheeks as he surveyed her injuries. She had a huge bruise on her left shoulder and across the left side of her ribs and there was a boot imprint on her right thigh. She had a black eye and a cut lip.

"Did they—ah—did they...?" John began.

"No. They would have, if you hadn't stopped them. They smacked me around for a while; I guess to soften me up first—dunked me in the lake." She shivered. "Hmmm. There are nasty people in the world." Caroline was quiet for a time and John waited. "Why do men think they have the right to treat women that way?" She looked him in the eyes as if searching there for her answer.

"Not all men feel they have the right," he responded quietly, lowering his eyes as though in shame at his gender. Once her wounds were tended, John returned to the bank to fetch one of the blankets to wrap her in while she dried off and dressed. Putting his arm around her shoulders, they sat together on the riverbank.

"John," she began.

"Hmmm," he replied.

"Why haven't the prison officials pursued us?" she asked quietly.

"The monsoon. Travel becomes very difficult at this time of year," John replied.

"Do you think they're still looking for us?" Her eyes pleaded with him to say 'no'.

Sighing, he pressed his cheek against hers. "They'll keep looking for me."

"Do you think we could go home soon?" she asked, sounding small and scared. John's eyes saddened as though in sympathy for her fear.

"I need to figure out exactly how we can get home," he responded. Leaning against him, she played with a frayed thread on his shirt.

"John, did you kill those men?" she finally broke the gentle silence between them, still fiddling with his shirt.

"Yes," he responded.

"Why did you drive them off the bridge if they were already dead?"

"They were likely on patrol. When they don't report in, someone will come looking for them. If it looks like an accident—like they got drunk and drove into the lake—then there's no reason to link them to us," he explained patiently. "Understand?"

She nodded. "John?" she began and stopped.

"Hmmm?" he answered.

"Why did you decide to become a spy, to join MI-5?" she inquired tentatively.

He responded slowly, a look of surprise flitting across his features. "My father wanted me to join the army. He said I needed the discipline to make something useful of my life. So I did, foolishly believing that it would please him," John responded bitterly. Caroline waited for him to continue. "During a special assignment, my men and I crossed paths with a team of MI-5 operatives working the same mission from a different angle. I guess they were impressed by me and, at the conclusion, they sent an agent to recruit me. I liked the idea of using the skills I had in this new and challenging way." He paused again then finished softly, "I thought my mother would approve of that." Caroline reached out and took his hand, lightly kissing him on the cheek.

When she was ready to move on, John helped her up and placed his arm around her, holding her tightly. They walked for a long time, Caroline feeling the need to put as much distance between her and the soldiers as possible. They hiked for several hours before coming to rest in a verdant, heavily leafed grove of trees that seemed to provide a suitable shelter. John used a stick to check for creepy crawlies before he allowed Caroline to enter. Spreading the blankets on the ground, they lay side by side gazing up at the bright and beautiful moon shining overhead.

"This is the same moon that's shines over Canada—" Caroline was thinking aloud, "the same bright, beautiful moon that shines over Singapore and India and Great Britain. What does this moon say to you, John?"

John was quiet for a time and Caroline wasn't sure if he would answer. "It tells me that the God who found me in a dingy, terrifying prison in Burma is the same God who gave me you. Whenever I see the moon on a clear night I'll remember that God loved me enough to send you to rescue me." Turning his head, he gazed deeply into her eyes as she lay beside him. Caroline rolled onto her side and put her arm across his chest, kissing his cheek and nestling into his side. "That makes my second life rather important then, doesn't it?"

"Oh yes. Oh yes!" They fell asleep in each other's arms.

CHAPTER 6

COLONEL SHING

Two more days of walking combined with John's tender consideration helped the pierce of Caroline's terror dull into an ache of apprehension. Lying under the moon one night, Caroline remembered the prayer John had made, patiently waiting for her to emerge from the fog. She glanced over at him as he lay beside her, one arm behind his head and the fingers of his other hand tapping out a rhythm on his leg.

"You're tapping," she said.

Confused, he replied, "pardon?"

Rolling onto her side, facing him, she reiterated, "You're tapping out a rhythm on your leg. You always do that when you want to ask me something." She slipped her hand into his, stilling his fingers.

"That's a 'tell'," he responded.

Now it was her turn to be confused. "Eh?"

"A 'tell' is a mannerism or a gesture that gives away something about you. I didn't realize I had a 'tell'." He stopped, gazing down at her hand where it held his, stroking his thumb across the back of her hand.

"Well?" she prompted him.

Glancing up at her face briefly then looking away, he said, "What if someone wanted to—well—wanted to—or maybe thought that God, maybe, was real and—well—wanted to—for instance—become a Christian or something. How would a person do that, if they wanted to?" He paused, still looking at their joined hands.

"It's simple really," she replied. "Just ask. Ask God to forgive you for your wrongdoings and to come into your life. Put him in charge."

Turning to Caroline, he asked, "Is that it?"

"Yep," Caroline answered. "When you want something—"

"Just ask, and trust God," John interrupted, smiling slightly. "You see, I am teachable."

Smiling at him, she confirmed, "You are teachable. John, God always keeps His word. He promised that if we confess with our mouths that Jesus is Lord and believe in our hearts that God raised Him from the dead, He would save us. When a person—someone—gives their heart to Him, they become His. He'll never walk away from His children. Whatever happens, He'd be with you—or them, as the case may be."

The next morning, John and Caroline exited the gloomy forest, flatlands stretching before them. They emerged from the trees, saw a few random bushes and then flat, dusty ground like the patted roads of a child's sandbox. The trees just ended, like a giant had taken a knife and cut a section of peel from an apple, leaving a band of white alongside the band of green. They found a shady spot on the edge of the flat and rested against a large rock, pulling out the soldier's map.

"I think we're somewhere around here," John said, pointing to a spot on the map. "The village of Hlelangu should be around here somewhere. If that's the case, we need to travel to here, Pyay, without being seen. I have a contact in Sinde, across the water from Pyay, who should be able to help us. Unfortunately, Sinde is on the other side of the Myitmaka River to us and there's no bridge between here and Pyay."

"That's a long way," she replied, more than a little awed by the distance.

"Hmmm," he acknowledged. "If we can walk along the edge of the forest, skirting the villages, we should be able to make it to Pyay in about a week," he explained, measuring the distance with his fingertips.

Caroline's jaw dropped. "A week? We'll be walking non-stop for another week?"

"At least we'll be able to walk in a straight line for a change," John mused, nudging her with his shoulder.

"Food?" she asked, disheartened.

"We'll have to stop from time to time to trap or find a way to acquire what we need."

"I don't want to steal," Caroline replied. John returned her gaze with a blank stare. She sighed at his response. "Well, if we're walking for the next seven days, I want to hear a story."

<><><><><>

Frantically, Captain Htet organized his desk. Perhaps if he looked organized, no one would notice his abysmal failure to collect any useful information about the escaped convict—the British spy—John Brock.

His office door slammed open. "Good morning, Htet."

Captain Li. Htet spat mentally but outwardly showed cautious respect. "Good morning, Captain Li. You are looking well."

Li held his body ramrod straight in the doorway. He was tall and thin but no one would make the mistake of calling him weak. He exuded calm and competence and his men were fiercely loyal to him. He was fiercely loyal to Colonel Shing. "I have been sent to escort you to Colonel Shing." Turning on his heel, he departed.

"I have tried," Htet called after him, causing Li to halt.

Languidly, he turned, removing the tiny oval spectacles from his nose and proceeding to clean them on his handkerchief. He met Htet's gaze. "Oh?" he inquired.

"Once the rains settled, I sent patrols throughout the ports of Yangon. I sent patrols east along the Thai border. I suspected those Karen people of aiding him but could find nothing. He has disappeared." As Htet finished his sentence, he knew he had made a tactical error. Li advanced on Htet who retreated until he was pinned against his desk.

"People do not disappear." Li moved in menacingly close, so close that Htet could count the cavities in his teeth. "Unless we disappear them." Replacing his spectacles on his nose, Li stiffly moved away, commanding, "Come!"

<><><><><>

"We have been walking for six days now and I've realized that for every question I've asked you, you have asked me ten." Caroline accused John, in mock seriousness.

"Is that so?" John asked, smiling as she poked him playfully.

"Yes. I have answered questions about my cousins, my dogs, my University classmates, and my favourite Indian dishes. What I still do not know is why you are here in Burma." Caroline grabbed John's arm and pulled him closer.

Spinning her into his body, he pinned her with her back against his chest. Running his lips lightly down her ear, he exhaled gently, causing her to shiver in response as she began to struggle halfheartedly. Gruffly, he whispered. "Vee Haff vays too make yoo tock." Kissing her neck, he released her.

"If you're quite through, I want to know NOW!" Caroline demanded. She launched herself, arms outstretched, ready to tickle him but he backed away, staying just out of reach until, in a flash of movement, she thrust her foot out, tripping him. Pinning his arms above his head, she commanded, "Tell me now!"

Laughing, John surrendered, "You're learning. I surrender. If you let me up, I'll talk." Accepting her offer of assistance, John rose and began to walk again, holding her hand. "Burma was a British colony until 1948." Raising his eyebrows at her, he waited for her to acknowledge this information before continuing. "Aung San was a military leader committed to establishing democratic ideals in the government following the move away from British rule. As a result, he was assassinated by political rivals in 1947. Conditions in Burma, once the British left, began to deteriorate immediately. However, they were able to hold multi-party elections until 1962 when General Ne Win led a military coup d'état. This allowed a communist influenced oppressive regime to take over—a totalitarian government—controlling and cruel. They called themselves the 'Burmese Socialist Programme Party' and they essentially impoverished their people. They kept foreign investment out and isolated the country from the rest of the world. You've already had a taste of the restrictions placed on the people and the surveillance that the government endorses coupled with the freedom it gives its military forces to do as they choose." Here Caroline looked down and shivered at the memory of the two soldiers. Holding her more firmly, John continued. "The indigenous peoples here lack even the most basic of civil rights. The military can force people into so-called 'volunteer' labour. The military can arrest, beat, torture—anything. Anyone criticizing the State Law and Order Restoration Council can be beaten or imprisoned. This land is bleeding and the world is pretending it can't see." John had stopped walking, lost in his thoughts.

Turning to face him, Caroline hugged him. "You really care about the people of Burma."

Sighing, he started walking, keeping his arm around her waist. "It's my job to know what's going on," he stated then continued, "In 1990, Aung San Suu Kyi, daughter of Aung San, finally won her bid for free elections in Burma when the SLORC allowed a multi-party election. Suu Kyi won a landslide victory even though she was under house-arrest at the time. Well, she's still under house-arrest and the SLORC are still running things." He shook his head in disgust. "Anyway, around that time, the Military junta decided that an isolationist stand wasn't working very well so they established a 'make money but shut up policy', encouraging international investment in Burma by major European, American, Australian and Asian corporations but not tolerating any political censure. So now, some can get rich as long as they ignore the oppression of their neighbours."

"What brought you to Burma?" Caroline asked, sadly.

"In 1990, I was tasked to approach Suu Kyi privately to discuss the part that the U.K. could play in investment AND change in Burma. With her advice—well assistance really—I was able to set up a network that provides intelligence to MI-6 about the political and economic interplay of Burma, Korea, Vietnam, China and India. Burma is in many ways the centre of a spinning wheel. In exchange, '6' aids Suu Kyi in ways that, frankly, I don't know. That part happened after I returned to '5'." John finished, taking Caroline by the arm and facing her.

"Caer, you mustn't discuss any of this with any person at all—ever—while we're in Burma. Do you understand?" He watched her intensely.

"I understand, John. I won't betray you," she promised.

Moving away, he walked on. "It's not just me, Caroline, it's not just me."

Following him, she assented, "I understand."

<><><><><>

SLAM! The Colonel's open palm slapped down on the table.

"This news you bring me is not good news, Htet. Explain then why we have paid you so much money—for this!" Colonel Shing paced beside his desk, his hands clasped behind his back.

"Sir, of course I grieve to bring you such terrible news. The Russian interrogator was careless, sir. He simply was not up to the grand task that you had set for him."

Colonel Shing stopped his pacing to bring his furious scowl around to face the Burmese prison warden.

"You seek to pass the blame on to our illustrious spy catcher do you? Be very certain that you understand what you are saying."

Captain Htet wilted beneath the Chinese Colonel's stare. He prevaricated, "Oh, sir, of course, I meant no disrespect to those who recruited him; of course, he should have been able to do the job he could—" SLAM.

"Enough warden, you have two choices: either you find the British spy for me or you will take his place. Do you understand?" The fire in his eyes matched the scorch in his words.

"Ye- yes sir. Uh, how am I to get men to accomplish this grand task I am privileged to undertake?" Htet flinched expecting a blow.

"I will send some of my own troops to accompany you. You will purloin appropriate uniforms for them and you *will* find him for me." The Colonel's voice gentled and the warden relaxed a little in response. "Or you will find that Vlad's techniques were lenient compared to what I will have done to you." Htet blanched and hurriedly left the room.

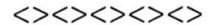

<><><><><>

John and Caroline stood, concealed in the bush, watching both the vehicular and pedestrian traffic pass over the bridge from Pyay to Sinde. Caroline noted many more pedestrians confined in a small space than she would have seen anywhere in Canada and the fact that many of the men, women and children were carrying loads balanced on their heads or hips.

"How are we going to get across without being noticed?" Caroline asked.

"Hmm, well, I guess we could just hide in plain sight," John replied.

Turning to him, Caroline inquired, "What does that mean?"

"Well, you hide but right where people can see you." he replied, expecting the gentle smack on the arm he received.

"Very funny, Einstein. Now, explain, please," she demanded.

"We try to blend in. Keep your head down, walk at the same pace as everyone else, move with the crowd and hope for the best. When we get across the bridge, turn left as soon as possible and I'll find you. All right?" John sought assurance that she understood.

Concentrating on the steps of the woman in front of her, Caroline crossed the painted iron bridge. It resembled a railway bridge back home but with an unhealthy dose of rust showing through the puerile green paint. She had no idea where John was as she took the first left turn and headed down a nearly deserted pathway. Uncertain whether she had taken the correct turning or not, she glanced ahead to see a couple of young men lounging against the walls of the alley. As she approached, they shoved themselves upright and moved to block her path. Glancing behind, she saw that while two of the youths had blocked her way forward, one more stood behind her, knife in hand. The young men in front of her looked to be about fourteen or fifteen. They were sleight, not excessively short or tall. The fellow behind her, however, was tall and broad and looked to be about eighteen or nineteen. He sported a neatly shaped beard and a switchblade. *Yea though I walk though the valley of the shadow of death, you are with me.* Caroline prayed the Shepherd's psalm as she began to shake, a vision of the soldiers at the Dawe sprinting across her mind. Frozen in trepidation, Caroline waited to see what would happen.

"Greetings!" she called in Burmese, her voice quivering pathetically. Turning, she backed toward one wall of the alley so she could see the young men in front and behind her. Raising her hands as she moved, she gestured to show that she had no possessions except her blanket roll. The young man with the knife motioned for her to drop the roll and she complied, tossing it a few feet away from her. Trying to watch all three youths at the same time, she missed the shadow that silently joined the stand-off.

The fellow with the knife ordered one of the other lads to pick up the blanket. As the lad moved forward, Caroline kept her eyes on him, trying to look confident. Picking up the blanket, he unrolled it, surprised when Caroline's treasured teak wood carving clattered on the pavement. Gasping, Caroline reached for it, brought up short by a knife held to her throat. Chasing the carving, the lad picked it up and studied it. Tears burned in Caroline's eyes. *No, of all things, not that.*

Suddenly, out of the shadows, a voice commanded in Burmese, "Leave it boys and go home. This lady has powerful friends."

"Ha!" The boys laughed, searching about for the source of the words.

"What will happen when the SLORC discover you have been accosting the wife of a magistrate?" The voice implied their doom.

Narrowing his eyes in suspicion, the young man with the knife snatched the carving from his companion and flung it against the wall, advancing toward the voice. As he moved away from Caroline, the two younger lads lunged at her, their advance energizing her body into motion. As one grabbed for her, she punched him in the face. The other swung at her and, as she dodged, he punched her in the shoulder. Kicking out, she caught him on the shin, causing him to hop around in pain. Unfortunately, as she fought off two of the lads, the third turned and, seeing his companions' situation, he came up behind her, pulling her hair back and pressing his knife along her throat. Caroline gasped but kept still.

"Show yourself or I'll slit her throat," the fellow yelled threateningly into the shadows.

All at once, the pressure on Caroline's hair vanished and the fellow's knife went spinning down the alley. Caroline looked around to see one youth unconscious behind her and the other two just turning to flee down the alley. Grasping the front of the would-be assailant's shirt, John pulled him up and prepared to readjust his nasal position. Caroline realized in a flash what he was planning to do and thrust her body between John and the young man. "NO, John!" John would have had to strike her in order to silence the assailant forever.

Pivoting angrily, he gestured at the fleeing youths. "And them?" he spat.

"They're just boys, John!" Caroline responded forcefully.

Keeping his distance from her, he strode over to the knife, first closing it and then pocketing it. Retrieving the carving, he tossed it to Caroline.

Confounded by John's mood, Caroline watched him speculatively. "Thank you," she said.

"What on earth were you doing down here?" he demanded, striding away.

John's tone spurred her to movement, following him out of the alley in the same direction as the lads. "What do you mean? I was only doing what you told me. You said to take the first left hand turn after the bridge."

"This is an alley. You don't go down dark alleys alone anywhere in Burma."

"Then why did you tell me to turn left?'

"Turn left down the first street!"

"Well then why didn't you say that?'

"Why did—?—" John muttered something unintelligible. She stopped. "Did you just say, 'women'?"

"No," he asserted.

"Better not have. Well, what did you say?"

"Nothing. It's complicated."

"What is?'

"Mixing necessity and emo—never mind, it's complicated." John sped up to end the conversation. Harumphing, Caroline followed him. *Complicated, indeed!*

They walked up and down streets for what felt like hours, taking a circuitous route through the town. Finally, John led them down a street that looked like wall to wall ghettoized barbie mansions—three story high, matchstick thin, aquamarine blue lace-like concrete walls with corrugated tin roofs. The height of the walls and the sardine squish of the buildings made Caroline feel claustrophobic. John led them to a tea shoppe sandwiched between a barber shop and a butcher shop. The smell from the street was less than appealing and Caroline wondered why anyone would want to eat or drink anywhere on this street.

As they entered the tea shoppe, they joined the queue and once they reached the front of the line, John ordered. "Manchurian Surprise with fresh mango. Is your mango fresh?" Caroline opened her mouth to give her order but he squeezed her hand sharply and she was quiet.

The waitress, a young woman with her hair pulled back into a ponytail, responded nervously, her eyes flitting across the customers in the shoppe. "I'm sorry, sir, but the mango did not arrive today. Please come back tomorrow."

Forged in the Jungles of Burma

"We'll settle for papaya instead," he responded.

The waitress frowned and replied, "We are also out of papaya, sir."

"Well, what would you recommend?" John seemed to be losing his cool.

"Come back tomorrow," she insisted.

Nodding, John pulled Caroline outside, walking to the first alley, turning right and walking around to the rear of the tea shoppe.

"What was she talking about? I saw mango and papaya behind the counter. And, by the way, what were you planning on using to pay for that tea? Have you forgot—"

John interrupted with a brusque, "SShhhh!" Fuming, Caroline was silent. He had, after all, saved her from the muggers in the alley. *I guess he deserves a little blind obedience.*

Positioning her in a dark alcove, he whispered, "Stay here." As he slipped into another shadow, she lost sight of him in the darkness, suddenly feeling very nervous and alone as memories of tea shoppes, airports and assailants assaulted her. They stayed like that for about fifteen minutes before a very harassed looking Burmese gentleman came muttering out of the back of the tea shoppe. He was a tall man with a dark complexion and a face marked with pox scars. Caroline watched as the man approached the spot where John was hidden and in one smooth motion, John had covered the man's mouth, twisted his right arm behind his back and planted him against the nearest wall.

"If you scream, I will kill you. Nod if you understand." The man nodded vigorously. "Now, Mr. Dara, you will explain why your waitress tells me your mangoes are not fresh when I can plainly see that they are." John whispered tersely. Slowly John moved his hand from the man's mouth and wrapped his fingers in the man's hair, pulling back hard enough to make the man gasp.

"Please—I cannot help you," the man simpered. "Military Intelligence has been alerted to the presence of a foreigner in the town. Apparently, a foreign couple masquerading as a magistrate and his wife assaulted three children in an alley across town. I cannot be seen with you. You must go, please." The man's voice was pleading.

"Where is Tomas?" John's voice was hard.

The man seemed to sag in John's grip. "He was taken—conscripted by the military as a porter. He has not been seen since. I cannot help you! Please go!" The man was becoming agitated. John covered the man's mouth again, in case he decided to scream in the silence of the alley.

John seemed to be thinking for a time. "Very well," he huffed. "First, you will do as I ask and then I will leave you in peace. Nod if you understand." John paused until the man nodded. "Has anyone been around looking for a foreigner, before today?"

The man shook his head and John released his mouth. "Not here. I've heard that Chinese and Burmese mercenaries have been searching for a British man in Yangon and along the Thai border. No one has been here—but after this attack today, word will spread." Mr. Dara ended on a threatening note but John brought him up short with a jerk to his hair.

"Very well. You will walk back into that tea shoppe of yours, remove one thousand kyat from your opium money stash, pack a satchel with fresh food to last three days and bring them to me. I will give you exactly six minutes to do this. If you do not return with everything I have asked for in under six minutes, I will ensure that your little side enterprise comes to the attention of the local military. Have you been attached to a car battery recently?" John's voice was menacing in the darkness. The man's legs were shaking in terror. He nodded then shook his head, confused. John released him, shoving him toward the back door of the shoppe and checking the imaginary watch on his wrist.

Looking over to Caroline, John pressed a finger to his lips and gestured clearly for her to stay hidden. Five minutes later, the quaking man returned with a back pack. Flinging it at John, he reentered the shoppe and locked the door. John darted forward, grabbing it. Quickly checking inside, he seemed satisfied. Donning the pack, he strode over to Caroline, grabbed her hand and, together, they ran out of the alley, along a back street and then headed over to a busier part of town. Flagging down a taxi, John ordered him to take them southwest along the highway to the town limits. The driver complied and thirty minutes later, John and Caroline exited the taxi, waited for it to drive back toward town and started walking west.

After walking for about an hour or so, they reached a small group of hills covered in trees. Pushing through the low-lying bushes with their long, wide leaves painted in natures pink, they forged ahead under the cover of the tall, thin branches of the forest. The narrow-trunked trees were heavily laden with narrow, green leaves and dotted with small, green berries. John led them well under cover before starting to cast about for a suitable shelter. Exhausted by the events of the day, Caroline collapsed onto the blankets and soon drifted off to sleep. John, however, remained awake long into the night.

CHAPTER 7
THINK, DON'T FEEL

It had been relatively easy to find the uniforms for Colonel Shing's men. Captain Htet had taken most of them from the dead bodies of his guards. When he had found Vlad's body after the Rebel's attack on his prison, Htet had known there would be serious trouble for him. He needed to make certain that no one realized it had been his idea to place the spy with the woman. Htet had learned later, after the Chin attack, from his Rebel informants that the woman had helped the spy escape. Beyond that piece of information, which had cost him dearly to obtain, no one seemed to know what happened to them. His only hope had been to pass the blame on to Vlad for his failure to retrieve any useful information from the British spy.

Initially, Htet had tried to distance himself from Shing, denying the connection but then Captain Li had shown up in his office. He had had no choice but to face the Colonel and hope to come out alive and, perhaps, have a second chance to regain his favour. Now, with the rains subsiding, here he was, journeying across Myanmar, pursuing leads to remote villages, barely accessible by confusing tracks and trails, accompanied by a dozen evil looking private soldiers. Htet was ostensibly in command but he knew full well that he was least in authority amongst them and that the Colonel had probably given them license to kill him at the first whiff of failure.

<><><><><>

Waking to the forest sounds of babblers and bushlarks in symphony with the barks of the deer and buzz of the mosquitoes, Caroline, shuddering, flicked a tiny lime green lizard off her hand and went in search of John. Finding him building a small fire, she joined him.

"Good morning," she greeted him cheerily.

"Morning," he replied evenly.

"You okay?" she asked, concerned by his response.

"Fine. Did you sleep well?" he asked, focusing on the fire.

"Yes, thank you." She paused, studying him. "Are you sure you're all right?"

John sighed. "I'm fine."

"I can tell you're not really fine," she said, laying her hand on his arm.

"I don't want to talk about it—not right now." Turning to her, his eyes were hard. "All right?"

Father, what is going on? "Okay," she answered slowly. "Why are these people so eager to capture you? For that matter, why did they bring you here to Burma in the first place? John, what's really going on?" she inquired, watching him carefully.

"They want my contacts in Southeast Asia," he answered as he passed her a piece of fruit.

"Who wants your contacts?"

"The only logical answer seems to be the Chinese. Well, not the entire Chinese nation but one Colonel in particular. The reason he's not a general, and will probably never be a general, is because of the work I did in Southeast Asia about twenty years ago," he responded. His body was close to her but his mind seemed far away.

"But, Vlad was Russian, surely. Why was a Russian interrogating you about a Southeast Asian network for the Chinese?" she asked, feeling very confused.

"Colonel Shing must have purchased his services. He did mention to me that he had been cast out by the KGB after he interrogated me the first time. You see, this isn't the first time I've met Vlad. He used to work for the KGB in the Soviet Union. When I was captured by the Russians twenty years ago, he was my interrogator. That's why he was so—um—enthusiastic. I didn't break last time for the KGB and he was determined to break me this time for Colonel Shing."

"I don't understand the connection between the Chinese and the Russians," Caroline stated, still watching him as a variety of emotions played across his visage.

Snorting impatiently, John replied tersely, "They just happened to want the same information as Colonel Shing. In the days of the Soviet Union, the two communist powers were competing for intelligence and influence."

"What would happen if you gave them the names?" she asked quietly.

"I can't give them the names. If I do, then dozens of people will be killed—tortured and killed. I can't do that. Some of my people have families. Some are just ordinary citizens who have agreed to help us preserve liberty in this part of the world. I can't give them up. I can't." He lapsed into silence then stiffened. "Enough! No more questions." John stood up, kicked out the fire, grabbed the pack and walked away westward, breakfast now forgotten. Caroline was left swallowing the lump of tears lodged in her pharynx. Checking the fire to ensure it was extinguished, she followed him, praying for herself, for John and for home.

<><><><><>

Captain Htet was very pleased with himself as he stood pacing back and forth slapping his riding crop enthusiastically. His connections in the local military police had paid off. He had received word that a foreign man and woman were being sought in connection with an attack in the town of Sinde in southwestern Myanmar. He and the twelve men Colonel Shing provided had just arrived in the town. Stopping at the local political newsagent's, he had ascertained the location of the alleged attack and had just arrived at the 'scene of the crime', as they said in America.

Turning the corner into the alley, he spotted—*Oh no. Captain Li. What is he doing here?* Htet fumed. *Why does he always look so calm and pleased with himself, standing there wiping his spectacles?*

"Captain Li, so good to see you, what brings you here today?" Htet simpered, resenting Li's arrogant posture.

"Captain Htet. I'm impressed. You are only twenty four hours late arriving," Li replied, replacing the spectacles on his nose.

Htet seethed inside. "Are you aware that a foreign man and woman are being sought here for a crime?" He hoped he had attained information that Li perhaps did not have.

"Hmmm, yes, are you aware that the youths were dispatched in a professional fashion. That the woman put up resistance? Have you interrogated the witnesses and established contact with the local law enforcement?" Li listed his triumphs as Htet's failings.

Htet's jaw dropped, and then, regaining his composure, he responded. "I believe I did tell Colonel Shing that the Christian woman was involved."

"The woman was reported to fight back expertly. I think that excludes your sweet little Christian, Htet. But the man could have been Brock—and the woman could have been one of his contacts." Li and Htet turned as a soldier ran up to them.

Saluting Li, he began, "Sir, we have interrogated three taxi drivers. Unfortunately, each gives a different story. One says he drove a foreigner west to the town limits, another says he drove a foreign man and his wife north and the third claims to have witnessed a foreign man and a Burmese woman entering a taxi which then headed east." Nodding and waving the soldier away, Li remained deep in thought.

"What should we do?" Htet asked.

Li scowled at him. "You will take your men and investigate the Chin uprising in the southeast; the uprising which led to your disgraceful loss of the spy, Brock, in the first place."

Stammering, Htet replied, "We-well, —there was a sweep of the area. What do you mean?"

"When?" Li demanded.

"As soon as the rains lessened."

"So, in fact, Brock could have been in some remote village for over a month. Is that what you're saying?" Li leaned in close, intimidating Htet with ease.

"We–well they went in as soon as the weather and roads allowed."

Grasping Htet's shirt in his fist, he pulled him close then flung him away. "Go and see to it."

"A-and you? What will you do?" Htet was quivering now.

"I will divide my men and pursue these possibilities—four to the east, four to the north and I myself will take three men to the west. Logic dictates that Brock will seek to escape the country as quickly as possible, and west into Bangladesh would be the quickest route out from here. It should be easy to track him down there." Li dismissed Htet, turned on his heel and departed.

<><><><><>

The rolling hills curved toward the heavens in undulating waves. Masses and masses of foliage traced the rise and fall of the waves. Bush twined together with tree to form a tangled web of green and brown, creased here and there by ruddy, muddy clefts in the sage. As beautiful as mountains were in theory, the reality of forging through the dense undergrowth, traipsing down one mountain only to ascend another, was definitely a disillusioning task, particularly with the added 'bonus' of clouds of buzzing insects always flying too close but just out of reach. Caroline felt she had been walking for ages, always spied on by the chief parakeet lookout that began his tutting as they approached a flock which was dining in the trees, and ending in a call to disperse the feathered aviators to the skies. Her feet were aching, her back was tired and her head was pounding. It still rained in the afternoons and the slippery ground made walking more difficult.

"John…John!" Caroline stopped, waiting for John to notice. He moved on a few paces then stopped and turned around.

"What's wrong?" John asked flatly.

"I need to rest, just for a few minutes. My feet are killing me." She walked over to a tree stump, poked a stick in it to check for creepy crawlies and rot, then sat on it. John walked over and dumped the pack on the ground beside Caroline.

Kneeling in front of her, he asked again, "what's wrong?"

"I'm okay but my feet are tired." John reached down and removed Caroline's left sandal, massaging her foot as Caroline groaned in pleasure. "Ahhh, the hands of an angel. Thank you." She closed her eyes and enjoyed the pressure of his hands on her feet. John finished with her left foot and treated her right foot to the same pleasure. Thanking him again, she slid back into her flip flops. Reaching a hand to her, he pulled her up.

"We need to crest this hill before dark if we can. There may be a clearing or something we can stop in on the other side. Come on, let's go." Caroline sighed and followed John. He kept her hand in his to keep her moving. Something had shifted in John since they had left the town of Sinde. Caroline couldn't deny it any longer. He was efficient, almost angry, and there were no glimmers of their earlier relationship. He never joked with her or shared his thoughts. Even when he touched her, it was like the foot massage, a kind act done with no emotion. Maybe this was the 'spy', the 'all business' John, emotionally cut off from her.

They walked along for another hour or so, stopping at the crest of the hill to survey the area around them and check the map to determine the best direction to head. Several metres along, they found a small tangle of bushes that formed a sort of cave in the side of the hill.

"This may be the best shelter we'll find today. Let me check it out. Can you find some dry wood for a fire?" He looked back at her and waited for her nod before entering the cave.

Caroline returned with a few sticks of dry wood. "The jungle is a difficult place to find dry wood," she complained as she collapsed on the ground inside the leafy cave.

"Never mind, there's some dry wood here under an overhang. We'll make do." John set about laying a fire.

"Why don't we make the raised shelters anymore?" she inquired.

"They leave too much evidence of our presence," he replied, evenly.

Once he'd started the fire, Caroline asked, "Now will you tell me what's wrong?"

John harumphed noisily, apparently annoyed by the question. "Nothing's wrong."

"Then at least tell me what your plan is," Caroline said.

"Don't worry, I'll get us out of here," John placated.

Poking his shoulder, Caroline demanded, "I need you to be honest and open with me, John. I think I've earned that, haven't I?"

John sighed, continuing to concentrate on the fire. "If we travel through the mountains, we stand a good chance of passing unseen. North of here is a town called Bagan, or Pagan. It is a town of temples, very unique." John paused thoughtfully. "Anyway, I have a contact there, or used to, who I'm hoping can help us."

"Help us do what?" Caroline replied.

"Help us find Brother Whatever's hidden something or other." John gestured the nothingness of the name.

"What?" Caroline replied, confused.

"In the far north of Burma, lost in a remote mountain valley, some Catholic Priest or Monk or something founded a hidden community. I'm hoping my contact in Bagan can help us locate it."

"Then what?"

"There's an MI-6 agent who uses it as a base between China and India and, if we can make contact with the agent, she can get us papers to assist us in crossing the border with India. Once in India, we can make our way to a British High Commission and then, home." John returned to cooking supper.

"Home," said Caroline wistfully. "What happens when we get to Britain?"

"What do you mean?"

"I'm Canadian. Britain is not my home. What do I do?"

"I'll deal with it," he replied.

"John, you don't get it, do you?" She knelt directly in front of him, becoming irritated by his unhelpful answers.

"Get what?" John asked, confused by her meaning

"Why do you feel you have the right to make decisions about *my* life for *me*? I am a fully functioning adult and can be trusted to make decisions for myself."

John was taken aback by her forceful statement. "You don't want to come with me?" John's voice sounded small and lost and then his eyes turned flinty.

Caroline sighed in suppressed frustration. "John. I *do* want to escape with you." She saw his expression relax slightly. "I do want to be with you. What I want you to understand is that I feel I have the right to be consulted on decisions. I want to *help* you decide what we will do."

John paused for a long time until Caroline thought he wasn't going to respond. She prepared her insistences and was just ready to launch her argument when he interrupted her thoughts. "I can't do that," he asserted tightly. Rising, he walked away from the fire, leaving a stunned Caroline behind.

The next morning, Caroline woke to a gentle shaking.

"Mmmm. Later," she muttered.

"Caroline. I need you to get up. Come on." John reached for her hand and helped her up. "We need to get going."

"Okay," she replied dejectedly as she complied with his request. *He sounds so distant. There's no—oh I don't know, Father—there's no affection in his voice. This is worse than prison. Back then, I didn't like him and he didn't like me. That was much easier than this. What is going on?*

The two hiked north for the next hour in silence. When John noticed that Caroline was slowing, he called a brief halt. Scouting the terrain briefly and checking the map, they soon carried on.

<><><><><>

Captain Li wasn't certain but he suspected that the foreigner the taxi driver had driven west had walked straight into the mountains. His soldiers and he had scoured the forested area just west of Padung. Too hilly for rice farming, this area of the river valley had been left to trees. However, it was well traversed by paths and after spending a day searching, Li was confident that he and his men had discovered a camp inhabited by at least one person for a short time. The diminutive Kyine, though his name belied the foul odour he always emitted, was an exceptional tracker.

Li and his men got into the jeep and drove along the bumpy lands just bordering the foothills of the western mountain range. Kyine felt the spy could probably have travelled about five kilometres a day in the mountainous terrain. Choosing a spot equivalent to that, Li and his men abandoned the jeep and entered the mountain range. Kyine knew this region well and trusted himself to find the most likely path the fugitive spy would take.

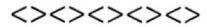

<><><><><>

"Just reach across and I'll grab you."

"No, John, it's too far." Caroline stood on one side of the collapsed section of the trail along a very steep hillside and John stood on the other side, coaxing her to cross. "Why can't we just climb down to that lower trail and travel there?"

"Visibility is much better up here. Just plant your foot and swing towards me, I'll take your hand and pull you across."

"It's too far. I won't be able to reach you."

"This would be so much easier on my own," he muttered.

Suddenly, the distant sound of voices filtered through to their ears. John and Caroline locked eyes with each other. Caroline planted her foot and swung across to John's reaching arm. As her leg crossed the open space, her fingers slid along his just before she began to fall. Caroline fell straight down the side of the mountain, feet first, hands scraping along the grasses and stones, trying to slow her descent.

"Caroline!" he called, sliding sideways down the mountain after her. Her feet hit first, her legs collapsing and bringing her backside into intimate relationship with the lower path she had been examining earlier. John landed a few feet ahead of her on the trail. He grabbed her hand, pulling her up before she took a breath. They ran. They ran as fast as they could for as long as they could.

"John," she gasped, slipping her hand from his. "Stop. Need. Breath." John slowed, looking up and around them to discover any sign of someone following them as he pulled her off the trail into some bushes at the side. Handing her the canteen of water, he sat beside her on the ground, as she took a number of short sips between gasps for air. She wiped her brow leaving a smear of blood. John took her hands gently in his and turned them palms up, swearing under his breath.

"I'm sorry," he apologized. Caroline winced as he poured water over her hands to clean the thin cuts made by the sharp edges of the sawgrass. "I'm sorry, sweetheart," he said again as he kissed her palms. Startled by the endearment after days of disengagement, she leaned forward and kissed his forehead, but couldn't keep the tears from flowing. He crouched before her, his guilty gaze fixed on the ground.

"Hug me, you idiot," she said as she poked him on the shoulder. He looked up to see her watching him, a small grin playing across her pouting lips. He smiled back, a small smile but enough to comfort her as he wrapped her in a hug. After a few moments indulgence, she took a shuddering breath and said, "Okay. What now?"

"We walk. We walk fast and hard. We've got to lose them in the mountains. We need papers to safely cross the border and we'll find them at the hidden community which we have to find without being tagged by Shing's men or Military Intelligence or anyone, for that matter. If we're discovered—well, let's not be found." John stood and shouldered the pack. Caroline rose beside him, took a deep breath and followed him out of the covering and onto the path. The two travelers walked and walked until Caroline was beyond thinking; simply placing one foot in front of the other, not even realizing she'd stopped until she felt John's hand squeezing hers. Crying out, she pulled away, his grip hurting against the cuts on her hand.

"....orry. We'll stop now. Caroline, are you listening?" Caroline was having trouble focusing on his words, swaying where she stood, head down, and eyes fluttering. All she wanted to do was turn off the bird noise and sleep. John took her by the shoulders and led her to an overgrowth of bushes where he placed the pack on the ground and helped her lay down. She was asleep before he covered her with the blanket, rousing briefly when he lay down beside her, after concealing their place of hiding. Rolling toward him, she rested her arm possessively across his chest.

"Caroline." John shook her shoulder. She groaned and swatted at him, rolling onto her side, clinging to sleep. He shook her more roughly, "Caroline."

"Everything okay?" she murmured, shuffling closer to him. It was lighter, morning had come.

"No," he responded. "There are two sets of boot prints right outside our hide." Suddenly alert, Caroline sat up straight, fear coursing through her as she listened to him. "They look like army boots to me."

"What does that mean?" she asked apprehensively.

"It means there is a potential danger in front of us and unknown dangers around us. We can't stay on the path. We're going to have to move very cautiously until we figure out where these men are and who they are. You're going to have to do everything I say without question." Gazing into his shuttered eyes, she nodded and followed him out. Surveying the lie of the land and studying the map, he chose a direction that led them down the mountain in a zigzag pattern toward the river. He strapped on the pack and they set off.

It was difficult to follow a straight path in the jungle as they were often forced out of their way to avoid obstacles, after which, they then had to reorient their direction. Caroline wished she could just slide down the side of the mountain on her pants but John had said it would leave too much of a trail for their pursuers to follow.

"I was only joking," she murmured to his back.

They stopped for food after a few hours but John didn't allow them long to rest. As they came out of one particularly dense spot of bushes, they heard a noise—a deep, thunderous noise—the river. John took her hand again and they began to move slowly toward the sound.

"The river will be out in the open so we need to approach cautiously," John told her. They scanned the riverbank from the safety of the trees for quite a while before John felt it was safe to venture out. The mist off the rushing river surrounded them as they walked out into the open.

"Crossing the river might be the safest path but I'm not certain how we can get across." John seemed to be thinking aloud, not requiring an answer from Caroline, so she gave none. "Perhaps if we walk upstream we'll find a place to cross."

They walked along beside the river in silence. Caroline walked behind John, talking to God. *I thought we had grown so close in the village. Now, he's retreated behind some kind of barrier.* Caroline pondered the change in John; the way he shut her out; the way he seemed to depersonalize everything. All the fun, all the laughter had drained out of him. *I just don't understand. What happened? What is he thinking? Has he always been this way and I just didn't notice?* She continued following John, talking to God until she was interrupted by a shoulder in her face. John had stopped and she had been so distracted by her prayers that she had walked right into him.

"John—" she began, annoyed. He clamped a hand over her mouth and pointed across the river. Two men in mottled green army uniforms were looking right at them. The men lurched into action, one advancing at a run and the other leveling his rifle. John pushed her and she was suddenly falling, hurtling toward the surface of the roiling waters below. She gasped for breath just before she slammed into the frigid river, water enveloping her body. She was plunged below, rocked and spun until she couldn't tell which way was up. Her body bounced off rocks like a pinball and her lungs burned with her desperate need for air. As the black edges of oblivion danced at the periphery of her vision, she was catapulted toward the surface and emerged only long enough to fill her lungs before she was again plunged below. Up, down and around, the dizzying journey seemed to last for ages.

Father, help me, she prayed. *Save John.* Her body slammed into a solid object and held. Opening her eyes, she scanned left to right. *Thank you, Father.* Her body was pinned by the rushing current against a large tree that had fallen across the river. The tree was slippery and wet. She kicked with her legs and slid her arms sideways to make her way toward the riverbank. With relief, she planted her foot on the bottom of the riverbed, using the extra friction to propel her out of the water and onto dry land. Shaking from the cold and shock, she moved away from the river into the edge of the bush but she knew she couldn't go too far in case John was searching for her. She had no idea what had happened to him. She remembered the soldier with the rifle. *Has he been shot? Did he run away or jump into the river behind me. Father, what do I do? I have nothing to use to build a fire. No food, no blanket, no supplies. No John. Is this his opportunity to forge ahead without me? No, he wouldn't.* Moving up against a tree, she sat with her back to it, curling her body around itself to preserve heat. As the angle of the sun shifted through the leaves, Caroline could feel herself succumbing to panic. *Father, I don't know what to do and I don't know where John is. Please send help.* Caroline jumped as something bumped her shoulder. She gasped and leapt up as a huge snake glided down the tree toward her. *Send a different help. I hate snakes!*

Not deterred by her feelings toward it, the snake continued to move toward her and she searched around to find some kind of weapon, her hand alighting upon a tree branch on the ground. She lifted and swung.

"You dirty rotten thing! Take that! Try to bite me will you." Thump. Thump thump.

"A python?" he questioned. Caroline spun around wielding her branch to see John, smiling from ear to ear. "You are a formidable woman." Caroline dropped the branch and flung herself at him. Squeezing him tightly around the waist, she buried her head in his chest as he brought his arms around her and pressed a kiss to her hair.

"You came for me! How did you find me?" she asked shakily.

Grinning, he replied, "I just followed the sound of your anger."

Looking abashed, she held him tightly. "You could have just asked," she remarked shakily as she clung to him.

"I beg your pardon?" John turned his puzzled face to her.

"I said I'd follow your instructions. You could have just asked me to jump in the river."

John began to laugh, a deep cleansing laugh, dispelling for a moment the tension of the last few days. "You are my mighty titan." After a few moments he released her, leaving her feeling disappointed and still shivering from her experience.

"What have you done to this poor python?" John asked, still smiling.

"Yuck. I hate snakes."

"I noticed," John responded wryly. Walking over, he nudged the carcass with his toe. "You have utterly destroyed the poor thing!" he remonstrated. She glanced at him as he finished with, "I hope you never hate spies the same way."

"That depends," she replied. He watched her with a question in his eyes. As she continued to watch the dead python, he realized, "we really should bring it along for food." Caroline shivered in distaste as John picked up the snake and coiled it into the pack. It must have weighed at least twenty pounds.

<><><><><>

"They could be anywhere now." Captain Li studied his companion with contempt. He didn't need the obvious stated.

"We have no option; we must follow the river downstream and catch their trail…or find their bodies." The two men started off, one hoping to find a place to rest and one hoping to find a living body to pay for this inconvenience.

<><><><><>

After travelling deeper into the bush and away from the river, John began casting about for fire wood. Caroline was shivering in earnest, shaking too much even to help as he cleared a space and lit a fire.

"Strip!" he commanded.

Caroline furrowed her brow. "Pardon?" she said.

"You need to take your wet clothes off. Come over by the fire and strip off." Caroline followed his instructions. She had promised to after all. John slipped out of his wet clothes as well and crouched by the fire. Hovering at a distance, Caroline timidly approached the fire feeling extremely self-conscious. *I've just spent weeks essentially living with this man, though not in the world's sense of the phrase. Why do I feel so embarrassed to be naked in front of him? This is a survival situation, isn't it?* John glanced up with a question in his eyes.

"Come to the fire," he commanded again.

Kneeling before the fire, she felt the warmth wash over her, a much more pleasant feeling than the wash she had had in the river. Closing her eyes, she basked in the glow of the flames. John was moving around and she opened her eyes long enough to see that he was wringing out their clothes and blankets and hanging them to dry. Adding more wood, he came back to crouch in front of the fire.

Caroline reached over and lightly touched his arm. "John, thank you for coming to find me."

Keeping his eyes on the fire, he responded, "You're welcome."

When he didn't offer anything else, she tried again. "What happened? I remember the soldiers with the rifles then I felt you shove me and—well, what happened next?" she asked quietly.

"When I saw the rifle leveled at you, I pushed you into the river and then jumped in after you. I was swept into a different current and hurtled past you almost immediately. I managed to angle my body toward a large rock in the water to halt my progress down the river." He stopped.

"What next?" she prompted.

"I was terrified." He spoke in a low voice that Caroline had to strain to hear. He kept clenching and unclenching his fists.

"I was terrified, too. It felt like the river was trying to squeeze the air out of my lungs." She shivered at the memory.

"I was terrified that I would never see you again. I've messed everything up. I'm sorry that I got you involved in all of this. I give you my word that I will protect you until I get you to safety." In a whirl, he changed the subject, talking at a furious pace, maintaining control over the conversation. "Shing's men will follow the river downstream to try to track us. We need to travel north, upstream, but we're going to have to stay away from the river for the time being. I think if we hike for the rest of today and as far into the night as possible, we can probably stay ahead of them." Caroline sighed. *Back to business. Father, you're taking care of us, aren't you?* **Trust me, my child.**

<><><><><>

Li was trying to decide why he had chosen to travel with this particular imbecile and not one of the others. He was plagued by pointless questions and statements of obvious facts. "Ah, here's a bend in the river. Oh, there's a deer path through the trees. Do you think the spy left the river on this side? Did you see the woman with him?"

The pair of soldiers had travelled for several hours when Captain Li called a halt, removing his spectacles and handkerchief.

"They must not be on this side of the river. We will travel ahead just past the bend in the river and cross where the water is calmer."

"What if the water isn't calmer past the—" Li's fist slammed into the unfortunate man's jaw. Li didn't wait for his companion to recover. He simply walked away downstream.

<><><><><>

It had been dark for several hours down amongst the trees. Caroline knew she was falling further and further behind and she desperately wanted John to notice—but he didn't. He forged ahead, forgetting her completely, allowing her to struggle along behind him in the gloomy moonlit shadows of the forest floor. *I'm so tired I can barely think. Maybe if I just rest a few minutes then I'll run to catch up. He'd probably be happy to lose me anyway. Why do I feel like I'm the burden he's dragging through the jungle?* She felt slightly guilty at entertaining such uncharitable thoughts, knowing it was her frustration and exhaustion speaking.

She sat down against a tree to rest briefly and slid to the ground, sound asleep. Launched from deep sleep to panicked wakefulness, Caroline cried out as she was seized and shaken. Adrenaline coursing through her, she struck out at her attacker, fist meeting shoulder as she was yanked upright. Yelling, she fought against the hand now clasped across her mouth, visions of soldiers parading across her imagination. Tearing her arm from his grip and punching at his chest, she struggled to be free only to be captured again, one arm twisted behind her back.

"John, help me!" she wailed

"Caroline, stop!" he barked, shaking her, terrified of the noise they were making. "It's me!" She stopped moving and John slowly released her, coming around to face her.

"What were you doing?" John accused her. "How could you do this to me? What am I supposed to do, search for you all night? Find you in the arms of Shing's men? I've jeopardized everything I've worked for—everything for what? How dare you treat me this way? Do you realize what could have happened? Shing's men are not far behind us. DON'T EVER DO THAT AGAIN!" Grabbing her upper arms, he shook her. Yanking her arms away, she gasped at his fury but it didn't stop the violence leaking through his body and his mouth. "I can't believe I risked everything for you and you let me down at the first opportunity! I can't believe I did it, I made the classic error. Don't get emotionally involved. Emotions compromise good judgment. I nearly blew the mission!" His angry words kept pouring out of his tortured soul, his voice growing louder and louder as his angst gathered energy. "If we're caught, I'll be tortured again. Everyone breaks in the end, Caroline. If I'm caught, no Chin invasion will save me this time. " He was panting with emotion.

"Is that what I am, a mistake—an emotional entanglement?" Caroline asked him quietly.

Spinning away without answering, he strode away from her through the verdant undergrowth, stalking off, not checking to see if she was following. She didn't see that he was shaking, so weighted was she under his fury and her grief. As he passed out of sight, Caroline was spurred to follow him, fearing Shing's men too much to desire being left alone, even if it meant walking with this man who loathed her. Anger and sorrow battled within her.

They walked on through the night, John striding far ahead, fury in his every pace, clenching and unclenching his fists. Caroline walked in sorrow which transformed into fury and back again in a loop. She had lowered the iron shutters of her mind. *I have had enough of this. How dare he treat me like that? Does he think I'm a naughty child who stopped to pick posies? I'm exhausted and he doesn't even care. What a fool I was to think that a man who lies for a living could ever care about anything but himself. I didn't ask to be dragged along on this nightmare.* She knew that God was trying to speak to her and that she should listen, but this last attack from John, as physical as it was, felt like the culmination of a disengagement that had been building between them for an undefined time. *God, help me* was all the prayer she could manage.

CHAPTER 8

FORGED IN THE JUNGLE

"Stop immediately!" Captain Li called out. "Don't move." Using his spectacles like a magnifying glass, he crouched low over the marks in the dirt on the riverbank. The oaf had almost obscured them with his lumbering steps but Li could clearly detect footprints leading up from the river and continuing along beside it—a man's footprints. Excellent! He had them now.

"Where's the girl, then?" Another useless question. Next time he travelled, he would bring Kyine along with him and let this oaf travel alone. Li was beginning to feel that this man would benefit from some reeducation in a laogai upon their return to China. He delighted in the scenarios his mind created for him.

As evening fell, the two men soon found the smaller footprints where the larger prints joined them and headed into the jungle. After an hour or so of searching they found the well hidden fire pit and followed the path the spy and his woman had taken.

<><><><><>

John and Caroline walked until the air began to brighten around them and the morning song of the birds, in rhythm with the insects, played its dawn symphony. Caroline kept pace, refusing to fall behind again. Stopping to rest, John cleared out a space amongst some entwined bushes and waited as Caroline took a drink of water. Brushing past him, she dropped the canteen beside him. Ignoring the gesture, he placed the blankets on the ground, pressing down the lumpy roots, vines and grasses. Not knowing how far behind Shing's men were, it wasn't safe to risk a fire, so they ate a cold supper and went to bed to grab a few brief hours of sleep. Caroline lay on top of the blankets and curled on her side to sleep. John tucked in beside her and reached his hand out to brush a lock of hair from her face. She ignored his touch and rolled away from him as soon as he removed his hand, putting as much distance between them as possible in the small shelter. Caroline lay, ignoring the still, small voice speaking gently to her heart.

Waking brought no relief to Caroline's torment. She had been dreaming of Henry in a horrifying loop. She saw him across a river and no matter how hard she swam she couldn't reach him. Then she saw John shaking Henry again and again and still she couldn't get to them. Sleeping with unresolved anger resulted in waking with unresolved anger. Rolling over, Caroline saw that John was gone and a moment of panic gripped her as she considered the possibility that he had left her. *But, no, he wouldn't leave me, would he? He came back for me last night. I don't know what he's playing at but I'm sure he wouldn't leave me.* Caroline sighed sadly. *I just have to accept that he's a violent man from a violent world. Whatever thoughts are governing his actions, he's not the man I thought I knew. He comes from a different world and our two worlds could never coalesce.*

As Caroline exited the shelter, she saw John crouched over a small fire. He had wrapped the python in large leaves and buried it in the coals. Walking over to the fire, she sat across from him, noticing the dark circles under his eyes. It looked like he hadn't slept at all. Silently, he handed her a portion of cooked python settled on a bed of leaves and she took it from him without comment. *I'm in Burma, eating a Burmese Python that tried to eat me.* She wanted to share her joke with John, but every time she tried, in her mind's eye, she saw his angry face, heard his angry words and felt his angry hands shaking her.

John wrapped a portion of the python in large leaves and placed them in the pack. Then, extinguishing the fire and burying the rest of the snake, he did his best to eliminate all traces of their camp. Packing the blanket and canteen, he informed her that they would have to return to the river today or they would run out of water. Pulling out the map, he tried his best to align himself on an oblique path that would lead them back to the river several hundred metres upstream.

They walked throughout the day in silence, stopping occasionally for short breaks to rest. Neither felt hungry but ate out of habit. When Caroline stumbled on the trail, John reached out to help her but moved away when she fixed him with a cold stare. When she looked at him, she noticed a complete absence of emotion on his face: no emotion; no tapping; no clenching. He was closed to her. Caroline waited for an apology from John but he never offered one. She felt the distance between them as an ache in the pit of her stomach.

Making good time, they reached the river in the afternoon. While John refilled the canteen, Caroline rested against a mossy rock, enjoying the green scent released as she rubbed against it. She wanted to know where they were heading. Actually, she was hoping that he would offer the information, but he didn't, and she couldn't bring herself to ask. *Oh Father, this hurts. Why did you ever bring this plague of a man into my life?*

That night they took shelter within an enormous tree covered in green and brown vines. The vines reminded Caroline of the python and she shuddered at the memory. They ate the python meat cold— adding to Caroline's feeling of yuck—as John decided that another fire would be too risky until they could get an idea of where Shing's men were. After their meal, he took the rest of the meat a distance from the tree and buried it. There was no point risking food poisoning or attracting predators in these circumstances.

Again, once they lay down to sleep, Caroline rolled away from John. **Caroline, Beloved.** *Yes, Father, I know. Help me to forgive. I'm sorry I haven't been listening but haven't I suffered enough pain? I just can't handle this emotional mess.*

The next day and the next they walked, following a zigzag course taking them to the river and away from it deeper into the jungle, always in a northerly direction. They walked in silence, ate in silence and slept coldly separated in whatever shelter or clearing was their camp for the night.

Caroline was becoming increasingly exhausted by the physical demands as well as the emotional struggle. On the third day, she stopped, coming to rest against a large tree. "John," she called, having no desire to lose him and risk a repeat of his behaviour the other night. John was deep in thought and didn't hear her call. "John!" she called louder. He paused and looked around. "I need to rest." He came back to pace in front of her. "I just need to rest for a while. I'm not an energizer bunny; I can't keep going and going no matter the cost." John turned a hard stare at her in response to her angry tone of voice. He stepped toward her, retrieving the canteen of water from the pack as he came. He handed it to her, flinging the pack at her feet, and moved to another tree to recline against it.

She drank deeply, sinking down into the verdure.

"Where are we going? You've been leading us back and forth for days now." When he didn't respond, she continued, prodding him for a response. "Didn't you say you'd consult with me?" she continued, feeling bitterness slip into her voice, "I realize I'm just a burden to you, but it's my life too."

Caroline saw his jaw clench as he brought out the map. Flattening it in front of her on the ground, he showed her a spot on the map. "I think we're here. Shing's men saw us here." He pointed to a spot southwest of their current location. "We travelled about this far down the river and we're now making our way to somewhere in this area." He pointed to an area in the mountains at the fork of a river. Folding up the map, he put it away. Shouldering the pack, he waited expectantly for her to move.

"Wait. If we're travelling that way, why do we keep zigzagging back and forth?" He looked at her intensely as she spoke. "Did you think I wouldn't notice?"

"The need for water, obviously." His voice was terse.

"Why don't we just walk along the riverbank then?" she spoke just as tersely, angry at his unwillingness to discuss the matter.

"Footprints, obviously." He sounded fed up with this conversation. Every word she said came out laced with ire and he was making it clear that he didn't want to hear her anger anymore.

"Then why do we have to walk so far into the jungle each time we zig?" Her voice was becoming more strident with each sentence she uttered.

"It's harder to track us amongst the trees, obviously." His voice was rising to match his frustration. Caroline sprang to her feet, all exhaustion leaving her.

"If you say 'obviously' to me once more, I'm gonna smack you." Her eyes were blazing with anger at his distant voice. He wasn't preparing to apologize for attacking her, he was challenging her.

"I'm only trying to keep us out of the hands of Shing's men. Stop acting like a b**** and keep walking!" Her slap knocked him back a step, his eyes widening in shock then slamming shut.

Caroline regretted what she had done the moment her hand let fly. "John," she called after him but he was gone, an icy stare had closed his eyes to her before he spun on his heel. He stormed away with his arms across his chest, as though holding in the broken pieces of his heart. "John," she called again then softer, "I'm sorry".

I can't believe I did that. Caroline berated herself. *Being slapped across the face is such a degrading way to be treated whether you're a man, woman or child. This is what you were warning me about, isn't it, Father. This is what comes of letting anger fester. Why didn't I just confront him after he attacked me that night? Then it would have been out in the open and dealt with. Now, I've hurt him. Now, **I'm** the one that owes **him** an apology.* She wept out her frustration and sorrow, praying for God's grace to flow into her. *I've been judging him without actually knowing him. He closed himself off from me but I never asked him why. I just assumed I knew what he was thinking. How could I know what he's thinking? He's not Henry. He's a completely different man with a different tale.* **Is his story different?** *No. They both came from crappy homes where they weren't given the love and support they needed and deserved. How would Henry have reacted in an extreme situation like this? If someone has never known love, real love, how would they handle a relationship in these circumstances?*

Caroline could hear John pacing nearby—John the spy; the man who saw her as a mistake, an emotional entanglement that 'blew his mission'. Still, he had also taken care of her, whatever his reasons. He was the same man who rescued her from the Burmese soldiers and the gang members in Sinde. She reminded herself of his tenderness after the soldiers had assaulted her, taking her in his arms and holding her, soothing her wounds and her fears. He was her protector and she had repaid him with spite and humiliation. The furious sound of his pacing ceased after a while, making Caroline wonder what was happening.

It seemed like hours had passed by the time John returned. Caroline had spread out the blanket and lain down feeling completely wrung out but unable to sleep. Hearing him approach, she rose to meet him.

"John, I'm sorry. I should never have hit you. I'm sorry." She looked up at him, expecting to see anger and hurt, but instead, he looked bright. He stood, his emotions carefully controlled with his fingers tapping out a rhythm on his leg. Breathing deeply, she started again. "John. I'm sorry I slapped you. It was wrong of me. You were cruel to me and I don't understand why, and you shouldn't have called me that, but that's for you to apologize. I can only be responsible for my own actions." She saw his cheek twitch but she thought that her words were not reaching through the barrier he had erected around his heart. "You know you are to blame for this situation as much as I am." She had a habit of filling the silence during arguments. Henry had known to give a response quickly to stem the flow of words but John was silent. "You started this whole thing by attacking me in the middle of the night." That was the right thing to say. He blinked rapidly. "You terrified me." Then softer, "you hurt me—you called me a—well, you know what you called me—but you didn't have the courage to explain and apologize."

"Are you finished?" he inquired gruffly.

"Yes," she sighed. When he didn't move, but remained—tapping—she moved over to the blankets and lay down. After a time, he came to lie down beside her, rolling away from her. *I guess I deserve that. It hurts surprisingly more than I thought.* Caroline's anger had fled the moment she saw the shock and hurt in John's eyes. God was helping her see the wounded man beneath the strong exterior. When she looked at John now, the arrogant selfish spy had disappeared and in his place stood a broken-hearted boy, rejected by his father, choosing a life of loneliness rather than subject himself to emotional entanglements.

When she heard his even breathing, she leaned over, gently kissing his neck and whispering, "I'm sorry" one last time. Still awake, John rolled over to face her, keeping his physical distance.

"I forgave you the first time you apologized."

"Then why were you so angry with me?" she inquired.

"I wasn't angry." He looked away, seeming to struggle with his answers.

"Then what? You completely closed yourself off from me."

"Self-preservation."

"What do you mean?" Caroline struggled to understand his meaning.

"Shut down your emotions and you can't get hurt." He paused studying his hands. "I thought—well, I thought that caring for you had compromised my judgment. I thought that letting my emotions lead had sabotaged my mission."

"Do you really think that? Am I just a liability?" Tears began to flow down her cheeks as she asked.

"I'm a fool, Caroline. You're no liability. You're my greatest ally. You're not an error in judgment. You help me make the best decisions I've ever made. Even if it had led to torture and death, I would still go back and save you." The intensity of his speech surprised her. "I'm sorry I hurt you and terrified you. I was so frightened that I had lost you. I'm sorry." John said beseechingly.

"Then, why?" she implored.

He sighed, not wanting to say the words. "In Sinde, I knew it was a tactical error to let those boys get away. I knew that word would spread and that we would be tagged because of it. I thought that meant that caring for you had compromised my judgment— emotion over intellect."

"Why did you close yourself off from me? Is it because you don't care for me?" Caroline asked, sorrow in her voice.

"Because I care too much." He closed his eyes.

"What do you mean?"

"I don't know how to think and feel at the same time. I've always shut down my emotions during an operation. It's the only way to keep your objective clear. With you, I'm afraid."

"Afraid? You're one of the bravest men I know," she responded, incredulous.

He snorted. "I would rather deal with a hundred gang members with knives—a dozen Vlads with whips—than one woman who cares about me. I don't know how to deal with emotions, in case you haven't noticed. When I'm on a mission, I put myself in a box; 'think, don't feel'. With you, I'm terrified all the time—terrified that you'll be hurt, terrified that I won't be able to protect you, and—" John stopped. "Anyway, I'm sorry for how I treated you—I'm sorry I tried to put my feelings for you in a box."

"Then, why—"

"Because I am an idiot," he responded humbly. "How could I ever think it was a mistake to care for you? You are the best part of me." John paused, breathing deeply to control his emotions. "Do—do you think you could ever forgive me?" he implored her.

Caroline reached out, brushing his fingertips with her own. "It's not that simple though, is it? I can tell you that I forgive you but how do I trust you again? I opened my heart to you once—my battered, bleeding heart and you have stomped all over it." John winced. "I don't know if I want to open up to you again, John. How do I open myself to someone I can't trust; to someone who doesn't trust me? I understand that neither of us knows where this is leading—to friendship, to love, to marriage, but I do know that I don't deserve to be hurt like that again."

John's eyes filled with sorrow. "You're right. You don't deserve this—any of this." He gestured around. "—and I don't deserve you—I don't deserve to have someone care for me." He stopped, gathering his thoughts. "But I do trust you, more than I've trusted anyone in my life—except perhaps my mother. I'm not asking you to forget what I've done, just to consider forgiving me, if you decide I'm worth it. I won't ask for anything else."

"Why John, what's changed?" she prodded him verbally.

"I realized tonight that I just can't do it. I'm not strong enough to protect you and to love you. My father once told me that I only bring pain to others." She gasped at the cruelty of the words, but he continued speaking. "He was right. I can't do anything right. Caroline," he paused waiting for her to look at him. "I've never met anyone like you before. I've never felt this way before, about anyone. I want to take care of you, to protect you but I also want to be with you. Even prison is bearable if you're there." He paused, tapping his leg.

"You're tapping," she stated.

Unexpectedly, he smiled. "I thought I had lost you tonight. When you slapped me, it felt like I had fallen into a deep, black pit. I realized that my father was right. I'm no good. I can't ever get it right and I don't deserve to be happy. So I gave up. I realized that nothing could help me. I was sinking into the darkness. Nothing I could do would stop me from careening to the bottom, so I called out to God to pull me out of the dark pit and make me His." Joy and light shone from John's eyes, visible even in the dimness of the forest night. "The burden lifted. I know I don't have to take care of everything now. God can deal with it all."

Reaching across to her physically and emotionally, the gulf between them vanished. He brushed a lock of hair from her face, tucking it behind her ear. As he returned his hand, she took it in her own and, shifting her body closer, reached her arms around him in a hug. Breathing shakily, he wrapped his arms around her, pulling her close and burying his face in her neck.

The next day, they journeyed again. John slowed the pace and offered more breaks. Caroline too, changed her behaviour. She spoke gently to him, was polite and encouraging. Impatient to settle things between them, she decided to push the boundaries of their relationship.

"Tell me about your mother, John."

John smothered his surprise at her gentle demand and sighed sadly.

"Caer, what do you want from me?" he asked morosely.

"I want to know who you are. Can you give me that?" she asked sincerely, knowing that the tale of his childhood was the crux of who he was.

He stopped, turning toward her and sighed. "My mother died when I was twelve." Caroline settled back beside him as he started to walk again. "She was awesome and I was wild. She always seemed to understand me. My father did not." He stopped. Caroline reached for his hand. He looked down at their joined appendages and smiled, releasing his breath on a happy sigh. And so he told her about his mother, about learning to ride a bicycle, and their trip to Wales together, pouring out his memories of the one person in his life who had shown him love.

"How did she die?" Caroline asked softly.

He sighed again, a long, sad sigh. "She died saving my friend and I from a prank that went bad. We ended up falling in a quarry. My friend couldn't swim well and when I tried to save him, he almost drowned me. My mother dove in and pulled him out. She got really sick after that and died."

"I'm sorry, sweetheart." Caroline's eyes misted.

"My father wouldn't let me see her. He said it was my fault. The next time I saw her was at the funeral and when I started to cry, my father grabbed me by the shoulders and shook me. He told me I had no right to cry. He told me that all I'd ever done was cause people pain." John seemed unaware that he'd stopped walking. Caroline stopped as well. John seemed to have shrunk into himself, too full of old grief even to cry. He felt Caroline shuddering beside him and assumed she was angry with him too for what he had done to his mother.

"Why that evil toad!!" she exclaimed. "How dare he do that to you? Is he still alive, because I'd like to get my hands on him and tell him a thing or two!"

John was shocked by Caroline's reaction. "Caroline? I don't understand."

She turned to face John. "He was totally one hundred per cent wrong John. Your mother loved you. She would've wanted to see you and she forgave you, didn't she." This was a statement, not a question. "You might never have heard the words but you know, in your heart, don't you, that she forgave you before she died?" She waited for John to respond. He stared at the ground between them. "John," she said firmly. "Answer me!"

He looked up slowly, pain etched across his features. "I don't know," he said.

"*John*, I am telling you as a mother, *your mother* forgave you." She stopped and waited for him to respond.

"Do you really think so?" he asked, childlike in his manner.

"Yes, definitely! And your Father was an evil toad. If my Henry had ever behaved in that way to our children, I would have beaten him around the head—severely—and I definitely would have haunted him and made friends with Zeus to plague him with lightning bolts to his privates for the rest of his life." Caroline's impassioned speech brought a small smile to John's lips.

The smile faded as he said, "I was a pretty rotten kid and a worse teenager."

"Oh John, aren't they all. Our children come as they come. It's not our job to make them someone else. It's our job to love them and point them in the right direction." She paused, gathering her thoughts. "You know that I know that you're not a perfect man. I think I've seen about the worst in you, haven't I?" John nodded. "I like you a lot. If I had to choose a best friend for the rest of my second life, I would choose you. Nobody's perfect, John but everybody can try to do the right thing. You always try."

John walked with a new lightness in his step. "My life will never be the same again, will it?" he asked with a smile on his face. She shook her head, returning his smile. "Thank you, God."

As they made a camp for the evening, gunshots rang through the night. John grabbed Caroline's hand, pulling her up and running back toward a narrow gully where he pushed her down into the verdant undergrowth, covering her with loose brush. There were at least four different male voices coming from different directions. They were surrounded.

"Ah, Mr. Brock, this is Captain Li. I believe we know each other, at least by reputation. You will come out now and I give you my word that we will not search for the woman." They could hear the footsteps getting closer, hemming them in a tighter and tighter loop. Caroline glanced at John to see what he was thinking and blanched at what she saw.

"Now now, let's not waste time here. You know that we have found you. We know that we have found you. If you would prefer my men to find and subdue your woman, then so be it. If not—well—I have offered you my terms." John placed his hand firmly on her shoulder and put a finger on her lips when she started to protest. He whispered directly into her ear. "Don't move, no matter what. Use the map and keep travelling north. When you get to the city of temples, find a Buddhist monk named Mo, he'll help you." He kissed her and was gone. In that moment, Caroline knew for certain that she loved this man; that she was never going to be whole again without him.

Peering through the thick foliage, Caroline watched as he jogged quickly through the bush, as quickly as he could, drawing the men further and further from her. *God, protect him,* she prayed. When he was close enough to the men, he raised his arms and clasped his fingers behind his head. Li walked up to him with a malevolent grin and punched him in the stomach. As he doubled over, Li clasped his hair, pulling him back up to a standing position. John crumpled as Li punched him again, kicking him in the groin and the head as he lay on the ground.

Having crept close enough to maintain a visual connection with the soldiers, Caroline watched as the man, Captain Li, beat John. She wept silently as they tied his arms around a bamboo pole fixed behind his back. He was trying to save her again. Well, this time she could do something about it. In the prison she had been powerless to stop the torture but now there *must* be something she could do.

<><><><><>

"Stop! Please!"

That woman's voice is becoming very irritating but perhaps she will convince her man to tell us what we want to know. These tribesmen really don't understand the politics of their own country. They think they can defy the government and escape the consequences. Htet paced off to the side as Shing's soldiers beat the helpless man. Two of the soldiers held the man's wife and child.

"Tell me, where is the spy?" The soldier called Ohnmar demanded, striking the man when he failed to respond quickly enough.

"North" the man gasped. "They were travelling north. I believe he was looking for someone there."

"Ah, now we're getting somewhere." Ohnmar responded with a pleased look on his face. "Beat him and take him to the prison. Take all the men to the prison. We must send a message to these people that they should not help the enemies of the SLORC."

"No, no!" cried Cho holding Khin tightly to her.

"And shut her up!" he commanded. Ohnmar walked away from the woman, blocking the path of Htet's pacing. "He is lying. No one in their right mind would travel north."

Htet looked at the soldier in confusion. "Well then why did you accept his answer?"

"You truly are a fool, warden. Brock will not travel north. He will find the quickest path out of Myanmar. No word has come from patrols along the Thai border so, if he has not left via the ports in Yangon, which are highly patrolled, then he will head to the next nearest airport and try to fly out."

Captain Htet was skeptical of this theory but leery of sounding stupid. He felt, however, that he needed to understand what was going on if was to maintain some semblance of authority over the other men, so he risked a question, "How can you be certain?"

Ohnmar shook his head in disgust. "We know he is too wise to travel south because of all the military patrols. Travel in the mountains is treacherous and if he does indeed have a woman along, she would never make it. We must check all the airports."

<><><><><>

Captain Li wanted to watch the hope drain out of John Brock. He kept him bound, forcing him to stand, while Li and his men rested and refreshed themselves. He showed his disdain for the spy in the way he allowed the men to relax and noisily

Forged in the Jungles of Burma

enjoy their victory as they discussed the rewards that awaited them. Li could see the ache of sorrow in Brock's features but yet, he did not see despair.

Li's thoughts were interrupted by Kyine, his inimitable tracker.

"Captain, you realize the woman is following us?" he asserted.

Li hadn't noticed, so focused was he on enjoying Brock's pain. "Of course," he responded.

"Shall we capture her? That could prove entertaining." Kyine licked his lips at the thought.

Pondering the idea as he spun his spectacles in his fingers, Li decisively shook his head. "No. If we bring her here, Brock will feel the need to protect her. It is better for us if he feels he's lost everything." He paused thoughtfully and then continued, "If she follows us, we don't have to feed her or guard her. When the time is right, we'll simply pick her up and see what entertainment she will supply."

"What can one woman do against us?" Kyine replied, confidently.

"Indeed." Li replied. "Be certain we don't lose her, we don't want her to miss out on the fun." He leered maliciously into the darkness.

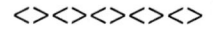

<><><><><>

Caroline used the vines twining themselves around the massive broad-leafed hardwood to climb to a large branch about eight feet up the tree. Clinging to the smaller branches for stability, she finally allowed herself to cry. *Why, God? Why is this happening? Why am I here in Burma?* Caroline's tears rolled down her cheeks making puddles on her arms where they lay across her knees. *I didn't ask for this. I just wanted to do something good with my life—something important—something for you. God, I wanted to go to the mission field.*

Why was that such a bad request? Caroline pulled out a blanket and, wrapping it around her shoulders, drew it across her face to stifle her sobs. *I made a mistake, though, didn't I? I thought I had to go to Singapore to serve you. I thought I had to "do" something. I didn't realize that you only wanted me to "be" something, to continue being yours. That's what I learned in prison: it doesn't matter where you are, it only matters whom you serve.* She shifted into a more comfortable position, leaning back against the massive trunk. *You gave me Henry and the children. Henry and the children were my mission field, weren't they, but I never realized that. I loved Henry, he was my best friend but I had no concept of what I was getting into when I married him. He came from such a crappy home but he never let his family interfere with our happiness and, as a result, we had an amazing relationship.* Her tears began to dry as her memories of Henry took over. *He taught me so much about patience and self-confidence. I taught him what a friend we have in Jesus.* The familiar tune began to play in Caroline's mind: "What a friend we have in Jesus, all our sins and griefs to bear. What a privilege to carry, everything to God in prayer.

O what peace we often forfeit,
O what needless pain we bear,
all because we do not carry
everything to God in prayer..."

Now, with John, I know what I'm getting into and I'm just not sure I can do it again. I know he's hurting. I know he's damaged. He's so closed, so hidden from me. Do I love him? I tried very hard not to love him. I tried very hard not to even like him. Is John my mission field? Isn't there someone else who could help him? Do I want someone else to help him—to be his? No, I love him. You knew I'd love him, didn't you? Do you trust me enough to be his? I do love him. **Beloved, love one another as I have loved you.**

<><><><><>

On the evening of the second day, Shing's men stopped to make camp. They shoved John roughly against a tree and fastened him to it with a rope tied around his chest. He'd had no food and not enough water for the last twenty-four hours. Li could read the torment in his eyes but didn't yet glimpse despair.

After their meal, Captain Li decided it was time for a little entertainment. The big man, Soe, hauled his massive frame over to Brock and gut-punched him so that as the skinny man, Thida, sliced the ropes holding John to the tree, he collapsed at their feet. They fastened his arms to his sides with a rope snugged around his chest and then hauled him over to the centre of the clearing where Li and Kyine were waiting to throw the rope over a low hanging tree branch. When John looked up from his position on the ground, Kyine and Soe were each holding a cut half of the bamboo pole which had been used to restrain him earlier. The men chuckled viciously at John's groan.

Li kicked him. "Stand up," Li ordered firmly, mentally wishing for him to move slowly and so increase the violence required. But Brock seemed to know the rules. He lurched to his feet and stood, swaying as he tried to catch his balance. Stopping to wipe his spectacles, Li started the game with, "Begin". Kyine and Soe then began taking it in turns to swing the bamboo at John's shoulders. When he fell to the ground, Kyine used the rope to haul him back up.

"What do you want?" John gasped.

Li held up his hand to stop his men. "Let's be clear about this, spy," he spat the title with derision, "I want nothing more than revenge."

"Revenge for what?" Each word emerged laced with pain.

"Try to remember." Li paused then turned to his men.

"Nya," John said.

"Exactly. I was having a lovely affair with her until you blew my cover and left me to the mercy of her husband. If Shing hadn't rescued me from the magistrate's court, I would have ended up in a laogai." Turning to his men again, Li commanded, "Begin."

The beating began again, this time targeting John's ribs. They planned to work their way down his body then finish off with his head.

"Oh God, help me," John cried.

Suddenly, Captain Li lurched forward, his spectacles spinning to the ground and blood seeping from his head.

"Put him down! NOW!"

"Caroline?" The men turned their shocked gazes from their stricken leader to—her. Caroline stood, quaking from head to toe, holding one of their own rifles on them. Kyine began to laugh, a deep and derisive laugh that echoed around the clearing.

"So you've come for your bit of fun too, have you?" He clutched himself suggestively and advanced on her.

Out of the corner of her eye, she saw John explode into motion in a howl of rage, launching himself at Kyine. Thida ran toward Caroline. She jumped in fear, reflexively squeezing the trigger, aghast as he fell in front of her. She turned to see Kyine push John up and off him as the smaller soldier pulled his knife and advanced on the taller spy. John held his ground. As Kyine lunged at him, John dodged and twisted so that the knife sliced down along the ropes holding his arms to his sides. The knife managed to draw blood on John's chest but now his arms were free. Suddenly, the big man, Soe, advanced toward John, casting his hollow eyes at Caroline before reaching the combatants. John had his hands around Kyine's throat when Soe's massive arms surrounded his chest and began to squeeze. Swinging the stock of the rifle deftly toward Kyine, Caroline slammed it into his head. She heard him gasp and sigh before falling to the ground, blood seeping from the wound behind his ear.

"I'll break his ribs if you don't step back." Caroline jerked her gaze from the felled man to the upright one. Soe glared at Caroline, squeezing John's ribs tighter and tighter, his face purpling with the blood that needed to travel south.

Tranquility descended on Caroline as she calmly picked up a rifle and, squaring up to the man, raised it to her shoulder, threatening menacingly, "Go ahead. But when he's dead, I'm going to obliterate your progeny." She cocked the gun and aimed it at the big man's head then deliberately lowered the muzzle to point directly at his groin. The man hesitated, flinching away from her steely gaze and glancing at the carnage around him. Setting John carefully on his feet, he began to back away. As he turned to run, Caroline handed John the rifle and he brought it down across Soe's back like a club, winding him and breaking the rifle's firing mechanism. John followed up with two knocks to the head before Caroline called out, "John, enough!" He stopped, surveying the clearing before bringing his eyes to rest on Caroline. Dropping the broken rifle, he advanced toward her.

"Why?" he asked desperately. "I thought I'd lost you. You were supposed to get away. Why did you risk coming after me?" he rasped.

"Because you're worth it," she stated calmly. "Come, we need to get out of here." She handed him the canteen Li had been carrying and waited for him to drink.

He coughed and sputtered. "This is whiskey."

She took the canteen from him, sniffed it, grimaced and tossed it away. "Come on, we need to move."

They ran through the trees, Caroline snatching up their pack, Captain Li's satchel and the last rifle as they passed the edge of the clearing. When John couldn't run anymore, they walked to put as much distance as possible between themselves and their pursuers. As the sky lightened toward dawn, John reached for Caroline's arm, "I-I need to rest."

She smiled grimly and replied, "Of course". Pacing back and forth, she waited for him to catch his breath.

"There's a cluster of vines and trees just over there." She pointed. "Perhaps we can take shelter there. Are you ready?"

John turned to face her, an enigmatic expression on his face. "It's scary, isn't it?" he asked.

"What is?" she replied.

"Trying to save someone, knowing that any minute they could be stolen from you." He got up, kissed her cheek and walked on in the direction she suggested. Caroline smiled. *I guess it is.*

The pair made their way across the hill where they found a large space covered by entwined branches, large enough and obscured enough to provide them with good cover. Caroline ordered John inside while she ensured that they wouldn't be discovered. When she was satisfied that it couldn't be seen, she came inside to find John sitting against one of the larger tree trunks, rubbing his left shoulder trying to restore normal feeling to it.

Caroline came over and knelt before him, undoing the buttons of his shirt. She pressed her fingers lightly over his stomach and ribs, checking for breaks and internal bleeding and avoiding the slice made by Kyine's knife. She moved her hands up to his shoulder, pushing his hands away as she checked to ensure it wasn't injured. Removing the canteen and a cloth from their pack, she began to wash John's face. He watched her as she worked but she avoided his eyes, concentrating on the cuts and bruises. Reaching up, he took her hand, kissing the palm. Stilling, she looked him in the eyes, brushing the fingers of her other hand across his forehead, down along his nose and across his lips.

"Why?" he asked softly, holding her gaze.

"Because I love you." She leaned in and kissed him, softly at first, not wanting to hurt him, then more firmly as passion washed over her. He pulled back first and she watched him closely to see his reaction.

"After all the things I've done—why?" he pleaded for understanding.

"It was because of the things you've done—and said—to me. I had a lot of time to think while I followed you—and to pray. I haven't been listening much lately, just demanding God fix my problems. When I started to listen, things started to make sense." She paused, her breath catching in her throat.

He paused, studying his hands. "I thought I'd lost you, for good this time. I pushed you away when you showed me only kindness and then, when I finally found my heart, you were gone." He paused, head still bowed. "Standing there in agony, watching those men eat and drink and rest, I realized what a fool I'd been to waste so much time; time I could have spent making you happy, and instead, I made you miserable. I realized I'd give anything to be back in your arms again, even if it meant being tortured." Looking up, he continued, "I prayed for another chance—with you." He stopped as though gathering his courage to ask the question he needed answered, "Do you hate me for what I've said and done? Have I ruined the fairytale?" She laughed a short laugh, then a longer laugh. He studied her in confusion, a look of hurt creeping back into his eyes. Caroline straddled his outstretched legs coming to rest on his lap. Placing her hands on his face, she kissed his forehead.

"This feels more like a horror film than a fairy tale. I wonder what the Brothers Grimm would do with our story."

"For me, this is a fairy tale," he responded blandly.

"If this is a fairy tale, are you my Prince Charming?" she asked him quite seriously.

John's eyes began to glisten with moisture and he pulled his face away. "What else could happen that would prove to you I'm no Prince Charming?" He snorted derisively at himself. She watched him for a few moments. He spoke, barely a whisper. "It would be so much easier to have never met you than to experience *this* and have you walk away."

"So, do you want me to love you?" She waited patiently for his answer.

He dropped his eyes, stroking his hands up her back, pulling her close. Kissing her collarbone, he rested his face against her neck, answering in a hushed voice, "Yes. Yes, I want you to love me." Continuing to rest his head against her, he clutched her to him and she held him tightly in return.

"John." He met her eyes again. "I love you."

Watching her, he asked, "Why?" sincerely not understanding.

"You're easy to love, John." He snorted derisively. "Don't snort at me you big grizzly bear." She smiled at him. "You're brave and intelligent, strong and skilled, sweet and kind." She brought out the carving he had given her in the summer time. He took it gently in his hands and rubbed his thumb over the children's heads.

"Why did you have that made for me? Why did you work four days in the rice fields to pay for it?" she asked.

"You were sad," he answered simply.

"Why did you care if I was sad?" she prodded him with her eyes.

"Because—well, because I care about you." He looked down at the carving in his hand.

Caroline placed her hand on top of his. "You are a wonderful man and I am lucky to have someone who cares about me that much." She paused. There was one more thing she wanted to tell him. "John, my Bear?" He smiled at the endearment. "I know that your life has been hard. I realize that you've never had love in the way it was meant to be given. One time you asked me if I could be patient with you, if I thought you were worth it. Well, right now, I'm telling you that I think you're very worth it and that I can be patient. Will you open your heart to me and see if this 'thing between us' is 'real forever always love'?"

"Caroline, my Beauty, I can't open my heart to you—" She frowned and began to protest. John placed his fingers on her lips. "Let me finish. I can't open my heart to you because you are my heart." She cried then and kissed him.

"You're supposed to be happy, not sad!" he exclaimed.

"I am happy, Bear—very happy." He held her close and she held him back until their legs told them that they had to shift position or never walk again.

"You were right," John asserted.

Surprised by his words, Caroline inquired, "What do you mean?"

"You were right. God is real and He does love us—and He does give people second chances." Smiling, she moved back over to him, kissing him lightly on the chin and burrowing into his chest.

"I know," she whispered.

They built a small fire together in the shelter and ate a meal. When John's thirst was finally sated, they laid out the blankets. John sat down and pulled Caroline against him, holding her close, running his fingers through her hair, kissing her cheeks and eyes. John slept that night with his arm firmly around Caroline, holding her tightly against him. She rested her head on his arm, entwining her fingers with those of the hand across her belly.

Caroline was raising a small fire in the shelter when John woke the next morning. "That's not some of Cho's tea, is it?"

She turned to look at him. "And if I say, yes?"

John moaned. "Why do I have to drink that stuff every time I get beaten up?"

She laughed and moved over next to him. "Good morning." Reaching up, he pulled her head down for a kiss. Resting her hand against his chest, he flinched and she quickly removed it, saying, "That's why you have to drink Cho's teas." She paused. "How are you feeling?"

"Awful. Stiff. Happy." She smiled at him and touched his cheek. *Be careful,* she admonished herself. *Take it slowly—for both our sakes.*

"Can you find us a route down to a stream or a creek while I make breakfast? We need to get you doctored a little better than I can manage in here." Caroline set some water to boil for tea and warmed a bit of the food they had with them. The water was taking a long time to boil and she was becoming concerned about moving on soon to stay ahead of pursuit.

"Do you think we have time to wait for this tea before we move on?" Caroline asked.

"We have time," he responded, keeping his eyes fixed on the map.

"Are you sure? I certainly don't want to be caught by those men again. They're going to be very angry."

"I'm certain," he replied, studying her back where she sat by the fire.

"John. Bear?" she wrinkled her brow, questioning him.

"Come here." His voice was gentle so she decided she could forego the 'please' as she moved over beside him. "What makes you think those men are still chasing us?" he asked.

"Well," she said, slowly, "why would they give up just because we got away? John, I don't understand where you're going with this. Is there something you need to tell me?"

"Not really. Just trust me. We have time for tea."

Caroline put her palm on his shoulder and turned him toward her. "Tell me," she said.

He looked her in the eyes and sighed. "Those men are dead, Caroline. They won't be chasing us." She leaned back against a tree, shock shooting through her body. Dead. She had killed last night. *What other choice did I have? I didn't mean to kill them.*

John was watching her closely. "Are you all right?" he asked.

Her eyes filled with tears. "I didn't mean to kill them, just to rescue you."

"Thank you for that, thank you for rescuing me. I don't think I've said that yet." John was watching her again so she sniffed back her tears and met his eyes.

"Thank you for telling me." She moved back to the fire to add the tea leaves to the steaming water. With her back to him, she felt she could let the tears fall. *Father, was there another way to help John? Forgive me if I did wrong and help me to handle this.*

"Aren't we supposed to be honest with each other?" John inquired.

Caroline took a breath and answered, "Yes."

"Then why are you pretending that you're not crying?" She sobbed and hugged her arms around herself. Moving closer, he turned her body to face him and brought his forehead to rest against hers. "Caroline, it's all right to cry about this. I've seen the results of having to kill and—well—you're coping remarkably well." He pulled her close and held her. "But Caroline, you didn't have a choice."

Quietly she asked, "Have you killed anyone?"

Grimacing, he responded, "Working for MI-5 isn't like those American spy shows where everyone sports a gun and shoots six or seven people a day. Being forced to kill is a rare occurrence in my world."

"Have you killed anyone?" she asked again, more insistently.

"Yes," he responded. She continued to cry miserably beside him. "I did exactly what you're doing now."

She sniffed, "Only once?"

"No, Caroline, more than once."

Does that mean he's killed more than once or cried more than once? I don't think I want to know, not right now. This is enough to deal with. Caroline allowed herself to weep freely until she began to feel calmer again.

When she quieted, John asked, "Do I really have to drink that tea? It's been steeping now for ten minutes. It'll be strong enough to melt my flip flops."

She sighed raggedly against his chest. "Whatever," she responded and then continued, "Let's eat and get going. I don't think we can assume we're safe yet. Let's find that hidden community and find a way out of Burma. It is a beautiful, lush country but I've seen quite enough of it."

They ate in a comfortable silence and cleared their presence from the area before heading down the mountain to find the stream that John had located on the map. Once they reached the stream, Caroline insisted that John's wounds be tended properly, concerned about the damage to his body.

"You go ahead and wash in the stream and I'll bring some cloths to help clean the wounds on your head and chest." John removed his clothes and waded awkwardly into the stream, gasping as he entered the water.

"Blimey, It's freezing!" he complained. Caroline glanced up and paused, watching his body. *He is such a handsome man,* she mused. Once he was immersed in the water she called to him to come and let her have a look.

"Just throw me the cloths," John responded.

"Don't be silly. Come here. I want to see how badly you're hurt," she insisted.

"You don't need to see. I'll look after it."

She was becoming annoyed at his resistance. "John, I've seen your body before. Just come here and let me see what those nasties did to you." Her voice was firm.

"No."

"Why are you being so difficult? I only want to help."

"Then pass me the cloths and go find some firewood while I deal with this." His voice was firm but softened as he added,

"Please." Caroline sighed. She left the cloths on the pack and walked into the trees to find some dry wood for a fire.

When she returned, arms laden, John was dressed and studying the map. He glanced up when she approached but quickly looked back to the map in front of him. Walking over, she began to lay a fire beside him.

"John—" she began.

"Nothing's wrong," he responded quickly without looking up.

"I only want to know if you're okay. I do have rather a lot of experience nursing a tortured man." She spoke softly, touching his arm.

He sighed. "There's bruising across my chest and shoulders. The cut on my chest is healing cleanly. It wasn't very deep. I don't have a concussion."

"I don't understand why you wouldn't let me help you."

"Do we *have* to do this, Caroline?" There was an edge in his voice that raised her ire.

"No. Fine," she snapped.

"Caroline," he started. "Refusing to discuss this does not mean that I won't let you close to me." He lifted her chin to look into her eyes. Sighing, she nodded, lowering her head sadly.

"Fine," he intoned in resignation. "Don't look up," he warned.

"What?" She glanced at him in confusion.

"I said *don't* look up. If you insist on being told, then don't look up." She smiled a little at that and lowered her head again.

He blew air out his mouth stridently. "Fine. They kicked me in the—and they're all swollen and—that's it." He sank down in defeat.

"Can I look up now?" she asked with a smile in her voice.

"It's not funny. Yes, you can look up. But don't laugh!"

She kissed him on the cheek. "I'm not laughing at your predicament. I'm smiling because you're sweet." She paused as he relaxed a little. "I had five sons. I know all about foreskins and testicles—believe me, more than I care to know." A laugh escaped his lips. "I'm sorry I embarrassed you, though. Next time, I'll let you deal with it on your own. Is there anything I can do to help?"

He looked up at her like she was crazy.

Then she blushed deeper. "I-I didn't mean—Well I didn't mean that!" She laughed.

CHAPTER 9
CITY OF TEMPLES

They set off after their meal, walking back into the tangled jungle and following a northeasterly path toward the fork in the river, their destination. They walked together in a comfortable silence and after a while, Caroline began to sing. John smiled happily at the sound of her voice.

"John," she interrupted herself. "How did you get here?"

He looked over at her. "Well, my mother and father got together and they went to the cabbage patch and they looked under every leaf until they found just the right—"

"What *are* you talking about?" Caroline grabbed his arm and stopped him.

"Well, I would have thought, with five children, you would have known how this all works, but if you don't, I can fill you in. The stork drops the baby under a cabbage leaf—" Caroline swatted him in the shoulder then shoved him, her mouth agape. John roared with laughter and started backing down the trail with Caroline chasing him, threatening all manner of punishments. He let her catch up to him, pinned her against a tree and tickled her then walked away backwards again along the trail as she lunged for him, missing him by centimetres. Caroline could see that behind him there was a fallen log or a rotten tree stump or something. She called out potential punishments again to keep his attention focused on her and, when he fell backwards, she pounced, pinning him to the ground. The look of pain on his face caused her to jump up. Rolling onto his side, he curled up, groaning wretchedly.

She sat beside him watching his misery. "I'm sorry. I'm *so* sorry. I wasn't thinking." She stroked one hand through his damp hair and tenderly laid the other on his shoulder. As his breathing settled, he rolled forward to get up, still clutching an arm across his battered ribs.

"Blimey, you weren't kidding when you threatened to make me pay." He groaned ruefully.

Caroline's eyes began to fill with tears. "I'm sorry," she sniffed.

"Oh, that hurts." He turned to look at her distraught face. "Don't cry. I'll be all right. I guess I'm just not up to active teasing yet. Just give me a minute and I'll stop whinging."

Caroline watched him carefully. "Maybe we should head back to the stream where you can soak in the cool water again," Caroline suggested.

"No, we need to keep moving. Shing may have more men; I can't imagine him sending only four. There are militant bands all over with a variety of allegiances and wildlife roaming all around us looking for its next meal. No, we need to keep moving."

As Caroline watched him limping about, she suggested, "Let's find another stream then, to head towards. The cool waters would help various parts of your anatomy. After Henry had his vasectomy—"

John, wincing, held up his hand. "No, please, stop there. You're only making it worse by using the V word."

Caroline chuckled. "Men are such babies when it comes to discussing these things."

"A proper lady wouldn't have said that," John admonished, "although, a proper lady wouldn't have threatened to obliterate someone's progeny. Thank you for that, by the way."

Caroline's face darkened at the memory. "I wasn't sure he'd even understand what I was talking about."

"Oh, he understood all right, when you aimed the rifle." Caroline brightened a little and helped him stand upright.

"Can you walk?" she asked. He nodded, resting his elbow on her shoulder as he limped along. After a few metres, John was able to walk upright again though he continued to limp slightly.

"John?" she asked.

"Hmmm."

"What's 'whinging'?"

Smiling, he responded, "I thought you spoke English."

Lightly nudging him, she smiled in return. "I only speak proper English."

"We invented it, ye ken?" John retorted.

"What is 'whinging', then?" she demanded.

"Whining." He adopted an aristocratic air. "Stop whinging or I'll bung you off for a snog."

"Oh yeah, that sounds really proper," she replied sarcastically. "What's a 'snog'?"

Grinning brightly, he pulled her close, "I'll show you." He kissed her firmly then more gently.

"Ah," she sighed. "Do you snog on demand?"

"Only for you." He kissed the tip of her nose. Twining their hands together, the two bedraggled travelers moved forward with renewed purpose along the trail.

"Tell me how you ended up in a prison in Burma," she demanded lightly.

John was thoughtful for a few moments. "I would...but then I'd have to kill you." John turned to face her as they talked, sporting a sly grin.

"Yes, thank you, James Bond." She grinned back at him, appreciating his flash of humour.

"I will tell you, but it would be safest if you didn't share this with anyone we may meet on this journey. Are you certain you want to know?"

Caroline nodded. "I think I've earned the right to know."

"Caroline, you've earned the right to every bit of me, but my question is, do you want it?"

"I want it. The whole entire bit of you, grumpy bear and all."

He looked confused. "Shouldn't that be grizzly bear?"

Caroline smiled back, "Well, you smell like a grizzly bear sometimes, but I think grumpy bear is a more fitting description." Caroline began to laugh as John grabbed her and began to tickle her. When he stopped, he continued to hold her. She reached up and kissed him on the cheek.

"You know that I work for MI-5?" Caroline nodded and he continued, "What you don't know is that I was recently promoted out of the field and into a desk job as a Group Leader within the Counter Terrorism branch of MI-5. After I'd been in the post about two months, word started coming down the pipe about a conference on counter terrorism which would bring together the heads of several domestic and international security services from the major countries, the U.K., France, Italy, America, China, India and Russia. It was decided that the conference would be held in India as it was geographically about the middle, roughly speaking. Four days before the conference was to begin, my colleague, who was scheduled to attend the conference, became very ill. Food poisoning, they said. Somehow, a request was made that I attend in his place. This made my more senior colleagues quite angry and that's probably why I didn't see the strangeness of it. It was too easy to believe that I was just better at the job than they." Here John sighed.

"Anyway, I arrived at my Hotel in Mumbai and headed over to the Hard Rock Café with the others for an evening of dancing and drink. Well, I drank—a bit too much. Not that I was alone in that, but now that I think back, I realize there were two Asian officials who were plying me quite liberally with alcohol." He sighed again then continued, "Around one o'clock in the morning I headed back to my room, drunk and jet-lagged. That's likely why I didn't set my usual security traps and why I didn't hear them enter my room. I woke to a huge hand over my mouth and an injection in my arm. I think there were four men in my room but there may have been more." At this point, John looked Caroline in the eye. "One of the men from the bar, the man who injected me with a sedative, was Captain Li." Caroline's eyes widened at the news.

"I woke once in a helicopter and was promptly sedated again. The next time I woke was in the back of the van as it delivered me to the prison."

Caroline watched her feet as she walked, trying to work through the information he had provided. "Why did they kidnap you? Was the entire conference a ruse?" she asked.

"It's hard for me to believe that the entire conference could have been arranged to accomplish my capture but I think it was seen as an opportunity upon which to capitalize. Someone at MI-5 must be a back door contact for Shing—a mole. I think Shing arranged to have my colleague poisoned and somehow put me forward to replace him. It must be someone high-ranking at MI-5 to have that kind of influence."

"And Shing wants the same network that the Russians wanted twenty years ago?" Caroline inquired.

"Yes. A few times throughout my career, I've been seconded to MI-6. It's actually quite common for the sisters to share agents back and forth. Well, twenty years ago I was a fairly new officer and eager to prove myself. I was sent to India to discover whether it would be possible to recruit agents willing to cross from India to China to gain intelligence on things like weapons accrual, movements of known terrorists, and so on. Instead of identifying potential candidates, I disappeared into the wilds of Burma, Laos, Thailand and Vietnam, recruiting a network of spies who would report back to a senior agent with information. This senior agent had a cover as an importer/exporter and travelled from China to India through all these countries on a regular basis. I was gone for 5 months. They thought I had died or been turned."

"Turned?" Caroline inquired.

"Gone over to the other side; joined the other team; defected," John clarified. He continued, "That network won me a huge promotion. I was able to move back to MI-5 which held my first allegiance."

"If you were back with MI-5, how did you end up captured by the Russians?"

"I was sent along with some agents from '6' to pick up a Russian defector from West Germany. We got cocky when the little fellow was late and went looking for him in East Germany. Two of us were captured. The other agent, Maryn Dale was held in East Germany but I was sent on to Moscow—where I met Vlad." John smiled ruefully.

They walked on in silence for a time.

"What happened to Maryn Dale?" Caroline asked softly. John smiled, enigmatically.

"What?" she responded to the strange smile.

"You're going to meet her," John said with a grin. "She's my agent."

John and Caroline travelled on, making their way through the jungle at whatever speed John's injuries would allow. He was recovering quickly and feeling excited at being so near their destination. He was so enthusiastic, in fact, that Caroline felt a small pang when he talked about being back in the U.K..

This is selfish, Father, I know. I've just grown so close to him here but I'm afraid of what life will be like when we get back to the real world. There are so many parts of him still hidden. How will I cope if he tells me something about himself that I can't live with?

Feeling that the imminent risk of capture was at least somewhat reduced, they returned to their practice of building raised shelters in the evenings, enjoying the greater comfort and safety they provided. One evening, as they sat around a fire cooking dinner, Caroline screwed up her courage and asked John, "What do you think will happen when we get out of Burma?" She continued to watch the food on the fire, not daring to look at him.

"What do you mean?" he asked, cautiously.

She sighed, realizing he wasn't going to make this easy. Trying again, she used a different tactic. "If I had been, say a tourist in London and we had met, say at a party or something, do you think we would have gotten together?" She held her breath waiting for his response.

"Is this about something?" he inquired warily.

Now it was her turn to be puzzled. "Pardon? What do *you* mean?"

"Caer, what is the question behind the question?" He seemed to have developed the ability to see into her mind which she found just a little intimidating.

"Never mind," she retreated, bashfully. He studied her for a moment then walked over and knelt beside her, taking the spoon from her hand and lifting the food from the fire. Laying his hand on her cheek, he turned her face to look at him, using those familiar words that always seemed to make her open up her mind to him. "Tell me."

Caroline sighed and closed her eyes, speaking in a rush. "I'm afraid that—" She stopped, unable to form her thoughts coherently; unable to reveal her vulnerability.

Bearing a look of solemn intensity, John watched her for a time, then, taking her hand, he drew her to her feet and walked over to their shelter where he perched on the edge of the platform and firmly placed her between his knees so that they stood and sat, face to face. Resting his hands gently on her hips, he asked, "What's wrong?"

Studying the top button of his shirt, she answered in a very quiet voice, "Do you think that this extreme situation created our relationship? Would we have gotten together under more 'normal' circumstances?"

John studied her for a long time before he responded. "I don't think you would have given me a second look if you had met me at a party."

Caroline glanced briefly at his face which bore witness to his disquietude. "You're very handsome. I would have noticed you."

"Caer, be honest. If you had met John the spy from prison, you would have said, 'Hi, how are you?' and walked away."

"Well, the same goes for you. What interest could you possibly have had in a 'stay at home mom' who worked part-time as a speech therapist, chasing children with Autism around all day."

Again, he waited a long time before responding. "I would have noticed you and I would have wished desperately that I could be the kind of man who could attract a woman like you. Then, I would have accepted that I wasn't that man, locked down my emotions and moved on. But I never would have forgotten you."

Touched as she was by his words, her anxiety wouldn't let her relax. "John, I'm frightened." She hugged her arms around herself. His hands tightened on her hips but he didn't draw her closer.

"What are you afraid of?" he asked, apprehension lacing every syllable of his question and every feature of his visage.

"I'm afraid that this—between us—is only a result of the circumstances—that when we get back to the real world, we'll—you'll regret what happened—between us." She was shaking and she pulled her arms tighter around herself, seeking comfort.

A catch in his husky voice, John replied, "Caer, if this was the only way you'd have me, I'm grateful." She looked up at his surprising words as he continued, "What is it that you're truly afraid of?"

Sighing at his insight, she finally unveiled her fears. "What if—Is there—I'm terrified that one day you'll tell me something I can't live with," she paused, "but I know that I could never be happy in a relationship where I knew that the truth was kept from me."

"What do you want to know?" His hands slipped from her hips to rest on his own knees, his eyes studying the ground between his feet.

Caroline raised her eyes, regarding the top of his dark head. "What is the worst thing you've ever done?"

Sighing, John rubbed his hands over his face, continuing to stare at the ground between them. "A few years ago, there was a rash of pipe bombs planted around market squares in Oxford. At first, the bombs were fairly small, only causing minimal damage to property, but we were having a very difficult time apprehending the perpetrator. Each time we failed, the next bomb was just a little bigger and just a little more public. People were starting to be injured, two little schoolgirls were killed. Finally, at one bomb site, he left a clue, a smudged fingerprint that sent us down a crooked path to his front door. Unfortunately, by the time we found his workshop, he was already setting his next bomb. We had everything we needed to find him but nothing we needed to charge him with a crime. I had to decide whether to bring him in or let the bomb explode, thereby ensuring his conviction in court and an end to the escalating violence. I ordered my officers to stand down and I let the bomb explode. Two people were killed that day, a father and his young son." John leaned forward, resting his elbows on his knees, scrubbing his face with his hands then remaining still.

"Do you regret the choice you made?" timorously, Caroline inquired.

"Every day," he admitted. "I went with the police officers to inform the wife. She lost control and started screaming and crying. The constable backed right out of the room, placing the blame on 'those shady spooks'—me."

"Would you make the same decision again?"

He sighed loudly. "I don't know. If I had warned the father, the bomber could have gotten away. If he had continued setting bombs, more people would have died. But I still see their faces in my dreams and I still hear the sound of the explosion when I'm alone in the dark."

Drawing a ragged breath, she asked tentatively, "Are you the same man who let those people die?"

He looked up in surprise, meeting her gaze. "Caer, I told you, I don't know what I'd do, now." He seemed distressed by her question.

"Are you the same man today that you were on that day?" her voice was stronger now, insisting on an answer.

Shaking his head, he replied, "I'm different—because of you—I'm not the same—because of God. Even though I'll return to my old life, I won't return to being who I was. I'm not the same man who arrived at Bourey Prison."

Taking a small step toward him, Caroline lifted John's hands and placed them firmly on her waist. Sliding her arms around his shoulders and taking a larger step closer, she pulled him into a tight hug.

"Thank you for telling me," she spoke tenderly into his ear.

He took a deep, shaky breath and pulled her closer, wrapping his arms around her.

"I'm sorry I'm not the man you deserve."

Pulling back a little, she framed his face with her hands. "You're the man I want. I love you."

His breath shuddered in his chest. "I don't know why—" he paused before adding, "but I'm so very grateful that you do." Then he kissed her, deeply and fully.

Emerging from the trees the next morning after yet another night spent in a raised jungle shelter, they looked out over a grassy plain that opened onto the most unusual sight Caroline had ever beheld. Buildings—stone buildings all across the plains: bulbous domes, receding terraces and concentric rings, monoliths, tiered structures, golden edifices, crimson towers, intricate carvings, elaborate structures. It appeared as though every cathedral in Europe had been sucked through a vortex and dumped in the plains of Bagan. Caroline gasped in wonder at the majesty and intricacy of the constructions.

"John, what are these?" she asked in awe.

"Temples. Buddhist temples," he responded. "My contact should be near the Shwe-san-daw pagoda." Taking her hand, he led her down into the valley, kicking up the dust as they walked. Caroline's head swiveled to and fro as she travelled, trying to take in the beauty and diversity of the workmanship around her. Finally finding the dirt path that led to the pagoda, John and Caroline moved between the walls of tall grass, dodging the goat herd along the way.

Purchasing two bottled orange fizzy drinks and fish balls at an outdoor food stop, John and Caroline passed the Toe Toe Win Buffet drooling as they watched the tourists partake. Reluctantly moving on, inspiration suddenly lit John's features and he retreated to the small food wagon they had visited earlier, telling Caroline, "I'll be right back." He returned with a third portion of food and, in response to her inquisitive look, simply replied, "It's for him."

After finishing their meager meal, they went to sit in the shade of the pagoda. In spite of the presence of milling tourists clad in all manner of western garb from jeans and chinos to bright purple University of Western Ontario sweatshirts, flashing pictures on cameras from digital to video to cell phones, Caroline fell asleep leaning against John's shoulder, eventually awakened by his enthusiastic cry, "Mo!" John gently shifted Caroline and stood to greet a gentleman with a shaved head and sporting a crimson robe. He was shorter than John, not much taller than Caroline, in fact. His broad, flat face, wrinkled, but happy, sported a broad, flat nose that looked as though it had been broken and reset to form a 'J'. Caroline could see fresh stitches on his head but it took her a few moments to understand why his face looked so odd until she realized that he had no eyebrows. Reaching out, John grasped the monk's shoulder and the men exchanged greetings in Burmese. *That looks like a happy conversation,* Caroline mused as John gestured for her to join them.

"Caroline, this is Mo. Mo is a Buddhist Monk. In Burma, the monks and the university students are the powerhouses standing against the oppressive military government. Mo has taken part in many demonstrations and if you saw beneath his robe, you would see the evidence of his resistance."

Caroline bowed and Mo folded his hands, returning her bow.

Scanning the area to ensure privacy, John began speaking in Burmese. "Mo, I'm in trouble and I need your help." As John spoke, Caroline pulled out her best linguistic skills to follow the conversation. "Military Intelligence…after me…need…safety. What…suggest?"

Pausing to think, Mo responded. "I believe, for you…Katafygio."

"The cata—what?" Caroline interrupted, speaking in English to John.

"The Katafygio," John replied quickly, turning back to Mo.

"Brother Phillip's…sits…mountains in the north… Chindwin River…border of India…show you…map…sent many of our Christian…risk of capture…" Mo explained.

John bowed to the man, showing humility. "I am very grateful to you."

"A monk has little…anything else…I can do?" Mo inquired.

"Yes. Do you know…transport…help us travel north… jungles?" John waited with bated breath.

"Hmmm. I may…'oozie'…travel north to Kalemayo… maybe…take you along. I trust him," Mo replied. John and Mo studied the map acquired from the soldiers at the Dawe, plotting a course north through the arbor-sheathed mountains.

John asked Caroline for the extra food he had purchased earlier and, when she asked, "how much", he replied, "this much," while making a bowl shape with his hands. "Buddhist Monks are required to carry nothing more than their bowl, depending on the generosity of others for their meals."

Turning back to Mo again, John spoke in deep gratitude, "Thank you, my friend. How can I repay your goodness?"

"You have repaid…send word…oozie…meet…Shin Boe Mae at dusk. I wish you peace—and enlightenment," Mo responded with a grin. John thanked him again and, after reviewing the route set out in the map, Mo departed.

"John," Caroline began, touching his arm to draw his attention from the retreating form of the monk. "Where are we going? What is the Katafygio?"

"Mo called it Brother Phillip's Haven of Rest. He placed it in the far north, nestled in a hidden mountain valley close to the Chindwin River and the border with India."

"I caught the bit about the Chindwin and India. What did he mean when he spoke of Christians and capture?" she inquired.

"He said that he often sends Christian dissidents there when the risk of capture outweighs the good they can do in resisting the oppression of the military junta."

"How are going to get there? Please don't tell me we have to walk the entire way. And, I don't even want an estimate of how many days it will take," she replied and John laughed at the look on her face.

When his laugh had settled into a smile, he informed her simply, "Oozie."

"John," she admonished. "What is an oozy? Not a gun, I assume."

Chuckling, he replied, "An oozie is an elephant driver. Mo knows an oozie who is on his way north of here to Kalemayo to train a new capture of elephants."

"Why on earth did I think I needed a more exciting life?" Caroline muttered to herself and John laughed good-naturedly in response.

Having a couple of hours to put in until dusk, Caroline and John wandered around the fantastic temples, slowly winding their way toward the Shin Boe Mae. John moved over and took Caroline's hand, kissing it and then continuing to hold it. She smiled in response. Trying to blend in with the tourists, John and Caroline attempted to hide in plain sight, not quite as successfully as they hoped, given the fact that three different groups of tourists asked to take their picture, a request which John politely denied. *I'm not sure why we don't fit in,* mused Caroline, wryly. *Could it be our wildly unkempt hair, our sun-burnished skin, our longyi and flip flops...* Her mind wandered through the plethora of characteristics dividing her from the people around her.

<><><><><>

Forged in the Jungles of Burma

Htet and his men pulled into the city of Bagan heading for the airport of Nyaung-u. Passing a Burmese couple holding hands amongst the foreign tourists and an elephant rocking in place as his driver stood in deep conversation with a Buddhist Monk, he marveled at the contradictions that were Myanmar: airports and elephants; resistant monks; patriarchy and passion; riches and poverty; freedom and restriction. Surely the regime he supported would one day bring untold wealth to his people—well, at least to him.

<><><><><>

Caroline hummed nervously as the elephant and driver appeared, fidgeting with John's fingers as she held them in her hand. The broad grey-brown beast lumbered closer with each unhurried footstep, its prehensile trunk swinging left and right like a very slow metronome. The barefooted oozie perched confidently across the animal's neck, his legs tucked firmly behind the large, flappy ears, swaying in time with the movements of the pachyderm as though beast and man were one creation. The only noticeable separation between the elephant and his human was the bright red shirt and straw hat worn by the driver.

"You're serious?" she asked apprehensively. "We're going to ride an elephant?"

John chuckled. "That hooked riding crop he's holding is a choon which helps to steer the animal. Elephants are still used instead of expensive machinery in many areas in Burma and all they require to keep them going are 'greens'. It's actually very environmentally conscious if you think about it, assuming, of course, that the beasts are well cared for." He slipped his arm around her shoulders and pulled her into a comforting hug.

"mgClapf. Prosperity to you," John called out in greeting to the Oozie who nodded in reply. Using his choon, he commanded the elephant to kneel so he could dismount. Approaching John, they conducted a discussion in Burmese with a little food and money exchanging hands. By way of conclusion, the Oozie waved John and Caroline onto the elephant. Demonstrating how to use the harness and saddle to pull oneself up, the Oozie hip-checked her onto the pachyderm's back. John followed, perching in front of her as the Oozie took up his place in the lead. Caroline grabbed John around the middle as the elephant lurched upright and began walking northwest toward the trees.

The Oozie was a most uncommunicative man and John seemed unwilling to converse while he was around, so the days passed in silence. Caroline often fell asleep pressed against John's back and dreamt of boats—sailboats, canoes, kayaks, fishing boats—all rocking on the waves. Caroline's legs were chafed and sore by the end of the first day's journey and John found her a nearby stream to bathe in to ease the discomfort. As exotic as it was to ride an elephant, it was also very uncomfortable. However, as Caroline learned ways to ease the chafing and muscle ache, she also learned to appreciate the fact that she wasn't walking.

A few miles from Kalemayo, the oozie helped them dismount, remounted and carried on east, along the road to the city. Leaving them with a curt wave, the Oozie disappeared into the distance, leaving the saddle-sore travelers on the edge of the dusty road. John and Caroline picked their way across a field of maize and resumed walking north in search of the mountain hideaway called, Katafygio, praying for the haven of rest and safety that the name promised.

CHAPTER 10
THE KATAFYGIO

Finding the tracks and trails up the side of the mountain, John and Caroline made slower, but still steady progress. Having grown comfortable together, they sometimes talked and sometimes just walked in silence. Caroline told John about her parents and childhood, about her job and about her children. She had told some of the stories before in prison but John had been in such a fog of pain and anxiety that he enjoyed hearing them again, filling in the gaps in his understanding of her life before Burma. He wondered aloud at how she always managed to find humour in situations that would discourage others. John talked about his time in the army, the beginnings of his time in MI-5 and his colleagues there. She found that she began to understand him and his reactions more clearly. They both learned how to communicate more successfully, relaxing into the actions and words that built on the foundations of trust that Burma was forging in their relationship.

When Caroline asked him about their route or their plans, John always answered, "I was wondering what you thought of this idea …"

To which Caroline would respond, "Can you explain the risks, please?"

"Of course, after all, you have a right to know."

They stopped to rest in a small clearing in the late afternoon, laying their gear beside a moss-covered palm trunk felled by the rigors of the jungle. Caroline had moved away a short distance, examining a low-lying bush laden with purple-red berries and leathery aciculated leaves tapering along a serrated edge to a point. The berries looked like small pomegranates wearing little green top hats. Where they'd been deposited by overly ambitious birds, Caroline saw through the splits in the rind what looked like marshmallows. While she examined the bushes, Caroline relaxed into the wonder of the world around her, singing along to "When Peace Like a River" which played in her head. When she heard an odd noise behind her—a low, huffing growl that sounded like a steam engine just starting up a hill—she assumed that John was playfully alarming her.

She called out to him, "Very funny, John, are you ready for something to eat?" His voice surprised her, however, sounding from her left.

"STOP!" John commanded. He was turned around, frozen to the spot, watching something off to their right. Caroline heard the apprehension in his voice and stopped.

"John, what is it?" she asked in a strident whisper, feeling the fear rise from the pit of her stomach.

"We're being tracked."

She looked around in fear, noting that the rifle was with the pack by the fallen palm at least ten feet away and John was further from it than she was. She began to creep carefully forward toward it.

"Stay still!" He scanned the area, his eyes focusing on the rifle.

"John, who is it? Is it more of Shing's men?" Caroline was beginning to shake with terror. "John, I'm afraid." He brought his alert eyes to her agitated face. Anxiety was coming off her in waves, her eyes darting around and her body visibly shaking.

"Caroline," he said calmly. "Beauty. Calm down. It's not Shing's men. It's an animal, I think. Slowly turn your head and look over your right shoulder, about waist height. Keep your body very still." She looked around and saw them: a pair of feline eyes watching them through the dank foliage.

"Leopard?" she inquired, breathlessly. "Jaguar?"

"Leopard, in these parts. We need that rifle." John inched slowly backwards keeping his eyes on the luminescent eyes in the jungle, crouching down, feeling the ground around him, and searching for the gun. "Where is it, Caer?" She stared back at him. "Caroline?" he asked more urgently. She turned her head to guide him to the rifle.

"Back a bit—a bit more. You've got it!"

Quickly and smoothly, he shouldered the rifle and pointed it toward the bush where the leopard seemed to be lying in wait.

"Walk towards me, very slowly." But slowly was too slow. Caroline's movement provoked the cat and it pounced, bounding toward her and knocking her to the ground. All the air gushed out her mouth at once, emptying her lungs. Struggling to inhale, the air rushed out again immediately in a scream as the leopard's claws sliced into her back—steel daggers parting flesh. Low growls sounded in her ear as the great feline bowed its head to her right shoulder. Struggling wildly, she pushed her arms against the ground, trying to propel the weight off her back, screaming and bucking all the while. Caroline cried out as the weight on her back suddenly lifted, an outraged snarl filling her ears. She could hear John swearing through the rush of blood pounding in her ears.

"Caer? Beauty. Can you hear me? We need to move. I-I couldn't shoot. I might have hit you. I clubbed it. I frightened it away but it might come back. Caroline? Answer me, please. Please, answer me."

"I'm okay. Help me up." She gasped as John reached around her and gently lifted her to a sitting position, crying out as he moved her. "Oh, John, it hurts!"

"Can you walk?" he asked. She nodded. Placing her arm around his shoulder, she clung to him as he half-dragged her back up the trail, searching for a shelter of protection; a haven of safety; somewhere to regroup and tend her wounds. A fresh snarl and growl erased their hope of shelter as the dappled tawny predator launched a renewed attack, this time catapulting onto Caroline from the left, throwing her against John. She bounced and rolled off his body, landing sideways beneath the cat. This time, the curved daggers shredded her shirt, ripping into the flesh of her chest and back as the head sought its preferred biting spot. Screaming, Caroline could see black crowding around the edges of her vision. Just before she blacked out, Caroline heard a familiar baritone, "The rifle—where is it? God, help us!"

Caroline roused when the dead weight of the leopard was lifted from her legs. She dimly recalled the sound of thunder—no—a car backfiring—no—gunshots? Too distracted by the dancing black circles in her mind, Caroline heard a buzzing sound in her ears that resolved into a voice. A familiar voice then an unfamiliar voice—*Leave her alone! Who are you? Not much gratitude in you, is there?* Now, someone was touching her shoulder.

"Oh," she groaned. *Was that me or the cat? Oh, be quiet. I want to sleep. Oh, the buzzing again.* A brief glance revealed a woman and two men within her line of vision. *The familiar voice again—Henry? John?* Caroline's eyes flickered open and closed, finding that the nausea retreated slightly when she only had to listen.

The woman spoke with a southern American accent. "The name's Delilah Grundy but you can call me Dolly." She offered her hand in greeting to—someone—John? The someone grabbed some cloths out of their pack and pressed them to her bleeding shoulder.

The familiar voice spoke again. "My name is John. This is Caroline. Who are you?" *Why does everything smell like a wet dog in a bog?*

The American voice drawled. "Well now I just told you who I am—yer a funny lad. C'mere lads and move this great cat out of the way." *The wet dog smell is gone.*

Caroline groaned as she felt herself rolled onto a stretcher and lifted. Something soft was pressed to her shoulder but she could still feel a warm dampness spreading. Each bump sent stabs of pain through every millimetre of skin that had been sliced and punctured by the leopard, until finally, peace and quiet. No more movement and then, opening her eyes, John, beside her. She tried to tell him she was okay but all that came out was a groan as her eyes drooped drowsily closed. Suddenly, she felt the sensation of lifting, pain searing through her shoulder at what seemed like a roller coaster of movement. *Why do they keep bouncing me around? Just leave me alone and let me sleep.*

Ah, finally, peace and stillness. A bed—now I can sleep. Oh no, not the buzzing again. Caroline opened her eyes to a man speaking to John. The man was slender and blonde with round glasses perched on the top of his head. His voice was gentle as he said, "I'm Simon—Simon Reldif. Here's your rifle. It's looks to be in pretty rough shape, the stock is cracked and the barrel's bent. It must have broken when you clobbered that leopard." He paused. "Welcome to the Katafygio. Dolly will bring the doctor. They'll be here shortly." John reached up to shake his hand but remained sitting on the edge of the bed.

Caroline reached out weakly, brushing her fingertips along John's leg. He immediately looked down and took her hand, holding it to his cheek. "Mmmm," Caroline responded.

Buzzing? Buzzing? Words? Who is that? Caroline wondered but nothing but a groan escaped her lips. *Key? Kyi? Doctor? Ouch?* Someone had stabbed Caroline, not once but twice—not stabbed, injected. *Where is Henry? I need him. Henry, why is he always late? But wait, Henry is gone—gone where? He's with the boys—our boys. Where are they? I miss them.* As the buzzing receded, Caroline floated away from the pain. It existed on some plane, somewhere in her mind but the colours and patterns kept pushing it away like the current in a river, bearing it away, away, away. Caroline rode the vibrant colours, traveling through countries of bears eating strangely shaped berries with marshmallow centres, pythons riding elephants and checkerboards flying through the air calling a tut-tut to all the other checkerboards feasting in the trees. The iridescent rainbows conveyed Caroline on and on through dreams of rivers and children and images of love and loss until they set her down on the green, golden-green grass of a garden. The blue of the sky matched her grandfather's eyes and the lilies were dazzlingly bright amongst the grasses which all waved in the gentle breeze. *More buzzing?* No, it was laughter, children's laughter. She could see children playing. They were running and leaping; chasing, yet never being caught; their infectious joy bringing a smile to Caroline's mind. She drew closer, wanting to join in the game; wanting to know these wonderful children: Aleck, Gabe, Teddy, Titus, Caleb. These were her children, her boys. "Mommy, Mommy," they called. "We're okay, Mommy! Don't worry. We love you!" They laughed and danced, waving their arms in glee. Then, there beside them, was Henry. They ran to him and hugged him. Waving, he called, "I love you, dearest. We're safe and happy. We love you. Be happy." The colours were blending around them, lifting her and carrying her away, and then they were gone, and there was another man—no, wait—a man and a boy. The man was sad and angry and cruel. He shook the boy as he cried. The boy cried out, "God, help me." She opened her arms to him and he ran into her embrace. Then he grew. He grew until he was a man and he held her in his embrace. Gazing into his face, she knew that she loved this man. Gazing back at her, she knew, without a doubt, that he loved her.

Feeling an unaccustomed softness beneath her, Caroline woke to see a slender, grey-haired Burmese lady entering the room carrying strangely familiar food on a tray, bringing a waft of clear mountain air through the door of the cabin with her. Caroline's confusion was growing as she gazed at her surroundings: a pillar, a blanket, warmth, dryness…and hurt. She remained still, cozy and warm, peacefully contented and unwilling to face the pain she knew was knocking at the door. When the hand she had not noticed, slipped from her fingers, she murmured sleepily, "John? John?"

"I'm here," his voice sounded from the floor beside her.

Following the sound of his voice, she gazed down to see him sitting up on a bedroll spread on the floor beside her bed. He looked freshly bathed and laundered, wearing a new beige-coloured longyi and a navy, long-sleeve button-down shirt , cuffs rolled back with military precision. She groaned softly, her eyes fluttering open and closed.

"Mmmm. I had a strange dream. I was in the river again and Henry and the children were on the other side. No matter how hard I swam, I couldn't get to them."

John's eyes saddened as he replied, "That must have been terrible."

She continued, "Hmmm, yes. But then you were there and you pulled me out of the river." She smiled in her dozy half-asleep state and he returned her smile.

Groaning as the pain seared back in, Caroline concentrated on John, ignoring the room she was in, begging, "Hold my hand." John reached over to take hold of her left hand, raising it gently to his lips and continuing to hold it against his face. Gently stroking her fingers against his cheek, she noted, "You shaved. Feels soft—manly, but soft." He chuckled softly at her words.

Focusing her pained, confused eyes on his worried features, she queried, "Where are we? What happened?"

"Do you want the short version or the long version?" he asked, reaching up and gently kissing her forehead.

"Long. I'm not going anywhere." She sighed.

"We had stopped to rest when you were attacked by a leopard. Do you remember that?" he asked.

"Mmhmm. Then there was noise—and people—and pain."

Sadness in his eyes, John continued. "A hunting party from the hidden village, the Katafygio, stumbled across us and shot the leopard. Dolly—she's an older lady with iron-grey hair, an iron disposition, and a body that an ox would be proud of—well, it's difficult to describe her entry; there you are lying on the ground bleeding and she's giving me the history of the world!" John stopped and shook his head. "I can even give you the history of Katafygio, if you like," he replied, amused at the memory.

She replied, "Why not?"

"Evidently, the name's based on the Modern Greek for haven, because—now listen carefully—Brother Phillip and his brother Brother Simon wanted to provide a haven of rest for those escaping persecution. It sounds like only Brother Phillip is still alive, Brother Simon having died years ago…" John went on to tell Caroline how Dolly had offered to take them to their community and "get yer lady fixed up". John's response of, "Great—Yes—Please" was accepted as consent. He explained how he and Simon and Myaing had lashed together a stretcher and carried her to the village.

"They made me carry the leopard for the first part of the journey. It smelled like a wet dog," he complained. *Wet dog in a bog, of course,* she remembered.

Continuing his tale, he explained that Myaing was half-Karen and that he and his twin sister, Nanda, were evidently the finest trackers in Burma. Mimicking Dolly's voice, he stated, "If it moves, they can find it. They know all the edible plants and all the secret ways." His voice returned to normal. "Apparently, they helped Brother Phillip find a secret place for his community and helped spread the word that the Karen peoples could find refuge here from persecution. The other fellow in the hunting party was Simon, a tall, blonde fellow with glasses."

"Hmmm, I remember him, tall, thin, glasses perched on his head?" she stated, softly.

"Looking like a four-eyed owl? Yes. Well, when we got here, Dolly brought a young Burmese doctor, Kyi, to see you. He gave you some antibiotics to fight the infection, and something to lessen the pain."

"By injection?" she asked. He nodded. "I do remember that. It hurt."

He smiled at her in wonder, beguiled by her fortitude. "You're attacked by a leopard and all you complain about is a little injection." She poked her tongue out at him and told him to keep going as her eyes fluttered shut again.

Chuckling, he continued, "They, Kyi and Dolly, cleaned your wounds and bandaged them properly. Dolly kept trying to make me leave but I stayed."

Caroline stroked her thumb along John's chin. "You've been with me the entire time, haven't you?"

"Yes. How did you know?"

She opened her eyes and smiled at him. "I could smell you." Her smile grew broader.

"What is that supposed to mean?" John asked, sounding insulted and pleased in equal measures.

"I dreamt about bears, too, for a while." She twined their fingers together, smiling. "How long have I been asleep?"

"Two days, give or take. Yesterday morning, you were quite feverish and I had to track down Dolly to find Kyi for me. He came and, together, we re-cleaned the wounds and re-bandaged your shoulder."

"Thank you, my love." John drew in his breath at her words and kissed her on her mouth, her cheeks and her forehead, his light kisses tickling her.

"You were delirious for a while yesterday. You were calling for your children—and Henry." He spoke softly into her hair.

"I dreamt about them. They were happy. Henry told me to be happy." Tears began to roll down her cheeks.

"I'm sorry, so sorry, Caer. Don't cry. I shouldn't have mentioned it. It's okay. Don't cry." John brushed her hair aside, patting her in panic.

Sniffling, Caroline tried to control her breathing—each shuddering breath causing shocks of pain to shoot through her shoulder. "John. John! Come up here and sit on the bed." He obeyed her, perching on the edge of the bed, careful not to lean against her. His eyes were sad.

"Bear. My children came to say good-bye. They're happy, and Henry is there looking after them—Henry and Jesus—there aren't many better caregivers than that! I'm okay." Reaching up, she tried to pull him down for a kiss but with one arm bandaged across her chest and the other beneath her, she couldn't reach. Taking her groping hand, he bent down and kissed her warm, sleepy mouth.

"I'm thirsty," she said.

"You ole romantic, you." John chuckled as he rose. Caroline's half-lidded eyes trailed him as he crossed the room to pour a glass of water from a ceramic jug on a carved wooden stand. Returning, she noticed a change in his gait.

Considering his freer movement, she blurted out: "You're not limping anymore."

"Kyi fixed me up," he replied, blushing slightly. In response to her raised eyebrows, he stated, "yes, with a needle—very scary." He shivered at the memory.

Grinning, she encouraged him, "I'm sure you were very brave."

Shrugging, he stated, "That's what he said."

Yawning, she decided that this story could wait as sleep beckoned her away to a drowsy escape from discomfort.

Caroline dozed on and off throughout the day while John puttered around the cabin, always within range of her needs. At the noon meal, Simon, rather than Lwin, brought lunch.

"Is that Simon?" Caroline whispered to John, looking self-consciously down at her attire of bandages and boxer shorts.

Seeing her discomfiture, he retrieved a longyi for her as he explained, "That's Simon, but not the Simon who founded the community. That's how Dolly introduced him to me the first time." John shook his head wistfully at the memory.

John brought her an emerald green longyi patterned with deep pink hibiscus flowers that, after admiring the beauty of the pattern and softness of the cotton, she configured as a sari, covering her legs like a skirt and her shoulders like a shawl. John smiled as he helped her wrap the cloth around her.

Simon approached, dressed in a strange mixture of Burmese peasant and Indiana Jones: dark brown longyi, khaki shirt and "vest of many pockets". "Brother Phillip asked me to share lunch with you today. He thought you might enjoy a game of chess, John."

"All right," John agreed, putting a pair of socks and sneakers on Caroline's feet to keep her warm.

"Socks and shoes?" she marveled at him. "No more flip flops?" Smiling, John nodded.

The three ate their lunch together. Out of bed and sitting up for the first time since arriving, Caroline surveyed the room more carefully. It was a rectangular structure and she could see several lattice lined windows topping the walls. Caroline sat on a bench that lined the back wall of the building and the men moved a small table and two hard-backed chairs over to sit in front of the bench so they could all eat together. To the left, there was a low wall separating the bedroom area from the rest of the cabin. The bed consisted of a twin-sized bedroll on top of a bed frame very similar to those in Zeya's house. A clay basin sat on a stand against the wall near the head of the bed. On the right there was a more substantial chair fashioned from logs, looking like an overgrown muskoka chair and, beside it, a small bookcase containing a few old volumes.

Simon was a quiet fellow. He didn't seem the least bit curious about how these strangers had appeared in the jungle. He just sat, eating and humming to himself with his glasses perched on his head. John seemed content with the silence but Caroline felt that it wasn't very polite.

"Simon?" He nodded. "How long have you lived here?" she asked.

"Ah, let's see—it's been about six years now," he responded then went back to eating.

"What brought you here?" She tried again, ignoring John's frown.

"I'm an anthropologist. I came here to study the indigenous tribes, and in the process found the Lord who led me to Brother Phillip."

This time when she began to ask another question, John not only frowned, he put his hand on her knee and shook his head slightly. "Why?" She mouthed at him, smiling at Simon when he looked up. John gave one terse shake and narrowed his eyes. She stuck her tongue out at him surreptitiously.

"I'm going to have my afternoon nap. Enjoy your game, boys." She gently smacked John on the shoulder as she passed, the jolt causing her more pain than him she was sure. Leaving the two men to set up the chess board and pit their wits against each other, she returned to her bed. While she felt exhausted from her brief foray across the room, finding a comfortable position that did not somehow push or pull at the leopard injuries was difficult. After several minutes though, her need for sleep overpowered the dull pain that bubbled just below the surface of the painkillers Kyi had left for her. She fell asleep, propped on her left side. Caroline slept fitfully through the afternoon and early evening, waking from time to time to watch the men play before drifting into sleep again.

The game was still ongoing as supper time arrived and Caroline sensed the palpable intensity surrounding the game. Simon spoke little but the simple act of lowering his glasses to cover his eyes before each move, spoke volumes. He was a talented player who, aside from the descent and ascent of his eyewear gave little indication of his interest in the game while John, on the other hand, was intensely competitive and seemed determined to gain victory. Caroline got up to use the toilet, startled on her return journey by a foraging tapir lurching out of the shadows. Her hasty return was completely ignored by the men engrossed in their game. She sat on the bench between the men and was completely ignored. She said, "I'm hungry" and was completely ignored. She flicked over John's king and received plenty of attention. John grabbed her hand almost immediately while reprimanding her.

"So you remember my name, at least." Bemused by the men's intense concentration on the game, she suspected there was a little more than friendly competition going on. "I—am—hungry" she tried again. John held her gaze with a flat expression as Simon looked on quietly, studying the two engaged in a battle of wills, Simon's face taking on a look of pity, perhaps, and concern. Caroline kept her eyes locked on

John's as she retrieved her hand and reached across the board to upright the fallen king.

"What if you feed me first and then play?" When she offered the compromise, he released his breath on a laugh.
"You know," Caroline continued, "if I hadn't stopped that leopard and let it chew on me, it would be you sitting here begging for food." Caroline's gaze never faltered as a grin pulled at John's mouth.

His eyes softened as he asked her, "What would you like to eat?"

Caroline thought about this for a few minutes. "Leopard." John's grin broadened and a sharp laugh escaped Simon's lips. Caroline finally had the chance to make her joke.

"I ate the python that tried to eat me, now I'd like to eat the leopard that tried to eat me." John laughed heartily at her joke, squeezing her free hand in affection.

"You were attacked by a python?" Simon inquired.

"Attacked?" John exclaimed. "By the time I arrived, it was nothing but a smear on the jungle floor."

John asked Simon to fetch supper, leaving Caroline briefly puzzled by the enigmatic look he shot at John before he left. Returning some time later with leopard steaks, noodles and greens, the three ate together. The food was an odd assortment of spices and sauces but such a change from their jungle fair that each bite sent waves of pleasure across Caroline's palate. Unfortunately, though, the meal was chased down with green tea. However, fortunately, Simon provided cane sugar.

"Sugar!" Caroline effused. "Heavenly sugar!" Simon appeared confused by her reaction but John smiled broadly, adding another teaspoonful to her tea. Once the dishes were cleared away, the men resumed their game. Caroline soon became bored and went back to sleep, waking later when John came to check on her in the darkening of early night. He pulled a chair to her bedside and sat on it.

"Mmm. Who won?" Caroline murmured, her eyes still flickering closed more often than open.

"Yours truly," he responded, proudly.

She looked at him and smiled. "Congrats! It's nice not to have to build a shelter tonight, isn't it?"

"Or trap supper."

"Or trudge through the damp grass."

"Or be eaten alive by insects."

"Or walk and walk and walk and walk," Caroline concluded.

"Caer?" he changed the subject. "We need to talk about our cover story."

She frowned, coming more awake. "What do you mean?" she asked.

"I don't know how long we're going to need to stay here but we have to be prepared for the fact that it may be a while. Fortunately, it's quite remote and certainly off the beaten track. I'm confident that this is the place that Maryn Dale uses as a stopover on her journeys between India and China. Maryn will help us get passports and visas so we can get out of Burma. This is a good place to hide."

"Maybe these people can help us. They must know Maryn if she comes here," she inquired.

"We can't let these people know why we're here. It would only put them in danger." John stated flatly.

She considered his words, sensing that there was more to this than he was telling her. "These are good people. They saved us. They saved me. Why can't we trust a few of them?" She had always tried to be honest and she didn't like the idea of lying to anyone.

"It's just not safe for them to know who we are. What if an official from the prison were to hear of our location? Technically, we're escaped prisoners." He waited while that idea sank in.

Caroline held his gaze with a doubtful expression. "Are you being honest with me or trying to frighten me so I'll do what you tell me to?" John looked startled and began to stammer a response. Caroline reached over and touched his leg. "Just be honest with me, my Bear."

John stopped and looked at her fondly, sighing as he kissed the tip of her nose. "I don't trust these people and I'm not willing to risk your safety or the people in my network on their discretion. They're an odd assortment of castaways and rejects and there doesn't seem to be any monitoring of who comes and goes. It would be simple for a government informant to blend right in with the group. Burma is not a country where havens remain safe for long." John waited for her response.

"Thank you for being honest with me." She touched his hand. "I don't want to lie."

"Then let's decide on something that we can agree on."

They agreed that the best story was that they were friends travelling to Singapore who had been brought to Myanmar on an emergency stopover because of mechanical difficulties. They had then been caught up in a freedom rally and were escaping north.

"The easiest way to lie is to include as much of the truth as possible," John explained.

"That isn't exactly my goal in life, you know, to find the 'best way' to lie." Caroline looked at him with a wry expression.

"If you don't want to lie, then just don't offer information. Answer only the questions asked or ask the interrogator a question—that's an old spy's trick."

"A trick for old spies or a trick from ages past?" she asked, grinning.

"Very funny." He shook his head in mock disgust at her pun. "I need to find out when Maryn is coming through next. She should be able to help us get out of here. I think there is someone in the village that is her contact but, so far, I haven't had time to work out who it is."

"Can we just melt into village life for now?"

"Yes. That's probably for the best but Caroline, you mustn't tell anyone about who we really are or who Maryn Dale is." She agreed.

"John," she began tentatively. He nodded, and she continued, "Do you think it'd be okay if—well, I'm cold but—just until I fall asleep—" Rising, John slipped into the bed on top of the covers, wrapping his arm carefully across Caroline's waist and breathing into her hair. Sighing contentedly, she laced the fingers of her left hand through his right where it lay across her belly. She murmured, "Thanks for looking after me. I love you."

John pulled her close at her words. "I'm still not used to that," he whispered into her hair.

As they snuggled together, they both knew they wanted more than just warmth from each other but they were each willing to wait, for better or worse, John trusting Caroline and Caroline trusting God's plan for love.

CHAPTER 11

PROXIMITY

While Caroline was convalescing, Kyi visited her regularly, checking on her injuries and answering any questions John had about her care. Caroline smiled fondly at how seriously John took his role as her nurse. Dolly charged in from time to time, bossing John around and always leaving Caroline feeling that she'd been speaking to a very loud, southern cyclone. Brother Phillip even came to visit one evening. He announced his presence with a knock on the door and a confident, "God's blessings on you, children." Entering the cabin, his bright, intelligent eyes scanned the room slowly, not afraid to let his visitors know he was studying them. Brother Phillip looked to be about eighty years old but could easily have been anywhere from sixty to a hundred. His stooped frame supported a full head of snow white hair and the brightest blue eyes Caroline had ever seen. He wore a black suit and a minister's collar. Asking John to pull over the log chair, Brother Phillip sat beside Caroline, humming a familiar tune.

"That's my favourite song," Caroline commented. "It makes me think of Job and how, through all his struggles, he knew that God was with him; that bad times don't imply abandonment. '…When sorrows like sea billows roll, whatever my lot…It is well, it is well with my soul.' I'm glad I had that idea firmly in my head from adolescence. Otherwise, I'm not sure how I would have survived." Her eyes still misted with the memories of the end of her first life.

"My child," Brother Phillip observed, perceptively. "You have known pain."

"Yes," she replied. "But I have also known joy." Following Brother Phillip's gaze over to John she was surprised to see him blush slightly and look away. *John's usually much better at going unnoticed when he wants to be. His spy radar is obviously on a low setting tonight,* she mused.

"Life is full of joy and pain. What brought you yours?" Brother Phillip asked, looking back over at Caroline.

"My husband and my children were killed in a bush plane accident three years ago. When I tried to move into a new life, a second life, I ended up here—" John dropped something and when Caroline looked over to him, he shook his head vigorously in her direction, reminding her not to give away too much information. "But my joy is also my children—and John." Caroline glanced over at John again to see him, perfectly still, watching her. She flashed him a reassuring grin.

"What brought you to the Katafygio, Brother Phillip?" she asked, honouring John's instructions to avoid telling too much.

Unexpectedly, he replied, "Burma is quite beautiful." Brother Phillip's gaze looked far away, seeming to focus on the clouds visible beyond the monkeys playing in the trees at the edge of the jungle. "I know they call it Myanmar now but it will always be Burma to me. I was a missionary in China in my younger days, before Mao rose to power, but my heart drew me to Burma. It holds the beauty of a diamond, clean and bright but with many facets. It is a beautiful glass, reflecting the things of this earth, but fractured by pain. My children were born here and some of them are buried here. My wife is buried here, also." Caroline noticed that John was still watching them.

"Where are your other children, now?" Caroline asked.

"My daughter and her husband are working in Hong Kong under the Methodist Church of Great Britain. My son is working with the Inuit in Northern Canada. As John Wesley once gave the great call to all Christians, so do my children obey. You know that call, do you not?" he asked and when Caroline shook her head, he quoted, "Do all the good you can, by all the means you can, in all the ways you can, in all the places you can, at all the times you can, to all the people you can, as long as ever you can." He paused. "My son is planning to be married next year. He wants me to come to the wedding but, aside from the obvious logistical problems of traveling in Burma, I'm not certain these old bones would enjoy a trip like that."

"That's lovely," Caroline asserted quickly, trying to keep up with Brother Phillip's abrupt topic shifts.

"This is my son's second marriage. Charles' first wife died of an aneurysm after their second year of marriage. It was very sad. He loved her so much that I didn't think he would ever find anyone else with whom to share his life."

"How does he deal with the love of two—um—wives in his heart?" Caroline asked, her eyes intense.

"Interesting that you should ask me that. I asked him the same question. You see, I never had the privilege of finding a second love, so my heart is full of the sorrow of past joy. My son told me that the great love he has for his first wife, Sharon, helps him to love his second wife, Tallini, even more."

"Does it bother his second wife—um, Tallini—that she is not Charles' first love?" Caroline asked.

"I admit that I also asked him that. Her name means 'snow angels'." Brother Phillip's gaze drifted far away, again. "Charles says that she is able to recognize that the love he felt—still feels—for Sharon only makes his love for her stronger because he understands what true love is all about."

"What is she like, Tallini? Have you met her?" Caroline was desperately trying to process the information and come up with appropriate questions.

"Charles says she is strong but gentle," he replied, studying the gold band still firmly lodged on his left hand.

"Where do they live in Nunavut? What do they do there?" Caroline inquired, enjoying even this small connection with home, the 'true north, strong and free'.

"Tallini is a nurse practitioner in their village on Baffin Island. You see, the people there have access to a doctor or dentist for only a couple of weeks in the year. The rest of the time, she provides most medical care needed or they must be flown south for treatment she is unable to give." He paused, looking at Caroline again. "My wife would have loved her, I believe. She loved women who were as strong as they needed to be. She had no time for vapid women who fainted at the least obstacle. However, she also had no patience for women without compassion. She always said that God gave women a wounded heart and men the employment of guarding it."

As Caroline pondered these words, she inquired, "What does your son do? How did they meet?"

Smiling, Brother Phillip replied, "They found each other through the meeting of minds and hearts of compassion. Charles is a teacher. He and Sharon had planned to teach in Nunavut, knowing that there were few of their colleagues willing to live in the frigid north. Charles decided to follow the call in spite of his loss. Their desire to help the children of winter brought Charles and Tallini together over and over until they realized that had each found a—hmmm—how could

I describe it?" He mused, tapping his chin as he pondered the thought.

"A kindred spirit?" Caroline proposed.

"A kindred—what?" Brother Phillip puzzled.

"It's from a Canadian classic, 'Anne of Green Gables' by LM Montgomery. A 'kindred spirit' is a best friend, but more than that. A friendship loyally bound by the meeting of minds and passionate affection; someone who thinks and feels the same way you do." Caroline looked triumphant at her definition. Glancing over at John, she saw him smiling fondly at her.

"Yes, daughter, that explains it perfectly!" Brother Phillip smiled broadly and slapped the arm of his chair.

Caroline swung the conversation back to China and Brother Phillip's work there, deciding that if he didn't have to maintain a logical flow of conversation then neither did she. As they spoke, she began to see that, although he had an eccentric approach to communication, he was a deeply insightful man and she began to suspect that his disarming nature was a tool for seeing into the hearts of those around him. She began to sense the gentle strength within him, reaching out, in spite of his own personal pain, to the hurting of the world.

When Caroline began to yawn, John insisted she be allowed to rest and firmly escorted Brother Phillip to the door. Clasping the younger man on the shoulder, Brother Phillip thanked John for his hospitality and left him stunned with the comment, "You are a wonderful man to have captured the heart of such a deeply committed Christian woman."

Caroline pulled John from his reverie by calling his name.

John startled at her voice, asking, "Why would he say that? He was visiting with you."

"He was studying you, I think," she replied, grinning that there was one person in the world at least that could set John off-balance.

Shaking his head in wonder, he checked in with Caroline, "How are you feeling?"

"Tired but I'm getting better. When do you think Kyi will let me out of this cabin?"

Walking over to the bed, John sat on the edge, leaning down to kiss her on the forehead. "We'll ask him tomorrow. I'd like to go for a walk. Will you be all right if I go out?" In response to her nod, he leaned down to kiss her cheek but she pulled his head to her mouth instead, kissing him deeply. "Hmmm, maybe I'll just keep you here forever," he decided. Smiling, Caroline bid him good night.

One more day confined to the cabin and then Kyi gave her his seal of health. Finally, Caroline ventured out into the life of the community. She was intrigued by the people she had met and was incredibly curious to meet the others and hear their stories.

The community consisted of a ring of houses all built after the fashion of a Canadian log cabin, complete with chimney and front porch. Within the ring of houses was a cleared area made to look like a village square with a pavilion at one end filled with chairs, chalkboard and desks. In addition, there was another covered area which contained a large hearth and cooking area. A stone well was evident beside the cooking area. The impression, though, was always that, as much as they attempted to maintain a clear area for living, the jungle encroached, threatening to take over and smother all traces of the community.

The community was the buildings but the Katafygio was so much more. It was an international mixing bowl. There were Canadians, Americans, Australians, Indians, Koreans, Chinese, and Burmese nationals including some from the Chin tribe and several from the indigenous Karen tribe. They had each come to the Community to escape something, but had stayed because of what they found.

Kyi was a doctor placed on an arrest list for refusing to give an abortion to a government official's mistress. Dolly had been a travelling evangelist in the southern United States who had come to Burma after watching a documentary on television about the religious division within the country. Simon was an anthropologist studying the indigenous tribes of Myanmar who had become disillusioned by professional pressure to suppress information that didn't support the current trends. Aayushi was a widow who had been outcast when she refused the supposedly abandoned practice of suttee, the burning of a widow on her husband's funeral pyre. Eijaz was a young man who had run away from his family at sixteen years of age when they arranged a marriage for him with a fifty year old widow whose children were older than he. The illuminating stories went on and on to cover each of the nearly two hundred people there. The residents of Brother Phillip's Haven of Rest, the Katafygio, had many stories and had travelled on many journeys, but they all felt that God had led them here.

Brother Phillip, Dolly and Archie were the unofficial leaders of the group. They attempted to live according to the ideals of the early Christian church. Those who could work worked cooperatively. Those who couldn't work helped in other ways, through organization, encouragement and prayer. Everyone shared what they had, not because it was the rule but because it was what Jesus would have done. Newcomers were welcomed into the Community. Brother Phillip said that part of the reason he had founded the community where he did was so that he could be sure that anyone who found it was surely led here by God.

For some reason John couldn't explain, Brother Phillip had taken an interest in him and came for him twice daily to walk around the village beneath the canopy of the coconut palms amidst the chattering of the Leaf Monkeys as they feasted in the trees, or perched on the roofs of the houses. More than once, John amused Caroline by telling her of one villager or another plotting the downfall of the pesky primates after some misadventure involving the mischievous creatures. One feud in particular, which had been ongoing for longer than anyone really knew, was between a rather timid older lady, Lwin, and a notable Leaf Monkey, known by the scalloped tear on his left ear. No one was willing to speculate on whether Lwin had caused the monkey's injury or not. Apparently, one day while Lwin was hanging her laundry out to dry, the monkey leapt down from a tree, grabbing Lwin's bloomers and swinging away. Curious about the bowl-shaped cloth, the monkey pulled them over its head and spent the afternoon dancing about on the roof of Brother Phillip's cabin, sporting the bloomers as a hat.

John, however, preferred the walks in the misty morning air, he said, when the monkeys with their black mohawks and white sideburns were quieter, to the afternoon walks which were filled with the cacophony of competing birds and animals and which were still regularly accompanied by rain. Brother Phillip was undeterred by the weather though, merely popping out his collapsible umbrella and donning his bright yellow rubber boots, his 'wellys', as John called them. John was intrigued by this old man and his ability to see to the heart of the world.

Not invited on the daily walks, Caroline began taking an interest in the running of the community. She began accepting chores, much to John's annoyance.

"You're hardly out of bed and you're accepting chores. You need to rest," he chided her.

"Kyi gave me a sling to wear and he says the wounds are healing well. He even gave me some exercises to help the muscles knit properly and to maintain range of motion in my shoulder and elbow. I'm okay," she reassured him.

"It's not just that. Once Maryn arrives, we'll need to depart quickly. How are you going to do that if you're so wrapped up in the people here?" John pressed her for an answer but the excitement of being with Christian brothers and sisters again; being with people of like minds; was so enchanting that Caroline chose to ignore the signals behind John's eyes.

Caroline made an immediate connection with a few people in the Community. She began spending more and more time with Simon and with Kyi's wife, Thuza. She also found that, although Dolly seemed the polar opposite of someone she would usually seek as a friend there was a level on which they connected perfectly. Caroline took to chattering away at John, telling him the stories of the villagers.

John reluctantly helped Caroline move in with Dolly who had one of the larger houses in the village while he remained in the guest house.

"I don't understand why you're doing this," John stated, pouting.

"We can't just live together," she replied.

"We're not doing anything we're not supposed to be doing."

"I know that and you know that but what will everyone else think?"

"Maybe it's none of their business." His voice had taken on a surly quality which Caroline found quite irritating.

"What is the real problem, here, John?" she asked, tensely.

"Nothing, just go."

Hurt by his words, she slowly turned away, answering with a tearful, "Okay." Before she turned fully away, he was there with his arms around her.

"I'm sorry, Caer. I'll miss you." He pulled her close.

"John. Can I tell you something?" He nodded. Whispering directly into his ear, she stated, "I don't want to move out, but I think it will confuse people if I stay. I'll miss you, too." Reaching up, she spread her fingers into his hair and pulled his head down for an intense kiss. "Okay?"

"I think I need another kiss, first." She smiled as she kissed him again.

Caroline noticed that, unlike her engagement in the community, John held himself back, following his habit of personal disengagement. Simon attempted to engage in regular chess games with John but was finding him more and more indifferent to the idea. Although John maintained an attitude of deep gratitude toward Kyi, aside from his daily walks with Brother Phillip, John kept himself out of the social loop, spending his free time either with Caroline or alone, trying to fix Captain Li's rifle. Brother Phillip was the only person in the community, aside from Caroline, who could draw him into a conversation that consisted of more than one word responses. His one consistent social exercise was to remind Caroline that they were waiting for Maryn Dale and then they would depart.

Life quickly fell into a routine for the sojourners. Their mornings began at sunrise with John knocking on Dolly's door and dragging Caroline into wakefulness from her preferred morning activity—sleep. They fetched water from the communal well and usually prepared breakfast together, fending off the early morning chill with coffee when they could get it and tea when they couldn't. After this, they would exercise in the thick verdure surrounding the village, wearing a path through the undergrowth and dodging the chattering monkeys, hares, squirrels and, particularly, the thorny Lynx Spiders which Caroline insisted were quite 'creepy'. This was John's favourite time of the day. Caroline helped John with sit-ups and push-ups and John helped her with her stretches, improving the strength and flexibility of the leopard-chewed shoulder, and holding her when tears of frustration and pain threatened to overwhelm her.

Upon their return, Brother Phillip would take John for a walk around the village, telling him of the spiritual journeys of the residents. During this time, Caroline would help with any chore Dolly assigned her, though she avoided anything that brought her into direct contact with the children. Since the plane crash, Caroline rarely sought out interactions with children and, though they still seemed to be drawn to her, she held herself at a distance, meeting their interest with dispassion. After spending the first half of her life working with, and raising children, she had been surprised by her heart's reaction, suspecting that this wound would never heal completely. That was one reason why the mission school had seemed like such a good idea. It would have allowed her to use her professional skills and training, but kept her at a distance from the children themselves. Caroline enjoyed it most when she was asked to help Simon in the adult literacy, history and mathematics classes in the village school. When John went looking for her each day, he often found her in deep discussions with Simon in the 'classroom'. Caroline was so enjoying the challenge of Simon's deep theological mind, that she hadn't yet noticed John's increasingly dark eyes when he came upon them.

After lunch, everyone in the village would head indoors for fellowship and Bible study. Brother Phillip had given John a Bible and Caroline had borrowed an extra of Dolly's. Caroline felt bathed in grace as she sat debating amongst her Christian brothers and sisters, recovering from the weeks and months since she had left Canada—a time when she had had so little fellowship and support. *No,* she told herself, *I had short times of sweet fellowship with Pastor Paul and Father Rory. I watched John give his heart to God. And I can't forget the way God has comforted and protected us.*

As Caroline enwrapped herself in the community, she was spending less and less time with John. She had noticed that he was becoming more and more surly with the members of the community, particularly with Simon whom he accused of being a 'prig', whatever that was. Baptism, the Trinity,

Nephilim—John clearly hated these discussions and Caroline had taken to ending them whenever he was near. She assumed his surliness was due to his frustration with the length of time that was passing as they waited for Maryn Dale to arrive. "I wish we'd never come," she heard him muttering more and more frequently.

One afternoon, about two weeks after John and Caroline had arrived in Katafygio, Nanda and Myaing returned from a 'walkabout' with news. Caroline commented to John one day that they reminded her of the Aborigines in Australia and their intense love of the land that called them from any idleness. Upon their return, the twins had sought Brother Phillip who happened to be having afternoon tea in the pavilion with Simon and Caroline. The trio was discussing ways to explain Jesus' sacrifice to the various indigenous tribes in terms they could understand: considering how the Karen had interpreted the appearance of western missionaries as a fulfillment of a prophecy indicating that God would send them a written language.

"Greetings brothers and sister, we return bearing dire news. As we passed through the eastern river valley, we observed five gunmen crossing the north in a western direction, stopping in each community they come across," Myaing explained.

Simon responded, "Guns mean they are either military, indigenous rebels or drug traffickers."

"They were not part of the Karen resistance and they wore no uniforms." Myaing said.

Brother Phillip wore an expression of concern. "When will they reach us?" he asked.

"Two days, three at the most," said Nanda.

"The local military are very interested in subduing the drug trade across the north. Could we select a small group to travel to Lon Ton and alert them of the presence of these men?" Simon inquired.

"Hmmm." Brother Phillip was deep in thought. "By the time the military arrived, these men would be long gone. We would need a plan to keep them here for a time without giving them the impression that we wanted them to remain for the long term."

"Perhaps John could help?" Caroline interjected, suddenly excited.

"John?" Simon responded skeptically.

Adopting an insightful look, Brother Phillip turned to Caroline, saying, "I believe you are right, daughter. Would you perhaps be willing to ask his advice?"

"Sure," Caroline agreed.

Simon continued to look doubtful. The glasses perched on his head made him look like he had an extra set of skeptical eyes. "I'd better come with you," he advised. Caroline shrugged as she stood, heading toward the guest hut.

Brother Phillip, Nanda and Myaing remained at the table, thinking in silence together.

Entering the hut, Caroline called out as John emerged through the side door carrying the broken rifle.

"Any luck?" Simon asked, sardonically.

John narrowed his eyes, not responding to Simon's sarcastic question.

"Hi." Caroline greeted John brightly as he flashed a brief smile.

"Caroline and I were hoping to ask you a question, John." As he spoke, Simon put his arm around Caroline. She gave him a funny look at the assumed intimacy of the gesture and, doing so, missed the fire in John's eyes. Slipping out from under Simon's arm, Caroline turned and asked him to fetch a map that they could study. As Simon departed, Caroline moved over to John, sliding her arms around his middle and resting against him. Unable to resist her proximity, he held her.

"It feels like it's been days since I've just held you," she murmured into his chest.

"It has been." He bent down to capture her mouth as she looked up inquisitively. One kiss led to another until Caroline's hair was messy from his fingers combing through it and her head was spinning from the urgency of John's need for reassurance. Breathless and slightly stunned by the intensity of emotion rebounding between them, Caroline pulled back, framing his face with her hands and smiling.

"Hello, my Bear."

Smiling tenderly, he brushed the hair back from her face, replying, "Hello Beauty."

Drawing him to the table, Caroline sat with John beside her as Simon entered carrying a map. Caroline noticed the palpable change in the atmosphere in the room at Simon's return but assumed that the change was related to the topic that needed to be discussed.

"Now, John, Caroline tells me that you may be able to help us a little with our current dilemma," Simon began, pulling his glasses down to cover his eyes. John's jaw clenched as Simon continued speaking. "Nanda and Myaing have reported that there are five gunmen, very likely drug traffickers, travelling this way. We plan to send a delegation to Lon Ton, the nearest town with a police force, to inform them of the trafficker's presence. The local police are very hard on drug traffickers even if the SLORC are not. We need some advice on how to slow their progress in order to give the police time to track them and, hopefully, catch them." Simon stopped for a moment. "I'm not certain what you can do to help but, since Caroline asked me to come, I wanted to give you the opportunity to assist us."

John picked up his rifle and began to clean the firing mechanism. "You're right," he said, eyes fixed on the gun. "I can't help you."

"Oh well. Thank you anyway." Simon rose to leave. "Come on, Caroline." He reached a hand toward her.

Caroline studied John for a moment. Not looking up, she dismissed Simon. "I'll see you later, Simon." Simon stood for a moment, waiting for her to look up, but when she didn't, he turned slowly and left.

Reaching out to touch his knee, Caroline spoke softly, "John—Bear—what's wrong? Are you okay?" In response to his unconvincing "fine", Caroline knelt beside him, staring intently at his face, both hands on his thigh and waited, "My love, what's wrong?"

Tenderness on his face, John shifted his gaze to meet her eyes. "How could anything be wrong when you're near me?" he asked.

"I love you," she declared affectionately, pulling his head down for a kiss. Setting aside the rifle, John held her close, sighing in pleasure.

"Do you have any ideas?" she asked tentatively.

Sighing again, this time in mild frustration, he replied. "Caroline, we are only here to wait for Maryn and a way out of Burma. We're not here to save these people."

"John," she repeated, softly.

"This is northern Burma, drug lords go with the territory. As long as the SLORC entertains the money they bring, the traffickers will use the political chaos in this region to its advantage. It's simply a fact of life."

"Simon says that there's a drug lord who enslaved one Karen village on the border with China by kidnapping the children and forcing the men and women to farm poppies for heroin as a ransom for the children. In the end, most of the children died of cholera anyway because of the poor conditions in which they were held. If this is the same group, shouldn't we do something about it?" she entreated.

Responding to her obvious distress, he kissed her on the forehead. "Caer, what will happen if the police find us here?"

Forged in the Jungles of Burma

She startled at his words. "What do you mean?"

"If the police find two unregistered foreigners here, they are going to be curious. Their curiosity will lead to a report which will lead to Military Intelligence which will lead to Shing." He paused for effect. "How many people will die then?"

Quietly, she asked. "Are we really more important than these people?" His eyes widened at her response. "Please help them John."

The silence stretched out until, slowly, he nodded. "All right."

John and Caroline went in search of Brother Phillip, finding him on the porch of his house conferring with Dolly, Archie and Nanda.

"Greetings, son," Brother Phillip called out happily as John approached with Caroline in tow. "Have you come to assist us in our time of need? Caroline seemed certain that you could help." Brother Phillip nodded at Caroline as he said her name.

Looking pleased at the fact that Caroline had praised him to the others, John seemed to renew his determination to help. Filling John in on the information available, Brother Phillip asked, "What would you recommend, John? How can we slow their progress so the police can arrive in time?"

"My plan does not involve keeping the traffickers here longer but rather sending them somewhere else where the police can meet them and hopefully arrest them. In Naungpin, there lives a retired major from Military Intelligence who is known to be corrupt and is suspected to be involved in a drug route through the north from China. If we suggest to these drug scouts that perhaps he has already offered us a deal to grow poppies, they will immediately head to Naungpin to discover if this is true. Suspicion breeds suspicion and I'm betting that, whatever his answer, their boss will suspect it could be true. If the police travel to Naungpin and arrive first, they can apprehend the five traffickers observed by Nanda and Myaing."

Eyes crinkling in a smile, Brother Phillip congenially smacked John on the shoulder, "You are brilliant, my friend, simply brilliant. Who would pass on this information to the traffickers and who would travel to Lon Ton?"

Before John could present his well-rehearsed reason why he and Caroline should not be involved, Archie responded, "I'll do it. I'll talk to the traffickers. Just tell me what to say." Two Burmese villagers John didn't know agreed to deliver the message to the police in Lon Ton and left immediately. John remained with Archie and the others as they spent the next hour planning and rehearsing. Dolly suggested that the majority of the villagers be removed to the secret hiding spot long ago prepared for emergencies but John suggested that it would be more dangerous than carrying on as normal. The trick was to merely suggest the idea and allow the men to jump to conclusions rather than let them feel they were being manipulated.

That evening, as John and Caroline sat at the edge of the trees watching the stars, Caroline asked, "How did you know there was a retired major in Naungpin?"

"You do remember what I do for a living, don't you?" John teased.

"Thank you for helping them." She nudged him with her shoulder.

"You're welcome." He pulled her against him and held her tightly.

Two days later, the five armed men arrived in Katafygio. True to form, they demanded hospitality, a very powerful tool in Burmese culture. Archie joined the men in the evening as they sat around the fire drinking a foul smelling alcohol, probably home brewed, from their flasks. He played his part beautifully, a tribute to the hours John had spent coaching him. In the morning, the armed men departed, heading for Naungpin.

A mini-celebration was held that night with John as the guest of honour, much to his chagrin. Caroline stood proudly by his side and in the morning, life returned to normal—well, normal for a community of outcasts and refugees escaping persecution in a hidden mountain valley in northern Burma.

<><><><><>

The next morning, Brother Phillip found John for their walk. He was determined to get behind the man's shield. Having seen the goodness and strength John demonstrated over the drugs issue, Brother Phillip was convinced the shield hid a brilliant and loving man. He had seen how John looked at Caroline and knew that there was more hidden within him than beneath the waves over a coral reef. To this point in their relationship, Brother Phillip had avoided asking John questions, using their time together to expound on the scriptures studied during Bible study. He spoke about his own life and how those verses had impacted the way he lived. Today he was determined to get to the root of John's impenetrability. Introducing a discussion of biblical families including Abraham and David, Brother Phillip asked,

"John, how would you describe your relationship with your father?" John froze. His eyes narrowed, he turned on his heel and strode away without a word.

"John?" Brother Phillip called after him. *Father, help that poor boy,* he prayed. *And help poor Caroline when he reaches her. Grant her wisdom.*

Caroline was deep in conversation with Simon when John strode over. As John approached, Simon's face became pensive and he reached over to get Caroline's attention by resting his hand on her arm.

Without warning, John firmly grasped her elbow. "Come with me," he ordered.

"What?" she gasped in surprise. "What do you think you're doing?" Becoming angry, Caroline pulled her arm from John's grasp. Simon stood to intervene.

John rounded on Simon, grasping his shirt and warning him, "Back off." He ground the words out, teeth clenched.

Caroline grabbed John's shoulder and tried to pull him back from Simon. She could see that his face and ears were flaming red and his jaw was tightly clenched. Her real concern, however, was the violent tapping of his fingers against his thigh. "John, leave him alone! Stop it!" She'd never seen John in quite this state before. He looked like he was going to lose control—but at whom, and for what reason?

Releasing Simon's shirt, John swung around and took hold of Caroline's arm again. "Come with me," he ordered again.

She dug in her heels again and retrieved her arm. "John. Stop!" Swallowing her anger and calming her voice, she sought to calm John. "I *will* come with you if you will just *calm down*." *Father, grant me wisdom,* she prayed. John held her gaze and nodded tersely. She breathed a sigh of relief.

Simon intervened. "I don't think you should go with him." He glanced at Caroline then kept his eyes on John. John began to redden again and Caroline thought he was going to plaster Simon.

She turned to Simon and set her hand on his arm. "It's okay, Simon, I'll be fine."

"Caroline." Simon covered her hand. "I don't think it's safe for you to go with him. Let me get some help." John took a step closer to Simon but Caroline braced her arm against his chest and stopped him.

"Simon. John won't hurt me. He's upset and he needs me." Her words had a strange effect on John and he seemed to calm before her eyes. Turning, he walked toward the guesthouse. As she moved to follow John, Simon held her hand tightly.

"Simon. Let me go." John turned swiftly at her words and punched Simon in the face. Caroline watched in shock as Simon dropped to the ground, his glasses spinning through the air and landing akimbo several feet away. John stood, shaking with visible effort as he restrained the urge to follow up his punch with another. People came running from every direction. Kyi ran up and sent Nanda off to get his medical bag. Some others crowded around Simon casting disparaging looks at John and pouring sympathy on Simon.

Brother Phillip approached with a sorrowful look in his eyes. John jumped when the older man placed his hand on his shoulder.

"Son, why don't we go talk," Brother Phillip said, softly.

Caroline stopped them as they turned to go, tears filling her eyes. "I'll go with him," she said to Brother Phillip and, taking John's hand, she walked with him back to the guesthouse.

<><><><><>

As John and Caroline exited the scene, the people in attendance turned to Brother Phillip, demanding justice.

"Look at that. We bring them in and shelter them and this is the way they repay us."

"They should be expelled. We don't allow any violent behaviour."

"Not the woman. She didn't do anything. That man is half crazy."

The comments flew back and forth over Simon as Kyi tended to him. Once Simon was standing again and the blood flowing from his nose had ceased, Brother Phillip called for silence.

"Brothers and sisters, quiet please." *How quickly we forget!* "We must not condemn John out of hand. He was a good friend, helping us with the drug traffickers." Reprimanding the crowd, Brother Phillip turned to Simon. "Simon please tell us what happened," and to the clamouring crowd, "with no interruptions!"

Simon began. "I was speaking with Caroline. We were discussing the debate over Baptism, infant versus adult; the age of consent; immersion as opposed to sprinkling. She made a very good point about the importance that Jesus placed on children and their ability to serve God...."

Brother Phillip interrupted him. "I'm certain it was a very interesting discussion, but we really need to know the events." Simon turned to Brother Phillip and apologized.

"I noticed that John was walking toward us with a violent look in his eyes."

Brother Phillip gently admonished him, "Tell us the facts, Simon, don't make judgments."

Simon nodded, "John was walking toward us with a very determined stride and his face was set in a grim look. Once he approached us, he grabbed Caroline by the arm. She resisted and I tried to intervene. Then he punched me." There was much murmuring from the crowd until Brother Phillip silenced them again.

"Did Caroline seem afraid?"

Simon thought about this for a moment, reddening at the implication. "No. In fact, she assured me that John would never hurt her." Simon looked down at his hands. Brother Phillip patted the younger man's shoulder.

"I'm certain you only meant to help but anyone who saw John when Caroline was injured must know that he cares for her very much. It is my opinion that he is a man with a deep hurt and that she is his one lifeline to the joy of the Lord." He turned to the crowd and remarked, "I believe this outburst, in fact, is my fault. Please, all of you forgive me." He looked directly into the eyes of each person in the crowd and waited for their nod or response before moving on to the next.

"I think we will let this matter rest now. Agreed?" Brother Phillip waited until all in the crowd had assented before moving away toward John's cabin.

<><><><><>

As they entered the guest hut, Caroline's tears of humiliation burst forth. Stumbling over to the bench, she sat weeping, her fists squeezed against her eyes. Standing determinedly by the door, John remained frozen in place as Caroline's tears flowed in streams down her cheeks until, head bowed in resignation, he walked to her side, kneeling before her.

"What was that all about?!" she shouted through her tears. "I don't know whether I feel more humiliated or angry?—or both with a dollop of pure fury added in."

John stood again, his anger held in check. "I'm not the one who broke their word." He spoke evenly, belying the ire in his words.

Caroline rose to her feet at his words, her brow furrowed. "What are you talking about?"

John responded frostily, "*I* didn't discuss *your* personal life with the people here."

Caroline found his cold blooded accusations more infuriating than his violent outburst. "I—have—not—discussed—you—with—anyone. Why would I?" She emphasized each word by poking him in the chest and finished by turning her back on him. But, before she turned, she saw in his eyes the hurt he felt at her dismissal.

"How would I know? Perhaps, Simon—" His angry words were cut off by a cough at the door. They looked over to see Brother Phillip standing inside the doorway.

"I knocked," he began, "but I don't think you heard me." Caroline was embarrassed to think this gentle man had heard them arguing. "I believe this grievous situation is my fault."

Caroline looked surprised as John remonstrated to reassure the old man. "No, Brother Phillip, it's not your fault." Caroline watched the interaction in surprise. "It's not your fault," John repeated.

"The young lady did not tell me anything about your past life, son. I have never asked her. I merely wanted to understand you better and help you understand yourself." Brother Phillip bowed his head. "I'm sorry for the grief I've caused."

John walked over and put his hand on the older man's shoulder. "No, it's my fault," said John. "I jumped to the wrong conclusion. I'm sorry."

"John!" Caroline exclaimed. "Your apology is very nice but what is this all about?"

"I asked John about his relationship with his father," Brother Phillip said simply.

"Ahhh." Now Caroline understood. "John. I haven't told anyone anything you've told me in confidence." She spoke softly, walking over to the two men. "I thought you knew that." She finished sadly and began to exit the guesthouse. John reached for her.

"Caer," he whispered. "I'm sorry." He drew her into a hug and she held him.

Brother Phillip began to shift from foot to foot, obviously embarrassed to be caught in the middle of this emotional scene. "I will leave you now," he announced.

"How's Simon?" Caroline asked innocently. John stiffened beside her and she turned to him with a questioning look.

Brother Phillip, noticing John's body language, reached out and patted her cheek. "Simon is fine, my dear, but you need to speak with John."

"John, what is going on?" Turning to John, Caroline asked, perplexed, "Speaking of Simon, if you were angry with me, what on earth possessed you to punch *him*?"

"Oh, I don't know," John answered sarcastically, "maybe because you spend all your time either with him or talking about him." Then more quietly, eyes down. "You've even started rooting for him against me during chess games."

Caroline was shocked. "Is that why you stopped playing? You're jealous?" John reddened at the accusation.

"Mmmhmm. I believe I will leave this discussion to you." Brother Phillip turned to exit the cabin.

"Brother," John began. "I am truly sorry for the disturbance I've caused." Shaking her head in dismay, Caroline stepped away from the men, sitting back down on the bench at the back of the room.

"Son," Brother Phillip again placed his hand on John's shoulder as he gripped his other hand. "You need to decide. You're trying to live in two worlds. You want God's help but you also want to live in your old ways. You want to be trusted but refuse to trust." At this, Brother Phillip nodded in Caroline's direction. John searched his eyes. "Romans 3:22 tells us that 'this righteousness from God comes through faith in Jesus Christ to all who believe.' It's there waiting for you but you need to step into the circle and grab it with both hands. You'll never grasp it by reaching in from the perimeter." He patted John's shoulder and departed into the growing noonday sun.

John stood at the door for a long time before walking over to Caroline. Sighing, he knelt on the floor in front of her.

His voice breaking, he asked, "Are you in love with Simon?"

"What?!" Astonished, she gaped at him.

"I can understand why you would be. He's kind and gentle. He's intelligent and—and—well—Godly, I guess."

Caroline's eyes softened. She caressed his face and bent down to kiss him. "You *are* a complete and utter idiot, you know," she said smiling gently at him. His eyes searched her face to discern her meaning. "I'm in love with you and you only. I'm pretty sure I've told you that."

"You've been spending so much time with Simon and—well—you seem to enjoy being with him so much, I—" His voice trailed off.

"I'm sorry, John." He looked up at her, searching her eyes. She continued. "I didn't think about how it must feel for you here. I feel like I've come—well, not home—maybe to my favourite aunt's house?" She chuckled then sobered. "But that's not how it feels for you, is it? I have enjoyed discussing theology with Simon but I love *living* faith with you. Simon's a nice guy and everything but—I don't know, I'm just not the least bit interested in him romantically! I have tons more fun with you! John, you're my best friend and far more."

"Did Simon really think I would hurt you?" he asked quietly.

"Yes, I think he did. You were pretty angry. I've not often seen you that incensed before."

"But you didn't?—think I would hurt you?" He appealed to her with his eyes.

"No." She waited for him to ask the question.

"Why?"

"You may make a lot of mistakes, my Bear, but you rarely make the same one twice." She chuckled at his look of chagrin.

Burying his head in her lap, he held her tightly around the waist. "What would I do without you?" he spoke into her side.

She brushed her hands through his hair. "Let's never find out, okay?" She felt him nod against her. They sat like that for a long time until Caroline broke the silence.

"You don't really trust me, do you?" she asked.

He gave a mirthless laugh. "That's just what Brother Phillip said."

"Is it because I've been spending so much time with Simon? I wasn't really very sensitive to your feelings. I was annoyed that you'd become surly but I would never be so faithless as to pursue another man right in front of you—or even behind your back. I love you. You can trust me—but you don't."

John straightened and held up his hand to stop her. "It's not that I don't *trust* you. It was just easy to believe you would prefer Simon. What do I have to offer you?" His cheeks flushed as he admitted his inferiorities. He continued very softly, "I seem to spread pain and disappointment wherever I go. Everyone eventually leaves me. " He moved away from Caroline and slumped to the floor in defeat.

"John, my Bear, I'm in love with you. I'm not going to leave you unless you force me away. You told me that you wanted me to love you but you don't really believe that I do, do you? You think that our relationship will inevitably fail." She continued speaking, keeping her voice level. "There is only one danger to our relationship. It's not Simon or Burma or Rin Tin Tin, it's you. It's the fact that you won't accept my commitment to you." She paused, gathering her thoughts. "The only reason you've ever hurt me, truly hurt me, is because you won't commit. You move toward me, get frightened and back away." She reached beside her and stroked his hair. "When I realized I was in love with you, I understood that God was asking me to commit to you. I understood that it would take patience. I didn't understand how deeply damaged you were." John's eyebrows rose and he started to protest. "No John! What I didn't realize was how high the walls were around your heart. Every time I think I've broken down a barrier, I find a new and thicker wall in my way." She stopped, concern furrowing her brow. He waited.

"The Bible says, 'Love is patient and kind. It always protects, always trusts, always hopes, always perseveres'." She paused again. "I have loved and lost and never expected to love again. Henry and I had a good life, but it ended and then you came along—you came and everything changed.

"When I first started to have feelings for you—well, have positive feelings for you—I was confused. It couldn't be God's will for me to find a husband. There are plenty of potential husbands back in Canada. I didn't need to travel through this hellish nightmare just to fall in love. But you know what?"

John interrupted with a ready response, "I've brought you more hell than anything else you've experienced?" He continued to sit on the ground beside her, looking defeated.

She chuckled wryly. "No. I realized that God is kind. He loves us and wants to bless us. You're my blessing." John raised his head a little. "And this is the only place I could have found you. I love you. Now, you need to decide. Are you prepared to let me in? Will you build a gate through which I can enter and stay? Will you make the decision and commit to it? Will you trust me to commit to it?" She crouched in front of John, gently holding his face, tilting his eyes to meet hers. "I love you. I will love you, always." She leaned in and kissed him, a deep passionate kiss. Touching his cheek with the back of her fingers, she rose. "Let me know what you decide either way. I love you."

John spent the next day, a Sunday, sequestered in his cabin. When he didn't emerge for supper, Caroline went to see Brother Phillip. The retired missionary welcomed her into his home and offered tea and biscuits.

"What can I do for you, daughter?" Brother Phillip asked as they sat down at the kitchen table.

"I'm concerned about John. He's been alone all day. He was so depressed when I left him."

Brother Phillip leaned forward and patted her hand. "Leave him to God, daughter. He loves John even more than you do." Caroline blushed. "Trust in the Lord with all your heart and lean not on your own understanding." She nodded sadly in response to his words.

Caroline walked slowly to Dolly's cabin. As the two women headed off to church that evening, Caroline saw John walking toward Brother Phillip's home. The two men met and spoke on the porch before John headed over to the community building where services were held.

After the singing and before the sermon, Brother Phillip rose with purpose in his old eyes and command in his voice, "We have a special announcement tonight, to which we will *patiently* listen. Please come forward, John." John walked forward looking very humble. He took his place at the front of the building, standing in front of the altar. He found a spot on the back wall and fixed his stare to it.

"I would like to apologize for my behavior, yesterday. It was inexcusable. I'm sorry." John stood at the front in silence with his arms clasped in front of him, eyes lowered. Silent tears slid down Caroline's cheeks. A movement off to the right caught her eyes and she watched Simon stand and advance to the front of the building, stopping in front of John and extending his hand. John looked up in surprise and shook the proffered hand. The two men returned to their seats together.

<><><><><>

Over the next several days, John spent a lot of time with Brother Phillip. They took each meal together and continued taking their twice daily walks. John began to attend Bible study and began to ask questions. He poured himself into reading the New Testament as Brother Phillip asked him to do. He learned to have a daily devotion and learned to expand his prayer life, to see God as his loving friend, not just a source of help in times of trouble.

"...Therefore, there is now no condemnation for those who are in Christ Jesus because through Christ Jesus the law of the Spirit of life has set me free from the law of sin and death."

"Brother Phillip, do you think that God can forgive us for murder?" John asked.

"Yes. The Bible tells us that all sins can be forgiven except the sin of not accepting Christ in this lifetime. Who do you suppose that you have killed, my son?"

Distracted by his thoughts, John responded before considering his words. "I've killed many people—in self-defense or in the defense of others. No, I mean murder. I am responsible for the death of my mother." John bowed his head in shame, expecting condemnation from the kindly man across from him.

"Tell me your story, John."

"I-I can't," John responded then remained silent.

Brother Phillip studied his bowed head. "Have you told Caroline the story?" Brother Phillip asked. John looked up in surprise and nodded. "What did she say to you?"

John smiled a secret smile at the memory. "She told me I wasn't responsible for my mother's death. She told me my father was an evil toad to make me feel that I was guilty of that sin. She told me that my mother forgave me."

Brother Phillip reached across the table and placed his hand on John's arm. "Caroline is a very wise woman."

John began to nod. "Yes. She is wise." His smile faltered. "My father once told me that I bring pain wherever I go." Brother Phillip fixed sad eyes on John who looked away in embarrassment. "I'm not trying to play the 'blame the parents' card but—" John paused, gathering his thoughts. "I just don't see how I can put Caroline through the trouble of a life with someone like me."

"Do you believe that she would leave you? Do you not trust her?" Brother Phillip asked.

"I do trust her, more than she'll ever know. No, the problem is that she *won't* leave me. How can I sentence her to a life with me? Wouldn't that be selfish?"

"Is that what is behind this grief that you carry like a cross, son?" John gave one terse nod in response to the kind man's words. Brother Phillip continued, "Jesus said, 'Come unto me all who labour and are heavy laden and I will give you rest. Take my yoke upon you and learn from me, for I am gentle and lowly in heart, and you will find rest for your souls, for my yoke is easy and my burden is light.' Let God carry that burden, son, and you be the kind of man you feel she deserves."

"How do I do that?" John asked earnestly.

"'Love the Lord your God with all your heart, soul, strength and mind and love your neighbor as yourself'. 'Husbands, love your wives, just as Christ loved the church and gave himself up for her'. 'Bear one another's burdens'. It's all there son, every answer you need, you just have to find it and do it." Brother Phillip held John's gaze.

John sighed. "If I give myself to her," he paused then continued, "how will I ever survive? When my mother died, she took all the joy out of my life." John shook his head miserably. "Everyone I've ever loved has left me. My mother left me. My father stayed physically but he left me. Mar—the first woman I had a long term relationship with left me, for a promotion," he added bitterly.

"I thought you believed that Caroline—" Brother Phillip started.

John shook his head. "Caroline would never leave me but what if she died? She knows better than anyone else—except perhaps you—what the loss of a deep love can do to a person. What if—what if she—" Brother Phillip urged him on. "What if she stopped loving me or if I made her miserable?" John sank within himself.

Brother Phillip took the time to pray before continuing. "Romans 8:28 says, 'And we know that in all things God works for the good of those who love Him, who have been called according to His purpose'. Does Caroline believe that the death of her husband threw her out of God's will?"

"No!" astonished, John responded. "She believes that God brought her to where she is today *in* His will."

"God is with us through the bad and the good. He will never leave you nor forsake you. Caroline is a wonderful woman but every man, woman and child will let you down. God won't. He created the universe and He created you. Proverbs 3:5 tells us 'Trust in the Lord with all your heart and lean not on your own understanding. In all your ways acknowledge Him and He will direct your paths'."

"What if I trust and someone gets hurt? What if my decision hurts someone I care about—Caroline or you, Brother Phillip? I've got to protect the people around me."

"Do you really have such a low opinion of the Creator of heaven and earth? Trust in the Lord with all your heart and lean not on your own understanding."

<><><><><>

That conversation proved to be a turning point for John. At the evening service, the pastor, a Korean man named Joo-Chan, opened the altar to those who wanted to rededicate their life to Christ. John went forward. He was baptized the next day.

Brother Phillip invited Caroline to attend the study on the book of Romans with John but cautioned her to allow John to find God's words for himself. So she did. She sat quietly during the studies, listening to John's questions and loving him more each day. She also avoided Simon, not wanting to distract John in any way.

Caroline was thrilled with John's spiritual growth. Many around her would comment on how different he was than before, but Caroline saw exactly the same man. He was still her John, just with Christ looking out of his eyes. She had hoped that when he rededicated himself to God, he would come to her and declare his love for her but he continued to stay away. Her heart saddened to think that in the wonder of his growth, she had lost him. She poured out her grief to Dolly.

"Caroline, there's somethin' I jest don't understand," Dolly responded as they sat around the table eating supper together.

"Yes?" Caroline replied, her sadness engulfing the word.

"What do you see in that man?" Dolly asked, confused.

Caroline swallowed her shock at the question. "Dolly, John is brave and fun—"

Dolly interrupted, incredulously, "Fun? I'm not quite sure Simon would call him fun, bein' punched an' all."

"He only punched Simon because he was jealous. Now, don't interrupt," Caroline admonished. "John is brave and fun, intelligent and kind. He would do anything for me," she concluded.

Dolly studied her dear friend contemplatively. "You think he's the kinda man who woos and weds? He seems pretty wild to me—wild and hidden. Brother Phillip keeps saying John's walls protect a deep hurt but it seems to me that man goes about hurting more than he gets hurt."

Feeling tremendously sad at Dolly's evaluation of John, Caroline defended him, "John has been hurt. I don't know how Brother Phillip figured that out but he's right. John has a lot of walls around his emotions but they're there for a good reason."

Dolly looked skeptical. "Walls is good for protection but without a gate, my girl, how you gonna get in?"

Morosely, Caroline replied, "I don't know."

"Ye've already been hurt by one man, Caroline, are ye really gonna let another man hurt you? Why take the risk?" The spinster in Dolly was peeking out from her psyche.

Beginning to lose her patience with this deconstruction, Caroline snapped, "I didn't ask to fall in love with John, Dolly, but he is a wonderful man and I don't really care whether you can see that or not."

As Caroline rose briskly from the table, Dolly grabbed her arm. "Ye'd marry him?"

Caroline halted, considering the question. After a long time, she answered, "Yes."

"Why take the risk?" Dolly inquired.

"Love is—" Caroline stopped, gathering her thoughts. "Love is joy and pain, affection and passion, adventure and monotony. To be happy, you need your best friend, a healthy dose of passion and trust, but most of all commitment. John is my best friend, I trust him, adore him and I will stand by him until the end of time."

"Yes, but does he feel the same way about you?"

A few mornings later, as Caroline sat down on Dolly's front porch to eat breakfast, Kyi's son Paul ran up to Caroline.

"Come, Miss Caroline, come." The boy gestured vigorously to her. Dolly began to rise as well but Paul motioned her back. "No, only Miss Caroline. Come quickly," he urged.

Following the boy to the big rock by the waterfall where the children liked to play, she saw wildflowers adorning the rock: pink orchids; white asters; red anthurium. When she turned back, the boy was gone. Returning her gaze to the flowers, she noticed a folded paper nestled amongst them. She read,

> How beautiful you are, my darling!
> Oh, how beautiful!
> Your eyes are doves.
> My dove in the clefts of the rock,
> In the hiding places
> On the mountainside,
> Show me your face,
> Let me hear your voice;

> For your voice is sweet,
> And your face is lovely.
>
> Song of Solomon 1:15, 2:14

Caroline looked around, tears in her eyes. "John?" she called.

"Yes," he answered from behind her, a look of peace in his eyes.

"What does this mean?" she asked, brushing the tears from her eyes impatiently so she could see him clearly.

He watched her confusion. "I've made a decision as you asked me to."

Her stomach fluttered nervously at his words. "What decision?" John moved over to her, sliding his arms around her waist and drawing her close as he began to kiss her with light featherlike kisses across her eyes and down her face to her neck. Her eyes fluttered closed as she lost herself in the sensation of his kisses. She rested her hands on his upper arms, breathing in the scent of him.

"What now, John?" she murmured.

"Well," John said between kisses, "I don't really know. I've never been in love before."

"No, I mean about the—John?" Caroline pulled back to look into John's face. His eyes opened slowly and he pulled her tenderly back toward him.

"John, are you sure? Please don't say it unless you're sure."

"Caroline, I love you more than breathing. I adore you and you are my best friend. I trust you, more than I've ever trusted anyone else in my life and I vow that I will stand by you until the end of time. I know I don't deserve you and I know I don't have a clue as to how to be worthy of you but, as you once said, I am teachable. I'm convinced that I want to be always, faithfully yours." He kissed her hands. "I've built you a long tunnel through all my walls straight to my heart and I promise that I will always keep it open. Do you want to come in—forever always?"

Caroline's tears fell unchecked. "Yes, John. Yes. I want you. I love you—forever always." She slid her arms around his neck and pulled his head down. He stopped a breath away from her mouth.

"I love you," he said and kissed her. Her stomach fluttered at his words. They kissed again, deeper this time. He stroked his hands up along her back, pulling her closer to him as she ran her fingers through his hair. He kissed her neck, resting his head on her shoulder, his lips against her neck.

She sighed, "I love you, my Bear," and she felt him smile against her skin.

Caroline was unable to sleep that night, so full was she of the emotions of John's declaration of love. Venturing outside under the full moon of Burma, she found him walking along at the jungle's edge long after the others were tucked up in their beds. Hearing her voice softly calling him, John turned and a wide smile encompassed his features from his ears to his eyes.

"Hello," he greeted.

"Hello," she replied as she stepped over to him.

"So, you can't sleep without me?" John reached out his hand and pulled Caroline closer as he spoke. Caroline gave him a shocked look. *Men!* As he wrapped his arms around her, she rested her head on his chest. "I miss you, too," he growled into her ear, causing her to shiver at the sensation. They stood together for a time, swaying to the silent music in the air.

After a time, he surprised her by asking, "When can we talk about getting married?" She pulled back to look directly into his eyes. He continued, "In case you haven't noticed, I'll tell you. I want to be with you always. I want to go to bed with you and wake with you every day for the rest of my life. I want to cook with you and clean with you and walk in the jungle and the snow with you. I want to laugh with you and hold you when you cry. I want you in my life, always."

"John?" she whispered, rendered voiceless by his words.

"I've surprised you," he murmured, pulling her close again.

"Yes," she finally answered, "but in a good way—a very good way." Caroline looked into his eyes again. "I want it all, too." Caroline stopped and then looked away sadly.

"But—" he started, waiting for her to fill in the blanks. "Tell me."

She smiled at him. "I think sometimes that you can read my mind." He was quiet to give her time. "We're so far away from home—so far away from little white chapels and wedding bells."

"Would you marry me if we were home?" he asked, holding his breath while she answered. Caroline studied his face. She closed her eyes and studied her heart, remembering her conversation with Dolly. John waited impatiently, prompting her, "If I took you to a fancy restaurant and gave you a diamond ring, would you marry me?"

"That's cheating!" Caroline challenged with a smile. "You have to ask the question first then get the answer, and, by the way, I don't want some goofy diamond. I want a garnet, deep and red—and—and you should definitely get down on one knee." She watched him closely, feeling her own excitement at the topic.

John took her hands in his, knelt down on one knee in the lush undergrowth of the Burmese jungle and began the next phase of their lives.

"Caroline, my beloved, I don't have a ring or a white chapel or wedding bells but I love you—with all my heart—I love you. Will you marry me?"

Caroline removed her hands and gently caressed his face. "Yes." His breath escaped in a rush as he swept her up in his arms. They kissed and set off in search of Brother Phillip with happy smiles and hearts full of warmth and wonder.

A sleepy, pyjamaed Brother Phillip responded to the pounding on his front door. When his yawn subsided, he looked with surprise at John and Caroline standing hand in hand with smiles wider than the Indian Ocean.

John began speaking in a rush. "Brother Phillip, are you a licensed minister? Wait, Dolly is, isn't she?" This was said to Caroline.

"You're right. Let's go to her cabin." Caroline added, oblivious to the older man's confusion.

Brother Phillip reached out to take them both by the arm firmly. "Children. Stop! What is this all about?"

"We want to—she said yes—can you believe it?"

"I don't know what'll happen—I don't know the first thing about being a spy's wife."

The two rushed on, speaking over each other.

Puzzled by the riotous cacophony of words, Brother Phillip picked out the word 'wife' and everything fell into place. He pulled them into his home and led them to the couch.

"You want to be married," he stated. They grinned so broadly, there was no doubt. "Now?" he added. They nodded vigorously. Brother Phillip began to laugh. He laughed and laughed. "Your mourning shall turn to joy. Yes, Father, this is good."

"Well, let's wake Dolly and get this underway. Who would you like to stand up for you, Caroline?"

"Thuza."

"Then I shall give you away and Kyi will stand for John."

The trio marched straight to Kyi and Thuza's and roused them from sleep. Thuza hugged Caroline and agreed. The two men clasped hands and they all strode purposefully onto Dolly's porch and burst inside, calling for the former evangelist.

When she emerged sleepily from her bedroom, Brother Phillip exclaimed, "Wake up sleepyhead, these young people wish to be married!"

Dolly squealed with delight, a sound that shocked them all coming as it did from this tough lady. Dashing to her room, she returned with her Bible and the Manual that contained the matrimonial service. She lined up her mini congregation and conjoined two of the most unusual people in her life, her dear friend and the man she inconceivably loved.

… "Do you, Bernard John,
take Caroline Gloria
to be your lawfully wedded wife?..."
"I do"
"Do you, Caroline Gloria
take Bernard John…."
"I do"

"I now pronounce you husband and wife." John placed his hands tenderly on Caroline's face and kissed her; a kiss of love and promise; a kiss of fidelity and assurance. When they looked up, the room was quiet and four pairs of eyes glistened with tears.

Dolly dashed away, calling over her shoulder, "Wait a minute." She returned with a small white New Testament, hugging it to her heart then handing it to Caroline.

"My mother gave this to me when I was sixteen for me to carry on my wedding day. I would like you to have it… no, don't argue, take it with love."

The group of friends accompanied John and Caroline to the guest cabin, standing around chatting happily. John and Caroline moved closer and closer to each other, falling silent as they realized that this was their wedding night, and there were four people standing between them and what comes next.

Caroline reached her arm around John's waist and began to stroke up and down his back. John brushed his fingers along her shoulder and curled them into her hair, his thumb caressing her neck. Caroline's hand slipped further down his back as he gazed at her with longing in his eyes.

Thuza had noticed the newlyweds' silence and the misty eyes gazing at each other. Nodding pointedly toward the newlyweds, she interrupted the conversation. "I believe it is time for us to retire." With that the four friends turned their gazes to John and Caroline and quickly excused themselves. Brother Phillip pulled the door quickly closed behind him, pronouncing rapidly, "God's blessings on you, children."

John turned to face Caroline and wrapped both arms around her waist, pulling her close while Caroline rested her hands on his chest, finding the spaces between his buttons. He gazed deeply into her eyes.

"I'm suddenly very nervous."

"Me too."

John leaned down and kissed Caroline on the mouth.

"I'm not nervous anymore," she murmured. He smiled and they moved together, finding a myriad ways to please each other as they became one.

CHAPTER 12
THE SOLDIERS

The next morning, news came to the community by way of two very serious looking Chinese gentlemen who entered the village square, passed by John and Caroline enjoying a late breakfast in the communal kitchen, and immediately went to Brother Phillip's home. Brother Phillip sent one of the children to find Archie and Dolly.

John watched the gentlemen intently, his eyes not leaving them, unaware that he spilled Caroline's tea on the homemade teak wood table.

"John! What's wrong with you?" she asked, touching his arm, lightly.

Glancing at her, he saw what he had done. "Sorry, Caer." He reached and grabbed for a cloth, wiping up the mess, all the time watching Brother Phillip's front door.

"John! Tell me."

Turning to her, he smiled and then frowned again. "Something's wrong. I'm going over there." Caroline moved to follow him, taking his hand. When they arrived at Brother

Phillip's door, John knocked, firmly. Dolly answered and invited them in.

"Ah, just the people we want to see. We need your advice," she said.

Dolly escorted them into Brother Phillip's front room where Archie was pacing by the window and Brother Phillip was sitting in his armchair, his index fingers tented beneath his chin and a contemplative look in his eyes. The two visitors sat tensely on the couch, drinking tea.

Brother Phillip welcomed John and Caroline as they entered. "Ah, children, welcome. Yes, I think it is right that you should hear this."

Caroline could feel John's tension and she held his hand tightly in response as he nodded at Brother Phillip.

The first visitor began, "We have come to warn you. There are soldiers everywhere. In every village we pass, there are tales of sorrow. The Warden from Bourey Prison has gathered Chinese and Burmese mercenaries to help him hunt for two escaped convicts, a man and a woman. People are being beaten and arrested across the country as the soldiers make their way further north. In one poor isolated Chin village near the Kayah state, half of the men were carted off to prison for suspicion of helping an escaped convict. One of the men was beaten in front of his wife and child. The Warden is offering a large reward for information on these convicts as they are very dangerous."

Caroline had blanched at the first mention of villagers. She thought of Grace, Zeya, Cho and Khin, of their kindness repaid with violence and imprisonment. John could feel her shaking beside him and he reached his arm around her waist, pulling her to him.

When the gentlemen finished their story, Archie showed them to the door and, calling Lwin, he invited them to share a meal in the community's kitchen before continuing their journey. When he returned to the sitting room, Dolly had moved to the window but John and Caroline remained frozen where they stood. The room was filled with silence.

Brother Phillip spoke first. "I think, son, you have a decision to make." John's eyes darted to the old man who looked sunken in his chair while Caroline sighed sadly and looked up into John's face. His eyes were flitting around the room and she could feel the tension in his body. "Trust," she whispered. He looked at her, his eyes full of conflicting thoughts, until suddenly, he came to a decision. Leaning down, he kissed her.

"My name is John Brock. I work for MI-5. I was abducted on the orders of a rogue Chinese colonel and taken to Bourey Prison to be interrogated for information that only I, and one or two other people in the world hold. *I* am the escaped convict to whom they refer. I've brought danger to your people, for that I apologize."

Dolly's and Archie's eyes were fixed on John as Brother Phillip sat weeping silently in his chair.

Eyes blazing, Archie asserted, "We trusted you." He forced the words out past his clenched jaw as Dolly moved over to Archie seeking solidarity by proximity.

Caroline moved over to kneel beside Brother Phillip's chair, resting her hands on his arm. "He was tortured, Brother. You can't imagine the things they did to him. We escaped when the rebels attacked the prison and some villagers gave us refuge until he healed and we could head further north—to here." Caroline stopped, realizing too late the implication of what she had said: that they had purposely travelled here; they had knowingly brought this trouble on these kind and Godly people. Caroline began to weep.

Dolly accused her, "So you are a convict as well."

John moved closer to Caroline as if to shield her from the accusation. "She was arrested for protecting a woman and her child from soldiers then given no legal representation and no access to her embassy." He paused trying to make eye contact with the elders in the room. "She saved my life—more than once." He paused again, trying to reach them. "You have to believe that this is not her fault, all the fault lies with me."

Brother Phillip raised his head to gaze at Caroline and patted her hand.

Archie intruded, "How do we know that any of this is true? Anyone can claim to be tortured."

John moved into the centre of the room and began to undo his shirt slipping it down his arms and off his body as he turned slowly to give them a full view. Gasping, Dolly began to weep as she saw the scars laced across his back. Archie moved closer to John as if in a trance, reaching out as though he meant to trace the lines of pain, his hand hovering in the air.

Brother Phillip patted Caroline's hand once more and walked over to John. "Put your shirt back on, son," he said. Turning to Archie, Brother Phillip spoke, "I, for one, believe him. We have lived peacefully in this valley so long that we have forgotten our mission. We are here to provide sanctuary to God's chosen. How can we expect to escape suffering when so many in Burma suffer daily?" Brother Phillip took John's hand and clasped it. "I believe that God sent you to us and I believe it is God's will for us to help you."

John protested. "No. I don't want anyone to risk anything for me. We'll leave now. I was waiting for a contact I have in the region to help us cross the border but—I'll—I'll find a way." Caroline walked over to John and wrapped her arms around his waist, holding him tightly.

"Who is your contact?" Dolly surprised them all by asking.

"Maryn Dale. She travels as an importer/exporter under the cover name of Maritza Dallish." The group turned when Archie inhaled sharply at the mention of that name.

He blanched. "Maritza?" he whispered hollowly. As John nodded, Archie continued forcefully. "You cannot wait for this woman."

John extracted himself gently from Caroline's hold, taking Archie by the shoulders. "What do you mean?" he hissed, his eyes quickly narrowing with suspicion.

Archie lowered his head, shaking it. "Before I came to this community, before I became a Christian, I worked as a trader in China. Maritza Dallish was my lover. When I became a Christian, I knew that she was one of the things I would need to give up in my life. What had seemed dangerous and exciting before God gave my life meaning now seemed foolhardy and tedious." He continued wryly, "She took the news of our breakup surprisingly well—it didn't seem to bother her at all. When I told her I was planning to seek out this community, she asked if we could still be friends and if she could visit me from time to time. I was flattered. Maritza—Maryn is a beautiful woman. She claims to visit me from time to time to maintain our friendship. She always arrives after dark and asks to remain anonymous, leaving before dawn so that no one here has ever seen her. I have kept her secret—I have foolishly believed her for a long time—a long, long time."

Caroline encouraged him to continue. "What happened?"

Archie continued, "When Jun and Lien arrived, escaping persecution in China, I happened to mention that I had a friend who often travelled in China. As I described her, they recognized her as the woman who had betrayed them to the secret police." Here Archie looked directly at John. "She has links to a Colonel Shing. She is also known to carry information back and forth between Shing in China and a General Akram in India." Archie turned to Brother Phillip. "I'm sorry, Brother, for keeping this secret—for being duped by foolish pride. I'm sorry."

Brother Phillip moved over and rested his hand on Archie's shoulder. "Our choices can be forgiven but that does not mean that the consequences of them disappear. But God is able to deliver us, either in this life, or the next." He turned back to John. "Now, what we need to do is pray." So they did.

As the time for prayer led into the time for action, Brother Phillip remarked, "I believe that we are missing faithful friends who could help us solve our dilemma." Brother Phillip turned to John. "Would you object to inviting Kyi and Simon to our meeting?" John turned to Caroline and when she nodded her consent, he gave his consent to Brother Phillip. Caroline offered to get the men and she set off to find them, locating them near the waterfall, deep in conversation. With little explanation except the expression of danger in the air, they immediately agreed to come when she asked them. As they walked back to Brother Phillip's home, Caroline stopped to invite Kyi's wife, Thuza, because she knew that Kyi considered his wife to be the wisest person he had ever met. Chairs were brought and Simon, Thuza and Kyi found places around the room. Dolly reviewed the recent events and John took over to explain their dilemma.

"As Dolly has explained, the two gentlemen currently sharing their repast in the village square have come to warn us that soldiers are on the lookout for Caroline and myself, claiming to search for dangerous escaped convicts. Dolly has also explained that we were, in fact, wrongly confined, even by the current laws of this country. I am an MI-5 officer who, many years ago, was responsible for setting up a network of agents across Southeast Asia. These agents were often common people who wished to see their countries free of terrorism, and oppression from elements outside their control. These agents were never asked to pass on information that would harm their own nation, only to help collect and pass on information about terrorist or guerilla activities. This network has been active for twenty years.

"When Caroline and I escaped from the prison, we headed here to Brother Phillip's Community because I knew that my agent, Maryn Dale, made contact with someone here."

Kyi interrupted, "Then Archie is really part of your network?"

John shook his head as Archie opened his mouth to protest. "No. Archie is not part of my network. I know of every agent in my network. There is no one here that is part of it. I can only guess that Maryn used the community as an escape or retreat of some sort. I haven't worked that out yet.'

Caroline interrupted, "If Maryn is a double agent then why did they need to kidnap you? Couldn't she have just given up the network to Shing?"

John smiled at her in admiration. "A good question. However, Maryn does not know the network. Her job is to carry information, or rather misinformation, from the Indian government to the Chinese government and back again in order to keep the countries from building too strong an alliance against the west. She also carries information from a few key contacts in Southeast Asia but she has never met more than a few of my network. She is, however, one of the few people who know *about* the network and she certainly knows that I am the one who set it up and that I travel every few years to check on my people."

Simon snorted. "Your people? When will the west stop interfering in the east? When will they learn to keep their meddling noses out of Burma's business?" Simon stood, arms crossed defiantly, daring John to argue.

However, it was Brother Phillip who took up the argument. "It is not for us to argue the politics of nations, Simon; it is our job to show God's love to a wounded and needy world." Simon nodded, accepting the older man's chastisement.

Caroline had been pensive during this discussion. Realization dawning, she stated, "Maryn was your lover at the time you set up the network."

John blushed in response to Caroline's words and he answered softly, "Yes." Caroline looked up at him, studying his face as he explained, "She broke off the relationship when I refused to take her with me to set it up. We had a huge argument when I decided to go out on my own. She took a job, a promotion with MI-6." John turned to Caroline. "I'm sorry I haven't told you. It's not exactly something I'm proud of—pretty embarrassing to be cuckolded for a promotion."

Caroline took his hand and, lacing their fingers together she brought it to her lips and kissed it. "We can't all get it right the first time round," she said, taking pity on his evident pain at the admission. John smiled down at her with relief in his eyes.

Thuza was the next to speak. "If you are to escape back to Britain and report your double agent, you need help to cross the border. The journey from here to India is demanding." Kyi nodded at that. "I believe I can help, or rather, my family can help." Everyone turned to her.

Dolly pursued this offer of assistance. "What do you mean?" she asked.

"What many people do not know is that, although my father was Burmese, my mother was Karen. Several years ago, during yet another wave of persecution against the Karen, my mother was killed. She was accused of aiding the guerillas and executed when my father's old carbine hunting rifle was found in the house. My father's grief upon his return was such that he took my brother and sister and left the country. At the time my mother was killed, I was older than my brother and sister and already pledged to Kyi. His family took me in and protected me. My father could not flee to Thailand as many of the Karen had done, so he traveled west across Burma into the mountains of India. He established a rice farm, remaining in seclusion there for many years—not many people know of these isolated farms in the mountains. Once a year, my father and the twins, Nanda and Myaing, would travel back into

Myanmar to sell their produce along the Chindwin River. Kyi and I would meet them in Hwebalan. When my father died, Nanda and Myaing returned to Burma. They rarely speak of that time but I believe their knowledge and experience can help you now as it has helped others in the past."

"Thuza," Caroline asked quietly. "How did your family come to be here?"

"Nanda and Myaing helped Brother Phillip find this hidden mountain valley years ago and when Kyi and I needed a place of escape, they led us here to Katafygio. Brother Phillip has always held a special place in his heart for the Karen." Thuza smiled fondly at Brother Phillip and, with a small smile and a slow blink, he inclined his head in a short bow.

"The Karen hold a special place in God's kingdom, do they not young Simon?" responded Brother Phillip, turning his gaze from Thuza to the anthropologist.

Simon picked up the tale. "The Karen are one of the indigenous peoples of Myanmar and Thailand. They are a fascinating and diverse people with varied traditions and even individual dialects that cannot necessarily be understood by the other sub-groups. They believe themselves to be orphans who lost their writing system after God handed it down to them but would have it returned one day by visitors from far away. They saw the first Christian missionaries as the ones God had sent to fulfill his promise. They were uniquely ready to hear the Gospel. The Missionary H.I. Marshall writes—"

Dolly interrupted him, "Thank you, Simon, but before ye launch into your thesis again, let's solve this day's problems." Simon grinned abashedly and nodded affirmation of her instruction.

"Kyi, you are a lucky man to have such a wife of such insight." Brother Phillip turned to John. "I believe we should ask Nanda and Myaing to join us and see if they will consent to be your guides."

Nanda and Myaing readily offered to accompany the couple on their journey, making use of their knowledge of geography and their connections within the Karen and Chin communities along the way. They knew all the secret ways of Burma.

John looked troubled. The others in the room were confused by his reaction but Caroline understood. She reached up and patted his cheek. "You see, John, God didn't wait for you to become a Christian to start planning for this day. He had this precious gift already in place for you. Let these people serve God by helping you. They love you." She smiled at him and kissed his cheek.

John looked around the room. For the first time in his life he felt surrounded by love. He gulped back the tears that threatened to overpower him and bowed his head in humble gratitude. "Thank you." He gulped again. "Yes," he said, more strongly. "I can make use of this precious gift." He hesitated. "But I don't—I don't want anyone to be hurt because of me. I'm so sorry to have brought you trouble, especially after you saved the love of my life. I'm not good at asking for help but—well—thank you," he conceded, humbly.

It was decided that John would work together with Myaing to pack and gather the gear necessary for the trip, and to plan a route. Thuza, Dolly and Caroline worked together to prepare food for the journey. Simon was asked to prepare any relevant cultural information that might be useful on their journey. Brother Phillip prayed. The day passed quickly.

When each member of the conclave turned in for the night they were exhausted from the preparations. John and Caroline walked to their cabin, hands woven together. Caroline walked through the door and collapsed onto a chair.

"I'm tired. All I want is sleep, sleep and more sleep." When John didn't respond, she looked up to find him leering at her in a most unchaste manner.

"Sleep, my wife?" He slowly made his way over to her. "Is that the best we can do?"

Caroline smiled as she wrapped her arms around him. "No, I think we can do a little better than that."

Caroline woke, confused by a heaviness until she realized that John's head was pillowed on her belly. Smiling, she curled her fingers into his hair, watching him as he stirred and moved to kiss along her ribs.

"John. My love?" she whispered. He muttered an unintelligible response and continued kissing toward her belly button. "John, there's one thing we've never discussed—one important thing—it may seem a little late but—" Another "mmhmm" was his reply. "Children."

He halted his progress and looked up at her. "Do you want more children?" he asked.

She shook her head. "I don't think I could handle it. I would always be afraid of losing them so much so that I don't think I could be a good mother. Do you want children?" She turned the question back to him.

"No. My life doesn't really lend itself to children. 'Be back in three or four months kiddies, once the bad men have finished torturing me'—but there is something I need to tell you. I didn't mean to keep it from you but I probably should have told you long ago." Caroline watched John carefully as he rolled onto his side and leaned on his elbow. "Five years ago, one of my colleagues was tasked to turn the wife of a Sudanese diplomat. He succeeded in making her an asset and obtained very useful information through her. She became pregnant by him."

"John! He slept with her—as part of the job?"

"When we're given an assignment, no one asks how we accomplish it; it's just our job to accomplish it."

"Have you ever—ever used sex to 'accomplish' your assignment?" Caroline held John's gaze steadily.

"No. Don't misunderstand me, I've done many things I'm not proud of and many things you likely don't want to know but I've never used sex to turn an asset. I always judged that to be cheating—and very risky."

Caroline touched his cheek. "I want to know everything about you—but maybe not all at once." John smiled softly in response. "What happened to your colleague?" Caroline inquired.

"The pregnancy was no problem. The wife just passed the baby off as her husband's but my colleague, Barry, couldn't handle it. He couldn't handle the thought of his child being raised by the woman's husband. As the pregnancy progressed, he became more and more reckless. I warned '5' to remove him but they wouldn't listen. They saw only the information he was retrieving. Eventually, the husband found out. They caught Barry and—" John faltered.

"John, I know what the world is like, please finish the story." She moved closer to him and rested her hand on his belly.

"They tortured him—castrated him and killed him. After they sent us the pictures, I decided that I never wanted to be in that position—ever. I went and had a vasectomy. I can't have children."

"Why didn't you tell me that when I told you about Henry's?" Caroline asked, disheartened.

John stroked his fingers along her cheek. "I'm sorry. We were close then but I—I just have never—My past sits in a box, Caroline. There's my 'good memories box' which, until recently, was very small. I pull it out when I need to escape from the present, for instance, when I'm being tortured, or during staff meetings." He grinned then sobered, again. "The rest of my life goes in this huge box labeled, 'do not open'. I'm not like other people. Key words and situations usually don't evoke a trip down memory lane. I've had years of practice at emotional disengagement."

Sadly, Caroline lowered her eyes, using her fingers to lightly trace designs on John's belly. "How do I get into that box, then?" Looking up to meet his gaze, she inquired, very quietly, "Where's my box?"

Smiling, John wrapped his arms around her and pulled her close, kissing her forehead. "I created an enormous box for you, labeled, 'I don't know why she loves me but I'm very glad she does'. I opened it the day in the prison when you forgave me and I've been filling it ever since."

Caroline smiled at him but the smile faded after a few seconds. "But how do I access the other box—the 'do not open'? How do I get to know you better?"

"Just ask. I don't often think about sharing my past with you because—well, because I'm just not used to sharing myself with another person, but I will tell you anything you want to know. I'm yours now, utterly and completely yours. I will give you anything you desire."

Smiling again, Caroline snuggled close to John, stroking her fingers through the ebony curls on his chest. Satisfied now with his response, she wanted to hear the outcome of the story that he had been telling.

"What happened to the woman and child?" Caroline asked, moving even closer to John.

"She had the child while they were still in London but I have no idea what happened to her once they returned to the Sudan. I never wanted to know. The diplomat merely claimed the child, a son, as his own." Caroline's face fell and they sat in silence for a time. "I'm sorry; perhaps I shouldn't have told you."

Caroline smiled sadly at him. "You can tell me everything, John. That's a very sad story." She lay for a time in John's arms. "I once thought," she began, "that you came from such a violent world that we could never bring our two lives together."

"I worked very hard to protect you from it," he replied. "But I simply wasn't strong enough to live without you."

She smiled against his chest. "Maybe that's what the Bible means when it says, 'we are made perfect in weakness'."

"Perhaps." Smiling, John resumed his journey to her belly button.

Joining the others at Brother Phillip's for breakfast that day, John and Caroline met with the conclave to confirm their plans. John repeatedly interrupted the meeting with objections, trying to eliminate any possibility of danger to the community. His protests ceased, however, when Brother Phillip huffed at him; "Exactly who do you think you are, young man?!" John was taken aback by the older man's indignation. "Do you think you are the only person with fortitude among us?" Brother Phillip gentled at John's wounded expression. "I am not afraid to die," he continued. "Death is not the direst consequence. I will stand true—and no middle-aged, overconfident James Bond is going to stop me!" John gazed at the older man with admiration, thankful to count this steadfast man of God as his mentor and friend.

Caroline surveyed the room, seeing her companions in a new light: she saw Kyi and Thuza, who had escaped persecution to heal others; Archie who had discovered that, when life has meaning, the reckless pursuit of danger loses its appeal; Nanda and Myaing, unflinchingly facing a life of persecution; Simon, disillusioned by the hypocrisy of academia; Dolly—was there anyone in the world quite like Dolly, unmarried and childless, yet she found unlimited patience, energy and enthusiasm for the children of the earth; and Brother Phillip, taken down by life but not defeated—a father to all those around him and, particularly, to her beloved, John.

Caroline's thoughts were interrupted as John summarized the plan, "All right, let's review. Nanda and Myaing will lead Caroline and me through the secret cavern which will bring us out at the base of this mountain. We will walk due west across the plains to Chaungzon where they have a contact, a Christian Chin family who will hopefully provide us with shelter and provisions. Then we move on to Kwaya where we will attempt to find a ride north to Tason and on to Hta Man Thi where I have a contact, a member of my network who will hopefully help us find a means of transport along the mining road west into the mountains. We will travel along the road as far as possible, climbing down to the river at that point and travelling along beside it. From there, Nanda and Myaing will take us through the secret mountain paths to India. At this point, Caroline and I will be on our own to travel down the mountain on the logging road until we arrive in Akhegwo where we should be able to make contact with the west. Once there, we will find our way on buses or trains to Kolkata and the British Deputy High Commission."

Myaing took over. "We should have no trouble finding ample water as there are many streams and rivers along this route. However, we are going to have difficulty finding transportation without money."

"We have a little money left from that fellow in Sinde," Caroline volunteered.

"Not much," John commented.

Brother Phillip left the table where the group was gathered, returning with a small pouch.

"When people come to this community, they are often escaping persecution or seeking retreat. Most arrive having lost all of their worldly goods while others feel that they can express their gratitude by giving up what little remains. No one is compelled to give, but some choose to." Brother Phillip turned to Dolly and Archie. "I propose that we send some of this money with John and Caroline to help them find their way home."

"I agree"

"As do I."

"Then it is unanimous." Brother Phillip handed the money to Caroline. It wasn't much but would hopefully be enough to get them closer to home.

"There is one other detail I feel I should mention," John began. "With the airport in Hwebalan, just south of Kwaya, it is possible that Colonel Shing will be able to track us once we reach the highway."

"Once we reach the mountains, we will be safe," insisted Myaing.

The group of friends finalized their plans and decided that the four travelers would depart at first light. The maps were folded and the packs filled. Later, as Brother Phillip put on the tea, they were interrupted by a knock on the door. Opening the door, they found little Paul, panting and out of breath, searching for his father.

"What is it, son?" asked Kyi, concerned by his son's apparent distress.

"Daddy, Daddy soldiers are coming."

Kyi took his son by the shoulders and asked him firmly. "What are you talking about?"

"Me and Danny and Gi were playing down on the path. I know we're not supposed to play there and we hided when the adults comed looking cause we wanted to see the giant tree that looks like a turtle but we got scareded when we heard the boots and bad words the men were saying. We peeked out to see and saw the soldier-clothes. Daddy the soldiers said they were looking for Brother Phillip's place. That's us, right?" The boy collapsed against his father as his words ended.

Kyi looked up at Brother Phillip. "Nanda, Myaing, take John and Caroline and get them out of here now!" Kyi ordered. "Thuza, gather all the mothers and children and take them to the secret place." No one moved. "NOW!" The word exploded from the usually mild man. Thuza grabbed Paul and left the house. Caroline grabbed her pack and slipped into her shoes. John, however, held back.

"Brother Phillip?" John asked, indecisively. "I can't let you fight my battles. I will meet the soldiers." Caroline blanched at his words. She reached for him but Dolly cautioned her.

Brother Phillip turned to face John. "The battle is the Lord's. Go, son."

John demanded, "Tell them we were never here. Tell them we're heading for China. Tell them anything." His sorrow filled his eyes.

Brother Phillip patted his arm. "I won't lie. Go now and never forget these people here who love you."

John tore his gaze from the man. Shouldering his pack, he took Caroline's hand firmly in his own. "Thank you, my friends." And they were gone. Running through the village past their cabin, past the children's play area, past the rock where John had declared his love for Caroline, behind the waterfall and through the crevice in the stone. They lit a torch and followed Myaing through the warren of caves and out into the dank valley below. Nanda brought up the rear. They made their way quickly along a path and then turned sharply left and plunged once again into the jungles of Burma. Nanda led them through the forested plains for the rest of the day and into the night.

<><><><><>

The conspirators quietly made preparations for dealing with the soldiers. They hid the evidence of their plans and attempted to look convincingly like a group of friends sharing tea.

Within the hour, soldiers entered Brother Phillip's Haven for the Lost, marched up the mountain by the warden of Bourey Prison, Captain Htet. The dozen or so soldiers, adorned in a mismatch of camouflage khaki, grey-green, and plain green uniforms, deployed throughout the village gathering all the people they could find into the village square. They ended their endeavour at the last house in the square,

Brother Phillip's. The soldiers stepped onto the front porch where Brother Phillip and the others stood, sadly surveying the soldiers' progress through the village.

"Come! Come!" the soldiers ordered. The companions followed slowly, praying for guidance and protection.

Once the remaining people had been gathered, Htet ordered a head count. There were seventy-five people remaining in the village, sixty-five of whom were men.

"Who is Brother Phillip?" the Captain asked. No one moved. He motioned to one of his soldiers who began to beat one of the villagers, chosen at random, with the butt of his rifle.

Brother Phillip walked forward. "I am Brother Phillip." All eyes were focused on the brave and gentle man.

Captain Htet walked slowly toward him. "Why did you not answer when I called you?" He frowned at Brother Phillip who shrugged.

"I am an old man," Brother Phillip replied, simply.

Htet's eyes narrowed as he studied the older man. "What is this place?" Htet demanded.

Brother Phillip responded, "A haven for those seeking peace."

Warden Htet glared at Brother Phillip. "Only men seek peace? I notice you primarily have men here. These few women must be kept very busy," he declared, suggestively. The crowd murmured in revulsion. Continuing, Captain Htet announced, "We are searching for two escaped convicts, dangerous people, disturbers of the peace—a man and a woman. We have evidence that they were seeking this place. Have they been here?"

Brother Phillip replied honestly, "We have no one here who fits that description."

The Captain looked skeptical. "You will all remain here in the village square as my soldiers search the buildings. Understood?"

Forged in the Jungles of Burma

Brother Phillip acknowledged his orders. "Understood." *I understand well, Father, the longer they take to search, the further John and the others will have travelled.*

The soldiers conducted a thorough search of the village and the surrounding area. Htet had a quiet discussion with three of his soldiers.

Finally, Captain Htet addressed the villagers again. "We will wait. There is a European woman who regularly visits your village. I know she is due here within the next two days. We will await her arrival. You will remain in the square under our 'protection' until she arrives. Understood?"

Brother Phillip agreed again. "Understood." The villagers settled in for a long day.

<><><><><>

Caroline was terrified to be traveling in the jungle again. Every vine looked like a snake and every movement sounded like the rustle of a big cat. John seemed oblivious to Caroline's fear, so consumed, she supposed, was he in fear for their friends, left behind to face the consequences of his actions. The travelers camped for the night in a tangle of vines at the base of conjoined trees, covered by Myaing's lightweight tarp which was strung between the branches of the trees with twine. After eating a cold meal inside the shelter, they rolled out their blankets on top of a nylon ground sheet to sleep. Very conscious of the fact that they were not alone, the married couple lay perfectly still, side by side, afraid to wind up spooning the wrong person. Seeking solace, Caroline rolled over against John and pressed her arm across his chest.

"You're humming," John commented. She began to shiver. He whispered into the top of her head, "Are you cold?" She shook her head and pressed herself more firmly against him, humming louder. He wrapped his arms around her. "What's wrong?" he asked, as she nervously fiddled with the buttons on his shirt.

"I'm frightened." She buried her face in his shirt.

"Of what?" he asked.

"Snakes." His breath escaped in a short laugh.

She poked him in the ribs. "It's not funny!" she reprimanded indignantly. John glanced over at Nanda and Myaing who seemed asleep, facing away from John and Caroline. John flipped himself to hover over Caroline, resting on his elbows. Her eyes were fixed on him and a small grin pulled at the corner of her mouth.

"You are my mighty titan. Why would you be afraid of snakes?" Caroline pulled him down into a full body hug. Folding his arms behind her head, he held her tightly until her shivering ceased, and then rolled to the side, pulling her against him.

"I will protect you. Trust me," he whispered into her ear.

"I trust you. I trust you even if you do smell like a panda bear." John hissed at her. "Why you—" He pinned her arms across her chest and began to tickle her. She giggled and kicked back at him.

"Shh! John, you'll wake the others. Stop." She spoke tersely between giggles. John stopped.

"Go to sleep," she commanded settling against him, her breathing calming as she succumbed to sleep. "I love you" she murmured just before she dozed off. "Love you, too" he replied.

As the first glow of morning broke through the forest canopy, glinting from oval leaf to spiny thorn, they gathered their things and started off, the fuchsia sunrise blending into the azure blue of the sky. This leg of the journey would be easy relative to the mountainous journey ahead. They walked across the forested plains, the turf springy beneath their feet and the broad leafed trees allowing easy passage. They were heading for the village of Chaungzon where there was a community of Christian Chin. The indigenous Chin were known as a lionly people who had fought and won a place in Burmese society, though they frequently faced cruel persecution. Myaing believed he could find shelter there and hopefully make a connection to help them find transport north.

The day passed quickly, the travelers taking short breaks to eat or rest. Completely unfazed by the journey, the siblings looked as fresh in the late afternoon as they had at dawn. John had kept himself quite fit in Zeya's village and in Katafygio, so only Caroline seemed to be suffering as the long day lengthened into evening.

"John." Caroline reached out and pulled on his shirt sleeve causing him to slow and take her hand, raising his eyebrows in question.

"I'm exhausted. I need to rest." He nodded, released her hand and paced forward to catch up to the twins. Caroline could hear him talking and saw their terse responses. She sighed. John was arguing but they were unmoved. She saw him nod as he slowed to let her catch up to him.

"They say we can't stop here. 'Rest later, not now.' I'm sorry, my love. I think we have to trust them." Caroline grimaced in spite of the fact that she was pleased to see her husband learning to put his trust in others.

"It's okay. Can you help me?"

John wrapped his arm around her waist. "Lean on me," he said. They walked on for another hour before Myaing came back to tell them to wait. They could see the outlines of houses in the distance and chimney smoke rising from the buildings. While Nanda and Myaing headed into the village, John spread a blanket on the ground, encouraging Caroline to lie down while they waited. Resting her head on his leg, she sighed and drifted off to sleep with John running his fingers through her hair.

"Mrs. Brock." Caroline woke to the words and the gentle shaking of her shoulder. She smiled up at him. *That's the first time anyone has called me that,* she mused as she forced herself fully awake. "Nanda and Myaing have found shelter for us." John waited for Caroline to rise before taking her hand. The four companions walked toward a house at the northeastern edge of the village where they were welcomed in and offered tea. *Poor John,* thought Caroline. *He's really come to hate tea but there he is, smiling gratefully and dutifully draining his cup.* Caroline leaned against him, eyes flickering in fatigue, as she attempted unsuccessfully to stifle huge yawns. Taking pity on her, their hosts showed John and Caroline to the one bedroom in the house. Caroline began to drift into slumber almost immediately but John was restless, unable to settle.

"You can go and talk, if you're not ready to sleep," she mumbled.

"No point," he responded. "I don't understand the local dialect. And they might offer me more tea." He grimaced at the thought. Caroline slipped her arm across him to still his fidgeting. As drowsiness pulled her under the waves of sleep, she slipped her arm under his shirt. He groaned softly and began to kiss her. When Caroline's hand slid lower down his body, his hand began to stroke along the outside of her leg.

She moaned. "Mmmm, what's wrong? Can't sleep?" she asked drowsily.

He rolled her off him and whispered in her ear, "I want you."

She woke a little more and whispered back. "We're in a tiny room in a tiny house."

He began to kiss along the side of her face. "How many more days will we have a bed in a bedroom on this journey?"

She smiled against him, running her hands along his back and around to his chest. "Hmmm, we'll have to be very quiet."

John smiled against her. "*I* can be quiet." He chuckled.

"What's that supposed to—" He cut her off with a kiss.

Morning found a sleepily contented couple. They awoke to Nanda's knock on the door and rose dutifully. Their host family fed them breakfast, replenished their provisions and sent them on their way with a blessing. Caroline was still tired from the day before but the walking was easier across the plains. The short grasses were dotted here and there with the massive, gnarled trunks of the trees whose entangled roots stretched along the ground and then plunged from the surface deep into the earth. Their branches looked perfect for climbing with lots of purchase for hand and footholds and Caroline wished they had time to stop and play.

Reaching Kwaya in the late afternoon, Myaing led them to a works shed in the middle of town. He and John left Caroline and Nanda sheltered behind the building as they went around to the front. Caroline soon heard John's voice speaking Burmese through the broken window above her head. When Caroline asked a question in Burmese, Nanda held her finger to her lips to shush her. After a while, Myaing and John returned. Caroline asked what happened.

"He is willing to drive us to Hta Man Thi but not until tomorrow. He has to pick up some tractor parts in Hta and deliver them to a client in Tason. I had to offer him most of our money to even consider taking us along. He's invited us to drink with him tonight." Caroline began to protest. "I don't think we can refuse." She opened her mouth again. "And you and Nanda are definitely not coming. This is no place for a half-Karen and a Canadian woman to be carousing." He paused and changed the subject. "Myaing's not certain where we can shelter. That fellow," John nodded toward the building, "has offered to let us stay here in his loft but my instincts tell me that's not a good idea. If he thinks he can get his money without the inconvenience of taking us along, I think he'll do it."

"Where will we stay then?" Caroline inquired.

"I'm not certain," John replied.

Nanda reached out and touched John's elbow. Turning to Caroline, John explained, "She says we should get something to eat and see what God provides." Caroline nodded and smiled at Nanda. The foursome trooped back out to the street, moving away from the works. Finding a small restaurant, they sent Myaing in to order the food and located a table under an umbrella outside. Myaing returned with four helpings of okra and split pea fritters. Handing out the portions, the four tucked in.

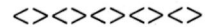

<><><><><>

At noon on the day John and Caroline reached Kwaya, Maryn Dale reached Katafygio in the form of Maritza Dallish. She entered the village square riding a handsome chestnut mule and accompanied by a husky Tibetan man leading a pair of donkeys loaded with packs. Maryn was a woman of striking beauty. Her midnight black hair flowed gracefully below her shoulders, perfectly straight. Her beauty always seemed magnified in the moonlight, when the reflected rays of evening's orb glistened on her hair and the grey of her eyes deepened to an ebony hue. She was tall for a woman, topping Htet's height with her five foot, ten inch frame, curved with slender perfection. The white of the furs wrapped about her body magnified the light tan of her skin, and the suede leather boots accentuated the contours of her shapely legs. Maryn sauntered over to Warden Htet.

"Ah, what have we here? It's my favourite prison warden. How are you, Captain Htet?" She leaned in and kissed the air by his left cheek.

"Ms. Dallish, it's so good to see you. Colonel Shing's message asked me to meet you here. Have you news of your errant spy?" He attempted to retain a look of coldness in his eyes but it was difficult to project more ice than Maryn possessed.

"Hmmm, Colonel Shing tells *me* that you let him escape." She accused the warden in a chilling tone of voice.

He flushed in humiliation and anger, frantically slapping his riding crop against his burnished boots. "If the Burmese government cannot control the rebels, what am I to do?"

She replied frostily, eyes narrowed. "I believe the idea was to confine Brock until his network was obtained." They glared coldly at one another. Htet dropped his eyes first.

Maryn continued. "As a result of your gross oversight, Colonel Shing asked me to meet you here. He also sent his soldiers to patrol the area around Yangon, the eastern Karen border and along the Chindwin River in the west. We will find him." Htet adopted a more humble attitude as he was reminded that Maritza Dallish was one of the few people that Colonel Shing made requests to rather than issuing orders.

"May I ask why we are here in this *Christian* outpost?" He spat the word out in disgust.

"I have a theory that, once John escaped, he would head here to meet with me, knowing that I could help him obtain papers with which to cross the border into India. What he does not know, is that I would actually hand him over to Colonel Shing and a new interrogator. Poor John, he really should have let me in on his little secret network while he still had the opportunity. Now when they find him, Shing will make him pay for this merry chase." She affected a pout then shook her head, sweeping her hair aside with the movement.

"He is not here. We have searched the entire village." Htet gained a little confidence in the supposition that Maritza was wrong.

"Perhaps." She walked over to the men huddled in the village square, walking amongst the crowd searching, it seemed, for one face in particular. Coming to a stop in front of Archie who refused to follow her movements, she crouched down in front of him.

"Oh, Archie, darling, how are you?" She reached out and patted his cheek, condescendingly. "I've missed you so much." Meeting her eyes, Archie held her gaze but did not respond. Dolly tensed where she sat beside him. Maryn watched the pair for a time before she made her move. She gripped Archie's chin, piercing the skin of his cheek with her painted red fingernails causing him to wince in response. Dolly gasped beside him and Maryn, rising languidly, turned a laconic stare toward her. Focusing her eyes on two of the soldiers, she indicated Archie and Dolly with a contemptuous nod and ordered, "Bring them here." The soldiers forcibly lifted the passively resisting Archie and Dolly, bringing them to a standing position in front of the group.

"Archie, my Pinocchio, I want to know if my little spy has been here." When Archie didn't respond right away, she slapped him, grazing his cheek with her nails. Archie's eyes watered.

"Maritza, what happened to you? Were you always this hard?" Archie asked. Maryn glared at him malevolently. She took a step back and borrowed a pistol from one of the soldiers. Unexpectedly, she brought the pistol around across Dolly's face, causing the older woman to cry out in surprise and pain as she stumbled back from the blow. Archie's arm shot out immediately to catch and hold her as a determined look crossed his face.

"Maritza, stop!" Archie commanded. "She has nothing to do with this."

"Perhaps before, but now …" Maritza cocked the gun and pointed it at Dolly.

Archie bowed his head for a moment and then straightened. "Ask me what you want to know," he said as Dolly gasped, "No Archie, not for me." He looked at her and smiled sadly. "Yes, for you—for a long time, for you."

Maryn seemed impatient with the interchange. "I am looking for a British man, though he is able to pass himself off as an Italian, Spaniard, or Russian, if necessary. He would be travelling alone."

Here Captain Htet interrupted, "We believe he is travelling with a woman, a Canadian who also escaped from the prison." *I'm only glad that Vlad is dead to prevent him telling Shing about my error in leaving them together.* Htet kept his thoughts firmly inside his head.

Maryn fixed him with a frigid stare, silencing him. "He may be travelling with a Canadian woman, who as far as I know, has no connections to the information I seek and, therefore, is of no interest to me. He is six feet tall with dark brown, almost black hair, brown eyes and a ruddy complexion. He would most likely be using a cover story as a journalist or an anthropologist. Have you seen him?"

"There have been no journalists here and we have only Simon, our very own anthropologist." At this, Simon bravely stood. Maryn walked over to him and ordered him tersely to sit.

"Archie, I believe you are lying to me. What happened to your god's orders against lying, Pinocchio?"

"I am not lying to you." Maryn moved in menacingly while nodding to a soldier to grab Dolly's arms. "Father, please protect those fleeing pursuit," Archie murmured then added clearly and decisively, "Leave her alone, Maryn. I will tell you what you want to know."

Maryn jerked around at the use of her real name. "How do you know that name?" She gripped his shirt in her fist as she hissed at him.

"John told me."

"Why would he do that?" she asked, brusquely.

"He is my friend."

"Now I *know* that you're lying to me, Archie. John Brock keeps his emotions safely locked away and he trusts no one." Maryn approached threateningly.

Brother Phillip stood, announcing in a calm and confident voice that somehow exuded a commanding quality, incongruous with the reality of being a captive, "People change."

She laughed, sardonically, "In the twenty years I have known him, no one has ever cracked the granite around his heart." She nodded to the soldiers who dragged Archie away and began to beat him.

CHAPTER 13

THE THINGS I'VE DONE

Sitting outside the little restaurant in Kwaya, the four travelers were becoming increasingly concerned by the middle aged Burmese gentleman staring at them from the shop doorway across the street. By the time the man pushed himself off the wall, walked over and arrived at their table, John had given Caroline a set of instructions for escape. Leaning his arms on the table, the man grinned, speaking in English softly, "You're Christians, yes? I saw you praying before your meal earlier." John tensed.

"Yes," Caroline responded, watching the man warily.

"God be praised!" he exclaimed. "He told me to come here today and watch this café and I would be given the opportunity to bless someone." The man reached across the table toward Caroline but John grabbed his arm and held him. The man's confusion was written across his features. Caroline studied the man before her. His smooth, round face was topped by grey-flecked black hair which was long but well-kept and clean. He wore a navy cotton jacket over a white shirt and a matching navy longyi tied up as pants. His bronzed legs peeked out the bottom of his pants, clad in well-worn flip flops. Caroline turned from her evaluation of the man and placed her hand on her husband's leg.

"John, it's okay." He turned to look at her and she repeated, "It's okay."

"No," John replied, casting his eyes up and down the street as though watching for enemies lurking nearby.

"There are four of us and one of him. It's okay," Caroline reassured her husband. Studying the stranger, the street and vicinity, John slowly released the man's arm. Caroline took it and shook his hand, a grin spreading across his face again.

"Hello, brother," she said softly as John watched her in surprise.

"My name is Maung. Come with me."

Caroline rose to follow the man but John rose to stop her, whispering tersely, "What are you doing?"

She smiled and squeezed his arm. "Trust me." Taking charge, she grasped John's hand firmly and dragged him along. Nanda and Myaing accompanied them.

They followed Maung along the dirt track that served as the central street of the village. The tall narrow trees lining the path reminded Caroline of the palms lining Sunset Boulevard in California except that the houses were thatch and board rather than beach houses and mansions and the women and children passing them were carrying burdens and dressed in longyi rather than bikinis and rollerblades.

The village was set out in a grid system and they travelled several blocks before turning right down a narrow dirt track that led toward the western edge of town, near the wide open rice fields to the south. Their journey ended at an over-large thatched house that looked as though it had been added on to repeatedly until it resembled a lopsided hexagon held together by duct tape and prayer. The muddy yard was littered with the evidence of much use and the jungle seemed to have surrendered the territory to its diminutive inhabitants. As they approached the house, they could hear the riotous sounds of many children playing.

"Come in. Come in. I will find my wife." Maung left the travelers inside the front door and went to locate his wife. John stood tensely beside her as Caroline gazed around at the simple home. The foyer where they waited, opened into what looked like a parlour on the right and, on the left, a dining room/sitting room/kitchen all in one. The rooms were brightly lit and children's paraphernalia littered every surface—a few books, wooden toys, homemade dolls and half-finished projects.

Maung returned shortly with a petite smiling woman, somewhere in her late thirties, heavily pregnant; on one shoulder lay a small blanket and on the other an infant. Her body seemed to be perpetually in motion, tidying, wiping or rocking the little one in her arms.

"This is my wife, Chit." Turning to his wife, he explained in Laizo, a dialect of Chin, "These are the brothers and sisters who God has sent to bless us." She beckoned them further into the house and prepared coffee for them in between setting the baby in a playpen for a nap, wiping up two spilled cups of diluted sugar cane juice and brushing the twigs out of another child's hair.

"Most people do not know that Myanmar produces some of the best coffee in the world. My brother-in-law works on a coffee farm near Bassein. He keeps us regularly supplied," Maung explained.

"Thank you so much for your hospitality. This is the best coffee I've tasted in a long time. Thank you." Caroline took another sip and continued in English, directing her words to Maung. "May I ask, please, what you mean when you say that God sent us to bless you?"

Once Maung translated, he and Chit laughed in joy together, interrupted by two children who came in from the yard in a heated discussion about what looked like a rock.

"Salai, Salai. ..." The children presented their cases to Maung, who responded, clapping each boy affectionately on the shoulder and sending them on their way with their conflict happily resolved.

Chit smiled at Caroline, explaining. Maung translated, "Who would have thought that two boys could argue over a stone?"

Caroline smiled, sadly. "I had five sons. Sticks and stones are the most precious things to boys." Caroline's sad recollection brought John's attention back to his wife and he watched her tenderly, wrapping his arm around her affectionately. Maung didn't translate the message but Chit patted Caroline's knee, sympathetically sensing another mother's pain.

"As to what I mean when I say that God has sent you to bless us, well—," Maung began. "I will begin at the beginning, as any good tale should. Six years ago, Chit's sister-in-law was killed during a wave of Karen persecution, leaving Chit's brother alone with two small children. He was unable to care for them and we took them in, not having any children of our own. Then, five years ago, a stranger showed up at our door with three children. He told me he had heard that my wife and I took in orphaned children. He told us that the children's parents were killed during the terrorist bombing of the airport in Hwebalan and that a benefactor had provided money for the children to pay for their upbringing and education. We prayed about it and took the children thus launching this." He spread his hands, gesturing around him. "The money given to us has allowed us to take in many children. We have 11 children with us at present and one on the way; one for each disciple, if we include this next precious gift." Here, he tenderly patted his wife's belly. "God has blessed us richly."

"Um, excuse me, Maung, but how does this explain meeting us?" Caroline asked. She glanced over at John who had a strange look on his face. Nanda and Myaing seemed completely unfazed by the entire incident

"Over the years since the first children arrived, God has sent me out and in each incident we have received another blessing. Last night, God told me to wait across from the café and he would send another blessing—and here you are! What can we do for you?"

In a mixture of surprise and joy, Caroline looked first at John, then at Nanda and Myaing, none of whom seemed able to answer. "We are travelling to Hta Man Thi and we believe we have a ride but have nowhere to stay tonight," Caroline declared.

Chit slipped her hand through her husband's arm and spoke to him. Nodding, he declared, "You will stay with us tonight. We have no vehicle so we cannot help you get to Hta Man Thi but we have many bedrooms and we wish to share them with you for this night."

Caroline smiled. "Thank you, thank you very much."

Maung showed them to their rooms and invited them to use the house as their own. Nanda and Myaing found a corner to sit and chat quietly. When John went off to wash, Caroline found herself at the front window watching the workers in the rice fields across the way. Twenty minutes later, Caroline jumped in surprise as John slid his arms around her and rested his chin on her shoulder. Recognizing his familiar form and scent immediately, she reached up and ran her fingers through his familiar hair.

"I love you," she said. They stood quietly for a time, before she added, "What's wrong?"

"Nothing's wrong," he replied, continuing to tap out a rhythm with the index finger of his right hand where it lay across her belly.

"Tell me." Caroline wrapped her arms across his arms, stilling their percussion, and holding him tightly against her.

He sighed. "It was me," John said.

Caroline twisted her head around toward him. "What?"

"I was here five years ago when we got word that there was a bomb attack planned for the airport. We managed to subvert the worst of the plot but six people were killed, two of them the parents of three small children who survived the blast. I gave my agent money to find good care for the children." Caroline turned in his arms and hugged him tightly.

"God's had his hand on you for a long time." John held her close. When he released her, she could see the wonder in his eyes.

<><><><><>

Archie's battered body was dropped at Maryn's feet, groaning as he hit the ground. Dolly knelt by him, weeping, as Brother Phillip's face hardened in determination.

Maryn addressed the crowd. "You will tell me now where John Brock has gone," she commanded.

"Or what?" She turned in surprise to face the elderly Brother Phillip who had spoken with steel in his voice. She couldn't hold his gaze and turned away to hide the fact. Turning back to him, she raised her firearm. She pointed the pistol directly at Brother Phillip's heart while calling for a volunteer from the shocked community of Katagygio. "Tell me or I will shoot your precious leader."

With a look of peace in his eyes, Brother Phillip faced Maryn Dale. As a shot rang out, echoes of his last words, "I forgive you" lasted beyond the reverberations of the gunshot. Astonishment rippled through the crowd. Maryn dropped her arm, a look of shock seizing her features. Kyi stood and walked forward to take Brother Phillip's place.

"You will need to shoot me, as well," he declared.

"And me as well." Simon took his place beside Kyi.

"And me." One after another the people of the village stood against the soldiers.

"Can sixteen stand against seventy-five?" Kyi demanded. The soldiers began to look very nervous. Htet's eyes flickered around the crowd. Maryn continued to stare at the body of Brother Phillip, who was smiling slightly in death.

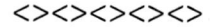

<><><><><>

John, Caroline, Nanda and Myaing joined Maung, Chit and the children for supper. They ate at a long table which was brought out for meals only. Between times it was folded and placed along the wall of the large room. The older children, boys and girls, served the others, the meal a loud and boisterous affair of stories and tales, jokes and gentle teasing. After the meal, the family gathered in the sitting room for songs and a Bible story. Caroline watched John's face throughout the meal. Normally so self-controlled, his face gave away his fascination with the loving way the adults and children interacted, father and mother joined in a united purpose: showing these children the love of Christ. Maung was a loving, gentle father but also obviously maintained discipline when necessary. When the toddler, Suu, "whomped" her 'brother' in the head with her doll, Maung was quick to remove the offending article and reprimand the child who, once she had apologized, was gathered into a hug and given a short, toddler-length lecture about telling your brother to move first before "whomping" him.

As evening fell into night, John declared that it was time for him and Myaing to meet the driver for a night at the local bar. Caroline was extremely uncomfortable with the situation but John insisted that they had no choice. After Myaing and John left, Nanda helped Chit put the children to bed while Caroline helped Maung tidy the house. Caroline's heart was assaulted by grief as every toy reminded her of her own loss. Once the house was put to rights, Caroline retired to her room to cry out the sorrow these memories brought with them.

Late into the night, she heard a commotion in the vicinity of the house. Looking out the bedroom window, she saw four men staggering, singing at the top of their lungs. Two of the men stopped part way along the dirt trail and returned the way they had come, waving repeatedly to the men left behind. The other two men continued reeling along the path, coming to stop at the front door of this house. Caroline crawled into bed and faced the wall, humming loudly. A few minutes later, John knocked and entered their room, pausing a moment before walking over to the bed. Caroline felt the bed dip as he sat on the edge. Reaching out he coiled a lock of her hair around his finger.

"You stink like a brewery," she muttered.

"You say the nicest things," he replied, evenly.

"You're drunk," she continued, louder.

John gently placed his hand on her shoulder and turned her toward him. "I'm not."

"I heard you, outside. I saw you."

John chuckled causing her to snap her gaze toward his face angrily. "You seem to forget, my love, that I am a spy; I am an expert at seeming to be something I'm not." Caroline paused, searching his face as he confirmed, "I would never come to you drunk." He leaned down to kiss her. She kissed him, tentatively, then winced.

"Blah! You taste terrible," she complained.

"You know, this is not good for my self-esteem." He paused and a small grin played across her face. "I did have some ale, it would have been suspicious not to, but I'm not drunk." Caroline ran her thumb across his lips and he kissed it sweetly. Heaving himself off the bed, he offered, "I'll go wash up. I'm knackered. However, I do have something important to tell you." John left to use the washroom. Returning, he crawled into bed.

"Better?" He leaned over, kissing her.

She smiled in response and kissed him back, curling against him. "Yes, much better. Thank you." John smiled at her. "What did you have to tell me?"

"There have been soldiers, Burmese and Chinese, travelling up and down the highway for the past two weeks."

Caroline froze. "Shing?"

"I think so. We need to keep a low profile. Staying in a hotel tonight would have been very dangerous. Just being a foreigner in these parts is enough to get us arrested by the Military Intelligence."

"Why don't they have to register us with a Form 10?"

"I asked Maung that, earlier, and he said that the Chief of Police here tends to turn a blind eye to this home as one of the children safely housed here is his nephew," John replied. They lay still for a time, each buried in their own thoughts.

"John, when will we be safe?"

He reached down, tipping her chin up, raising her head to look directly into his eyes. "We'll be safe from Colonel Shing if we can get into the bush to the west of Hta without being tagged. As for how long until we're really safe—probably not until I draw you the most luxurious bath in my house in London." She kissed his chin and settled her head on his chest.

<><><><><>

Captain Htet could see his soldiers becoming nervous in the face of seventy-five men and women who were willing to die rather than tell them anything else. He looked over to Maryn who seemed frozen, her eyes fixed on the dead man.

"Lower your weapons!" Htet ordered, tucking his riding crop under his arm. Failing to retrieve useful information could be explained to Colonel Shing but losing a dozen soldiers would definitely result in a one way trip to a laogai. Htet raised his arms in a placatory gesture as he came to stand before the assembly, declaring, "You have harboured a fugitive. This is a subversive act. The State Protection Law dictates that each one of you should be imprisoned for three to five years," Htet expanded the legislation to meet his current needs, "but, I am generous. I will not arrest you. However, your goods are forfeit and will be destroyed by fire." He added in a rush, "Once this forfeit is paid, we will leave." Htet wanted there to be no doubt that the soldiers would leave if the villagers remained passive, for he knew if these villagers were no longer afraid and if they decided to act, they could wipe him out and all of his soldiers in a flash.

"Set the buildings alight!" Captain Htet commanded. The soldiers obeyed their commander's orders. Watching the soldiers sadly, the villagers wept as their village burned.

Kyi had been studying Maryn for some time. He moved over to her and placed a hand on her shoulder. This seemed to break the spell she was under and she jerked away, trying to camouflage the fear in her eyes.

Maryn quickly made her way to Captain Htet. "Where to now, Htet?" she asked huskily.

"Do you still believe that Brock will head for India?" She nodded. "Then we head down the road to Hwebalan. That would be the quickest way for him to escape. We wait for him at the airport." Maryn nodded again. She moved over to her man who, after helping her mount the patiently waiting mule, goaded the donkeys into action and rode back down the mountain without another word.

<><><><><>

Caroline, John and the twins bid their hosts farewell in the morning with many thanks. The foursome made their way back to the works shed by 7:00 am and waited around the side of the building for their driver to arrive. He showed up bleary-eyed about half an hour later. The travelers waited impatiently for another half hour as their hung-over chauffeur filled the truck's gas tank and replaced the spark plugs which he produced from a pocket where he kept them to prevent theft. Then, he decided to have breakfast. Finally, just after 9:00 am they piled into the back of the truck and set off for Hta Man Thi. The driver provided them with thick car blankets to increase their comfort.

John suggested that they hide under the blankets until the truck passed through the town in order to avoid being seen by any of Shing's men who could be patrolling the road. They needn't have bothered. As soon as the truck passed the last house in the village, it began to rain—hard. The car blankets combined with Myaing's tarp were helping a little but the rain driven under by the wind was slowly defeating its repellency. The intensity of the rainfall, however, helped to camouflage them from cars passing by. When the rain made visibility too poor to continue, the group huddled in the cab of the truck with the driver.

Aside from the difficulties presented by the rain, one other problem existed: Caroline's decidedly foul mood. John kept asking if she was okay and she knew her responses were becoming increasingly rude, for which she felt guilty. Nanda and Myaing were casting sidelong glances in her direction and had taken to remaining silent unless huddled under their own blanket in the flatbed of the truck. When Caroline cast a withering glare at the driver for smoking in the cab of the truck, he had been so intimidated, that he was now flicking the ash of his cigarette out the window every few minutes. Each time he opened the window, the occupants were dashed with a soaking spray of water. Caroline just couldn't seem to shake her dark and stormy mood.

"For better, for worse," John muttered when she responded to his latest question with a hard stare and sarcastic, "wonderful". Soon, back in the flatbed under the ever dampening blanket, John bravely tried again to shift her mood.

"Caroline." She ignored him. "Caroline," he said, sternly. Turning to him, her eyes grew dark as she furrowed her brow. "Come sit here." She allowed him to move her to sit between his legs with her back leaning against his chest like a chair.

"Comfortable?" She nodded and she felt her mood thaw a little. "Tell me how we should redecorate when we get home." She turned to him, quizzically, and, meeting her gaze, he smiled softly, encouraging her.

"What do you mean?" she asked, interested.

"Well, when I bought the house, I just called in a decorator and had the house done. I stuck up a few pictures, had a safe installed and—voila—home. But now it's your home and—well—how do you want to decorate it?"

Caroline studied his face for a time. "Well—what does it look like?" she inquired, warming to the idea.

John began, "When you walk in the front door, into the foyer, there is a door on the left that leads to the garage and a door on the right that leads to the spare room."

"A garridge, is that the same as a garage?" she asked, mimicking his accent and smiling slightly.

Grinning, he replied, mimicking her accent, "It sure is, eh."

Laughing, she continued, "How is the spare room decorated?"

"In white—white bedding, white bed and white walls."

"Could we paint it blue—maybe sky blue with darker blue trim?" she suggested, tentatively.

John kissed her cheek and answered, "Of course."

"I would probably want some sort of colourful print with blue in it for the bedding." She began to enjoy the discussion. "What else?" she prompted.

"There are some steps up to the great room which is open concept. On the right hand side there is a sitting area with a couch and two chairs. The chairs face the fireplace and there's a television off to the side. Behind that, there's my desk and computer. Directly across from the stairs is another small couch and two high backed chairs for entertaining people who drop in for tea. Around the corner to the left there is a large walnut dining table and, off to the side, a galley kitchen."

"Are all the walls the same colour?"

"Yes."

"What colour?"

"Brown. Although the kitchen is a lighter brown."

"The bedroom?"

"Another shade of brown."

Caroline turned her body to stare at his face. "Are you serious?" He nodded in response. "The kitchen definitely needs to be yellow—a soft but bright yellow. I think each area should have its own feature wall ..."

Caroline became more and more excited about redecorating and John listened contentedly. She felt him smile into her hair, relaxing into the sound of her happy voice.

Sometime later, Caroline woke John by gently prodding his ribs. "We've reached Tason," she whispered.

The driver left to get lunch. It was agreed that Myaing would take some money and purchase lunch for the four who would eat in the cab of the truck. After their hunger was satisfied, Nanda and Myaing went in search of the driver, hoping to bring him back before he found the local drinking establishment. John pulled Caroline close and leaned against the passenger side door.

"What was bothering you this morning?" he asked.

Caroline sighed and pulled his arms more tightly around her, shifting slightly so she could see his face. "When it started to rain, the whole journey just got to me. It feels like it is interminable, like I'll be running away forever." She continued more quietly, "And then when it's over, I don't even get to go home." John's expression saddened at her admission. "But then you made me feel like I am going home. I can picture our home now and I have lots of ideas of what we can do with it."

"If you don't like the house, we can buy another one. Because of my job, I have to work in London but we can live anywhere you want within reach of that." Caroline moved away from John and turned to face him directly. Resting her forehead against his, she slipped her arms around his neck. Taking her face tenderly in his hands, he kissed her.

"Thank you," she said.

"You're welcome."

<><><><><>

Htet, Maryn and the soldiers had been at the airport for two days. The trip along the road in their jeeps had gone fairly quickly. Htet was pacing up and down the so-called lounge in the airport which really consisted of a cordoned off area in a large, drafty—obviously built in world war II—Quonset hut containing dusty-musty space and a few hard backed chairs. Maryn was silent, as she had been for much of the journey. *She was purported to be tough as nails, the ice queen,* Htet thought in irritation. Htet had finally had enough. If the ice queen wasn't going to give them some direction, he would have to. He did not relish another interview with Colonel Shing where he could be held responsible for a failure. He was certain that she would direct any blame to him, probably quite successfully. Ordering the jeeps to be brought around, he instructed four soldiers to remain at the airport and sent the rest out in trios to patrol north and south along the Chindwin River.

<><><><><>

The afternoon passed without incident as the four travelers remained huddled under the sodden blankets, the rain continuing to hide them from prying eyes. They arrived in Hta Man Thi tired and wet. Thanking the driver, John paid him the rest of his fee plus a few extra kyat for his silence. Then, the weary crew plodded across town to the northern outskirts of the village, attempting to keep a low profile as John led them to his contact. Along the way, they purchased Mon Lon Ye Paw, eating them as they walked.

"When we get home, I'm never eating rice again," Caroline stated emphatically.

John smiled at her. "When we get home, I'm never ever drinking tea again." Caroline took his hand and kissed it continuing to hold it.

"We're here!" John exclaimed. As they walked up the path to the house, a girl of about fifteen or sixteen came around the corner of the house, singing to herself, freezing when she saw the travelers approaching. Caroline was concerned that they had frightened the girl until she let loose a squeal of delight and, running down the path, flung herself at John, stopping short of actually embracing him. "U-lay. U-lay....." Then she launched into a rapid flow of Burmese that confounded Caroline and made Nanda and Myaing glance at each other in bewilderment. The girl grabbed John's hand and hauled him toward the house. Apparently, John was not moving quickly enough, as she released his hand and disappeared into the house, calling for her mother and father. A man about John's age or a little older came running from the edge of the forest beside the house. Recognition dawning, he slowed, dropping the axe he was carrying with a broad grin spreading across his face. Moving toward the man, John called out a greeting and they met in a broad hug.

"George Davis!" The man greeted John in English. "It has been many months since I have seen you—many, many months. How are you, my friend?" Just then the girl returned, dragging her mother by the hand. The mother stopped and began to weep when she saw John. She moved forward, taking his hand and bringing it to her cheek, pressing it there. Her husband put his arm around her shoulders and gently held her.

"George Davis—welcome! And welcome to the friends who come with you." Here she indicated Caroline and the twins.

John took over the conversation. "Arun Naing, these are my friends Nanda and Myaing and this," here he put his arm around Caroline and pulled her close, smiling grandly, "is my wife, Caroline." The woman began to weep anew as she took both of Caroline's hands in hers and pressed them to her lips. Arun bowed in respect.

"This is my wife Aung and my daughter Htay, for whom I owe your husband the most eternal gratitude." Arun bowed again. Aung released one of Caroline's hands but held the other as she led her into the house. Once the guests were seated, tea and food were provided in abundance. Aung and Htay made several trips back and forth to the kitchen to ensure that everything was perfect while Arun and the guests waited in silence so that Aung wouldn't miss any of their conversation. Once the seven were well supplied with refreshments, Caroline finally released the question she'd been impatiently holding.

"In what way does my husband deserve your gratitude?" She couldn't read his look as John watched his teacup.

Arun answered. "Ten years ago, your husband was travelling through western Myanmar on a—uh, how do you say?—a scientist's visa studying the Chin. He and I came across one another several times as our work—uh—intersected. You see, I am a shnei nei—a lawyer who specializes in the rights of the indigenous. Aung and I invited him to stay with us after a time and we became ahswei—friends. George left us after three months, only to return six months later. Unfortunately, his return coincided with a Typhus epidemic. Myanmar is a divided country and in our division, the care for the sick—

healthcare has fallen by the wayside. The privileged left the area, the rest were left to die.

"Aung and I chose to stay in the area because of our work with the Chin people here. Three days before George arrived, Aung and Htay succumbed to palei—disease. I could not afford the medicine to help my wife and daughter but George, somehow, found the medicine we needed and pjau—saved Aung and Htay from death. He stayed on and helped me care for my family until they were well again. Without George, I would stand before you alone and aggrieved."

Caroline reached over and took John's hand. He looked at her as though he expected to be reprimanded. She was confused by his reaction though none of the others in the room seemed to notice. After a time spent chatting with Arun about his work and about Htay and her schooling, John and Arun wandered to the back room of the house that Arun used as an office. Nanda and Myaing joined Aung in the kitchen and Caroline was left in the sitting room with Htay.

"What do you want to do when you finish school?" Caroline asked.

"Teacher." The shy young lady responded. "Papa says there is a special school where only the Chin can attend and maybe I could teach there." She kept her eyes lowered demurely. The two were silent for a time.

"Miss?" Caroline turned her face to the shy girl. "How did you meet Mr. George? My Papa said he was a man who could give kindness but whose heart was impervious to the touch of woman or man." She paused while Caroline tried to think of how she could respond. "Mama says he's like an attractive book that was closed with a lock, like a diary with no key." Caroline studied the girl not knowing what to say. The sixty minutes they had spent with this family had shown her more about John than the sixty days prior.

As darkness bathed the sky in night, John came in search of Caroline. Taking her hand, he urged her to, "come with me". They walked across the side yard, through a stand of trees and into a clearing beyond. John spread the blanket he carried on the ground and lay down on his back, pulling Caroline down beside him.

"Close your eyes," he instructed. She complied. "Now, open them." A panorama of sparkling diamonds danced across a velvet expanse.

"It's beautiful, John." She reached beside her to take his hand and lace their fingers together.

"How does it make you feel?" he asked.

"Humble. Inspired. Grateful."

Leaning up on his elbow, he gazed into her face. "That's exactly how I feel whenever I look at you. I love you."

Startled at the power of his words, Caroline's eyes filled with tears as she reached out to stroke his face tenderly. "I love you, too," she declared.

He leaned in slowly. She kept her eyes locked on his, her heart racing and her breath catching in her throat at the passion facing her. A fraction of a breath from her mouth he slowly changed direction and kissed her chin, her cheek bones, her eyelids. She could feel his strident breath against her face and the expectation in his frame. Reaching up she plaited her fingers through his hair and, drawing his head closer to her, she guided his mouth to its desired location. He lightly brushed his lips across her mouth, barely touching, a moan escaping his throat at his self-imposed torture.

"John," she whispered. His eyes fluttered closed as he possessed her mouth completely and then gave her complete command of his.

"I'm glad you married me because I would hate to go home to Dolly's after a kiss like that," Caroline alleged. John grinned at her and pulled her against him as he rolled onto his back.

"How do you think they are?" she asked, reminded of Dolly's plight in the community.

"Can you picture any man getting the best of Dolly?" John answered.

Caroline smiled then sobered again. "I'm worried about them."

"Brother Phillip would tell you to— "

"Trust God." Caroline finished his sentence. Pondering the fates of their friends, they had no way of knowing for now but Caroline knew that John would find a way to know later.

Suddenly, Caroline remembered something. She turned her head to John. "Does Arun have to register us with a Form 10?"

Smiling, John responded, "This far north, the MI doesn't bother to post a man." She pondered that information for a time.

"Bear?"

John smiled at the endearment. "Mmmhmm."

"What happened here? Do they know who—or what—you are? Why did you tell them my real name?"

He tightened his arm around her. "Caer? Are you upset with me?" He asked very quietly. She lifted herself to look directly into his face. He flinched.

"Why would I be upset with you?" she puzzled.

"You're not upset?" He breathed a sigh of relief.

"No. But I do want to know what happened here. Was George Davis your cover name? What were you, a biologist or what?"

"My cover is George Davis, anthropologist."

"Is that why you told me your name was George in the prison?"

"Yes, it was an automatic response. When I travel across Southeast Asia, I travel as an anthropologist studying the indigenous tribes. I find the tribesmen are often the best source of information regarding social and political unrest and are generally far enough away from the seat of power to allow me to keep my anonymity."

"I thought you were intentionally lying to me."

"Well, in a way, I was. I had no idea who you were or why I had been imprisoned with you. I just knew, from the first moment I saw you that I was going to need a strong defense to keep you from taking my heart." He dropped his hand to her waist and hugged her to him.

"I got it anyway." She rested her hand on his chest and her head on his shoulder.

"Yes, you did."

"So, why did you give them my real name?" she inquired.

"I didn't want you to have to lie."

She pondered her next question. "If you travelled as an anthropologist, is that why you hated Simon?"

"I didn't hate Simon. He had designs on you and I was desperate to keep him from succeeding."

She looked up at his face again to see if he was teasing her. "You're serious," she alleged.

"I loved you for a long time before I acknowledged it to myself, but that doesn't mean I was daft enough to walk away and let that pillock have you." John slipped his right arm behind his head, raising his eyes to meet her gaze.

She leaned in and kissed him. "Simon never had a chance, my love. It's always been you." John pulled her close again and kissed the top of her head.

"Tell me what happened here," she demanded.

John shrugged. "Arun was a good contact—connections with various indigenous groups, poor enough to welcome help and devoted to his wife and child—a perfect asset. It took some time to gain his trust but once I had it, he was quite free with information. When I returned after my initial groundbreaking visit, the area was riddled with Typhus. I almost didn't come, but when I slept at night, I couldn't get the image of their little girl sick with a fever, dying, out of my mind and in the end I came. When I saw how ill Aung and the girl were and how distraught Arun was, I just couldn't walk away. I got permission to purchase the medicines they needed."

"Did you gain their gratitude that way?" she asked carefully.

"I know what you're asking. I told '5' that it would purchase their gratitude and lead to years of valuable information, which it has."

"But— " she prompted.

"Caer, what if there isn't a 'but'? What if that's it? What if that's really who I am—the heartless blaggart?" John studied her face as she composed her answer.

"I don't believe you. The man who beat back those prison guards, the man who tenderly called me back from despair after the soldiers beating—that man is not a heartless anything, he is my husband and I love him."

"Truly?"

"Truly—always." Sliding his knee between hers, he grasped her waist, pulling her so close they couldn't tell where one body ended and the other began.

"Let's go to bed my beautiful wife."

Caroline woke alone. She heard voices under the window and looked down to see John, Myaing and Arun covered in grease, doctoring two motorcycles. Glancing up, John caught sight of Caroline watching them and waved happily. *Boys and dirt,* she thought, *a perfect combination.* Caroline bathed and dressed quickly, descending to the kitchen to help with breakfast, only to find a mini-feast laid out before her. Htay had left for school already but Nanda and Aung were deep in conversation when Caroline entered. They spoke in a combination of Chin and Burmese that Caroline was unable to follow. She bade them good morning and eagerly awaited an invitation to indulge in the delectable looking repast.

As Aung noticed Caroline's entrance, she greeted her warmly. "We will wait for the men," she stated firmly. After half an hour had passed and Caroline was still offered no food, she decided that something had to be done. Politely excusing herself, she went in search of her husband. Finding the three men still removing and refitting motorcycle parts, she greeted them. Just before she called John, she remembered that here, in this place, he was not her John but George Davis—a man who surprisingly shared all the best characteristics of her husband and none of the annoying habits. She grinned to herself. *I wonder how many men I'm married to.*

"Mr. Davis." John looked up, a twinkle in his eye. "I believe that the women are waiting for the men—for breakfast—even though they are *very* hungry." She smiled at him, ironically. He fixed her with a steady stare but his eyes continued to sparkle.

"And— " He left the sentence hanging, teasing her.

"And, I believe it is in your best interests to wash up and come **now**." She stressed the last word, narrowing her eyes at him in emphasis.

John turned to the other men. "Gentlemen, I believe I'm ready for breakfast, what about you?" Myaing and Arun exchanged a glance, avoiding Caroline's intense stare. They nodded.

"Excellent choice," she responded. "I will see you in five minutes." She grinned at them, turned on her heel and walked back into the house. Entering the kitchen, she announced, "The men are ready for breakfast. They'll be here in five minutes." Aung's smile grew broader and broader until she finally broke into an unexpected guffaw.

Breakfast was cheerful and delicious. As the women cleared the table and washed the dishes, the six adults chatted sociably. Once the kitchen was spotless, John invited Caroline to join him and Arun in Arun's office. Nanda joined Myaing as he returned to the motorcycles to finish preparing them for a journey. Approaching the desk where a map was set, already spread, John motioned Caroline over, and he and Arun showed her the route they would be taking.

Feeling extremely disheartened as Arun began to explain the terrain, Caroline asked, "About how long do you think this will take?" John narrowed his eyes, sending her a 'softly softly' message telepathically. She sighed. *I'll never figure out exactly who I'm supposed to be in this situation.*

"It should take you about a week or so to travel up the mining road and along the river. That will bring you to those farms you wanted to study. How long do you think you'll need to be there?" Arun asked.

"I think we'll send Nanda and Myaing back with your bikes once we find a farmer who's willing to cooperate. They should be back to you in two or three weeks. I don't want you to be without transportation for any longer than necessary," John replied.

"It's no problem, my friend. I owe you much more than two motorcycles, tents and a little food. What are you hoping to learn from your study of the farms?" Arun inquired.

"I'm looking to see whether these so-called isolated farms form a community. I think that would make an interesting paper," John replied.

"Well, Aung and I can make do with our bicycles for a few weeks. I'm happy to be able to begin to repay our debt to you." John nodded at Arun, accepting his gift of thanks. Then, taking the map, John and Caroline left Arun to his own work as they exited the room to help prepare for their departure. Caroline knew that John was hoping to leave by mid-morning. He was chafing at the wait, muttering his complaints to her, while Nanda and Myaing finished with the bikes. When he could no longer contain himself, he marched out to the yard to hurry the twins along. Caroline followed. As they turned the corner of the house, they came upon the siblings involved in a heated argument. John slowed and halted.

Caroline prodded him in the side. "What are they arguing about?" she whispered tersely.

"Who gets to drive," he responded, humour in his voice.

"Go Nanda!" Caroline whispered and made a small gesture with her hand. John turned and watched her, eyebrows raised in question.

"You want to drive?" he asked.

"Yes," she responded.

"Why didn't you tell me?" he wondered.

She shrugged, "I dunno." She looked down, studying the grass.

"Cogent argument," he smiled sardonically. Reaching into his pocket, he removed the key and handed it to her.

A grin split her face and, looking up, she thanked him. "Of course you realize, the last time I drove a motorcycle, I dropped my passenger off the back," she stated, grinning again.

"Oh great, now you tell me," he replied, ironically.

John and Caroline returned to the house to bid farewell to Arun and Aung. Caroline thanked them several times for their kindness until John pulled her hand and whispered, "Enough". She pretended to ignore him but moved on to farewells. John and Arun carried the extra gas cans, packs of food and water, and the two tents and bedrolls to the motorcycles. John dropped half of the gear at Myaing's feet and loaded the rest onto the other bike. Handing Caroline one helmet, he fastened the other on his head and waited for her to hop on. Myaing watched the couple with interest and then surprise. As Caroline started the bike and John climbed on behind her, Nanda punched her brother in the arm and grabbed the key from his weakened grasp. Within ten minutes the quartet had departed. The mining road was quickly located and they set off at a furious pace, the women enjoying the free feeling of the wind and the control of steering their course. Caroline found the dirt road was narrow and bumpy but each mile took them closer and closer to home.

<><><><><>

Htet's jeep stopped in Tason to find that no one had seen any foreigners in the area in the past two weeks. When Maryn suggested that they had been too slow leaving Hwebalan, Htet lost his temper, calling her every name in the book and threatening to contact the Military Intelligence to inform them that a British-Chinese-Indian spy was in their midst.

"How dare you?! How dare you?!" She screamed, emerging from her subdued state. She moved in threateningly close to the prison warden and told him in no uncertain terms that a trip with the MI for her would equal a trip to a laogai for him. Remaining uneasy allies, they moved on to Hta Man Thi.

<><><><><>

After a break for lunch, Caroline gave John the key with a huge kiss. Nanda, however, retained control of her key, much to Myaing's frustration. They journeyed through the afternoon, stopping at twilight and making camp. They cooked supper over a fire and set up their tents. Nanda wondered if the men wanted to share one tent while the women shared the other but John let her know in no uncertain terms that he would be sleeping with his wife.

Lying in their tent, each trying not to disturb the other, John and Caroline remained awake. The day on the motorcycle had been exhausting but not tiring. Finally, Caroline broke the silence.

"Are you asleep?" she whispered.

"If I said 'yes', would you believe me?" To which he received a jab in the ribs.

Caroline rolled against him and said, "I can't sleep. I feel tired but restless."

"Too much travel and not enough exercise. We'll have to find a way around that tomorrow," he replied.

"Can we talk?" she inquired, softly.

"All right," he responded, in a whisper.

"Anything?"

He tipped her face up to look him in the eyes. "What is it that you want to know? Go ahead and ask me."

"When we were with Arun and his family, why did you expect me to be upset with you?"

"Well, it was the first time you had been confronted with my job—with the sorts of things I've done."

"Those are the things you've done *in the past*."

"Caroline, this is my job. Using Arun, the danger that would put him in if my real purpose was discovered, that's—well, it's—very small, shall we say, compared with some of the other things I've done," he stated evenly.

"I'm not naïve. I understand what it is that a spy does." He looked skeptical as she paused, studying him. "I do want you to tell me everything, John. In order for us to be truly one, we need to share our lives with each other. I'm not afraid of what you would tell me."

He laughed without mirth. "Perhaps, I'm afraid of it."

"Are you ashamed of what you do?"

"Yes, of some of the things I've done—of my job, no. I save hundreds of lives every year and help keep my people free and independent." He lifted his chin defiantly.

"Will you keep doing it when we get home?"

He kept his eyes steadily on hers. "I don't know. It's the best and the worst of me."

"Then how will you know whether or not to return to MI-5?"

"Wait and see. I've noticed there's this extra voice in my head, now, since I became a Christian."

Caroline smiled. "Don't worry. It's the Holy Spirit, not schizophrenia." She laughed gently at her own humour.

"What would Brother Phillip think of working for MI-5, I wonder?" John said.

"Well, I guess it depends on whether you're a pimp or a politician."

"Pardon? Please clarify that statement."

"A pimp who became a Christian would be good to his prostitutes. He would provide healthcare benefits. He wouldn't beat them up. I mean, wouldn't the world be better off, if all pimps were Christians? However that scenario still has a problem since being a pimp is inherently sinful—worse than sinful, it forces others to sin. So in truth, a pimp who becomes a Christian simply cannot continue to be a pimp.

"Politicians, on the other hand, are purported to be liars and cheats. When a Christian becomes a politician, he can no longer lie and cheat. He can no longer take advantage of others and manipulate situations for his own ends. However, being a politician is not inherently sinful. It merely provides a position wherein sin can be accomplished. A politician who becomes a Christian can continue to be a politician if he changes his behaviour."

"I'll figure it out," he asserted.

"We'll figure it out together," she responded.

He pulled her close.

CHAPTER 14

MOUNTAINS, RIVERS AND FARMS

Htet and Maryn reached Hta Man Thi the next day. As they passed through the village, they came upon a group of villagers having a heated discussion at the northwestern edge of town. Maryn ordered one of the soldiers to remove his uniform and approach the group in civilian clothes to discover the point of the debate. Blending into the edge of the group, he returned after a time and reported.

"It is a debate about men's rights and women's rights." Htet shook his head in disgust.

As he returned to the jeep, Maryn sought to clarify the soldier's discovery. "What prompted the discussion?" she asked.

"Apparently, two motorcycles were driven out of town yesterday. Women were driving them both," the soldier replied.

A slow, malicious grin dawned on Maryn's face. "It's them," she stated firmly. Htet turned and returned to her.

"How do you know?" he asked slowly.

"What Burmese man would allow a woman to drive? We've got them. Call Colonel Shing and have him order a helicopter. Contact the Burmese MI and tell them we've located a British spy on their soil."

<><><><><>

Three more days on the motorcycles and they reached the end of the road, literally. John and Myaing drained the gas tanks and dug holes to hide the cans of petrol in case the bikes were found. Nanda and Caroline cut branches to hide the bikes. A quick meal and they climbed down to the river. The river was narrow enough to swim but much too fast to risk. Flowing downstream, the clear blue waters bounced and jumped over the rounded rocks littering its depths. Travelling upstream, the walkers were usually forced to trek along the raised, densely forested riverbank but occasionally found game trails that allowed them to approach the water.

The feeling of being far from people gave Caroline a sense of liberation, prompting her to burst into song as they threaded their way through the mix of soft and gentle broadleaf trees and the scratchy, poky needles of the conifers lining the riverbank. John smiled at the sight of his wife so happy and relaxed. The others joined in the songs when they knew the lyrics in Burmese or English.

Around lunchtime, they found an easy slope and made their way down to the water to cook a meal away from the hugging arms of the forest. John sent Caroline to cool her feet in the rippling water as he prepared the meal. Nanda and Myaing attached lines and hooks to sticks they had foraged above and fished.

Responding to John's call, Caroline gingerly made her way across the rocks, carrying her shoes. She reached over to flick water on him when he froze. When she reached out to tickle him, he grabbed her hand, demanding silence. Above the trees floated the unmistakable sound of a helicopter. John kicked the small fire apart and buried it under stones to reduce the smoke then tossed their gear into the bush.

"Put your shoes on!" he ordered. Caroline dropped to her seat and put her shoes on as quickly as she could, her feet still wet and sticking to her socks.

John hollered to Nanda and Myaing who came running. "Put your shoes on!" John yelled, again. Her eyes began to fill as she hurriedly obeyed. John grabbed her hand and the foursome ran up the riverbank and into the trees. John insisted they run as far as possible away from the spot they had stopped. He kept them near the riverbank so he could get a look at the helicopter. Secreting them each under a heavy bush, he planted himself along the edge of the tree covering. After about ten minutes, he sighted the helicopter, flying perpendicular to the river. It then banked east, travelling downstream away from them. Once he was certain it had disappeared, he called the others out of their hiding places. Caroline charged at him, terrified and furious in equal measures. She punched at his chest and collapsed against him. He held her tightly against his body as he spoke calming words of comfort into her hair. Her shoulders shuddered with the force of her tears. When she had calmed, he brushed the hair back from her face and kissed her cheeks.

"Okay?" he asked. She nodded and drew him close again. Releasing her after a moment and shouldering his pack, he walked upstream, drawing her to him again, holding her firmly around the shoulders. Nanda and Myaing followed. Calling a halt at sunset, John took Caroline aside to talk to her.

"Caer? Darling?" He tipped her face to look at him. She sighed in sadness. "Want to talk about it?" he asked kindly.

"I'm sorry. I just went from feeling so free to feeling so terrified, that's all. I'm sorry I hit you. Suddenly, it was just all so overwhelming." She paused. "John, I want to feel safe again. I'm tired of it all." She began to sob against him, the tears rising up from an unknown, seemingly never ending depth. John held her tightly, stroking her hair and murmuring love to her.

Apologizing again as she regained her composure, he kissed her in response then released her. "Can we talk now?" he asked tenderly. She nodded, leaning against his shoulder. "I think we should send Myaing and Nanda back. If that helicopter was looking for us, then we're all in peril. I can't ask them to follow us into that danger. What do you think?" He encouraged her to answer.

"Of course. You're right. I'll miss them." Her voice wobbled as she responded.

"At least we'll finally be alone." He smiled kindly to show that he was joking. "I'll go and tell them now," he said. She nodded and began to weep again, softly this time. Nanda and Myaing refused, insisting that they could lead them all to their father's old farm and hide safely there until the pursuers gave up. John returned to Caroline, tenderly comforting her through the night.

Nanda, Myaing, John and Caroline continued walking upstream through the rustling trees along the riverbank. After about half an hour of hiking west, they changed direction to travel south-southwest toward the twins' childhood home. They emerged from the trees into a cleared area. The farm looked active but the fields contained a type of millet, not rice. There were two buildings in the clearing, a house and some sort of outbuilding which really just looked like a thatched roof suspended over a half-wall of lattice. The only plants taller than the millet were the small fruit trees planted right against the house which was constructed of palm fronds and grass wrapped around wooden posts with a small covered entryway shading the front door. John and Caroline investigated the house and Nanda and Myaing went to check the outbuilding.

Passing through the entryway of the house, pushing aside the palm screen, and stepping onto the cool dirt floor, Caroline thought she detected a mewling sound from inside. Their calls, however, met with no response. *Perhaps they have cats*, Caroline mused. The inside of the house was divided into a living space and a sleeping space. An unpleasant odour drifted across the room on the slight breeze and, upon investigation, they discovered a macabre secret—a woman, about thirty years of age, lying dead. John estimated that she had been dead between twelve and twenty four hours—and, there, huddled in the corner of the room was a small child, a boy of about three, arms clasped firmly around his knees, mewling and rocking back and forth. Caroline was paralyzed at the sight of the suffering child but John approached him calmly, urging him to come. The boy allowed John to lift him, hanging limply in his arms. Squeezing her elbow to urge her forward, John carried the child outside to a nearby well, drawing Caroline along beside him. He pumped some water into a basin and looked around for something to clean him. Caroline began to hum.

"Caroline. Caroline," he insisted. "Please find me some towels or washcloths or something." Shaking her head, Caroline backed away. She needed to get away from here—too much sorrow—too much pain. She needed to get away from the unpleasant odour of mortal sickness. She walked away, far enough to feel she had escaped but close enough so she could still hear John. He was calling her. She found a tree to sit against where she could watch what was happening. Nanda and Myaing returned with a dairy cow in tow. Nanda pumped water for the cow and then milked it.

"There is a man about forty or so, dead in the outbuilding, dead for some days, I would say." The words and sentences floated across the breeze to Caroline's ears.

John nodded at what Myaing said, and added. "The mother is dead in the bedroom—maybe a day or so. It looks like she died of some kind of fever. Did you find any sign of others?"

Myaing shook his head. Gesturing toward the boy, he said, "I believe he is alone now." As those words drifted across the grass to her ears, Caroline began to shake.

John nodded again in response. "Nanda could you please find me some clothes for this little fellow?" She turned to do as he bid and when the boy was washed and changed, they moved away from the house to fix a meal.

Caroline needed to move. She rose and walked in and out of the trees surrounding the farm. Her mind seemed to have shut down. She could hear John speaking to her as he approached. She could understand his words but she couldn't seem to get herself to obey his instructions. *I just can't do this!*

"Caroline, supper's almost ready. Can you come and help me with the boy? Please?" John asked firmly, annoyance leaking into his voice.

"No." She turned and walked away from his shocked expression. She heard him jogging behind her then felt his firm grip as he spun her around to face him. She turned to him, her face flushed and sweating. She tried to listen to her husband but she needed to escape. Her heart was pounding, her hands were shaking and she needed to get away.

"All right. Please just come and eat then. Nanda will feed the child. All right?" Her gaze flickered to his face then away again. He took her shaking hands in his own and a look of worry crossed his face. *Okay. I'm sorry.* She nodded and let him lead her back to the fire.

The group ate in silence. Nanda fed the child who, once his belly was full, struggled down and climbed onto John's lap where he promptly fell asleep. *I can't do this. God, help me!* Springing to her feet, Caroline announced, unexpectedly and with force, "I need to go for a walk!" The others watched her in shock.

"Caer, just wait a few minutes, and I'll walk with you," replied John, sounding annoyed and apprehensive in equal measures. Beginning to shake again, she sat back down.

Once the meal had been consumed, John opened the obvious topic of conversation.

"The searchers are on our trail again, Myaing, it's time for you and Nanda to head back home. Go back to the bikes, return them to Arun and head home—with our deepest gratitude. I will nee—"

"Take the child." Caroline interrupted in a strained voice.

John turned toward her. "Pardon?" he asked.

"Nanda and Myaing should take the child," she said, her intonation rising and tightening with every word. "Take it to Maung and Chit. They will be happy to have another blessing." She stood up suddenly, and declared, "I need to go for a walk." John reached for her hand but she pulled away and protested, "No! I need to get away. Now!"

Caroline heard John rising and following her. The feeling of pursuit made her walk faster until she was running into the trees.

"Caroline!" he called after her. Once she reached the edge of the forest, she faltered and slumped against a tree, panting.

"What is wrong with you?" he demanded.

"Let them take it to Chit. She'll care for it." Her voice sounded strange even to her own ears.

"And how exactly are they supposed to carry him? Strap him to the back of the bike?" She shrugged and he grasped her shoulders, preventing her from turning away.

"Take it to Chit," she said again, her voice rising. *Why won't he listen?*

"This boy is Indian, in case you hadn't noticed." John sounded angrier as this conversation continued. "Taking an Indian orphan into Burma would not be the most compassionate choice, now would it?" He shook her once.

Her head snapped to his and she slapped his hands away. "What do you propose to do?" Her voice had lost the strained edge and now conveyed anger rather than panic. She stared him directly in the eyes—a flaming red glare.

"We can take him with us to India and leave him in an orphanage or something. At least then he would be with his own people. I could arrange to pay for his care once we're home."

"If he's going to an orphanage, what difference does it make where?" she argued.

"It matters and you know it matters. Stop this Caroline! I am not walking away from another child. I can save him and that's what I am going to do." He stalked away from her and back to the fire.

"John," she called hotly after him. "We're walking into danger. Villains are pursuing us. Just exactly how long do you think he's going to survive?"

John stopped and turned to her, anger in his face. "At least you've finally acknowledged that he's a person and not an 'it'." He turned again and left her there.

Nanda gathered some of the child's clothes and a few small toys. Myaing formed a small funeral pyre and the three adults held an informal funeral for the boy's dead parents as Caroline hovered on the periphery, watching the proceedings. Nanda had found a necklace and a few other pieces of a personal nature in the house. She put these with the boy's clothes so he would have them when he was older. Once the fire had been doused, John led the way back to the river, carrying the boy. He took Caroline by the arm as he walked past her. His grip propelled her forward.

Before departing, Myaing confirmed, "You remember the way I showed you?"

"I remember," John confirmed.

At the river, the twins bade them farewell and headed downstream toward home.

John, Caroline and the boy, whom John had decided to call Digby after his favourite literary character from childhood, walked upstream. They walked through the evening and camped under the camouflaging shelter of the trees that night. Caroline watched John feed the boy and lay him down in the tent. Once Digby was asleep, John approached her where she sat against a tree, studying her carving; the carving John had given her. She heard him take a deep breath but rather than speak, he sat beside her and waited. Gradually, when she realized he wasn't going to scold her anymore, she shifted her position to lean against him, drawing comfort from his warmth. He wrapped his arm around her shoulder, reaching over to trace the carved heads.

"I'm sorry," he said. She shrugged in response. He continued, "I'm sorry. I didn't understand. All you needed was a little understanding and all I could do was scold you. I'm sorry." Kissing her cheek, he whispered, "Tell me."

She sighed sadly and turned her face into his shirt. "I suddenly felt like I needed to get away or I would die. It hurts too much."

"Tell me why," he urged her gently.

Silent tears began to fall down her cheeks. "I don't want another child I care about to die. I can't do it. I never want to hurt like that again."

"What makes you think that you will?"

"What if he catches whatever his parents died of? How would we care for him? What if Shing's men find us? What if he's attacked by a leopard?" She raised her eyes tentatively to look at him. He traced his fingers along her cheekbone and down across her jaw to her chin. Leaning in, he kissed her tenderly on the lips, holding her chin gently with his thumb and finger to keep her gaze on him.

"What if he survives and we find a safe place for him to stay? What if I manage to protect you *and* him?"

"I don't feel like I can do this."

"I know," he said. "I know." He rocked her gently as she wrapped her arms around his waist.

"I'm sorry," she whispered into his shirt.

"For what?" he replied, mildly. "For not being perfect? For not meeting every impossible situation with perfect equanimity?" She raised her eyes to his face, searching it. "I'm proud of you." He paused. "And I'm grateful to you, for letting me do something right for a change." Smiling, he gazed down at her, kissing the tip of her nose. "I love you." She nodded and followed him to bed. Entering the tent, Caroline lay as far away from Digby as possible while John lay down between them. The little boy snuggled into John's warmth.

<><><><><>

"Sir, we've located two individuals walking along the river heading back into Myanmar," the helicopter pilot reported to Captain Htet who grinned slyly at Maryn Dale, gleefully slapping his riding crop against his gloved hand.

CHAPTER 15

INDIA

Caroline awoke to a pointy elbow in her ribs. She felt beside her, in search of John's hand, but instead, she found a little hand which grasped hers in response. Looking down, she saw that Digby had wiggled to firmly plant himself between her and her husband, finding the warmest, most inconvenient spot to sleep. Turning on her side, she studied the little boy's face, peaceful in repose.

"I know you're watching me," she stated, shifting her gaze to John who was reading her face from beneath half-closed eyelids.

He grinned. "He woke me with his shivering, so I put him between us, to keep him warm," John explained.

"I'll go sort out breakfast," she said. Getting up, she put her blanket over Digby.

John came out of the tent as she was laying the fire and organizing the food. Approaching her, he slid his hands over her hips. "We'll reach the mountain today and then, just a few more miles and we'll be on Indian soil." He gently patted her bottom and she swatted at him playfully.

"Okay, Father Goose, junior needs to get up and get going." John smiled at her, darting back to goose her.

"In honour of my name." She smiled at this as she swatted at his hand again.

The trio ate and headed off toward the secret way. As they emerged from the trees to take the hidden path, they heard them again—the whirr of chopper blades. The helicopter seemed to rise above the trees directly ahead of them. John grabbed Caroline's hand and pulled Digby tightly to his chest, the boy sensing the danger and clinging like a monkey to him. The chopper seemed to be heading directly for them. There was only twenty metres until they could reach cover.

<><><><><>

"This is air traffic control Azawl. We have an unidentified flight occurring along the border with Myanmar. Request permission to notify the military?"

"Permission granted."

"This is air traffic control Azawl, notifying military personnel of an unidentified, unregistered flight crossing the border."

"This is Air Force control acknowledging your message. Thank you, air traffic Azawl. Over and out."

"Air Force control, please send two Jaguars to intercept unidentified flight, exact coordinates to be sent en route."

"Air Force control, Jaguar one and two on intercept course. Do we have permission to engage?"

"Permission granted. See them off, men."

"Jaguar two, confirm, fire warning shot."

"Confirmed."

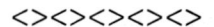

<><><><><>

John and Caroline ran as fast as they could over the rocky terrain, the sound of the helicopter growing ever louder. Suddenly from the west came the awe inspiring roar of two fighter jets. The jets zeroed in on the helicopter and let it know in no uncertain terms that it was an unwelcome intruder in Indian skies. John grabbed Caroline and pulled her down beneath him as one of the jets fired near the helicopter. John and Caroline looked back to see the helicopter veer away to the east. The fighters followed it to a certain point and then turned back. John and Caroline cheered, sending thanks miles high to the fighters, "Yeah to the Indian Air Force!" John yelled, hugging the confused Digby to him.

John, Caroline and Digby crossed the secret way and began the long trek down the mountain to Akhegwo, India. They walked and rested, walked and rested. On the second day of their journey, they hitched a ride on a logging truck which left them at the bottom of the mountain, half a mile from Akhegwo. People stopped and stared as they entered the village and John used this curiosity to find the location of the post office which turned out to be a desk at the back of the general store right in the middle of the village. John took Digby to buy him some milk as Caroline called home, reversing the charges.

"Dad? Daddy. Is that you? It's Caroline. Yes, yes, I'm alive. You'll never believe what I've been through, but for now, Dad, I need you to wire me some money. Yes, about two thousand American dollars—in rupees...I know...I'm stuck in Akhegwo, India, close to the border with Myanmar. Once I get to England, I'll contact you again, okay? Daddy, thank you. I love you. Give my love to Mom as well, okay? Here are the details to send the money..." Caroline gave the details to her father and went in search of John and Digby, finding them chatting with the cashier. Digby sat on the counter drinking milk through a straw.

"Caer. This woman thinks that Digby is her cousin's son. When I described the farm, she said it sounds like it could be them." He returned his attention to the cashier. "She says she's willing to take him. Her daughter has just been married and she is finding the house very empty."

Caroline whispered, "Does Digby like her?" John smiled broadly at her and nodded. The boy happily embraced his new 'Aunty' and John and Caroline watched as she fussed over him, patting his head and pinching his cheeks. They handed over his possessions including the few personal pieces Nanda had gathered. John tousled the boy's hair and Caroline kissed him tenderly on the cheek. Now, there was nothing the couple could do until the wire transfer of money was completed so they walked around the village, searching for a place to sit and rest. After walking a few minutes in silence, Caroline nudged John with her shoulder.

"What?" he asked.

"Do I have to say it?" she inquired.

"Say what?" he asked, indicating that, yes, she did need to say it.

"You were right—about Digby. You were right and I was wrong." His eyes softened as he watched her discomfiture.

"I told you I was teachable," he replied.

She gave a short laugh. "I'm sorry," she said contritely.

"There's no need to apologize. I think I understand—attachment means pain." He rested his arm around her shoulders.

"I guess we're not as different as I previously thought," Caroline mused.

"We share many scars in common. We're a matched set," John stated. She nodded and slipped her arm around his waist.

"I love you," he said as he kissed her cheek.

"I love you, too, my Bear."

After Caroline returned to the post office to collect the money her parents had sent, John purchased two bus tickets and determined the route of the bus that would take them to the next village, where they could flag down a bus, to take them to the train that would eventually deliver them to Kolkata.

As Caroline joined him, he asked, "Did you get the toilet paper?"

"Excuse me?" she responded in confusion.

"The toilet paper—did you get the toilet paper? And we'd better get some bottled water, as well." John paused. He reached over and grabbed a handful of rupees. "Be right back. If the bus comes, just step into the road and wave your arms. Don't let it leave without me!" He spoke over his shoulder, leaving a baffled wife as he jogged back to the post office.

John returned carrying two rolls of toilet paper, some bottled water and a box of cookies. When their looked-for transport appeared, he stepped into the road, waving his arms to gain the driver's attention. As the bus pulled up, Caroline saw the crush of people, packages and animals already loaded. Firmly holding Caroline's arm, John boarded the bus, grateful that they had no luggage to worry about. He forced his way to the middle of the bus and intimidated an adolescent into giving up his seat. John positioned Caroline in the seat and stood guard beside her. The bus lurched forward and the longest, hottest, smelliest, noisiest, most miserable bus ride of her life began. With the canvas shade missing, dust floated in through the uncovered window, blanketing everything inside in a light coat of earth. Caroline noticed that the young man beside her had a coin in his ear and raising her eyebrows in query, she sent John a nonverbal question.

"Wait and see," he responded. After a few miles, John nudged her with his knee and nodded out the window toward a small Hindu shrine at the side of the road. The young man removed his coin and tossed it toward the shrine. "To ensure a safe journey along the mountain roads," John explained. Caroline was amused at first, until they began to traverse the hairpin turns through the mountains at high speed. The passengers rocked to and fro, clinging tenaciously to any mobile or immobile object that might steady them. The driver seemed determined to catapult them to the floor on more than one occasion.

"I get it now," she said to John. "I understand why my father always prayed for 'travelling mercies' before we left on any trip." John smiled in response.

After changing buses four times and waiting a total of six hours for connections, John and Caroline finally exited the last bus and made their way to a train station. They bought tickets to Kolkata but noticed that not everybody bothered with that formality. On the trains, the women were expected to travel in their own compartments apart from the men. Caroline squeezed herself onto a seat with four other women. She spent the journey fretting about how she would find John again once they disembarked.

A trip to the bathroom, with her toilet roll firmly in hand, revealed a small room with two porcelain foot-shaped imprints, a handle on the wall and a hole. As Caroline placed her feet on the imprints, clutching the handrail firmly, she watched the railway ties speed by beneath her. *Well, at least it doesn't smell.*

Finally, after hours of dusty, exhausting travel, John and Caroline found themselves in the bustling city of Kolkata. John appeared as Caroline stepped off the train and, locating a taxi outside the train station, John once again used his powers of persuasion to find them a spot in the loaded taxi and asked the driver to deliver them to the British Deputy High Commission.

Paying the taxi driver, John firmly took hold of Caroline's hand and together they approached the gate to the High Commission. There was a line of people down the street waiting to enter the gates but John bypassed them all, with Caroline in tow, and approached the guards at the gate.

"I'm sorry, sir, but you'll need to wait in line," the guard warned the oddly attired couple.

"I am a British citizen—" John began.

"Then show me your passport," the guard interrupted.

John fixed the man with a steady stare and a low, calm voice full of warning, "Corporal! You will not interrupt me again. Find your way inside and tell the Secretary that you have an agent out here with clearance code M5JB Zulu Bravo Charlie." John's bearing left no mistake about his authority. The guard saluted and quickly strode to his call box where Caroline could hear him reciting the code that John had given him. Two minutes later the guard returned and politely ushered them inside the gate. John kept a firm hold on Caroline but the guard never even considered her presence in his haste to obey the instructions given from inside the building.

John was greeted by the Deputy Secretary and immediately ushered into an ornate office to await the Deputy High Commissioner, who entered shortly thereafter.

"Mr. Brock, your people have been very concerned about you. You look as though you've been lost in the jungle for weeks."

"You're not far off the mark, Deputy Commissioner. Is MI-5 still searching for me?" John inquired.

"Indeed. I've sent them a preliminary message to the effect that someone with your personal clearance has arrived at my door," the Deputy High Commissioner said.

"May I contact my people on a secure line, sir?" John asked.

"Of course. I will give you a moment. Perhaps your companion will join me for some tea," the Deputy Commissioner suggested. Caroline's eyes filled with fear at the thought of being separated from John in this unknown place but when he nodded at her, she followed the other man out of the room.

"My name is Daniel, Daniel Johnson. I am the Deputy High Commissioner." He stopped and offered her his hand in greeting. She looked at him blankly for a moment before realizing that he wanted her identity.

"Sorry. I'm Caroline." She reached out and shook his hand. He seemed satisfied with that and continued on down the corridor.

"You're not British, then. Are you an American?" he inquired.

"Canadian," Caroline responded. She felt completely overwhelmed by this situation, so far removed from her experiences of the last several months. John seemed to slide right into the role that this situation demanded but she was floundering and she knew it. *Father, help me get it together,* she prayed as Daniel opened a door and ushered her through. Entering a sitting room, Caroline saw a lovely, immaculately dressed woman sitting primly on a settee beside a table set for high tea.

"This is my wife, Emma. Emma, this is Caroline—" He left the sentence hanging, prompting Caroline to fill in the blanks.

"Wells. Caroline Wells," she replied. *Wait, no, Brock—I'm Caroline Brock now. Oh well.*

"Will you join us for tea?" Emma asked in accented English—an accent Caroline couldn't identify.

"Yes, thank you," Caroline responded. Emma set about serving tea, passing plates and milk, sugar and cucumber sandwiches.

John entered as the last sandwich was offered and accepted. Emma sent her servant to bring more sandwiches as John approached the table. As his gaze rested briefly on Caroline's face, she nodded to let him know that she was okay.

"Emma, my dear, may I present John Brock, one of Her Majesty's Servants traveling abroad. John this is my wife, Emma." John shook her hand politely and took a seat beside Caroline. The servant arrived with more sandwiches and the tea party continued.

"The weather has certainly been mild this year, wouldn't you say, my dear," Emma began, carrying on a conversation of complete and utter inanities. Caroline was glad of John's calm and composure as she was expending all her energy not giggling at the woman's vapid questions. If she only knew what they had been doing for the past months. Eventually, the bizarre tea party drew to an end but Caroline would forever hold the image of the Belle dressed in her beautiful lavender silk dress, coiffed hair perfectly in place, serving the two strangers clad in sneakers and Burmese longyi, hair wild and tangled and clothes filthy from weeks of travel. As the last of the second helping disappeared, a message arrived for Daniel that forced him to leave for a few minutes. Upon his return, he informed John that there was a call for him.

Turning to her husband, Emma continued. "Now, my dear, you simply must offer our guests a place to rest. Darling," here she patted Caroline's knee, "you simply must be craving a bath and a nap. I always have a bath and nap in the afternoon. The servants can wash your clothes, if you like. Or perhaps," here she stopped and looked at her husband. "Could we perhaps find them some—um—fresher clothes to wear?" At this Caroline blushed. *I don't know why I'm embarrassed. I've been chased through the jungle for months. Of course I don't smell very 'fresh'.*

Daniel patted his wife's hand. "Of course, my dear, I'm certain the servants can see to that. Why don't you take Ms. Wells to the Arthur Suite and she can rest?" Caroline rose as Emma rose.

"What about John?" Caroline asked Daniel.

"I'll bring him to you when he finishes his call. Would that be convenient?" Daniel asked. Caroline nodded and thanked him, suppressing the panic she felt every time John was away from her in this place.

Emma showed her to a beautifully decorated room and bade her rest well. The first thing Caroline did was sink into the down quilt on the bed before surveying the room and noticing through an open doorway, a copper bathtub with steam rising from the surface. *A hot bath—oh exquisite pleasure.* Caroline disrobed and slipped into the steamy water, sinking down until it threatened to leak over the sides before sitting back up and soaping herself from top to toe, not once but twice, enjoying the feeling of being clean. Once she was satisfied that she had gotten the most out of the bar of soap, she lay back in the tub and closed her eyes.

Not realizing she had slept, she awakened to firm hands massaging her shoulders. Looking up she stared into the deep brown eyes of her husband who was watching her with a look of unconcealed lust. Grinning with pride that she could evoke such passion in him, she reached up and brought his head down for a kiss. As he stood and turned to face her she realized he was naked. Taking his hand, she invited him to join her. Reaching between her toes, he removed the plug long enough to give his body room to join his wife and, once he was settled, he asked, "Why did you tell them you were Caroline Wells?"

She grimaced slightly. "Sorry. It was just a reflex. I've never introduced myself as Caroline Brock before. Did it bother you?" she asked, concerned she had hurt his feelings.

"No, I understand, but it took me ten minutes to convince Emma that I really was your husband and that she could let me come to your room."

Caroline laughed. "If she had seen *that* look in your eyes, she might have locked you away."

"What look?" he replied innocently.

"That look—the look that makes my tummy jump and my heart race."

"Oooh, this look." John moved toward her, sliding his hands along her arms until he reached her neck where he slid them into her wet hair. She reached out for him and he kissed her sweetly and soundly.

When they were both clean, dirty and clean again, they dried and moved to the bed where they found new reasons to bathe until they fell asleep contentedly in each other's arms.

CHAPTER 16

MI-5

Coffee? Caroline inhaled the amazingly exhilarating aroma as she shifted in the bed. *Clean sheets?* She patted the bed beside her until a hand took hers. She slowly opened her eyes, groaning at the effort, as a hazy John appeared beside her.

"Good afternoon, sleepyhead," John said as he smiled at her.

"Mmmm, how long have I been asleep?" she asked.

"Sixteen hours. Feel better?" He brought her hand to his lips.

"Dunno yet. Coffee?"

He chuckled and nodded at the cup on the bedside table.

She sat up in bed and reached for it, grimacing at the bitterness. "Cream and sugar?" she asked. He reached across her and held the sugar for her while she scooped two teaspoonfuls then reaching back across, he poured in some cream until she nodded. Sipping again, she closed her eyes in bliss.

"How is the coffee? I haven't had a chance to have one yet," John inquired.

"Kiss me and find out," she replied. So he did, smacking his lips appreciatively. "Good kiss or good coffee?" she asked playfully.

"Both," he replied, enjoying her playfulness. "However, it *is* time you were out of bed." She groaned in response and pulled him closer, suggesting he join her instead. Kissing her cheek, he pulled away from her. "We can't stay in bed all day," he offered.

"And why not? We're married." Grabbing his shirt, she pulled him closer again, but, grinning, he shook his head at her.

"You know that I am a big fan of sleeping with you but I have a surprise," he explained.

She looked at him doubtfully. "A good surprise?" she wondered. He nodded. "Not a leopard—or a python—or a psychotic colonel?" she mused.

John laughed and kissed her hand. "A good surprise, I promise," he assured her. As she started to get up, she realized that she had no clothes. John, appreciating her dilemma, brought a pile of clothes over to her from the chair where they had been placed by a servant.

"There should be everything you need here," he stated. She pulled out some navy blue track pants, a white t-shirt, a navy zippered hooded sweater and undergarments. Wondering how he managed to get the sizes right, she dressed and took John's proffered hand. As they left the bedroom and entered the sitting room, Caroline saw a table set with china and crystal, two candles in silver holders as the centre piece, along with a bouquet of local flowers. Filling the glasses with ice cold water, a servant pulled a chair out for Caroline to sit. John nodded to the fellow who placed a covered dinner plate before them both and left the room. John walked over and locked the door after him.

Caroline watched John with wonder in her eyes. "What have you been up to?" she asked softly.

He moved over to kneel in front of her. "This is the closest I could come to a fancy restaurant and I haven't managed to organize the white chapel or the wedding bells but I did manage to find this." He reached into his pocket and pulled out a small teak wood box inlaid with beautifully coloured stones to form a picture of a flower. He opened the box to reveal a yellow gold band set with three garnets, a large one in the middle and two smaller garnets on the side bordered by tiny diamonds.

"I love you each day more than the last. Will you marry me again?" He removed the ring and reached for her hand. Once he had placed the ring on her finger, she framed his face with her hands and kissed him, she kissed him with all the love and passion she contained. When she felt she had emptied her love into him, he filled her with his own.

"Can I take that as a yes?" he whispered hoarsely.

She nodded, joy beaming from her eyes. "You remembered."

"I remember everything you tell me," he assured her. She slid down to her knees and he drew her close to him in a firm hug. Breaking apart after a time, he asked, "Shall we eat?"

"Mmhmm, I'm hungry." Removing the silver lids, they breathed in the scent of the curry and rice. Delicious. As their hunger began to abate, and their mouths had free time to talk instead of chew, Caroline asked, "What did you mean when you asked if I would marry you again?"

"I was speaking with Daniel and, well, basically, Dolly's credentials are going to be difficult to chase down. It's probably easier if we just marry again." Watching her closely, he waited for her response.

"What do you mean? Is he saying we're not really married?" she asked, concerned.

"He's saying that the marriage would not be recognized in the U.K. so we can either be legally common-law after the requisite time or get married again. There are three people here at the High Commission who are licensed in England to perform marriages." John's face expressed his concern at her potential reaction.

"I'm not going to be common-law anything. We were married before God, John. I don't quite understand the problem." She was becoming more concerned by his concern than by the situation. It didn't actually surprise her to hear that the marriage was not being accepted. "John what is the real problem? Ask me the question behind the question."

Releasing his breath on a sigh, he smiled at her. "You're not bothered?"

"No, I guess it's not surprising that the British don't want to accredit a retired southern evangelist who has been living in Burma for who knows how long. But I can tell that there is something going on in your mind. You're concerned about something."

"If we return to the U.K., we can apply for a check on Dolly's credentials, hold an investigation and have the marriage approved and registered. That, however, will take time, probably several months." John paused, gathering his thoughts. "I would like to get married again, here, before we reach the U.K. so that we enter the country as a married couple." He stopped.

"Because—" Caroline prompted.

"Because, if things go badly during the debriefing stage, they could decide that it's in the countries best interests to— uh—deport you to Canada. I've travelled across the country of Burma chased by psychotic colonels, leopards and pythons. I will not let my own country deprive me of the best thing that's ever happened to me." His voice gained strength as he spoke, finishing with an impassioned declaration of his love for her. Caroline reached across the table to entwine her fingers with his.

Smiling, she said, "I will marry you as many times as it takes, darling." She paused, thinking. "If we get married a third time, can I have a necklace?" A grin broke across John's face and erupted as a deep, cleansing laugh. Joining his laughter, Caroline walked over and kissed him. Pulling her onto his lap, he kissed her again and again.

That evening, John and Caroline were joined in matrimony again, by the Chaplain at the British Deputy High Commission in Kolkata, India. As the ring service approached, Caroline wondered whether the Chaplain would merely skip this part but John produced a beautiful gold wedding band to place on Caroline's finger and one for his own.

"With this ring, I thee wed.
With my body, I thee worship.
With all my worldly goods, I thee endow," promised John.

"With this ring, I thee wed.
With my body, I thee worship.
With all my worldly goods, I thee endow," promised Caroline.

They kissed to seal the covenant again. Emma Johnson wept and hugged Caroline, apologizing and assuring her that she had led John to Caroline's room only because he had convinced her they were married, while Caroline explained for the third time that she and John were, in fact, married in Burma by a real minister. John watched, shaking his head in humour, until a call interrupted the festivities and John accompanied Daniel to his office. Returning later, John took Caroline's hand and excused them. They walked hand in hand back to their room.

"That's a little obvious, don't you think?" she prompted.

"Hmmm." John replied, still absorbed in his thoughts. He opened the door to their room, standing aside to let Caroline enter first. Locking the door, he walked over to the stereo and turned on the radio.

"John? I said, don't you think it's a bit obvious if we leave our wedding reception early to go to our bedroom?" She remained by the door, waiting for his attention to shift to her.

John moved around the room peeking in lampshades and turning over pictures to examine the backs. He paced across the floor in front of the couch. Caroline began to slowly undo the zipper on her sweater, prompting John to turn his head to watch her. She sported her best 'come hither' look and crooked her finger to invite him closer. He stopped pacing and changed his direction, coming to stop in front of her, his fingers beating a tattoo on his thigh.

"What's going on?" Caroline asked, concerned. John's eyes flickered from her body to her face. Taking her hand, he sighed heavily. They walked past the stereo where John increased the volume and brought her to sit on the couch. Leaning in, he spoke directly into her ear.

"The room is bugged." She raised her eyebrows quizzically. "The electronics can't hear us through the music." She furrowed her brow in concern. "One of my friends called to warn me that MI-6 received intelligence suggesting I may have been turned in Burma. They've asked the Deputy Commissioner to turn on the listening devices and monitor my activities. MI-5 is sending people over to meet with me before they'll let me back in the country." Caroline looked up at him in shock. "Fortunately, they're sending Blake and Donnehy who are loyal to me—at least, they were," he finished dubiously.

Choking back tears, Caroline asked, "What's going to happen?"

"If they believe me, Blake and Donnehy I mean, MI-5 will escort us back to the U.K.. Once back in the U.K., they'll debrief us until they're satisfied that I didn't give away any useful information, and, only after that, will they allow me to return to work."

"What if they don't believe you?" Caroline's eyes were large with grief.

"Well," John paused for a long time, "if they think I've turned, they'll bring about a curtailment of my continued existence through proxy." John's voice was grim.

"What does that mean?" Caroline's voice shuddered as she spoke but his look told her all she needed to know. "Why?" she asked, sobs chasing her every thought.

"Someone high up has convinced the Home Secretary that I arranged to disappear from Mumbai; that I was working with Shing all along. The Director General is unconvinced, or I would be dead already."

"So what you're telling me is that your own country could end our happiness faster than leopards or pythons or Shing?" John nodded. Caroline collapsed sobbing in his arms. John was far too angry to cry.

After a night of fitful sleep, John and Caroline bathed and dressed. John's eyes were bright with anger but Caroline's were dark with grief. Emma Johnson bubbled away in her inane manner at breakfast, oblivious to the pain of her guests. When Daniel did not arrive at the table, John bitterly asked Emma if Daniel was avoiding them.

"Of course not, my dear, he is a very busy and important man, you know," Emma replied, continuing her commentary on the weather. *Who would have thought anyone could have so much to say about the weather!*

After breakfast, John and Caroline moved to the library to browse the books while they awaited the MI-5 agents' arrival.

"Just tell the truth, Caroline," John commented.

"Pardon?" she asked, confused by his topic shift from D.H. Lawrence to truth.

"Whatever they ask you, just tell the truth. They may try to trick you by telling you that I said this or that, but, if you always tell the truth, you'll be fine. Oh, and don't get carried away with storytelling, answer the question they ask, nothing more." Frowning, Caroline walked across the room and wrapped her arms around her husband.

"John, I'll do my best. No matter what happens, we're in this together? Right?" she asked, uncertainly.

John gazed down at his wife with love in his eyes. "We're in this together," he assured her, wrapping his arms around her and resting his face against the top of her head.

They found an old Bible on the shelf in the library and, opening its worn pages, they found within it the comfort and assurance they were seeking.

Harry Blake and Alexa Donnehy arrived with a third person just after the noon meal. Daniel came for John who insisted that Caroline should join them. John greeted his colleagues cautiously but Harry and Alexa soon let him know that he'd been missed. Harry clasped John's hand firmly and Alexa seemed eager to wrap him in a hug but settled for slapping him on the shoulder.

"John. You are a sight for sore eyes. Some tried to convince us you were dead but we knew you'd make it. No wannabe general could get the best of our own Ironheart," Alexa asserted effusively.

"Why do you call him Ironheart?" Caroline asked, interested by the woman's obvious charisma.

Alexa and Harry turned, as if noticing her for the first time. Alexa replied, "Our John may bend but nothing can break through his iron walls." Pausing, she intensified her gaze at Caroline then inquired. "And who might you be?"

John walked over to Caroline and took her hand. "This is Caroline—Brock—my wife." Harry raised his eyebrows in surprise and Alexa dropped her jaw in amazement.

"Your wife?" Harry gulped.

John grinned in response and replied, "Who won the book, then?"

Harry clapped John on the shoulder, laughing heartily. "I'm not certain anyone would have taken the bet."

Alexa turned to Caroline and shook her hand firmly. "Now, how did you find our man, here?" she asked, curious.

"I found him quite obnoxious, at first, actually." Caroline replied with humour in her voice. John grinned and squeezed her hand while Harry laughed loudly. Alexa narrowed her eyes, studying Caroline.

"uhHmm" Daniel cleared his throat to gain their attention. "I am Daniel Johnson, the Deputy High Commissioner. I am at your service." Harry and Alexa shook his hand, introducing the third in their band.

"This is Dr. Baxter. He's come to provide any medical care needed," Harry explained. "Is there somewhere he could set up? And would you be so kind as to let us borrow another room—a clean room, if you don't mind." Harry emphasized the word 'clean' much to Caroline's puzzlement.

Daniel nodded and led them to an interior suite of rooms on the second floor of the building. He excused himself when it was made clear that his presence was no longer required. Dr. Baxter led John and Caroline into the bedroom in the suite and began to set out his instruments. John gently instructed Caroline to sit in one of the chairs in the room while he moved over to the bed where the doctor stood.

Dr. Baxter removed a clipboard and pen from his medical bag and donned a pair of surgical gloves. Asking John to remove his shirt and sit on the bed, the doctor examined his eyes, nose, ears and throat, stopping every few minutes to make notes. When he brought out his stethoscope and proceeded to apply it to John's back in order to listen to his lungs, his attention was arrested by the marks there. He turned John and began to study the scars crisscrossing his back, moving his fingers along as though counting the lines on a piece of paper.

"Mr. Brock, you were flogged?" he asked.

"Yes." John replied. The doctor moved around to study John's chest.

"And beaten?" he asked.

"Yes."

"Ribs broken?"

"Yes."

"Complications?"

"Pneumonia, I think," he replied, glancing at Caroline to confirm this.

"Hmmm, we'll need an X-Ray when we return." The doctor instructed John to remove his trousers. John complied.

"Hmmm. Burns. Electrical burns—you were electrocuted?" the doctor observed.

"Yes," John responded.

"You had good care." John didn't respond. The doctor continued his examination until every millimeter of skin had been inspected. "Okay, you may get dressed now. Mrs. Brock, could you please come over here?" Caroline waited until John nodded before moving over.

"Were you tortured, Mrs. Brock?" the doctor inquired.

"No," she responded. The doctor checked her eyes, nose, ears and throat. When he moved her shirt aside to listen to her heart and lungs, he paused and asked, "What's this?" noting the scars on her shoulder.

"I was attacked by a leopard. There are more scars on my back," she explained. The doctor asked her to remove her shirt to get a better look.

"These have been very well cared for. A cat's scratch can be very risky because of the danger of infection," he stated.

"I had a doctor to care for me, a Burmese doctor," she explained. Dr. Baxter nodded and completed his examination.

As Caroline dressed, she heard the doctor beginning his report.

"First patient, male, forty-five years of age, healing scars on the ...."

John and Caroline left the doctor alone with his tape recorder and found Alexa and Harry in the sitting room. There was coffee and biscuits on a tray and John poured a cup for himself and one for Caroline.

"All right, John," Harry began. "I've set up a signal scrambler so we should be able to speak freely. Tell us what happened."

Alexa moved over and put her hand on Harry's arm. "Perhaps we should hear from Caroline, first."

John studied Alexa then nodded slowly. Turning to Caroline, he asked, "Is that all right?"

Caroline nodded. "What do you want to know?" she asked.

"Tell us everything—from the moment you first met John," Alexa instructed her.

Caroline studied John's face, trying to read any message there while Harry studied the looks passing between them.

She began, "I met John in Bourey Prison, somewhere outside of Yangon, Myanmar. He was brought to my cell one day." She stopped, trying to follow John's rules about not giving too much information.

Alexa prompted her, "What were you doing in a prison in Myanmar?"

Caroline took a deep breath, her nerves becoming obvious. "I was arrested for slapping a soldier." She stopped again.

Alexa was becoming impatient. "And—" she snapped. "What on earth possessed you to slap a Burmese soldier?"

"Alexa!" John silenced his colleague with a word. He turned to Caroline and put his arm around her. "It's okay. Just tell them what happened." He waited for her to look him in the eyes before giving her an encouraging smile.

She released a breath and nodded. Looking up at Alexa, she apologized, "Sorry."

Harry prompted her again. "You were telling us about the soldier."

Caroline nodded. "While I waited for my flight in Yangon, I went into a tea shoppe with some of the other passengers. While we were in there, two soldiers began molesting a young woman and her daughter. I—well—I couldn't just let them take the little girl. I—I couldn't believe that no one helped them!" She looked at her interrogators miserably. "Anyway, I stood up to intervene, and when the shoppe owner grabbed my arm, I pulled away and slapped the soldier. One of the women escaped with the little girl while they were arresting me." The emotions of that day came flooding back into Caroline's belly. She hugged her arms around herself. John could feel her shaking and he pulled her tighter to himself. She looked up at him gratefully.

"What happened next?" Alexa's voice was gentler than before.

Drawing a deep breath, Caroline persisted. "I was arrested, tried and sentenced to Bourey Prison. They refused to let me speak to anyone from the Canadian Embassy."

Harry interrupted, directing his question more to Alexa than Caroline, "Is there a Canadian Embassy in Burma?"

"I'm not certain but there's certainly an affiliated—" Alexa was interrupted by John clearing his throat. She brought the conversation back on topic. "What were you charged with?"

"I'm not sure what my sentence was or exactly what I was charged with." Caroline's hand was shaking as she rested it on John's leg. He reached for it and curled it up in his own.

Harry encouraged her, "What happened once John arrived?"

"Well, basically, they tortured him," she replied, looking up at Harry. "They did terrible things to him. I don't know how he endured it." She threw a defiant look at the two MI-5 agents. "I think he's very brave," she stated with conviction.

The corner of John's mouth twitched into a grin. Leaning over, he kissed her temple.

Alexa relented. "I'm certain he was. You realize he's been tortured before?" she asked, probing. Caroline nodded. They all waited but Caroline didn't know what they were waiting for. The silence was broken by Alexa. "What did John tell you about his mission?" she asked.

In a rather forceful tone, she retorted, "Nothing. He was quite obnoxious about it, actually. I mean, really, what difference did it make to me why he was there? I'm presented with this difficult, wounded man who resists every attempt to help him because he thinks I want something in return. Life in prison is bad enough without having to live in the presence of anger every day!" Caroline finished her impassioned speech. Harry looked slightly shocked by her outburst. John watched his colleagues carefully to note their reactions.

"Why do you think they put John in a cell with you?" Alexa inquired.

"I'm not really certain," Caroline began, "but I think it amused them."

"Amused them? How?" Harry asked.

"The warden, Captain Htet, was irritated by the fact that I had encouraged the prisoners. I—"

Harry cut her off, "Encouraged them how? To escape, to revolt, passive resistance hunger strikes—in what way encouraged them?"

Caroline looked at Harry like he was loony. Arching her eyebrows, she responded slowly. "I—encouraged—them—to have hope."

Harry frowned. "Hope in what?" he asked, confused.

"Hope that, even in terrible circumstances, good things can happen." John barely suppressed a smirk at Harry's obvious discomfiture and Alexa's confusion.

Alexa clarified. "You encouraged them to have hope?"

Caroline nodded and added, "Hope is what keeps us from despair."

"Is that what you did for John?" Alexa asked quietly.

Caroline leaned into John, resting her head gently against his shoulder. "I think so," she responded.

The room was silent for a long time with Alexa and Harry exchanging several coded looks.

"She's not a mole, is she John?" Alexa asked him quietly. John shook his head, his eyes bright. Puzzled, Caroline watched the interaction.

"Tell us what happened, John," Harry demanded lightly.

John proceeded to give his colleagues the facts of his abduction, imprisonment, torture and escape. Caroline marveled at how John managed to cleverly give accurate information that never really told the whole story. She watched him carefully as he spoke. He never gave away what was the whole truth and what was part. Harry and Alexa interrupted with questions from time to time but seemed enthralled by John's version of events as though he was Scheherazade with her thousand tales.

"Vlad? Vlad the Impaler? That ex-KGB scumbag slash psychopath?" Harry inquired.

John nodded. "Yes. Vlad was brought in by Shing to interrogate me. Guess what he wanted to know?" John replied.

"Not the Southeast Asian network? Not again." Alexa added. "How did you escape?" she asked.

"The Chin Liberation army attacked the prison. We escaped on a truck with the other prisoners but got dumped in the middle of the jungle. Some villagers took us in and nursed us until we could move on. We made our way to that hidden village there in northern Myanmar and escaped west through the mountains to India," John finished.

"Is that the one where Maryn Dale has contacts? Did you run into her?" Harry asked. John's eyes darkened briefly at the name of his former lover but Caroline didn't think the others noticed.

"No, we weren't able to make contact."

"Now, you know I need to ask you this, John. Are you an agent working for Shing?" Alexa asked, narrowing her eyes to study his response.

"No. Shing sent more men. They caught up with me once but I managed to escape."

"Did you give any useful information to the interrogators?" Harry asked.

"No. I never told them anything. It's easier not to speak than it is to weave a tale of deceit, as you well know," John replied. The three spies studied each other for a long time before John broke the silence. "Is there anything else?"

Harry responded, "We got some intelligence from '6' stating that a helicopter was caught in Indian air space three days ago. The numbers on the helicopter were traced to a pilot hired out of Hwebalan in Myanmar by Chinese agents. We've had several reports of increased Chinese activity in Myanmar and we know that Shing has been very agitated lately, sending half his private staff to a laogai last week." Quiet descended as Harry and Alexa exchanged a long look, seeming to consider all they had heard and seen and then finally expressing agreement with two nods.

"Ready to go home, John?" Harry rose, extending his hand toward John.

"Definitely!" John rose to meet him, finally releasing the smile he had kept under control since seeing his old friends. He shook his colleagues' hands in turn and reaching for Caroline's hand, he pulled her up into a hug. She smiled in relief.

"Good. There's a flight out first thing tomorrow morning. How shall we celebrate tonight? Night club? Dancing girls?" Harry suggested. Caroline raised her eyebrows, pulling a face that spoke volumes about her opinion of his ideas. Harry continued, "Scotch, Tequila—Electric Jello?" Caroline's face grew darker and darker. John burst out laughing, unable to contain his humour at her discomfiture. She threw a dark look in his direction, swatting at him.

"John!" she exclaimed.

"What?" he laughed incredulously, "I'm not the one suggesting it!" John slipped his arm around her waist. She jabbed him in the ribs, sulking.

Alexa laughed. "How did you two *ever* get together?"

"Just luck," John intoned.

Caroline pulled away to stare at him in disbelief. "Luck?!" she exclaimed.

"Sure," he responded. "You were just lucky I was available." John grinned wickedly as Caroline's jaw dropped. Grabbing a pillow off the couch, she walloped him in the head. He spun her around, pinning her pillow hand and pulling her back flush against him. He lowered his head to speak directly into her ear. "Now, Mrs. Brock, we have company. Behave." Caroline shivered as his voice vibrated in her ear.

Leaning her head back against his shoulder, she asked, "*Who* needs to behave?"

He spun her back around and pulled her close. "Me?" he inquired.

"Indeed," she replied, smacking him with the pillow again. He grinned in response.

Alexa and Harry stood watching in bewildered amusement, exchanging a look that seemed to ask, *"Have you ever seen or heard of anyone who has ever witnessed the 'playful' side of John 'Ironheart' Brock?"*

"Well," Alexa began, uncomfortable with this side of her colleague, "If you two are quite through, we should celebrate. Mr. Stuffed Shirt Deputy Commissioner must have some champagne around here somewhere. Let's go find him and see what torment we can prepare for him. That could prove to be quite entertaining." Turning to John she continued, "Welcome back, John. You were missed!"

Alexa went in search of food and Harry went in search of alcohol. John and Caroline sat back on the couch awaiting their return. Caroline was still annoyed at being the butt of a joke and John was too amused to try to deflate the situation, knowing he would only make it worse.

Harry returned with an exasperated steward in tow, gesticulating wildly that the champagne belonged to Mrs. Johnson and that she would be most displeased to find it missing. Harry responded, "If it's missing, she's not going to find it, is she? Now, you have a choice, sir. You can either report this to your mistress or," he paused for effect, "you can join us."

The steward stopped moving and after a brief pause, replied, "I'll find us some glasses," he replied and soon returned with six glasses and the upstairs maid.

Harry placed a bottle of champagne, a bottle of scotch and two beers on the table. "It's all I could purloin," he explained. Whispering to John, he added, "The guy in charge of the liquor cabinet was much bigger than this fellow." John chuckled.

Soon Alexa returned with cheese, mangoes and sausage. The friends dug in and regaled Caroline, the steward and the maid with tales of parties of the past. After a time, the steward began to nod off and the upstairs maid decided it was time to leave. Once the maid had removed the drunken steward, the stories turned to humourous tales of events that John had missed during his incarceration.

"Then, Robert, you know how much he loves surveillance, comes roaring out of the van, straight into the hotel and punches the mark on the nose." John and Harry broke into fits of laughter. "So, then we find out he'd fallen asleep while watching the video feed and woke up in time to hear that the fellow was actually sleeping with Robert's girlfriend." Harry and Alexa doubled up laughing but John sobered a bit, seeing a new side to this tale that would have totally missed him in the past, just as it missed his colleagues.

Alexa picked up the story. "Next thing we know, Robert is hauled up on the carpet before the DG himself and scolded for half an hour about protocol during surveillance. You know how formidable the DG can be when he's incensed."

"Formidable," John interrupted, "if you want to hear about formidable, how about a prisoner who scolds her prison guards?" A tinge of pink crawled up Caroline's cheeks. Harry and Alexa leaned forward and waited.

"The guards drag me back into my cell, I'm soaking wet from being dunked all night and Caroline starts to yell at the guards. 'Why is he all wet? What do you think you're doing?' I'm telling you, she was so fierce, they sped out of their like their fathers were chasing them with sticks." Harry gaped at Caroline. Alexa nodded, a grudging respect forming for her.

"Me," Caroline interjected, "What about you?" She turned to Alexa. "Vlad decided to send for John at night but the night guards didn't know which bed he was sleeping in so, in the dark, they grabbed me and dragged me out. The next thing I know, John is launching one of them across the room and telling them, 'don't ever touch her again'. And do you know what? They didn't. They scurried out of there."

Alexa asked incredulously, "You got away with that, John?"

He shook his head grimly. "No, they came back with two more guards and beat the crap out of me, but they never came after Caroline again." Caroline placed her hand fondly on John's leg.

John, in a lighter tone of voice, said, "But, if you want to hear about a 'formidable' moment, how about the python?" He turned toward Caroline. Blushing, she shrugged.

"Well," John began, "we were cascading down this river—"

"Which you pushed me into," Caroline interrupted.

"Well, it was either that or be shot by Captain Li!" John exclaimed.

"You could have just asked. I told you that—but, oh no—," here she turned to Alexa and Harry, "He shoves me into this river and the next thing I know I'm spinning and bobbing down rapids until I'm finally flattened against a huge tree."

"What did you do?" Alexa asked, enjoying the excitement of the story.

"I crawled sideways out of the river. I was freezing, soaked, exhausted. I knew I couldn't move too far from the river in case John was looking for me—"

"What do you mean 'in case'? Of course I was looking for you," John interjected.

Caroline gazed at him, recalling the feelings of those unhappy days. "Of course you were," she whispered, reaching up to kiss his cheek as he brushed his fingers along her jaw. Harry coughed to break the moment and John continued the story, still gazing at Caroline for a few more moments, looking back at his colleagues as the story gained momentum.

"Well," John went on, "the next thing I know, I hear this angry, threatening voice and, as I walk into a small clearing, she almost brains me with a tree branch. She was actually scolding a Burmese python."

"It had the audacity to try to eat me." Caroline defended herself, pouting playfully. Harry slapped his leg in amusement.

"Were you able to scare it away?" Alexa asked.

"Scare it away?!" John snorted. "She obliterated the poor thing! By the time I arrived, it was completely decapitated, the skull in two pieces. Then—then, she says we've got to bring it along for food! That thing must have weighed fifty pounds!"

Caroline sniffed. "Fifty pounds—more like twenty, at the most."

"And now, Mrs. Brock, who had to carry it?" John asked, feigning insult.

Caroline reached over and gently patted his cheek. "You did, my love—and thank you, by the way, it tasted delicious."

Alexa and Harry just sat and shook their heads. Who were these people?

During the lull in conversation, Harry noted that John and Caroline were only drinking water. "John Brock, my friend. Have you turned teetotal?"

"Not particularly. But she won't kiss me if I drink."

Harry looked at him, perplexed. "What do you mean?"

"She doesn't like the taste of alcohol. If I drink, I don't get a goodnight kiss."

Alexa smacked John companionably on the arm. "They're that good are they?"

John smiled wickedly, "What do you think?" Caroline blushed and smacked him on the other arm.

Soon after, John and Caroline excused themselves, using the early morning flight as a reason to head to bed. Once they were back in their room and the outside world was locked out, Caroline turned on John. She grabbed his shirt and backed him up until his knees buckled against the edge of the bed then, leaping on him, she straddled his body, pinning him.

"Now, husband, first, you will explain to me the contents of electric jello and then, you will explain to me why Harry thought you would want to spend the evening at a night club with dancing girls. Next, you will—" John moved and, in one fluid motion, flipped Caroline onto the bed beneath him.

"Pardon?" he asked, in his most innocent voice.

"Never mind," she replied, evenly.

John moved his hand up along her sides. "Pardon?" he asked, more firmly, lightly stroking her ribs.

"Nothing. Good night, dear." She closed her eyes and pretended to sleep. John stood up and backed away.

"Hey!" she called after him. "That's not how you play the game!" she exclaimed, reaching out to grasp his shirt, pulling him back toward the bed. He moved in closely and kissed her deeply.

"Better?" he asked.

"Oh yes," she replied.

"I love you," he repeated between kisses.

"I love you, too."

CHAPTER 17

FRIEND OR FOE

Morning came early but not early enough for John. He was up at first light, pacing the room in anticipation of finally going home. Caroline had thrown all the pillows at him to make him be quiet and was now chasing sleep, resting her head on a bunched up patch of duvet. Finally, she gave up and invited him back to bed. If she couldn't get some sleep, she could at least enjoy being awake.

John, Caroline, Alexa and Harry arrived at the airport in good time and boarded their plane. Alexa had conveyed John's passport and managed to acquire a temporary visa for Caroline Brock from the Deputy Commissioner. The flight from Kolkata to Mumbai was bumpy and crowded, and, after a brief stopover in Mumbai, the quartet boarded their plane for the eight hour flight to Heathrow in London, England. John and Caroline managed to organize two seats together and were even blessed to find the third seat empty. Harry and Alexa were spaced elsewhere in the plane. Once the plane had ascended to cruising height, John settled in for a nap.

"You're certain you don't mind if I sleep?" he asked Caroline. She shook her head, though he was soon disturbed by her fit of giggles when she realized the choice of movies for the flight included 'Anna and the King' and James Bond. Once she had settled, he resumed his siesta while Caroline tried to read the magazines in the seat pocket, soon becoming bored and restless. She welcomed Alexa's company when she moved forward to sit in the empty seat next to Caroline.

"Hi." Alexa opened the conversation.

"Hi," Caroline responded.

"He asleep?" she asked, nodding in John's direction.

Caroline nodded, wondering if this conversation was going anywhere, anytime soon. Caroline waited for Alexa to speak again but when nothing was forthcoming, she broke the silence, "The other night, when the three of you were reminiscing, what did John mean when he asked 'who won the book'?"

Alexa gave a short laugh. "Spies are a strange breed. We spend our time either in mortal danger or crushing boredom. When we're bored, we bet. We bet on who can shoot an elastic band the furthest, or on whether Zoran can get a date with the sandwich lady or whether Tessie will have the nerve to finally ask Jason out. We call that 'opening a book'. However, as Harry told John, no one would ever bet that he would get married, so no one opened a book." She concluded her explanation.

"Why is it so hard to believe that he's married?" Caroline inquired.

"John's a hard man. I'm not saying he's cruel or anything, but I've never seen—or heard of him—doing anything that wasn't a direct result of cold-blooded necessity." Caroline studied Alexa, trying to amalgamate this John with her John. Alexa continued. "No one, and I mean no one, has ever cracked the granite around John's heart. He never gets angry and he never cries." Alexa's eyes grew distant. "He's had women—no question, but he doesn't keep them around. Maryn lasted the longest of anyone I know of, but even she only lasted a few months. How *did* you two get together?" Alexa asked in bewilderment. Caroline was still wincing from the mention of 'women' as Alexa turned to her with that query.

Caroline paused for a moment to consider her answer. Smiling, she said, "It was a long and turbulent journey and the rain came down in torrents." She glanced over at John then turned back to Alexa.

"You're not going to tell me about it, are you?" Alexa asked.

"I don't really think I should. It's his story," Caroline replied.

Alexa frowned and then sighed. "You can hardly blame me for trying," she stated, patting Caroline's arm and returning to her own seat.

Caroline sat for a time, questions swirling in her mind.

"You can ask me anything, you know." Caroline jumped as John's voice broke through her reverie.

"I thought you were asleep," she said, turning to him.

"Uh uh, can't sleep when you're awake." He reached over and took her hand, shifting his body more upright in the seat, continuing to watch her.

"Did you sl—uh—have a relationship with Alexa?" Caroline asked.

John kissed her hand. "No. I never date junior officers."

"Is she a junior officer then?"

John grimaced. "Well, she was when I left."

"Have you been with a lot of women?" Caroline asked quietly, studying the seat back in front of her.

"A few. I have quite a reputation, you know." He smiled slyly. "I've always found the mystique of the 'unattainable man' to work to my advantage but I've never lived up to the stories." John paused until Caroline looked at him questioningly. "Mostly, my life was lonely, consumed with duty and responsibility."

He reached over to stroke his thumb along her chin. "Caer?" She nodded, her gaze captured by his eyes. "I love you. I'm completely and totally yours, you believe that, don't you?" Caroline studied his gaze for a moment seeing only love.

"Yes," she replied, just before she kissed him.

Once the plane landed in Heathrow and the travelers had passed through customs, John and Caroline were ushered into the back of a waiting sedan and transported to the Best Western in downtown London. A network of rooms was regularly used at this Best Western by the Security Services. The Home Secretary had been ambivalent about letting John Brock enter the city before his loyalties were confirmed but had capitulated after the DG insisted. Once they arrived at the hotel, Alexa and Harry disappeared to report their findings to their superiors while John and Caroline were escorted to the Honeymoon Suite on the top floor of the hotel.

"Look, John, there's even a fruit basket," Caroline commented as the Bellboy waited impatiently at the door until John informed him that unless he wanted Burmese kyat or Indian rupees, he was out of luck as far as a tip was concerned. The young man huffed out of the room, shutting the door rather loudly behind him.

"What now?" Caroline asked.

John sighed sadly. "Well, they'll probably let us rest tonight but debriefing will begin in the morning and continue until they're satisfied." He paused, pacing the room as Caroline watched his agitation.

"John. ... John." She waited for his response. "John, come here!" she insisted while he stood clenching and unclenching his fists, his mind far away. "J~o~h~n," she sang at him. Briefly, he glanced over at her. Caroline shook her head in dismay. Entering the washroom she began to run a bath and soon, once the ideas of BATH—CAROLINE had coalesced in

John's mind, he found his wife and spent what could be their last carefree time together for a while.

Tubbed, scrubbed and content, John and Caroline began to think about supper.

"You know what I want?" Caroline asked.

John wrapped his arms around her and pulled her close. "What?" he whispered into her ear, causing her to shudder and smile.

"A hamburger—wait, no—a cheeseburger with fried onions, mushrooms, bacon—"

John interrupted smirking, "Canadian bacon?"

Chuckling, Caroline continued, "—and a Caesar salad—with coffee—no wait—I want a cola. Mmmm." Caroline's eyes glazed over. "What do you want?"

"Hmmm. Steak and kidney pie, green olives, chips and—hmmm—a strawberry milkshake." John's eyes glazed over.

"Bear?"

"Mmhmm."

"Can I call my parents before we go down to supper?" Caroline inquired.

John sobered. "They'll be monitoring our calls," he mumbled. "Don't really know when we'll be home." Looking into Caroline's pleading eyes, he smiled with just a tinge of sadness. "Go ahead and call them." He paused. "But remember not to tell them anything over an open line." He paused again, thinking. "And, well, I'm not certain when they'll release us to meet with your parents." Pausing, he added tenderly. "Tell them I'll pay for their tickets to come see you."

Caroline reached up and pulled his head down for a kiss. Huskily she whispered, "Thank you." *When will we be truly able to relax?* Caroline wondered.

"I'll see about supper. You go ahead and call." John left the room in search of the duty security officer.

Forged in the Jungles of Burma

Collecting her thoughts, Caroline dialed her parent's number—her number—the telephone number she'd memorized when she was five years old.

"Hello?" her father answered.

"Dad, it's Caroline." Caroline's heart was hammering excitedly in her chest.

"Caroline! Are you okay?" her father inquired, apprehensively.

"Yes, Dad, I'm fine. Are you and Mom okay?"

"Yes. Wait Caroline. Let me get your Mother. Can you hold for a minute?" her father asked, coming back to the phone to add the last question.

"Yep." Caroline heard steps and her Mother's name in the background until she heard the telltale click and her mother's weeping voice on the extension.

"Caroline, my darling, are you safe? Are you well? We've been so worried about you! Where are you? When are you coming home?" Her mother delivered her questions in rapid speech. Caroline laughed. *It's so good to hear them.*

"I'm fine. I'm safe. I'm in England. I've been on a huge adventure and I'm very *very* glad it's over."

Her father took over. "When are you coming home?"

"I can't come to Canada right now but I'm going to fly you here—if you'll come." Her voice changed. "Will you come—to see me? —here in England?"

Her mother and father answered in unison and then laughed. "Of course we'll come."

Her father continued, "But why can't you come here?"

Caroline took a deep breath. "Well, it's a little complicated to explain. It's not for a bad reason, and I *so* want to see you. Will you come?"

"Yes, sweetie, yes, we'll come," her mother reassured her. "We just want to know what happened. You disappeared without a trace and showed up months later asking for rupees."

"Mom—Dad—I will explain everything when you get here. It will be a day or two before I can arrange the tickets but I'll contact you as soon as I can."

"Is everything okay, dear?" her mother asked.

"Yes. It's just—well, it's a really big story but, yes, I truly am fine."

"But?" her father asked, knowing there was something she still wanted them to know.

"You're going to find this hard to understand—I wonder about it myself sometimes—but—well—When you come, you'll meet him anyways—" Caroline fumbled, trying to find a way to break the news.

"Just go ahead and tell us, dear," her father insisted.

"When I said that I would send you airplane tickets, I really meant that John would send tickets." Caroline eased into the subject.

"John?" her mother asked. "Oh darling, have you met someone?"

Caroline chuckled. "Yes. John is my husband. I'm Caroline Brock, now." Shocked silence screamed down the phone line. Biting her lip, Caroline waited.

"Uh," Her father began and stopped. Caroline heard his humph in the background, imagining her mother walking over to him, cordless phone firmly in hand, and elbowing him in the ribs.

"That's lovely, dear. We're so happy for you." *Good ole Mom.* "Is he good to you?" subdued, her mother inquired.

"He saved my life, Mom. He saved me from the prison guards. He saved me from the soldiers who attacked me. He saved me from the leopard. He's kind and good and brave," Caroline stated emphatically, then more gently, "I love him."

"Then I'm sure we'll love him, too," her mother replied with confidence.

"Is he there with you? Can we speak to him?" her father probed.

Caroline smiled to herself. *Fathers protect their daughters. I wonder what would have happened if John had to ask for my hand as Henry did.*

"He went to see about supper. Just a minute and I'll see if he's back yet?" Placing the telephone receiver on the bedside table, she walked out of the bedroom and into the suite's sitting room to find John entering quietly. Crooking her finger, she beckoned him over.

"My father would like to speak to you," she informed him quite seriously. He looked like a deer caught in headlights. Walking over, Caroline took his hand and dragged him to the phone.

"Why do they want to speak to me?" he whispered.

"Because they want to meet you," she whispered back, handing him the receiver. "Just be yourself."

He frowned at her. "Hello," John began, "John Brock here." Caroline rolled her eyes at him. 'What?' he mouthed back at her, shrugging his shoulders and furrowing his brow. She shook her head, amused by his formality.

"John. This is Caroline's father. I'm pleased to meet you." His speech was stilted and formal.

"Pleased to meet you too, sir," John responded, all business.

"Oh for goodness sake," her mother interrupted. "John, this is Caroline's mother. Feel free to call me 'Mom'. Thank you so much for taking care of our daughter. I'm sure you'll make her very happy."

"Yes, ma'am—um, Mom? I—well—I love her—very much." John's words came out stilted but warm. Handing the phone back to Caroline, he sat heavily on the bed beside her.

Caroline put the phone to her ear. "I need to go now Mom, Dad. I'll call you in a day or two. I love you. Bye."

"We love you too, dear. We're both looking forward to seeing you—and John," her father replied. "Bye."

Caroline replaced the receiver. Sighing, she turned to John and wrapped her arms around him.

"Sorry," he muttered.

She chuckled. "You were very sweet."

"Sweet!" he replied indignantly.

"Uh huh. A real tweety pie." Caroline giggled as John tickled her in response. She tackled him, momentarily pinning his arms between them. "They'll understand when I've told them the whole story."

John stilled beneath her. "You can't tell them the whole story," he declared. "Not without getting them to sign the Official Secrets Act, and having them formally vetted."

Caroline leaned down and kissed him. "I'm hungry. When can we eat?"

John shrugged as if to let the topic rest for the present; as though not wanting to upset Caroline when there was no immediate need. "The hotel's restaurant is filling our orders as we speak. Last one down there is a rotten egg!" He flipped her over and off him and raced to the door. Caroline grabbed a pillow from the bed and flung it at him, racing behind. They reached the door to the corridor breathless and laughing.

"Now, Mrs. Brock, wife of John Brock, MI-5 officer, we must show some decorum in front of my fellow officers who are placed all around this building, so kindly compose yourself as you join me for a dignified dinner." John opened the door and bowed, graciously allowing Caroline to exit first. At the last minute, she shoved him backwards, grasping the door in both hands and pulling it shut. She ran to the elevator and tapped the down button repeatedly. John emerged to see Caroline's extended tongue mocking him through the rapidly closing elevator doors

Caroline peered left and right carefully as the elevator doors opened onto the lobby. *No John in sight. Ha! I beat him.* She strolled haughtily toward the restaurant until her progress was halted by a hand across her mouth and a firm grip on her arm. As she began to struggle, the hands spun her around—face to face with John, grinning broadly. Breathing a sigh of relief, she whacked him on the shoulder.

Hand in hand they entered the restaurant. Once they were seated and their orders confirmed, Caroline asked, "How did you do that?"

John wiggled his eyebrows at her. "Trade secrets, my love."

"Okay, smarty-pants. Teach me something right now."

John thought for a moment. "All right. How many security officers are in this restaurant?" he tested her. She looked around examining the patrons for what she imagined could be telltale signs. Shrugging, she raised her eyebrows at him, indicating that she didn't have a clue.

Waiting until the server had set their meals before them and departed, John enlightened her. "Six." Bowing for grace, they paused to give thanks for their safety and for familiar food.

"Which ones?" Caroline asked.

"Spook number one—waiter who keeps bending over a little too far to fill glasses. He has a mike in his lapel. Spook number two—maitre d' who keeps adjusting his cufflinks which contain a camera. Numbers three and four—couple, three tables over, she has a directional mic under the napkin on her lap. Number five is hiding behind the plants by the window and number six is approaching from the elevators." John finished, looking over toward Harry who was approaching from the elevators.

Caroline chuckled as Harry greeted them. Giving her a confused look, Harry asked how they were doing. After the pleasantries were completed, Harry informed them that their 'meeting' was arranged for 9:00 am tomorrow in Rooms 406 and 408. Then, bidding them good night, he departed.

John frowned into his meal, displacing the food with his fork listlessly. Caroline watched his bowed head sadly.

"Shall we go upstairs?" she asked, placing her hand over his to still his fork. He nodded, waving for the waiter and signing the bill. "Want to go for a walk, first?" she inquired, taking his hand. He nodded, motioning her to wait while he rose and walked up to the man hiding by the windows, sporting a lopsided grin as he returned. The man he'd left behind had flushed a beetroot red and now mumbled into his wrist.

"Amateur," John muttered.

It felt good to be outside again. After spending so many weeks outdoors, it was refreshing to once again feel the breeze, even if their walk looked like a parade—two security officers walked ahead of them and two behind. There was also a car following them that Caroline suspected was part of the surveillance.

Ignoring their entourage, Caroline moved in close to John and slipped her arm around him. Smiling at her, John placed his arm around her shoulders.

"Tell me," she demanded.

"What do you think—of all this?" He gestured around him.

Caroline walked in silence for a few minutes, gathering her thoughts. "It's all been rather weird." John stopped and looked at her. "Not you, the situation," Caroline clarified and continuing, she added, "In Kolkata, on the airplane, here. At first, I tried to rationalize the John they knew with the John I know." She stopped, wrapped in her thoughts.

"And—" John prompted.

She began walking again. "And then I realized that they don't know you at all. Not one of them has ever bothered to look behind your eyes and see the real you."

John pulled her to him and lowering his forehead to meet hers, he stated, "Except you."

Caroline smiled tenderly at him. "Except me. Have I seen the real you?" she posed the question on her mind.

Whispering, "Only you," he leaned in and kissed her. Straightening, they walked on, oblivious now to the officers watching them.

"John? Bear."

"Mmhmmm."

"Tell me."

Smiling sadly, John sighed. "No escape?"

She shook her head and insisted, "Tell me."

"Tomorrow, they'll want to know all that happened in Burma."

"Yes. Are you worried about what they'll think of you?" Caroline asked, trying to understand.

"No." Caroline pulled him against a wall, cupping his face in her hands, holding him until he looked at her. Observing the pain behind his eyes, she slid her arms around him as he rested his head on her shoulder, his lips warm against her neck.

Holding him close, she insisted, "Tell me, Bear."

"In order to tell them what they want to know, I'll have to put myself back there." Caroline, though confused, remained silent, giving him the time he needed to formulate his response. "I have to immerse myself in the memories so that I can tell them everything." His sorrow sat like a burden on his shoulders.

Caroline took his hand and began to walk again. "The first time you walked through the door of my prison cell, covered in welts and blood, I wanted to wrap you in my arms and kiss your pain away." John stopped, watching her.

"The day they shocked you, I remember holding you in my arms and singing until you roused and began to respond to me." John turned fully to her, beginning to understand her strategy.

"The day you awoke in the village—well, all I can remember is your warm brown eyes staring at me and the great wave of relief I felt. I missed your company so much when you were ill."

John appraised his wife in amazement. She knew that he understood. She was trying to attach a good memory to every horrible situation so that when he remembered it for re-telling, he could also remember her love for him.

Morning found Caroline in John's arms, exhausted from keeping vigil with her husband. Praying together, they had traced back through every major event so Caroline could find some tiny fragment of joy to attach to it. At 8:00 am, John woke her, continuing to hold her close, as though drawing strength from her body.

"Hmmm, John?" He murmured "yes" into the top of her head. "I remembered the one I was thinking of last night. 'Come to me all ye who labour and are heavy laden and I will give you rest. Take my yoke upon you and learn from me ... for my yoke is easy and my burden is light.'"

Turning to look her in the eyes, he reassured her. "It's enough." He paused. "Caroline? Darling?" She nodded. "Will God stand by me through this, even if I've done things he couldn't approve of?"

"You're His now, Bear. Trust him. Follow his rules now, even if you didn't at the time. He loves you." She held him as they prayed before starting the day.

"John. I will stand by you no matter what, you know. If we end up pig farmers in Arthur, Ontario, I'll be right there with you."

Humbly, he responded. "My life—I can't—this is all beyond my comprehension. Thank you."

Following breakfast, Caroline was escorted to one room and John was delivered next door. Caroline's morning passed in a haze of questions. She spent one hour with an individual who spoke so quickly that she was never certain which question she was answering and several times caught herself staring up into an expectant face realizing she didn't have a clue what she was supposed to be saying. They allowed her a half hour break at noon to eat and pace about on the balcony then brought her back into the room for another round.

At three o'clock, a powerful looking man, glasses perched on the end of his nose, and a brilliantly coloured tie hanging loosely on his neck, entered the room and introduced himself.

"Hello. I am Sir William Jacen, Director General of MI-5." He extended his hand and Caroline shook it firmly. Continuing to hold her hand, he moved closer to her, clasping his other hand on top of their conjoined hands. "We are very impressed by your responses today. You have been very brave."

"Thank you," Caroline replied, thinking that, although she desperately wanted her hand back, she liked this man. He was strong, but she read no condescension in his manner.

"May I ask you one more question?" he asked.

"Of course," she responded. Behind her, one of the interrogators snorted and reminded her, "Sir".

The DG sent him a withering glance and he was silent. "Britannia no longer rules the waves, Nicholas," the DG defended her.

Nicholas didn't dare snort again but his face told her all she needed to know as she glanced at his profile in the mirror. "You wanted to ask me another question, Sir William?"

"What prompted you to help John when you were in prison? As I understand it, you helped him even at times when you were very unhappy with him," he inquired.

"Christians are called to do the right thing in spite of feelings, not because of them," she explained as well as she could.

"I believe I would like to know more about your definition of that term—perhaps another time." He escorted her into the hallway.

"Sir William, where is John? Is he okay?" she asked.

"He is fine, my dear. John is a professional. He knows what he is about." Sir William patted her hand. "You go on to your room now and get some rest."

Caroline was escorted to her room by yet another unnamed security officer. Settling into the bathtub, she relaxed with a soak and then napped on the bed. Waking at seven o'clock, she looked for John and was again assured that he was fine and that she should feel free to have supper as he would be taken care of.

After supper and a walk, accompanied by Huey, Dewey and Louie as she called her security escort, Caroline returned to her room at nine o'clock and found that John still had not returned. Frustrated at the lack of answers from the security officers, Caroline went in search of her husband, remembering how exhausted she had been after just a few hours of interrogation.

Asking her security detail for directions to the sauna on the first floor, Caroline entered the elevator, pleased that Huey and his pals waited behind, calling down to the agents on the first floor rather than accompanying her. Taking the elevator down to the fifth floor, she exited, quickly moving to the stair well and descending to the fourth floor. *Now, my interrogation took place in room 408 and they said they were also using 406. Father, help me find him.* Scanning the hallway as she crept along the edge, she noticed the DG in conversation with two men in suits. She saw Alexa deep in conversation at the opposite end of the hall with another man who had shed his suit jacket and loosened his tie. Praying all the way, she moved closer and closer to her goal. Waiting for the guard to turn away, she slipped into the alcove two doors away from her target room—406. Just then, a man exited the room, scanned the hallway and turned left toward the DG. Before the door slammed shut, Caroline slipped through.

The room was large, much larger than the room they had used for her. The beds had been removed and the only furniture was a small table and two wooden chairs in the middle of the room. Three men hovered around shouting, whispering and threatening and there, in the middle, sat her John, stripped to a t-shirt and shorts, looking pale and exhausted. Each question was answered, each threat acknowledged. Caroline saw the other men in the room drinking from water bottles but there were none anywhere near John, as he sat perspiring—the heat in the room had been turned up to ninety degrees Fahrenheit.

Caroline stood aghast and immobile, unable to believe that his own people would treat him this way, until one man grabbed John by the hair and the other one slapped him. Then, something exploded in Caroline's chest. She launched herself across the room, punching the slapper in the face, wheeling and slapping the hair puller. Wrapping herself around John, she yelled, "How dare you?!" Two men converged on Caroline, each grasping an arm. John exploded out of his chair, dispatching the two men holding his wife and warning the others drawing close, "Don't you dare touch her!"

"Enough!!!" The DG's voice echoed through the room and every MI-5 agent in the room and the hallway froze.

Caroline, not to be cowed by anyone until she had been heard, reprimanded the boss. "How can you treat him like this? He's one of yours. Have you any idea what he's been through—what he's suffered in order to keep your secrets? And instead of rewarding him, you punish him. You treat him like a criminal. How can you?"

The snotty man, Nicholas, moved closer, "You do not know anything, you colonial." His voice was low and threatening.

Caroline returned his hard stare, unflinching. John extended his arm toward Nicholas. "Back," he warned.

"Mrs. Brock." Caroline turned to the DG as he spoke. "We do not believe that John is a criminal or a traitor."

"We have to be certain, sir," Nicholas demanded.

"I am certain," the DG responded, "and so is the Home Secretary. This interrogation has ended." Turning to John, he extended his hand in congratulations. "Welcome back, John. You've done very well—very well, indeed." John sighed in relief, taking the proffered hand and, releasing Caroline, he ran his fingers through his hair. "Get yourself cleaned up, John and get some sleep. I'll expect you at the office on Monday." The DG nodded to the officers, waiting as they preceded him out of the room. "Look to your wife, son. By the by, I think my wife would enjoy meeting your wife sometime soon." The DG nodded to John and exited the room. John turned to Caroline who was still standing in the same spot, shaking with spent emotion.

"Caroline," John called to her gently. "Caer, can we go, now?" he asked, extending his hand to her. Gripping his hand, she silently followed him to their hotel room. But once she crossed the threshold, she collapsed on the floor, wrapping her arms around her knees and dissolving in tears. John sat beside her and held her until she calmed.

"Thank you," he said.

She took a deep breath and released it. "Why do you want to work for those people?" she asked.

"They just want to be sure. Nicholas was the one passed over for my job. He's done all right for himself, I see, in spite of that, but I think he's the one who whispered 'disloyalty' into the Home Secretary's ear. The DG needed to be very certain and prove without a doubt that I'm innocent because I work very closely with the HS. But don't misunderstand me, I'm very grateful for your intervention," John explained.

Caroline leaned into him. "You stink," she observed, smiling.

"You say the nicest things," John observed, rising and dragging her to her feet. "Bath—wife—bed." And they did.

CHAPTER 18

CAROLINE'S SECOND LIFE

Finally, after months of exile, pain and despair, John and Caroline Brock went home. John's description had been so perfect on that day in the back of the truck on the highway to Tason that Caroline felt like she was returning to a place that was warm and familiar. John provided a tour of the house, starting with the all-white guest room and finishing with the master bedroom where they remained until their stomachs cried out for food. The service, MI-5, had stocked the fridge and made certain the house was clean and temperate for their returning hero. After a stir-fry for supper, John and Caroline walked to the park behind the house, returning to build a fire in the fireplace and watch the first TV they'd seen in months. Quickly bored with the inane sitcoms on offer, they returned to bed, never tiring of the intimacy of privacy and clean sheets.

"What day is it?" Caroline inquired the next morning.
"Thursday, I think. Did you want to call your parents and invite them to visit?" John wondered.

"I think maybe I'll wait until Sunday to call them. It's rather nice to be alone and safe with you. We've spent a lot of time with Digbys and Nandas and Myaings and so on. I'd like to just experience you for now." She flipped over to sit on John's legs. "Can we help the people we left behind?" she asked.

"Help them how?" he wondered.

"We need to send money to Digby's aunt, enough to educate and feed him and maybe even send him to college. We need to find out what happened to Zeya. Was he imprisoned? Can we buy him out of prison? Maung and Chit could certainly use some extra cash. Katafygio—we need to find out what happened."

"Once I'm back at work, I can investigate those things. As for money, I have a good savings but I won't be able to—"

Caroline interrupted. "I have money."

John sat up. "What do you mean?"

"I haven't done anything with the life insurance I received after the plane crash. I could never bear to spend it. I'd like to use it to help all the people who helped us.

"That's your money, darling, you should spend it on yourself." John sounded confused, uncertain how to respond.

Smiling she stroked his face. "I have everything I need right here."

"I'll get the information you need and then you can decide what to do," he assured her.

"Thank you. But for now, we have four measly days until paradise is shattered by the real world. What shall we do today?" she asked, a grin playing across her face.

"I don't know about you, but I'm knackered." John lay back, his arms behind his head, and closed his eyes.

Watching him closely, she stroked her fingers through the hair on his chest. "I've been thinking lately that I'd like to write my name on your chest. I'll go and get the tweezers." As she moved to rise, he grabbed her hips and pulled her back.

She continued, "Well, I suppose if I had something else to do, I could let that little fantasy slide."

"You are a persuasive person. I happen to have a better idea of what I can do with *your* chest."

"John!" she exclaimed.

Thursday, Friday, Saturday, Sunday. Inevitably, Monday did arrive. John rose early and dressed in a suit and tie while Caroline watched mournfully from the bed.

"I don't want you to go," she said, dolefully.

Sitting on the edge of the bed, he replied, "I don't want to go."

Tears filling her eyes, she mourned, "We've been so happy. I don't want things to change. Can't we just go back?"

"Back to Burma?!" he asked in astonishment.

Laughing through her tears, she replied, "No. How about Sunday?"

"You were miserable Sunday, anticipating today."

"Saturday? Shopping was fun."

"If you like. I would suggest Friday." He grinned.

"We didn't get out of bed all day."

"Exactly!" John pulled her close. "I love you."

Tears forming again, she replied sadly, "I love you." Holding him close, she observed, "Your tie doesn't match."

"Pardon?"

"Your tie doesn't match your shirt," she repeated as though it was the worst news she'd ever received.

Bemused, he responded, "Can you choose a new one for me?"

Rising from the bed, she chose a deep blue tie that matched one of the pinstripes in his shirt. Settling back on the bed, she watched him tie a Windsor knot, straighten his collar and wait for her approval.

"I've programmed my numbers into your mobile."

Nodding, she asked, "What time will you be home?"

Grimacing, he replied, "I don't know. They seem to be in the middle of a crisis and, until I'm up to speed, I won't know how the day will progress." John pulled her up into his embrace, sliding his hands intimately over her bottom and kissing her deeply. "I will love you no matter where I am or what I'm doing," he promised, his voice hoarse with passion.

Nodding, she let him go.

Tuesday, Caroline's parents arrived. John left for work at 6:00 am after five hours of sleep, promising to meet Caroline at the airport by 11 o'clock to greet her parents. He arrived breathless, in time for a quick kiss before the gate was opened and her parents' relieved and curious faces appeared.

Wrapping Caroline in a hug, they wept for their daughter who had disappeared almost a year ago; their daughter who had suffered so much. Standing beside John, she introduced her parents and, still uncertain how to behave around these people, John was stiff and formal, shaking her father's hand. But her mother would settle for no less than a bear hug, finishing by kissing John on the cheek. A small grin remained on his face, causing Caroline to smile again.

Dropping them at the house, John returned to work. Settling her parents in the very white spare room, Caroline went to the kitchen to make coffee. For the rest of the day, she told them her story, starting with her flight to Singapore, the emergency stopover in Burma, the tea shoppe and the soldiers. She told them about the turmoil in the country. How Myanmar was still Burma to the common people, how it was the name used by the various resistance forces. She talked about the persecution of the indigenous peoples and the oppressive military junta. She told them of her time in Bourey Prison, of Captain Htet and his irritation with her. She told them of Hla and Mya, of Paul and Rory. Then she told them about John. She told them about his angry resistance. She told them about his suffering and courage. She told them about the epiphany that drove him to a leap of faith, rewarded by an answering, loving God. She spoke of the Chin Liberation Army, of their attack on the prison and escape, of the loneliness of abandonment in the jungle and the kindness of Grace, taking them in and caring for them and the risk that set for the family. She told them of their flight from the village into the jungle, of the soldiers in Bago, the muggers in Sinde and Captain Li in the mountains. She told them of the Katafygio and the friends they made there. She described their escape to the Chindwin and through the mountains to India. The day flew by. Caroline's parents listened, wept, laughed, rested, ate and listened again. By the time John arrived home at 8:00 pm, the story had arrived in the U.K., although many incidents remained for later tales.

"I'm home," he called as he ascended the stairs.

"We're up here," Caroline replied. Turning back to her parents, she continued. "There were MI-5 agents everywhere. When we went for a walk, it was like a parade! There were—"

John cut her off. "What are you doing?" he demanded.

The smile left her face. "What do you mean?"

"Can I speak to you in private?" His eyes told her there wasn't really an option. Nodding, she excused herself and followed him to the bedroom where he closed the door.

"What are you doing? I told you that you cannot discuss my work with anyone!" He paced beside the bed.

"They're my parents, sweetheart. They won't tell anyone."

"Being a parent does not imply infallibility." He turned to look her in the eyes.

Caroline studied him for a time, before responding, "I explained the risks to them and had them sign the Official Secrets Act. I told them the cover story that you're a civil servant working for the Home Office."

John was shocked. "How did you get a copy?"

"I called your office to ask you but got redirected to a computer guy named, Aubrey. He told me how to open your home computer without setting off alarms all over the country and he emailed me a copy and explained how to use the form." She paused, uncertain how to respond to John's evident surprise. "He said you had given orders for them to provide any assistance I requested." Quietly, she added, "Thank you for that."

Gob-smacked, John stared at her. He pulled her into his arms and began to laugh, a laugh that burst from his heart. "You are amazing!" he stated emphatically.

Smiling, Caroline hugged him back. Tentatively, she asked. "You're not angry?"

"I was never angry, just terrified. I know you love your parents but it's simply too risky to tell anyone the whole truth." Tilting her chin, he gazed into her eyes. "How would I ever survive if something happened to you because of my job?"

Caroline paused, praying for guidance on how to explain her parents to him, knowing his own history with his family. "You trust me, don't you?"

"Of course. I'd trust you with my life," he replied sincerely. "I trust you with my heart."

"Then trust me. My parents won't tell. They raised me. I am who I am because of them. I won't tell my brothers or sisters or friends or anyone else but my parents need to know the whole story. Otherwise, they'll never understand you and that would be more than I could bear. They need to understand so they don't spend the next twenty years mourning for their daughter. They need to know," she finished simply. When he remained pensive for a time, Caroline touched his arm. "Tell me what you're thinking," Caroline insisted.

"Brother Phillip once told me that I needed to divest myself of the responsibility for my loved ones; he told me that I needed to trust God. I can try to do that," John replied, pulling her into a hug. Removing his tie, jacket and shoes—he was having difficulty readjusting to wearing confining dress shoes all day and wished for flip flops— John and Caroline joined her bewildered parents in the living room.

"Is everything okay?" Caroline's father directed his question to his daughter.

Smiling, she responded. "Yes. I'm going to make an omelet for John. Why don't you three get acquainted."

As she prepared John's supper, she noticed the moment when his 'all business' explanation of the Official Secrets Act, evolved into his more relaxed storytelling mode. Re-entering the living room, she heard...

"... then I heard this angry voice, and I thought, I've heard that voice before." Caroline's father chuckled in response. "I walked through the bush and there she was, your lovely daughter, beating the living daylights out of a Burmese Python." Caroline's parents laughed.

"You love telling that story," she accused as she placed his supper on the coffee table in front of him then perched on the arm of his chair.

"She's always been terrified of snakes!" her mother exclaimed.

"Well," Caroline began, pouting. "It annoyed me." The quartet burst into laughter again.

"As annoying as Captain Li?" John asked, turning to her.

Her face darkened. "He was *really* annoying." The atmosphere in the room changed.

"Who is Captain Li?" her father prompted.

Caroline slid her arm along John's shoulder, seeking comfort from the memories of that terrible time. "You tell them," she urged.

"At one point in our flight, I was captured by a vile man named Captain Li who worked for—well, let's just say he worked for a very bad man. They—"

"They tied him up and dragged him through the jungle with no food and barely any water for two days, then—" Caroline faltered, tears in her eyes. "Then they beat him with bamboo sticks." She became silent. Reaching his arm around her waist, he pulled her onto his lap, murmuring comfort.

"Sorry," she muttered, apologizing to her parents for breaking down during the story.

"Anyway," John continued, "the next thing I know, men are falling all around me. She took out four trained soldiers and rescued me." He watched his wife with pride.

"Not really, you dealt with two of them," she offered, still subdued.

John laughed. "You are a formidable woman." Kissing her on the cheek, he hugged her tightly. Caroline smiled and hugged him back.

Conversation continued for the next few hours until Caroline's parents begged leave to retire, but it lasted long enough for them to remark privately to Caroline that they could see the courage of their new son-in-law and the love he felt for her.

In their bedroom after her parents had gone downstairs, John mused, "You're right. It felt good to tell them. I've never—" He stopped.

"I know," she said. "But you do now. Come here," she commanded. And he did.

Caroline's parents remained for two more days before returning to Canada. They were pleased to know that Caroline had found a man who loved her passionately and would bravely protect her, but were concerned by the fact that his job kept him away from her for twelve to eighteen hours a day. They knew their daughter well enough to see that struggles lay ahead for the newlyweds.

Once her parents departed, Caroline felt at loose ends. John had taken to leaving the house at dawn and returning at midnight. When Caroline tried to stay up and wait for him to come home, she usually failed and awoke in the morning feeling miserable on the couch, curled under a blanket. She tried setting her alarm for 6:00 am but John just turned it off before he left. Caroline felt all the happiness draining out of her life. Here she was in a strange country, away from family and friends. She had no job, no hobbies. John kept promising to take her out to practice the right hand drive but he never seemed to have time for her anymore. She tried to hold a pretence of happiness when her family telephoned but her mother saw right through her.

"Come home, darling. Just for a visit. Come home for a little tender loving care." But all that did was remind her of what she and John had had. How long had it been since he'd used that term of endearment on her? Why did things have to change? Why couldn't he just come home and stay the same?

<><><><><>

John himself was struggling with his return to work. The atmosphere at home was more and more oppressive as he felt Caroline's unhappiness like a burning burden on his heart. He was unhappy too. He knew it affected his behavior by the looks his officers gave him when they thought he wasn't watching, his few months of married life warring with twenty years of the service mindset. Finally, one day, three weeks after he returned to work, he demanded an appointment with the DG and presented his terms, hoping he wasn't too late to rescue his marriage.

<><><><><>

Three weeks after John returned to work, Caroline received a letter from Burma. Her hands were shaking as she opened the missive.

My Dearest Caroline,

I know that you have arrived safely in the U.K.. John sent word some time ago. We all rejoice at your safety. As you have probably already heard, Brother Phillip was killed by Maryn Dale during the soldiers' occupation of our village. We are saddened by his loss but know that he is happily reunited with his wife in Jesus' arms. Kyi seems to have naturally taken his place, helping us rebuild after the soldiers burned the village. We are all pleased by this development.

Speaking of changes, did John tell you that Archie and Dolly were married? Evidently, they've been in love for some time but neither wanted to spoil their friendship by broaching the subject. God continues to bring good from bad.

We all miss you here and hope to hear from you.

Love, Simon

Caroline's heart filled with joy at the letter. She cried over Brother Phillip and laughed at the thought of Dolly and Archie. Her heart burst with pleasure that her friends thought of her and missed her. What would she give to have those few happy days back again?

With a renewed sense of energy, Caroline decided to clean the house, something she hadn't done since arriving in London. In fact, she realized she'd spent the last three weeks moping around the house, mourning for something that hadn't really been lost. *I know how to live,* she thought. *I always thought that when Paul said, 'I have learned in whatever state I am to be content', he must have been referring to a time of action but actually, he was in prison. He was speaking from a time of frustration and solitude. Thank you, Father. I can be content, help me when I fail.* As she cleaned, Caroline sang, for the first time in weeks. She dusted and vacuumed—hoovered, as John called it—emptied the hall closet of shoes and coats and suitcases, washed and folded laundry. Her foray into the yard was interrupted by John's voice.

"Caroline. Caroline!" John's voice echoed through the house.

"Hi. You're home early." She greeted him gaily, her smile disappearing as she saw his face. He looked agitated, upset. "What's wrong?" she asked, concerned. *Why is he home early? Why is he so upset?*

"The suitcase," he said, sounding furious and despondent at the same time.

"I was cleaning the hall closet and forgot to put it back. Are you okay?" *What is going on? The suitcase—does he think I'm packing?* "John, you don't think I'm—"

"The letter."

Caroline could see the crumpled letter in his shaking hands. She paused, puzzled. *The letter? The letter from Katafygio?* Understanding dawned. *The letter from Simon!* She rushed across the room and threw her arms around him, relieved when his body melted into hers. Pulling back to look him in the face, she saw tears falling down his cheeks.

"Oh, my darling! I'm so sorry. I'm not going anywhere, I promise. I know I've been miserable lately but I'm not leaving— I'm certainly not leaving to be with Simon. You were right about him. He does have a thing for me." She paused, trying to prompt a response from him; to confirm her suspicions of what he was thinking. "You won't let him get me will you? Please?" She grinned, kissing his cheek.

He shook his head vigorously. "I—I—you—you've been so unhappy lately and I heard your mother ask you to come home the other day and—the letter—the suitcase. Caroline, don't ever leave me. I'm sorry I'm a lousy husband. I promise to fix things. I love you." Misery and desperation drove him to his knees.

Caroline followed him down, holding him tightly. "I'm not leaving you—ever. Do you think you can get rid of me that easily? No. I agree that things need to change but part of that is me changing. Instead of moping around the house all day missing you, I need to find something to do to fill my time. I do think we need to do something about your job too—but—well, I feel like we can make this work. I love you, John." She murmured reassurances. "I finally listened to what God was telling me instead of just moaning at him."

"I did that, too. I went to see—wait. Will you make us some coffee, please, so I can explain?" he asked.

Smiling, she answered, "Of course. Wash up and we'll start this conversation all over again."

They cuddled up on the couch and took a few moments to enjoy being together during the middle of the day. John finally broke the silence.

"I went to see the DG today. I told him that things simply weren't working for me and that unless changes were made, I would be resigning at the end of the month."

Caroline gasped. "John? —but you love your work," she announced, astonished.

"I love you more," he stated simply, kissing her forehead then continuing, "I told him that I simply couldn't put in these long hours, that most of the time there was no need for me to actually be in my office, just to be available. Then I asked him, if I were to be available, say never more than thirty minutes away, could I flex my hours around needs."

"And?" Caroline asked.

"He agreed." John smiled. "He did warn me that a schedule such as that would put paid to any hopes I had of promotion but—well—frankly—I can live without a promotion."

"What else?" she prompted.

"Well, my administrative assistant retired while I was in Burma and no one has replaced her yet. I told him I didn't know if you'd want to but—well—I demanded that I be allowed to offer the position to you, first." He finished with a rush, watching her reaction.

"Me? —You want me to be an assistant—for MI-5?"

John looked uncertain of her response. He clarified, "Not just an assistant, you'd be my administrative assistant. You wouldn't have to work for anyone else. You'd keep my diary, do research, type and file reports, maybe do a little analysis from time to time. I know it's not what you're trained for but we'd be able to work together. You'd be privy to what's going on. You can work part time if you like. I can hire a second part timer to do all the things you don't like. What do you think?" he paused, holding his breath.

Finding his eyes with her own, she threw her arms around his neck and said, "I think you're the most amazing husband in the world!" John released his breath in relief and held her tightly against him. "That would be brilliant. I don't want to go back to what I used to do. This would be a whole new challenge. We could work together?" John nodded, grinning. "I would know what you were working on—Oh John, yes yes yes."

"I have one more thing to tell you. I informed the DG that my wife and I had never had a honeymoon and I demanded two weeks off so, starting Friday, we are off for fourteen consecutive days to go anywhere you want to go. The DG really likes you, you know. I think I probably could have gotten a raise if I'd asked on your behalf! But I got what I wanted."

"John, I love you. Thank you. I accept."

"I love you."

Together they forged ahead into a new life. There would be many bumps along the way and the adventures were certainly not over, but they would meet each day together, one hand in the other's hand and one hand in God's.

EPILOGUE

THE HAPPY ENDING

Caroline had lived two lives. She thought of her first life as "Henry". She grew up, went to University, met and fell in love with Henry Wells. Their love blossomed from the seeds of friendship, attraction and commitment. She and Henry married and had children together. Her Henry life was good. Caroline's first life ended on the day the plane crashed. That crash left Caroline a childless widow, struggling to make sense of the loss; trusting that in all this there was a purpose.

Caroline's second life began with John. With John she escaped from prison, travelled the length of Burma evading capture, and fell in love. Their love was forged in the jungles of Burma. She and John married. They had no children together but they did buy a dog. Her life with John was continuing on into the future. Her life with John was very good.

LaVergne, TN USA
08 September 2010
196357LV00001B/21/P